A RARE FIND

JOANNA LOWELL

BERKLEY ROMANCE

NEW YORK

BERKLEY ROMANCE
Published by Berkley
An imprint of Penguin Random House LLC
1745 Broadway, New York, NY 10019
penguinrandomhouse.com

Copyright © 2025 by Joanna Ruocco
Readers Guide copyright © 2025 by Joanna Ruocco

Book design by Katy Riegel

Library of Congress Cataloging-in-Publication Data
Names: Lowell, Joanna, author.
Title: A rare find / Joanna Lowell.
Description: First edition. | New York: Berkley Romance, 2025.
Identifiers: LCCN 2024048317 (print) | LCCN 2024048318 (ebook) |
ISBN 9780593549742 (trade paperback) | ISBN 9780593549759 (ebook)
Subjects: LCGFT: Queer fiction. | Romance fiction. | Novels.
Classification: LCC PS3618.U568 R37 2025 (print) |
LCC PS3618.U568 (ebook) | DDC 813/.6—dc23/eng/20241021
LC record available at https://lccn.loc.gov/2024048317
LC ebook record available at https://lccn.loc.gov/2024048318

First Edition: June 2025

Printed in the United States of America
1st Printing

The authorized representative in the EU for product safety and compliance is
Penguin Random House Ireland, Morrison Chambers, 32 Nassau Street,
Dublin D02 YH68, Ireland, https://eu-contact.penguin.ie.

For Joey, always.

And for the Js, who know themselves.

Dear Readers,

I hope you enjoy Elf and Georgie's journey. They have many adventures on the bumpy, boisterous road to their happy ending. Please note that one of these adventures involves a dangerous interlude in a confined space. Elf and Georgie also confront casual and callow misogyny, most often perpetuated by Elf's father. And they grapple on-page with the legacies of parental abandonment and death. Elf's father is an antiquary—a person who studies antiquities. He and some of his cronies express problematic ideas about England's origins that are implicitly linked to racist ideologies and imperialism, ideas that are challenged within the novel.

The queer characters in A Rare Find are living full lives. However, given the social and legal censure on LGBTQ+ relationships in Regency England, they deal with various degrees of emotional and material strain due to the conflict between the world they live in and the ways in which they love. The term nonbinary didn't exist during the Regency, and people didn't have a practice of sharing their pronouns, as we do in many community organizations, schools, and workplaces today. If Georgie could step out of these pages and join our present reality, they would likely identify as nonbinary and use they/them pronouns with everyone. In the novel, they use they/them pronouns only within their intimate circle of friends, with whom they're able to talk about their particular experience of gender.

A Rare Find is about two people finding all sorts of things. Passion. Community. Queer ancestors. The dream of a bigger, better, freer world they want to try to bring into being together. And last but not least, treasure!

Happy Reading,
Joanna

A
RARE
FIND

1

DERBYSHIRE
1818

THE BUSHES THRASHED violently. Elfreda put down her trowel and sat back on her heels. The bushes began to growl.

"Wolves," she guessed. "Two ferocious, green-eyed wolves from the Dark Peak."

One bush gave a loud gasp: "Are there wolves in the Dark Peak?"

The other bush made a shushing noise.

"Most certainly," said Elfreda. She liked inventing legends as much as she liked reading them. "The Dark Peak is where the wolves went when mean old Edward Longshanks tried to have them all killed. You can hear them howling when the wind blows from the north."

Both bushes squealed.

"Is it far?" asked the one.

In an instant, Elfreda understood her blunder. She could already imagine her sisters skipping into the craggy wilds.

"Terribly far." She adopted a commiserating tone. "And the way is closely guarded by a regiment of aunts armed with curling tongs."

The bushes, which had been rustling excitedly, now observed a horrified silence.

It had been nearly three years since Aunt Susan had returned to

Surrey, but her tenure at Marsden Hall had left an indelible mark—not the improving one that she'd intended.

"And castor oil," added Elfreda for good measure. "These aunts won't let anyone step foot near a wolf. They are the sort who prohibit dogs in the nursery."

She couldn't see her sisters' faces, but she thought the foliage drooped. Good. Dejection was better than them running off and someone finding them a thousand years from now in a peat bog on the Howden Moors.

She turned her attention back to her work. She'd been digging for weeks, cutting trenches across the wooded bluff, a slow and solitary effort. Once Papa had lost interest, he'd stopped paying the laborers who'd helped break ground. Part of her wondered if it was folly to dig so long without assistance, and without result.

Take this trench. She'd exposed a layer of loam, and then marl, and then clay, and then something darker—possibly char from ancient cookfires. No buckles, though. No nails. No fragments of pottery. No proof.

All her hopes rested on an entry in a local annal included in Papa's manuscript copy of *The Anglo-Saxon Chronicle*, an entry for AD 868.

This year the heathen men overran Mercia as far as Twynham, burning and breaking, so that many were slain. They remained in Mercia, and there fixed their winter quarters.

The heathen men wouldn't have fixed their winter quarters in Twynham, a small settlement, exposed on all sides. They'd have looted St. Alcmund's, and the abbey, and moved on, until they reached a defensive position.

This bluff. The closest to Twynham, and the highest ground for miles. It towered above the river and sloped down to what was now her family's parkland.

A few inked lines had brought her here, and also intuition and common sense.

This was the spot. The one *she* would have chosen if she were a seaborne raider.

Ergo, she refused to give up.

More growls made her turn her gaze on the undergrowth. She could see Hilda's foot protruding, a foot shod in a badly scuffed boot with trailing laces. Unless it was Matilda's foot. The six-year-old twins shared only a passing physical resemblance, but they were equally ruinous to leather. And muslin. And velvet upholstery.

"Let me guess again." Elfreda pretended to ponder. "I know— you are giant, growling moles!" She beckoned with the trowel. "Come, dear moles. Let us tunnel together deep into the earth, where we shall find the silver ingots of the Great Heathen Army!"

"We are bears." Hilda crawled from the bush. She'd a long red scratch on her cheek and a moth-eaten fur tippet wrapped around her head. She rose onto her knees, hooked her fingers into claws, and bared her teeth. "And we are ravens."

"Ravenous!" Matilda crawled after her. "We aren't *ravens* bears. Ravens bears have feathers. We are ravenous bears. We have a great hunger, like the hunger of 1044. Papa says it was a sign of doom."

Elfreda frowned. Whenever Papa was in a sulk, he had his children gather in the library after dinner so he could recite to them all the grimmest episodes in the history of the English nation.

"There's no such thing as doom." Elfreda said it brightly.

"Isn't *that* a sign of doom?" Hilda was considering Elfreda with a frown.

"What?" Elfreda held her breath as her sister crawled closer and hovered a fingertip between her brows.

"Oh," said Elfreda, swiping at her fringe and almost certainly leaving another smudge. "It's dirt."

Hilda was still considering, so Elfreda offered an alternative explanation.

"It is a sign that I am an archaeologist."

The twins surprised her by nodding at once.

"That's why you dig holes," said Matilda.

Elfreda nodded too. This acceptance—swift, uncomplicated, and absolute—did something strange to her heart. The Albion Society of Antiquaries didn't allow female Fellows, and only Papa's name appeared on *Two Dissertations on the Saxon Grave Hills of the Peak District*, even though she'd authored the second dissertation in its entirety. Elfreda Marsden was nobody. Painfully awkward at social gatherings, unable to speak in front of a group, let alone sing while plinking along on the pianoforte, and with nothing else to show for herself.

But children saw possibility where adults did not. Hilda and Matilda were bears, and Elfreda was an archaeologist, and that was that.

She smiled at the roly-poly, round-faced little cubs, smiled so widely her forehead itched. She scratched and flakes showered down.

Dirt. From the Old Norse, *drit*.

The Great Heathen Army had left behind many of their words. What she needed was one of their swords.

"Go off home." She made a shooing motion. "Assuage your great hunger with seed cake."

The twins shot to their feet.

"You can bother Agnes!" Elfreda shouted after them as they ran through the trees. "But don't disturb Papa! He's with Mr. Clutterbuck!"

At least, she hoped he was with Mr. Clutterbuck. The visit—Mr. Clutterbuck's first in over a year—could last well into the afternoon. Mr. Clutterbuck and Papa had been friends and colleagues for decades and always had much to discuss. On the other hand, the visit could have ended as soon as it began, with shouting and broken china. Mr. Clutterbuck was now the president of the Albion Society, which had involved stabbing Papa in the back.

Elfreda had poured the tea and raced to the bluff immediately after, praying—foolishly, desperately—that today was the day. She'd dig something up in time, before Mr. Clutterbuck continued on his way to Wales. Something to show him what the twins believed, what Papa seemed to believe when it was just the two of them, rambling from barrow to barrow in the countryside.

She *was* an archaeologist.

For another hour or so, she sifted the soil. Nothing. Pebbles clunked in her sieve, and she tossed them one after the other onto the pile behind her. The one in her hand now—it felt odd. Its shape, the weight of it. She tried to peel the caked dirt with her nails, to no avail.

She sprang up, and swayed, vision going white, spots dancing in the air around her. She gripped the not-pebble tight in her hand. It steadied her. She launched herself forward, skirts tangling about her legs as she ran.

The River Thorn was the closest source of water, but the bluff dropped down to the bank so steeply it might as well have been a cliff. She ran away from the river, down the mellow slope toward the park. A slight deviation of course brought her instead into the woodland, which would open eventually into a clearing with a fishing pond dead center.

Technically, their neighbor, Henry Redmayne, owned the woodland, but he was in France, and his insufferable sister Georgina was in London. The pair had always considered themselves too dashing for the retirement of country life. Things had been quieter in the neighborhood during the five years they'd been gone.

Elfreda sometimes snuck away from her sisters and read by the pond, her back against the trunk of the willow tree. But today, the pond would provide more than serenity.

Her sides were heaving as she burst into the clearing. She paused to catch her breath. The spring afternoon was bright, and the pond lay before her, flashing in the sun.

She crouched on the bank and dipped her fist. The cold itself felt bright.

She scrubbed the pebble clean with the pads of her fingers and flushed with anticipation as she withdrew her hand.

There it was, a leaden object an inch in length, topped by a shorter perpendicular arm.

A hammer.

Or rather, an amulet shaped like a hammer.

A thousand years ago, a living, breathing Northman had worn it close to his skin as he pulled the oars and rowed across the whale-road, leaving the shores of his homeland behind.

Papa, Mr. Clutterbuck—they had only to glance.

She stared at it herself now in wonder, her scrutiny finding delicate traceries in the metal surface.

It had been engraved.

She scrambled to her feet, heart pounding in her throat. The hammer felt heavier by the second in her palm.

The Great Heathen Army had, in fact, overwintered on the bluff. No one had ever corroborated a literary reference to one of their winter camps.

Until now. *She* had. Elfreda Marsden.

She needed to run like the wind back to the house.

She allowed herself one more moment, just her and the hammer.

She didn't realize she'd closed her eyes until the darkness shattered into stars. Her breath whooshed out as her ribs compressed. Whooping cries pierced the hush, and she was off her feet, lifted bodily into the air, and then she was falling, falling—splash! She felt a frigid slap of water, and the pond closed over her head.

2

EORGIE! WHAT HAVE you done?"

Elfreda registered a shocked, high-pitched voice with one ear. The other ear was underwater. She pushed off the pond's mucky bottom, struggling to her knees.

"You tried to drown a perfect stranger." The scolding continued. "It was absolutely sinister."

"She's not a stranger," came the low reply.

What Elfreda saw on the bank belied the claim. Strangers. Two of them. A tall young woman in a peach-blossom walking dress, blonde ringlets peeking from a bonnet of blue crepe. A hatless gentleman in top boots, buckskin breeches, and a riding coat, thick russet hair waving upon his brow.

There was no time to wonder how or why.

She relaxed her fisted fingers with difficulty, then gazed with horror into her hand.

It was empty.

She'd let go. When that *sinister* sprig of fashion had attacked, she'd let go.

"No." She flung forward. She plunged both hands through insubstantial silt, buried them in clinging mud, and scooped.

Tadpoles. A slimy twig. A pebble. Another pebble. Another pebble. Pebbles by the hundred. By the thousand.

"No, no, no." She pivoted wildly. Every movement spread billowing brown clouds through the water.

"Elf," said the gentleman. "Did you lose something?"

She froze.

The gentleman strolled toward her. He had a loose-limbed, athletic stride, a way of moving that epitomized smugness. And that face. That unmistakable face.

She stared, spellbound by incipient dread.

The hair was short, and darker than it had been a half decade ago when she'd seen it last, arranged in shining twists and braids. The wicked slant of the brows was the same. The high cheekbones. The square jaw that framed a deceptively sweet-looking mouth. The pale blue eyes edged with long black lashes.

Certainty struck like a lightning bolt.

Her mouth went dry. She was dripping everywhere, but she could barely unstick her tongue from her teeth.

"Georgina," she croaked. "Damn you."

She'd imagined uttering those words on innumerable occasions.

Saying them now brought no comfort.

Georgina Redmayne gave her a dazzling smile. "I've certainly been trying."

Elfreda stifled a scream. She punched the pond instead, dredging up another handful of mud.

"Oh," murmured the young lady, looking between them. "You *are* acquainted. Georgie, you tried to drown someone you know?"

"I thought she was Rosalie." Georgina waved a hand. "Something about the hair. From behind."

"You tried to drown *Rosalie*." The young lady sounded outraged. "Your dearest friend. You are a monster."

"Dunk, not drown." Georgina sat and tugged off a boot. "She knocked me out of the boat the other day. You weren't decrying attempted murder then."

The young lady ignored this.

"Lucky for Rosalie, she escaped," she said. "Most *un*lucky for poor . . ." She trailed off as she picked her way along the bank, her ribboned slippers disappearing in the rushes at the verge. "Should I call you *Elf*?" she asked Elfreda, bending down, as one did when addressing a child. "I gather you and Georgie grew up together? I don't believe I've ever seen you in town."

"She doesn't go to town." Georgina tugged the second boot, more sharply. "She molders in Marsden Hall. The pile on the hill."

"The pile on the hill!" The young lady beamed. "I adore it. So picturesque. I'm delighted to meet you, although I understand if you don't return the sentiment at present. I hope we can renew our acquaintance when we both have dry feet."

Elfreda didn't offer her response.

I would rather dry my feet in the fires of hell.

She let the mud in her hands plop into the water.

"I'm Anne," continued the young lady, undeterred, "Anne Poskitt, of the Halifax Poskitts. Did you lose a ring? A fish might have swallowed it. Fish are always swallowing rings, in fairy tales anyway, which usually have some truth to them. Did you know Bluebeard was a real person? And apples can poison you if you eat the seeds."

Elfreda made a choking sound as she clawed up more mud. More pebbles. Her head was hot, and her toes were nubs of ice.

"Why were you wearing a ring?" Georgina splashed barefoot into the pond. "Don't tell me you're married."

"I'm not telling you anything." Elfreda rose to standing, rivulets streaming down her legs.

"Good Lord, you are married. How can that be?"

Elfreda pushed past her.

"Who is he?" Georgina followed. "Did he dress in sprinkled calf-skin and trick you into thinking he's a book?"

Elfreda spun. "You—" She failed to finish the insult. Georgina was an inch away, emanating dryness and warmth, her gaze the blue of woodsmoke. Mesmerizing as a flame.

"Me?" drawled Georgina. "A favorite topic. Go on."

"Go to the devil," muttered Elfreda and waded for the bank.

"Not until I find your ring," called Georgina. "It's the least I can do."

"For God's sake, I haven't lost a *ring*." Elfreda turned back. Georgina stood where she'd been standing, arms crossed.

"You're *not* married," she said, triumphantly smug. "I didn't think so."

Elfreda bristled. She was three and twenty, more than old enough for marriage—approaching old maid. All the girls who'd played hoops with Georgina on the village green had been married for years. Certainly, Georgina herself. Whenever she'd been in residence at Redmayne Manor, suitors had arrived from each of the cardinal directions, leaving swathes of flower-denuded meadow in their wake.

"I haven't felt inclined to marry," said Elfreda. "I've been doing other things. Interesting things."

"Like what?" Georgina raised her brows. "Traveling?"

"A bit," said Elfreda, cursing herself for taking the bait. "A few rambles. Barrow digging."

"Barrow digging." Georgina cleared her throat. "Barrows are graves, yes?"

"Ancient burial mounds."

"Ah," said Georgina. "Charming. What about parties? Any cavorting with people who have flesh on their bones?"

"I attended an assembly at Thornton."

"One dance in five years?"

Elfreda frowned. Aunt Susan had forced the issue, singeing off most of her fringe with the curling tongs in the process. That one dance had been more than enough.

"I socialize," said Elfreda, stiffly. "Lord Fawcett still hosts those Venetian breakfasts. You must remember them. The last time you went, you poured brandy in the lemonade and let John Worrell take the blame."

"He was delighted to take the blame. He lived to impress me with his gallantry. Whatever happened to John Worrell?"

"He married Jane Slater."

"My favorite of the Janes." Georgina shook her head. "What else? Have you made any bosom friends?"

Elfreda's frown deepened. "No."

"Romantic conquests?"

"I've been doing things that *I* find interesting. If you are attempting to compare our recent activities, you can stop now. You won't hit upon similarities."

"I am sorry to hear that," said Georgina, with exaggerated gravity. "Because I've been having a tremendously good time."

"I've no doubt." Elfreda was shaking, with cold and with rage. Georgina always had a tremendously good time, at the expense of whoever she pleased.

"Elf." Georgina came toward her. "We haven't seen each other in half a decade. Can you blame me for hoping you hadn't spent the *entire* time reading?"

It was too much.

"Blame you?" Elfreda sucked in her breath. "You were the bane of my existence. Every day you didn't return from London was the best day of my life. And suddenly you're here, and you've already managed to ruin everything!"

"Ruin what? What did you drop?" Georgina halted a step away.

Elfreda squeezed her eyes shut. This wasn't real. It was a nightmare, a very vivid, very wet nightmare. That explained Georgina's breeches. In dreams, details didn't follow any discernible logic. The girl from across the lane could appear in the guise of a Corinthian. But in waking life, it wasn't very likely.

She opened her eyes. Georgina was still there, still in breeches, arms crossed, giving her an appraising look.

This wasn't a nightmare. It was worse. It was real.

"Why are you wearing your brother's clothes?" She blurted it out.

"Harry's clothes? I would never." Georgina raised her brows. "I went to a tailor. I like my garments to fit." She glanced down at herself, mouth quirking in satisfaction. "I look well, don't I?"

Without a word, Elfreda marched out of the pond. There was no retrieving the amulet, and nothing to be gained from conversation with Georgina.

Anne Poskitt emerged from the fountain of willow fronds, smiling. "I wasn't eavesdropping."

Elfreda kept squelching through the grass. Her clammy dress plastered her body and slapped at her shins.

"You were very loud, though." Anne fell into step with her. "I heard everything, despite attuning my ears to the birdsong. Are you Georgie's age? Four and twenty? I'm one and twenty, and my father wants me married by Michaelmas."

Elfreda reached the footpath, but she felt as though she were entering a new circle of hell. A hell where Georgina's minions popped out from behind every tree to flaunt their fine figures and accomplishments and deliver lectures on matrimonial duty.

Anne continued, "That's why I'm running away to Italy."

Elfreda blinked. But she didn't let surprise get the better of her. She walked faster. "If you started in London, you're headed in the wrong direction."

"We did start in London," said Anne. "We arrived the day before yesterday. Georgie, Rosalie, and myself. Well, and my chaperone, but she's been indisposed. Bad fish pudding at the coaching inn. I don't mind spending a fortnight in Derbyshire. Georgie wanted company, and I'm not running away until July at the soonest."

Elfreda couldn't begin to parse this nonsensical chatter. She latched on to the bit that mattered. "A fortnight?" Thank God. She could endure a fortnight.

"Yes, a fortnight," agreed Anne. "Rosalie and I can't stay longer. Poor Georgie will have to carry on without us."

Elfreda nearly tripped. "Georgina isn't going with you?"

"Oh no, Georgie's here forever. Unless Major Redmayne changes his mind."

Henry Redmayne was a *major* now? Shouldn't he have been content to purchase himself a captaincy? The Redmaynes were awful, ostentatious people.

"But—" Elfreda bunched up her skirt, wadding so hard water dripped from the fabric. "What about her husband?"

"Lord Phillip?" Anne gave a little hop. "Georgie didn't marry him! You didn't hear? About the broken engagement? And the duel? And the curricle crash? It was a terrible scandal." She laughed at Elfreda's blank expression. "What do people talk about in this neighborhood? Livestock? The sheep *are* remarkably fluffy. I've never understood counting them to lull oneself to sleep, but now I can imagine napping on one, in an orchard, perhaps. All that warm, clean, fluffy fleece, and leafy shade, and the smell of apples."

"I gave up the search." Georgina overtook them at a lope, slightly breathless, hair in raffish disarray. "It's difficult when you don't know what you're searching for."

The path wasn't wide enough for three to walk abreast. Georgina insinuated herself right in the middle. Elfreda didn't budge an inch, which meant Anne was bumped to the side and had to stumble over roots and through brambles.

"Ow," said the girl, good-naturedly.

"I found a flask." Georgina held it up, a slim vessel of heavily tarnished silver, streaked with mud. "But it's not yours. Unless one of your interesting activities is *drunken swimming by the moonlight*, but I think that's too similar to one of mine. Also, there's a monogram. *H. J. R.* I wonder if Harry has missed it." She gave the flask a shake. "Full. But of whiskey or pond water is the question. Shall we investigate?"

Elfreda couldn't walk any faster. Her feet were sliding in her slimy boots. But the woodland had thinned, and just ahead, she could see Holywell Rock. She swerved from the path and plodded over to it, pressing her hands to its rough surface.

"Not another step," she warned, twisting around as Georgina and Anne came up to her. "You're on my land now."

"This boulder marks the boundary of your estates?" Anne leaned forward to touch the rock with a gloved fingertip. "How deliciously medieval."

"It is medieval," said Elfreda. "Holywell Rock is named in the Domesday Book."

"How do you do?" Anne curtseyed to the rock. "I've never met such a distinguished boulder." She smiled at Elfreda without a trace of sarcasm. "Is your family in the Domesday Book?"

"No," said Elfreda shortly. "My family bought the estate in the sixteenth century."

"And they sold my family the majority of it in the final quarter of the eighteenth century." Georgina unscrewed the lid of the flask, sniffed the contents, and made a face. "And have hated us ever since."

"Why's that?" Anne looked between them.

"They didn't know us before." Georgina tipped the flask and a pale brown liquid streamed out.

"Be serious," said Anne. "I'm fascinated by feuds."

"Feud overstates the case," said Elfreda. "Our families have had little to do with each other."

"They think we're upstarts," said Georgina.

"Really, we don't," said Elfreda. "We don't think of you."

"You see?" Georgina looked at Anne. "The overconscious display of superiority? They find it lowering to share a property line. Because my grandfather tied parcels to earn the money he used to pay *her* grandfather the money he needed after he squandered his fortune."

"Never mind what I said." Elfreda pushed off Holywell Rock. "There is a feud. It starts today." She tried to make her eyes into daggers as she stared at Georgina. "You are my enemy."

Georgina's eyebrows shot up.

Elfreda addressed herself to Anne. "Goodbye. I hope you enjoy your holiday."

She gave herself a shake and considered too late—as droplets flew—her resemblance to a wet dog.

She started on her way, embarrassment pinching her shoulder blades together.

Georgina's voice carried on the breeze, a low murmur, not meant for her ears.

"She's an eccentric, but she comes by it honestly. That grandfather of hers thought he was a druid."

"You are ignorant." Elfreda whirled. "Knowledge looks like eccentricity to fools." She stepped toward Georgina. "Do you really want to know what I dropped in the pond?"

Georgina was studying her with an expression that mingled mirth and surprise.

"An amulet," Elfreda said, and that strange thing happened again to her heart. She pushed her fringe from her forehead and scratched at the dirt, at the sign on her skin. She *was* an archaeologist. "An amulet that verified the presence of the Great Heathen Army on the bluff above the river."

"Oh my." Anne gazed eagerly in the direction of the bluff. "And everyone has been talking all these years about the threat from France."

Elfreda gritted her teeth. "The presence of the Great Heathen Army in the *ninth* century."

Anne deflated. "That's much less exciting."

"It's incredibly exciting!" Elfreda threw her arms in the air. "It's incredibly *significant*. I've dreamed about such a discovery for *years*."

Georgina's eyes had narrowed. She seemed about to speak.

Elfreda heard a rumble, more a faint vibration of earth than a sound. It took her a moment to understand.

When she did, her stomach made a sickly plunge.

"That's a carriage." She spoke her fear aloud. "That's a carriage on the lane. He's leaving. Mr. Clutterbuck is leaving. I'm too late."

She hadn't covered ten yards when her left foot slid from her ruined boot. She wobbled and fell to her knees. From her knees, she watched Georgina sprint past, long legs devouring the ground.

Three more heartbeats, and she'd vaulted the low stone wall and vanished into the hedges.

3

CHASING A CARRIAGE down a country lane was fine sport, for a highwayman. But a highwayman would do it on a black stallion, not like this, stumbling along on two less-than-Thoroughbred legs.

Georgie ran for longer than was sensible, and in the end, as was obvious from the beginning, the carriage's lead proved too great.

A pity.

It would have been satisfying to see something besides accusation in Elf's bottomless black eyes.

The walk back up the lane dragged on. The landscape was the same as ever, a rolling green patchwork, green fields stitched together with darker green hedgerows. Georgie had an unobstructed view of Marsden Hall. Fortresslike, it jutted from the highest hill, heavy wings of gray stone pierced with lancet windows, crenelated tower etched against the cloudless sky.

Redmayne Manor lay less than a mile south. A redbrick mansion in the Georgian style, airy and symmetrical, with large sash windows and a bright white portico.

The houses themselves would feud if they were able.

You are my enemy.

Elf had been pale with fury when she said it.

Georgie kicked a stone and kept kicking it, following it back and forth across the lane, concentrating on its progress.

"Are you drunk?"

Georgie looked up. Anne was on the lane, and fast approaching, cheeks pink with exertion, blonde curls bouncing.

"You are drunk!" she exclaimed.

"You're mad." Georgie glared at her. "How could I be drunk?"

"That flask."

"There's nothing in the flask but a few unhappy tadpoles."

"Well, you were walking like you're drunk."

Georgie gave the stone a final kick. It bounced on the packed earth and struck a booted ankle. Muddy boot, no ribbons.

Georgie winced in recognition. Elf. She must have been close on Anne's heels, and she'd picked just the wrong moment to step around her, out into the line of fire.

Another accident.

Georgie could explain, but explaining to Elfreda Marsden had never produced the desired effect.

"Georgie," said Anne in a scolding voice. "That was childish."

"That was a bull's-eye," said Georgie, fetching up a cocky smile. Anne shook her head in reproof, but Elf advanced as though she hadn't even noticed.

"Mr. Clutterbuck?" she asked. Her eyes weren't accusing, but hopeful, and that actually felt quite a bit worse.

Guilt flooded in, followed by a crashing wave of irritation. She was twisting the screws. She could see for herself that Georgie's crackpot dash had failed to answer the purpose.

"Gone." Georgie gave a careless shrug. "Drove off like the dickens. Seemed to have somewhere else he'd rather be. I can sympathize."

Elf's throat worked. She was still pale, dark snarls of wet hair straggling around her pointed face.

"Who *is* Mr. Clutterbuck?" asked Anne. "A beau?"

Elf plucked at her dress, which clung to her body in all the places that Georgie tried hardest not to look. "He is the president of the Albion Society of Antiquaries."

"Society of Druids," Georgie translated for Anne. "When my father was a boy, he used to see them walking about in long robes. Her grandfather was the president. Until he tried to sacrifice his rivals in a wicker man."

"Lies," snapped Elf. "Invented *by* his rivals." She turned to Anne. "The Albion Society is a glorious institution for bold inquiry into the human past. A proud association of lamp-holders dedicated to shining light through the mists of time. They organize and fund excavations all over Britain. You don't exist as an archaeologist unless you're a Fellow." Her voice took an uncharacteristically wistful dip, and her dark eyes seemed to swim with tears, but a moment later, they hardened into obsidian, so Georgie was left to doubt.

"I planned to tell Mr. Clutterbuck about the amulet," she continued, in a sharper tone. "But he's gone to Llangollen."

"Llangollen!" Anne gasped. "To see the *Ladies*?"

Georgie tried to catch her eye, to signal *stop*.

"What ladies?" asked Elf.

"The *Ladies*!" Anne had begun to sparkle. "Lady Eleanor Butler and Miss Ponsonby. All sorts of people pay visits to their cottage. Poets and such. Wordsworth said in a poem that theirs is *a love allowed to climb / Ev'n on this earth, above the reach of time*. I hope to visit someday myself, when I've more to offer in terms of conversation and experience. I so greatly admire them."

Anne clipped articles about the Ladies from the papers to paste in her scrapbook, and she wrote poems herself in praise of their way of life.

Which Elf might not like.

Or perhaps she would.

Georgie tamped down that train of thought.

Elf was frowning. "Mr. Clutterbuck didn't mention any ladies."

"Why else go to Llangollen?" Anne gave a little sigh. It was a rhetorical question, but Elf turned owlish.

"To survey the northern stretch of Offa's Dyke. The earthwork King Offa built to defend his kingdom from the Welsh."

"Was this also in the ninth century?" asked Anne brightly, blue eyes slightly glazed.

"The eighth," corrected Elf.

"King Offa stole his territories from the Welsh." Georgie smiled. "That makes his earthwork an offense, not a defense."

A strange look passed across Elf's face.

"What do you know about King Offa?"

"Nothing," said Georgie. "But my mother was from Wales, so I know a few things about thieving, murdering Anglo-Saxons and marcher lords."

Elf's chin shot up. "I wish there were a dyke between our properties."

"Let's build one." Suddenly, Georgie was laughing. "Why not? I don't have anything else to do."

Elf went still.

"I do," she said. She passed a hand briefly across her eyes. Dirt made lunar eclipses beneath her fingernails.

"I must tell Papa." She was speaking to herself, gaze turned inward. "An amulet on the bluff. He'll understand that we need to dig in earnest."

"I can help." Georgie offered without thinking first. "You lost the amulet because of me. I'll find you a new one."

"A new one." Elf's lip curled, and her gaze focused. She stared so hard and long, Georgie's muscles went rigid.

Five years ago, during their last encounter, they had stared into each other's eyes. Their faces had come so close that Georgie had smelled the strawberry lemonade on her breath. Their mouths had nearly touched. And then they'd both started in shock.

Another accident. One Georgie hadn't forgotten.

How did Elf remember that night? That moment?

She was already walking away, arms stiff at her sides, left heel pulling out of her boot with every step.

Georgie gazed at her retreating figure, which seemed so small and fragile, and then up at Marsden Hall—uncountable tons of stone, and the weight of history besides.

God, it was gloomy.

Anne broke the spell. "You could go after her."

"I don't want to go after her. I want to go back to London." Georgie started kicking a new stone down the lane.

"You *should* go after her." Anne followed. "It *is* your fault, about the amulet."

"It's Rosalie's fault." Georgie sent the stone sailing into the grass. "Where is Rosalie? She was supposed to meet us at the pond. Why aren't you worried?"

"Because I know where she is. She's sleeping under the willow. Bedded on the moss like a fairy. Cowslips all around. She looked enchanted, so I didn't dare to wake her."

"I dare," said Georgie darkly, and quickened the pace.

"Yes, you're very bold." Anne skipped to catch up. "Soooo." She drew it out. "Elf."

"Elf," muttered Georgie.

"Is the name derived from her appearance? She looks supremely elf-like."

"How's that?" Georgie snorted. "She looks . . ."

Dark eyes that could drown the sun. Elf always seemed on the verge of a frown. It was the shape of her lips. They had a downward turn. Coaxing them into a new shape would make for a challenge. One might start with a featherlight touch. Trace their outline with a fingertip. And then—

"She looks . . ." prompted Anne.

"She looks like she looks," finished Georgie, with a scowl. "Her name is Elfreda. Hence Elf. I say it to annoy her. No one else calls her that."

"I see," murmured Anne. "A pet name. Something just between the two of you."

Georgie examined Anne's profile suspiciously. A dimple dented her cheek. "It's not like that."

"Of course not."

"She's not like us."

"Of course not," said Anne. And then: "How can you be sure?"

"I'm sure." Georgie wasn't sure. It was maddening. "I'm sure. And it doesn't matter. She hates me."

"She seemed to."

"I hate her."

"Mm."

They'd reached the part of the lane enclosed by hedges.

"Is that where we came in?" asked Anne, pointing to a gap. "I squeeze through there, get back to that boulder, and then I'll see the path to the pond?"

"Why are you asking me?"

Anne swung around and caught Georgie by the biceps. They stood like that, face-to-face. Anne wore a tiny smile.

"Because I don't want to wander in circles while you convince your elfin queen to forgive you."

"Ha," said Georgie.

Anne let go. "I'm sure you'll succeed. You usually do."

Georgie gave a groan and half turned, looking down the lane. Back and forth, again, and for what?

The hedges rustled with country birds. And with Anne, slipping away, leaving Georgie alone with their thoughts.

4

ELFREDA WAS HALFWAY home when she spied Papa striding through the park.

"Look what Clutterbuck gave me!" He gesticulated wildly as she approached, something tiny pinched between his fingers. "A halved penny struck in the name of Empress Matilda. The pompous arse discovered a buried pot packed with coins from the Anarchy, near Watford. He wanted to rub it in that I wasn't invited to the Watford excavation, or to Llangollen."

"Perhaps he gave it to you because of Matilda," suggested Elfreda, trotting to keep up.

"Matilda?" Papa stopped short, thunder on his brow.

"Your daughter. Matilda. He is the twins' godfather, after all. Perhaps he meant it for her."

"Oh." Papa started walking again. "No, indeed. He meant to humiliate me. I shall hurl it in the river."

"You mustn't." Papa liked to be begged not to follow through on his threats, as though there was a chance he would. "Add it to your coin cabinet. You've made such important contributions to the study of British numismatics. Mr. Clutterbuck knows that."

"He knows nothing. He has not so much brain as earwax. Mark

my words. I will pen my letter of resignation this very night. I, Harold Marsden, esquire, refuse to carry on the works of the Society another day under a hog's turd such as Walter Clutterbuck!"

When Papa began to mix the insults of Shakespeare with the insults of Chaucer, there was nothing to do but play along.

"Don't resign from the Society, Papa," she begged. "You hate London. You skip three-quarters of the meetings. That's why the Fellows elected Mr. Clutterbuck. They don't respect him more than they respect you. It's just that he's there. The president attends Society business in Gray's Inn. No one believed you would take up residence in town."

"I wouldn't. If I were president, Society business would come to me." Papa stopped walking again. "That is what Bartholomew Mortimer intended."

Bartholomew Mortimer, the previous Society president, had died last spring, leaving the office vacant. Elfreda had wished for Papa's appointment as fervently as Papa himself. If Papa were president, he'd rally the Fellows to submit a supplemental charter for her admission. Mr. Clutterbuck would be much harder to convince.

"You were Mr. Mortimer's rightful successor." Elfreda spoke in soothing tones. "He held you in the highest esteem."

"Yes, I was. Yes, he did." Papa turned his gaze on the clouds. He was a big man, with a large beard and white hair that waved back from his brow to end in a perfect curl below his ears. When Elfreda was a little girl, she'd thought that he looked like God, or at the very least, like King Alfred.

"Clutterbuck, Clutterbuck." Papa sighed and put on his quoting face. Of late, he had been comparing himself alternately to Caesar and Macduff.

Silence settled over them.

Elfreda guessed Caesar.

"This was the most unkindest cut of all," said Papa. "The toad-hearted knave. The wretch. The traitor! I championed his candidature for fellowship. I read a testimonial on his behalf before the whole Society. See how he repays me! With a stolen presidency and a rotten half penny!" Papa opened his hand and glared at the fragment of silver in his palm.

The moment had come.

"Papa," she said. "The Fellows won't care what Mr. Clutterbuck finds in Watford, or Llangollen. Because *I* have found something extraordinary. On the bluff." She stood straighter. "An amulet. Hammer shaped, cast in lead, about the size of my thumb." She paused, the engravings appearing in her mind's eye. Her finger twitched and traced the angles in the air.

"Papa," she said. "It was inscribed with runes. From the alphabet of the Northmen."

His expression altered. "Youngling. Are you saying what I believe you are saying?"

She nodded. "The Great Heathen Army made their camp on the bluff." She gazed over the green sweep of the park, up to the towering bluff, and the miracle of it hit her again.

"The Northmen were there, just there," she whispered.

"Oh, my dear girl!" Papa was all smiles. "Tonight, we celebrate with a saga. And you can drink a glass of my Canary sack. Out of the green goblet."

Elfreda's chest warmed. Papa never shared his sack. And the green goblet had been Grandpapa's. Fourth century, Roman. Touching it was absolutely forbidden.

"Now." Papa tucked the penny into his pocket and held out his hand. "The amulet. Show me."

The warmth in Elfreda's chest leached away. She hadn't thought this part through.

"I don't have it."

"You don't have it." Papa blinked rapidly, trying to make sense of her words.

"I found it." Elfreda swallowed. "And then I lost it."

Papa's lips moved inside his beard, but no sound came out.

"The army camped in Twynham." She tried to push her certainty through her eyes. "It says so in the *Chronicle*. And the hammer is proof. Once we mount a serious excavation, we will—"

Papa laughed, not a nice sound. "You propose I hire more laborers? Incur enormous expense? On what basis? You've shown me nothing. For all I know, you had a whimsical experience with a pebble."

That stung.

She spoke softly. "It wasn't a pebble."

"This isn't the first time you've succumbed to whimsy." Papa began to pace. "You are prone to it, as was my mother. But she didn't have the benefit of the education I've given you. I educated your understanding, not your sentiments. I educated you as I would have educated my own son. And yet you still behave like a silly daughter."

That stung more. And Papa hadn't finished.

"I haven't forgotten you thought the old rabbit warren by the orchard was a barrow. I told you it wasn't, but you insisted the rabbit skeletons were the remains of miniature men."

Elfreda's eyes smarted, and she had to bite her lip to stop its trembling. "I never thought it was a barrow of miniature men. That was a game of make-believe with Agnes. And it was years and years ago. I'm hardly ever silly anymore. Papa, the amulet is real."

"Then where is it?" He stepped to her and loomed, like Thor himself demanding his lost hammer. "Did it sprout wings and fly away?"

"More like gills," came a pleasant voice. "The amulet is in my pond."

Papa's head snapped around. Georgina was sauntering toward them. "And it wasn't any fault of your daughter's." She smiled as she drew up to them. "I knocked her into the water—accidentally, of course. We collided."

Elfreda felt Papa's eyes move over her.

"You *are* wet, aren't you?" He cocked his head. "Child, you look as though you were wallowing like a swine."

"Not at all," said Georgina. "She was more swan-like than swine-like, in truth."

Papa's eyes swung back to her.

"Good afternoon, Mr. Marsden," she said. "It has been too long."

Papa clearly did not agree. His nostrils flared. "Did you see the amulet? A little lead hammer? Did you see it?"

Georgina hesitated.

"As I thought." Papa stroked his beard disapprovingly in Elfreda's direction. "Go up to the house before you take ill. And you"—he addressed Georgina—"you *accidentally* knocked my daughter into the water. I assume you have wandered *accidentally* into my park. I bid you remove yourself." He inclined his head. "Good afternoon, Captain Redmayne."

Elfreda's mouth dropped open. Her eyes met Georgina's.

"Actually," said Georgina, with a hint of a smile. "It's *Major* Redmayne." She tucked one hand into the front of her coat, the ubiquitous pose adopted by war heroes in portraiture.

"Major." Papa nodded. Elfreda turned to stare at *him*. Could he truly have mistaken *Georgina* for her brother? Georgina was tall, but Henry Redmayne was over six feet, and much heavier. Their coloring was the same, and they shared the same abhorrent cockiness, and Georgina had *dressed* for the part. Was that what convinced him? Breeches made the man?

Papa continued, "I thought you were still in France."

"Oh, I am in France," said Georgina, smoothly. "Stationed in Cambrai with the Army of Occupation. But they have to let us officers put on mufti and pop over to our country estates every now and then. Ride to hounds." She glanced at Elfreda. "Build a dyke or two."

Elfreda's blood boiled.

"Georgina—" she began.

"Is also here," supplied Georgina. "With two very dear friends, Miss Poskitt and Miss Mahomed. They request the pleasure of Miss Marsden's company, for dinner."

Papa's eyes narrowed. "And where will *you* dine?"

"With the other officers, of course." Georgina smiled an ingenuous smile. "In Thornton."

"There are no officers in Thornton." Elfreda felt as though she were chewing glass. "The militia disbanded in 1816."

"Did it? That's a shame. The neighborhood will be wanting a bit of dash, then. I suppose I'll dine at home." Georgina bowed to Elfreda. "If Miss Marsden doesn't object to having me at the table."

Miss Marsden objected with every ounce of her being. She objected so strongly her throat closed up like a fist.

As for Papa, his face had turned a strange shade of puce. "You are designing. But I can easily penetrate your scheme."

Elfreda caught her breath. So Papa *wasn't* fooled.

Georgina didn't have the grace to look sheepish. She looked amused. "Designing, am I? And what is my design?"

"My land, Major. You are after my land. I assure you, your money cannot buy the rest of it. Nor can you gain it by marriage. I would never consent to such a connection."

Elfreda's cheeks flamed and she made a choking sound.

Georgina's cheeks had pinked too, but not with embarrassment, with anger. Even after all this time, Elfreda knew her expressions well enough to know the difference. The anger crackled around her for one long moment, and then she smiled, nonchalant.

"You will never have to consent. I am happily engaged. To a French countess. The adorable Marguerite. Marguerite Marie-Rose de Champagne. Her whole family was put to the guillotine, even the lapdogs. I am very much in love."

Pure nonsense. Elfreda knew, too, when Georgina was poking fun. She was laughing now at Papa's expense.

"That," Elfreda spit out, "is the most preposterous thing I've ever heard."

Georgina studied her gravely. "I am sorry to disappoint you, Miss Marsden." She paused and added, in an encouraging tone, "But I have no doubt that the right suitor will one day come along."

That did it. She was going to scream.

"Tell Georgina," she said instead, to Georgina, her voice impressively calm, "that I would rather eat a lapdog than sit at a table with any of you."

She stalked off, head held high, but her sense of triumph faded with every step. She was itchy and damp and so bitterly disappointed. Today's discovery should have changed everything. Instead, it had changed very little. And Papa's dismissal had planted a seed of doubt in her mind. Maybe she *had* fallen under the spell of a funny little pebble and let her fancies run away with her. Now she'd never know for sure. She'd keep digging, of course. She'd dig on the bluff for twenty more years, if that's what it took. And it might. Digging was slow work when you dug alone, and only during those hours you could rob from other tasks.

She risked a glance over her shoulder. Papa and Georgina had parted company. Papa was walking northwest, not toward Marsden Hall, but not toward the river either. The Empress Matilda penny was safe.

Georgina wasn't anywhere. She was fast, though. Perhaps she'd already reached the lane, disappeared through the hedges.

Elfreda veered into the orchard, a sparse grouping of gnarled apple trees, more dead limbs than flowering boughs. Crows perched high in the crowns, pecking at last year's withered pippins.

She sat on a stump by the old rabbit warren, brooding. Her grandmother had first taken her to the warren, opened it up with a shovel and showed her the tiny bones. It was her grandmother who'd made digging seem magical, a way to make time fold over, so that the past and the present touched. She never felt closer to Grandmama than when she was digging. Grandmama, Grandpapa, Mother—they were all in the churchyard. But when she had a shovel in her hand, Grandmama was digging with her. Grandmama had been an archaeologist as well, although no one ever acknowledged her as such. She'd accompanied Grandpapa to Stonehenge, and the drawers of her writing desk contained not only diaries but notebooks filled with observations in her own hand, some of which Elfreda recognized from Grandpapa's published books.

"I wish we'd had longer," Elfreda said to her, rupturing the orchard's hush. "There are so many things I would have asked you, now that I'm grown." Grandmama had died when Elfreda was ten, six years before her mother, whose memory had faded much quicker. Mother had been faded too, in life. Grandmama was vibrant, then and now. Elfreda could almost see her, between the trees.

"You would have believed me about the amulet," she said. "You would have helped me figure out what to do next."

A twig snapped. Three crows hopping around the stump flapped suddenly into the air.

Her skin prickled.

It wasn't Grandmama ducking under an apple bough, coming toward her.

"Do you enjoy talking to yourself?" asked Georgina. "Is that why you scorn the very idea of friendship?"

Elfreda hunched on the stump, too tired for surprise, let alone outrage.

"Go away," she said dully.

"What a lackluster retort." Georgina plucked an apple, sniffed its wrinkled skin, and frowned. "Try harder. Tell me that talking to yourself is the only way to have an intelligent conversation."

She gave a minimal shrug. "I wasn't talking to myself."

"Who were you talking to?" Georgina glanced about, intrigued.

It seemed wrong to let Georgina force her from her own orchard, but she'd developed a chill, and the stump had unfortunate protuberances, so she stood, ceding territory without any fuss.

"I'll go, then. You can stay. I wouldn't eat that."

Georgie let the apple drop. "This orchard is a bit morbid. Crows. Dead trees." She kicked the apple. "Mummified apples."

Elfreda turned without a word.

"Elf." Georgina caught her arm.

She froze in Georgina's grasp. She felt lightheaded, and she smelled balsam, a bright, evergreen scent cutting through the orchard's heavy fragrance of fermentation and moss.

Slowly, she rotated until she was looking into Georgina's face. The sun struck red glints from her hair, and her straight black lashes framed her narrow blue gaze.

"I'm sorry," said Georgina. "I'm sorry about the amulet, truly."

Elfreda pulled back and felt a moment of resistance before Georgina released her hold. Georgina had sounded sincere, which most certainly meant she wasn't.

"Your apology doesn't interest me in the slightest."

Georgina folded her arms. Her shoulders made a straight line, and her bosom was flat—or seemed flat. Elfreda's could never compress to such dimensions.

Georgina's hips were narrow. She'd always been slender, but in a tight coat, and tighter breeches, she appeared lean and muscular. Her legs were very long, and it felt a bit shocking, *seeing* them. Two of them. Their contours.

Elfreda realized that her eyes were tracing Georgina's body. Georgina had realized too.

"*Something* interests you," she drawled. "Whatever it is, I'm amenable."

Suddenly, Elfreda found it difficult to think. She found it difficult to breathe. She didn't understand the implication of Georgina's words, and she didn't like not understanding.

A crow flapped out of a tree, cawing, and she jumped. To cover her confusion, she went on the attack, folding her own arms, glaring.

"You know you can't go strutting around impersonating your brother. My father is terrible with faces, but no one else would be taken in."

"I'm handsomer." Georgina's smile spread. "I'm aware."

She ignored this. "Why, though? Why do it at all?"

"I never had any intention of impersonating Harry. Your father came up with that on his own."

"But you *are* wearing breeches."

"I got into the habit in London, on the stage."

"On the stage!" Elfreda gaped. "Is that how you got into so much trouble? Acting?"

"The acting hasn't come to light, thank God. How do you know I got into trouble?" Georgina squinted. "I don't imagine you read the scandal sheets. Not enough mildew."

"Your friend, Miss Poskitt, told me."

"Of course she did. What else did she say?"

A broken engagement. A duel. A curricle crash.

Elfreda wouldn't be distracted. "You act men's roles? In the theater?"

"I act as a man, in the theater." Georgina leaned closer. "In daily life, I act as a woman, or as a man. Either. Sometimes neither. Sometimes both. It depends on various factors."

Elfreda wasn't chilled any longer. She felt too hot, her mind working, the efforts fast, furious, and futile. It was like being confronted with a page of text written in a language she couldn't read.

"Maybe I'll put on a private theatrical." Georgina straightened. "*Romeo and Juliet*. We'll take the title roles."

Elfreda smiled thinly. More than four strangers in a room and her tongue locked in place. Georgina had witnessed her humiliations in countless parlors. She was mocking her now.

"My family dislikes your family." Elfreda spoke in a brittle voice. "Your family dislikes my family. But I'd abhor you all the same if your surname was Mowbray or de Burgh."

"My God." Georgina's laugh was low. "Even de Burgh? The snobbery."

"It's not snobbery. What I'm saying is I abhor you for *you*."

"Because I teased you when we were children."

"Teased me? You nearly put out my eye."

"I was eight years old. And I said *en garde*. You were supposed to raise your stick and parry."

"I was using my stick to roll my hoop, like everyone else."

"No, you weren't. Your hoop was on the ground. You couldn't roll it for your life. You were standing there looking furious, and I thought you'd benefit from a bit of swordplay."

"You cut off my braid in church."

"Also at a callow stage of life. And I'd brought the most cunning little pair of grape scissors. I had to cut something."

"Why bring grape scissors to church?"

"Good question." Georgina paused. "It was just the tip of the braid."

"You rode me into a ditch."

"I didn't see you. You matched the lane. I recommend brighter colors."

"The time at Mrs. Pattinson's."

Georgina's eyelids flickered. "Which time at Mrs. Pattinson's?"

"The ball. The ball before you went to London. You were nineteen."

Some quick, complex expression passed across Georgina's face. Then she gave a small, negating twitch. "It wasn't what you imagined."

"I don't care." Elfreda wished she hadn't brought it up. Memories of that night were stupidly tender, like bruises in her brain.

"Elf." Georgina stepped closer.

"Stop." It was overwhelming. The amulet. Georgina. The odd light in her eyes. Elfreda swallowed and met those eyes directly.

"Go fritter away your life," she said. "Dance and drink champagne and play whist with your pretty friends and snicker at wallflowers and put on private theatricals and—"

"How is that frittering?" Georgina interrupted. "That *is* life. Except for the snickering at wallflowers. You've got me all wrong there."

"Do as you please," Elfreda continued. "Engage in all the superficial pursuits you like best, just as long as you do *not* come near me ever again."

Georgina stared. "If I was born a thousand years ago, and buried in some barrow, you'd collect my buttons and hairpins. My frittering would seem significant."

Elfreda did not concede the point.

"You weren't," she said. "And it doesn't."

With that she started walking up the rutted road to Marsden Hall.

"So I'll see you at dinner!" Georgina called after her. "Seven o'clock. Lapdog fricassee."

This time, Elfreda didn't glance over her shoulder. She hoped she'd already seen the last of Georgina Redmayne.

5

T HE FIRST TIME Elfreda saw Georgina Redmayne, she was
five or six. Grandmama was still alive. Mother too, of course,
but Mother had been inside, abed, and it was Grandmama
who'd taken her out into the park. While Elfreda was weaving a
necklace of dandelions, a little, impertinent girl astride a too-big
pony trotted right up to her and asked to see the dragon. Elfreda
hadn't yet heard the neighborhood gossip that had painted Grandpapa as a dragon breeder, as well as a druid, and only stared at the
girl, who went red with pique to the roots of her red hair, and let her
pony eat the dandelion necklace before cantering off.

That was the beginning. This was the end.

Elfreda would avoid Georgina like the plague.

Papa was avoiding *her* like the plague. After his walk, he'd locked
himself and his Empress Matilda penny in the library and wouldn't
even open the door to receive his dinner. She'd left the tray in the hall.

Now it was well past eight in the evening. Elfreda sat contemplating a plate of cold pork bones at the kitchen table with her sister
Agnes beside her and the housekeeper opposite.

"I'm not going up to bed," announced Agnes, pulling her chair over to the hearth. "I'm practicing for London. Beatrice says it's terribly provincial to sleep between dinner and breakfast."

Beatrice Parker was Agnes's bosom friend, sixteen years old and out in society. Every day, Agnes paced the entrance hall, hoping for another of Beatrice's letters from Mayfair, where her family had taken lodging for the Season. These letters tended to produce either a storm of weeping, a bout of excessive curtseying, a vociferous craving for frozen punch, or some particularly annoying combination of all three.

"I can't ride Æthelstan anymore," continued Agnes. "Beatrice says none of the girls ride donkeys in London."

You're not going to London anytime soon. Elfreda almost said it aloud. Papa always had money enough to buy a rare book on Paternoster Row. Not so when it came to things he considered frivolous, like gowns and slippers. He would never pay for a debut. And the other option had been foreclosed.

"You love Æthelstan," she said instead. "Æthelstan loves you. He kicks everyone else."

"I want to take Æthelstan to London, of course," responded Agnes. "But I can't *ride* him there. I'll walk him on a leash, with Beatrice, when she walks her Pomeranian."

Elfreda put on a vague smile and started clearing and stacking plates. Lately, Agnes showed every determination to style herself like a conventional young miss. The harder she tried, the more peculiar she seemed.

She would admire Anne Poskitt excessively. Perhaps Elfreda should have sent her to dine at Redmayne Manor. An evening of French food in fashionable company. Elfreda wanted that for her. Except, Redmayne Manor. Except, Georgina.

Georgina.

Elfreda slammed the crockery.

"What's a better waltzing partner?" Agnes stood up from the chair and wandered the kitchen. "A broom? A jug? A bellows?"

Eventually, she did go up to bed, but only after Elfreda resorted to chasing her around the table with an onion, repeating, "Promise me the next two dances!" at the top of her lungs. Agnes hated onions.

Elfreda dropped the onion back into the basket, knowing she'd been silly, even before Mrs. Pegg said to the low rafters, "Did ever anybody see the like?"

She crept to her own bed, dejected, a silly daughter who'd embarrassed herself one too many times.

In the morning, Mrs. Pegg prepared breakfast for Papa and Agnes, while Elfreda cooked porridge for the twins and carried it up to the nursery.

"Heavens," she said upon entering. "Hilda and Matilda have vanished! Wherever could they be?"

The nursery was a small, dim room, with narrow windows. Elfreda had done her best to relieve the chill of the stone with carpets and tapestries and whatever upholstered furniture she could drag up the stairs. This had resulted in a warmer, cheerier atmosphere, but it had also furnished the children with dozens of attractive hidey-holes.

"Are they under this rug?" Elfreda asked, lifting a corner of the rug with her toe.

She heard stifled laughter, and Hilda exploded out of a mound of pillows. The fur tippet was wrapped around her neck, and she'd added a muff on each arm.

"I'm not hungry," said Hilda. "I ate Hilda for breakfast."

"Ah," said Elfreda. "Did you also eat Matilda?"

"I ate Matilda," said Matilda, crawling out from beneath the bed. She was wrapped in a raggedy shawl and wearing mittens. Grendel, the elderly beagle, waddled after her.

"Hilda and Matilda weren't very big," noted Elfreda. "I'm sure you have room for porridge." She set the tray on the table.

Matilda crawled over to the table, climbed into a chair, and began to lick at a bowl. Hilda followed suit.

Elfreda put her hands on her hips. "Spoons, please."

Matilda raised her head. "Bears can't use spoons."

Elfreda opted for logic instead of silliness.

"Bears can't speak English either," she said in a brisk, stern voice. "Therefore, you are not . . ."

Matilda was looking crestfallen. Hilda raised her head too and pawed sadly at the oats stuck to her cheeks.

Elfreda sighed. "You are, therefore, magical bears. Ready?"

The twins nodded.

"Abracadabra." Elfreda stretched out her arms and wiggled her fingers. "Now. Try to use a spoon."

Brow furrowed, Matilda picked up a spoon and held it clumsily in her mittened hand.

"Miraculous," said Elfreda. "Magical, spoon-using bears."

Unfortunately, the magical bears followed her up to the bluff, where they transformed into magical, trowel- and sieve-using bears. They kept stealing hers, which made it difficult to proceed with her dig. When she brought them back to the house, so Agnes could mind them, all three started crying, so loudly the wails summoned Papa from the library. He looked distraught and disheveled, with ink on his fingers and smudges on the lenses of his spectacles. He didn't meet Elfreda's eyes as he lined his children up by age on hard chairs and began to read to them from the Venerable Bede. But he did, when his throat grew hoarse, pass the Venerable Bede to her, so that she could pick up where he'd left off, and he nodded along in a way that signaled his sulk was almost over.

Later that night, he showed her the letter of resignation he'd written to Mr. Clutterbuck, and after she'd begged him to tear it up, he did so, ceremonially, for the good of the Society. They went back to work, together, on the book that he hoped to publish, *Ancient Derbyshire*, which expanded upon their pamphlet, *Two Dissertations on the*

Saxon Grave Hills of the Peak District. By dawn, clouds blew in and deluged. She couldn't dig in such weather, or get on with laundry day, and so she continued working at Papa's side, their pens scratching in unison. It was almost as if Mr. Clutterbuck hadn't visited, as if she hadn't found the amulet, and lost it again, at Georgina's hand. She was almost relieved by the rain, for the pocket of peace it provided.

The next night, she was less relieved. The rain hadn't ceased, and the stain on the ceiling of the blue room began to bulge, droplets pattering down onto the threadbare rug, and more upsettingly, onto Grandmama's writing desk. She couldn't ask Mrs. Pegg for help. Mrs. Pegg looked sweet and soft, with her lace cap, white hair, and dimpled face, but she was implacable. Papa had tried and failed to sack her with the rest of the staff. She'd boxed his ears. As the sole remaining servant, she acted as cook, nurse, *and* housekeeper, but within limits. Her rules stipulated no tower, no library, no blue room.

Elfreda positioned the ash bucket under the leak, wiped off the desk, and pushed it, with difficulty, to the drier side of the room.

"Papa," she said, tiptoeing into the library, "the ceiling is leaking again, in the blue room."

He was reading a topographical survey in a wingback chair and didn't lift his gaze. "Catch it with the ash bucket."

"I did. But the leak is bigger than before. Don't you think it's time I ask Mr. Hibbert to come by?"

Mr. Hibbert was Twynham's master builder. He employed several stalwart carpenters in his workshop in the village. They could fix the leak in a trice.

"No, I do not think." Papa raised his head. "I won't have that villain in my house."

"But Papa—"

"Not after what he did to St. Alcmund's."

"He was responsible for the repairs, not the . . ." She hesitated. The restoration committee had called the alterations to the church "improvements," but she knew better than to repeat the word.

Her delicacy made no difference. Papa's mood turned explosive.

"Desecration!" He thundered it. "That man carted Anglo-Saxon masonry out of an eighth-century nave and used it to mend the road. He should be subjected to rat torture. I won't have Marsden Hall disfigured by brutes. Better the ceiling collapse. Now, bring me the opodeldoc. My shoulders ache."

When Papa used that tone, her *head* ached. She pressed her lips together and went for the opodeldoc. The bottle was empty. In the kitchen, she mixed a fresh ointment with extra rosemary oil. She brought the bottle to Papa, put the twins to bed, gave up on Agnes, and peeked once more into the blue room, to assure herself that the ceiling hadn't, in fact, collapsed.

It hadn't. But Grandmama's desk was still wet. Or rather, it was wet again. Water dripped from the ceiling directly above. A new leak. She pushed the desk all the way over to the fireplace. No drying warmth emanated from the fireplace—Papa forbade fires after May Day—but at least there weren't any leaks on this side of the room. Yet.

A horrible thought occurred to her.

She lowered the desk's fall front. As she'd feared, the water had seeped inside. The poems Grandmama had written on scraps of paper and stuffed in the pigeonholes—also wet. Mostly just the edges, but on a few, the inked lines had lifted up and run together.

"No," she cried, not for the first time that week. "No, no, no."

She extracted poem after poem, carrying the damp scraps to her bedchamber, where she could spread them out. No poem had been rendered truly illegible, but even so, she felt shivery and sick, and furious with herself. Why hadn't she ever made a fair copy of Grand-mama's magnificent sonnets? She'd treated Grandmama's desk like a cabinet of wonders, each scrap a one-of-a-kind object.

As soon as the poems dried, she'd copy them all.

She moped back to the blue room and was blotting the little puddles inside the desk's emptied pigeonholes when she noticed something else.

The central walnut panel dividing the pigeonholes had popped slightly forward along its left edge. The panel was, in fact, a little door, if not deliberately secreted in the desk, so discreetly engineered, she'd never registered its existence.

She let the rag drop.

An instant later, she was prying the little door open with her fingernails.

Folded papers filled the space behind.

She smoothed them as best she could and read the first, the second, the third. She read faster and faster, forgetting even to blink.

Still reading, she burst into the library.

"Hwat!" Papa cried out when she touched his shoulder. It was his most guttural, Beowulfian cry.

She fell back a step, but only a step.

"Wretched heathen men!" She waved the papers, bouncing on her toes. "Papa, another reference to the Northmen in Twynham! Tenth century!"

"You are waving sheets of foolscap." Papa glared at her over his reading spectacles, his expression severe. "Foolscap is not tenth century. Foolscap is *paper*. Plant fiber. In the tenth century, scribes wrote on parchment, or vellum. Animal skin. Youngling, I despair of you."

"Paper, I know! I mean, Papa. Papa, I know the difference between paper and parchment. There's no need for bears. I mean, despair." She was tripping over her words in her eagerness to explain. "This is Grandmama's writing. She is writing *about* a tenth-century manuscript. It must be here, in the library. *The Chronicle of Sexburga of Twynham*. She was a nun at the abbey. Look, there's a section called 'Concerning the Wretched Heathen Men.'"

She thrust the relevant page under Papa's nose. He snatched it from her but spared it only a glance.

"This is English." He handed back the page.

"Sexburga wrote in Latin, of course. Grandmama was translating. Papa, have you ever seen Sexburga's chronicle, the original? We have to find it!"

She didn't add: *And then dig again on the bluff.* Surely once Papa beheld the finely lettered leaves of parchment spelling out the story of the Northmen in Twynham, he'd agree that digging on the bluff was now compulsory.

"*The Chronicle of Sexburga of Twynham.*" He gave an incredulous snort. "You may refer to the shelf list. That chronicle is not here. Because it doesn't exist."

"It must. Grandmama—"

"Was writing a novel," interrupted Papa. "Your grandmother had only the rudiments of other tongues. She couldn't translate Latin, or Saxon, or anything else."

"Oh, but she did. Both." Elfreda shuffled the papers again. "See here, she copied out the abbey's charter. The boundary clause would have been in Latin, but with the landmarks in Saxon." She read the landmarks aloud. "Old manure heap. Wild iris patch. Swing gate. Thorn tree. Wolf pit."

"Novelists often pretend to write true accounts." Papa shrugged. "What novel doesn't include invented documents and letters?"

He had a point.

But novelists invented those documents and letters to serve an artistic design, to heighten the drama and further the action.

"There are pages on the regulations introduced by the new abbess," said Elfreda, with more shuffling. "On customs and dues. The price of flax. Papa, there's no *plot*. There are hardly any incidents whatsoever. It's not novelistic in the least."

Papa sighed and shook his head. "Good mother. She was unable to distinguish between the important and the trivial. She read all my father's papers, but unfortunately, his erudition clogged her mind with superfluities."

Elfreda glanced at the portrait that hung between two of the tall mahogany bookcases, Grandpapa in his druidical robes. He had died long before her birth, but based on everything she'd ever read, of his and of Grandmama's, *she* was the intellect.

Papa saw it otherwise. So did the Albion Society. The whole world.

Papa was still speaking. "She loved ruins, but because she thought them beautiful—not because she perceived their relationship to great events, to war, to government. She wrote poems about Twynham Abbey. I'm not surprised she was also writing a novel." He sighed again. "*How the dark age stones do crumble*," he quoted, and Elfreda's mouth fell open. Papa, too, had lines of Grandmama's poetry by heart? He'd never let on.

Before she could formulate a reply, he rose and began to pace.

"She resented my father for breaking the entail," he said, pacing up to Grandpapa's portrait before turning back and pacing up to Elfreda. "But it was lose a few hundred acres, and the abbey, or lose everything. Mother didn't understand the necessity."

"She understood the necessity! She resented what made the necessity necessary." Elfreda gulped as Papa's brows lowered. But if he'd read through Grandmama's diaries, as well as her poems, he'd know that she'd kept accounts and disapproved of her husband's spending.

Grandpapa had drained the family coffers carting full-grown oaks from Wiltshire to plant in his own sacred grove. Printing one thousand gilt-edged, lavishly illustrated copies of his final book, *Druid Temples and Their Origins*. Nobody had ever bought one. They'd been stacked for decades in the gatehouse.

"*You* presume to understand?" Papa gripped the collar of his great-coat with both hands. "*You?*"

Elfreda held her tongue.

After a long moment, Papa's glare drifted away from her, toward the windows, which rattled with wind and rain.

"I resent that glorified fishmonger," he growled. "John Redmayne. He's to blame. He swore he'd preserve the abbey. Instead, he built his crass, common-rate manor right on top of it. And now his grandson, the scheming *Major*, comes sniffing around my property. Mark me. He's a fox, and a fox always leads with his nose. He wants this hall. He wants to smother it with stucco, and carpets, and wallpapers. Destroy its character and change its name."

"That will never happen," soothed Elfreda. Despite herself, she pictured Georgina with her fox-colored hair slinking through the house.

"Never." Papa agreed, but his glare was all for her again. "He won't. He can't. Remember that. Should he prevail with you, I shall raise my voice to declare to one and all, *I have no such daughter.*"

Disquiet swept through her. It was horrible to hear Papa disavow her, even hypothetically, even knowing he misperceived the Major's threat in every way.

She shifted, restless, poised to tell him he'd met the other Redmayne, the more dreadful one, the girl, but something held her back, the desire to spare his pride, and spare herself his outburst.

Surely not the desire to protect Georgina.

"He will not prevail," she murmured. "I will always be your daughter."

Papa's expression softened. "Yes, child. And I would not part with you, even to a man more worthy. You know you have my preference among your sisters."

He'd said as much before, many times, and in the past, she'd reveled in his regard, and felt its rightness. It meant he recognized her as cut from the same cloth.

Tonight, she felt her disquiet increase.

She had to give herself a mental shove to regain her focus. She shuffled the papers again. These papers deserved her attention, and his.

"This section." She cleared her throat. "This section about the wretched heathen men. It says they made their camp not a mile from the abbey. They left behind a hoard, and two nuns discovered it. They hid it again, fearing the army would return. What if it's still there? A hoard, Papa. Imagine the objects."

In the little silence that followed, she perused Papa's person for hints of excitement. The tilt of his head was promising.

He reached out and tugged the papers from her hands. He walked closer to the nearest candle, and for a long, tense moment, he read.

Finally, he looked up.

"Drivel. Rubbish. Balderdash."

Elfreda's teeth sank into her lower lip. She felt her heart bump each rib on its painful descent toward her stomach.

"Your face is long as a parsnip." Papa gave a sudden laugh. "Well, I have news that will put more apple in your cheeks. William Aubin-Aubrey is coming to Derbyshire. I had a letter this afternoon. He praised the diagrams of the tumuli in *Two Dissertations*. And promised to back me for president."

"Mr. Aubin-Aubrey praised the diagrams?" Elfreda's hands clapped together. William Aubin-Aubrey was known as the Barrow Prince. He was one of the younger Fellows, a man with a true genius for antiquity, the author of the book she kept on her bedside table, *Sepulchral Anecdotes*. And he'd praised the diagrams—*her* diagrams! For she'd drawn almost all of them, the ones in her dissertation, and most of the ones in Papa's.

"Will you tell him about the camp on the bluff?" Her face was all apples now. "Papa, will he dig with us?"

Papa tossed Grandmama's papers onto the library table. "He plans to open barrows in the Peak. I've been invited to go with him, and I'd intended to extend the invitation to you. But if you'd rather chase after figments, you are welcome to stay here and swoon over pebbles and nuns."

"It wasn't a pebble." Elfreda heard the pleading note in her voice. "And Mr. Aubin-Aubrey will—"

"Here." Papa strode across the room and tugged a book from the shelf. "Take this, to cleanse your mind. I will test your declensions in the morning."

The book was Edward Thwaites's *Grammatica Anglo-Saxonica*.

Elfreda took it. But when the clock chimed midnight, she crept into the library and retrieved Grandmama's papers, and it was those papers she read, until her candle stub burned out.

6

"Aᴏᴛʜᴇʀ ʀᴇᴀsᴏɴ I hate the country." Georgie stood at the parlor window, watching the rain bucket down.

"It rains in London," said Rosalie, with detestable reasonableness. She was stretched out on the pink brocade sofa, a teacup and saucer balanced on her breastbone.

"Let's play whist." Anne dealt at the card table, but none of them were used to the three-player variant, and the game disintegrated.

It was the third day of rain. It felt like the three hundredth.

Anne's chaperone had revived, and after luncheon, she sat with them in the parlor, which spoiled Georgie's plan to smuggle champagne up from the wine cellar. Anne was forced to filigree a basket. Rosalie situated herself beneath a lap desk and made unnervingly anatomical sketches of her own hand. Georgie wrote letters. Desperate, wheedling letters. To Harry. To everyone.

When a yellow sunbeam shot into the room, a collective cry of relief rang out. Mrs. Herridge couldn't have stopped the stampede to the door if she'd tried. Mercifully, she didn't.

"Another reason I hate the country." Georgie stood in the garden by a marble column of the wisteria-cloaked pergola, watching the clouds scud through the washed blue of the sky. "There's nothing happening out here either."

Anne and Rosalie stepped into the pergola's shade and squeezed together on the bench. There was no need to squeeze. The bench was long. They looked at each other and then at Georgie. Clearly, the bench wasn't so long it could accommodate a third wheel.

"Right," said Georgie. "I'm off."

Off to where, though?

Georgie headed nowhere, walking out of the garden into the park, kicking at the clinging wet grasses.

Harry had picked his punishment well.

In London, Georgie could have paid a call to one of a hundred acquaintances, fritterers by Elf's standards, but only because they had pulses. Because they looked at the horizon instead of down at the dirt.

Here, Georgie could pay a call on a childhood friend. But they were all married, if not confined, too busy with domestic life for more than perfunctory engagements. Certainly nothing fun. Who did that leave?

Not Elf. Or as Anne had called her, *the elfin queen*. She'd always seemed otherworldly. Utterly removed from the here and now. Once, Georgie had sat beside her in a carriage, when Mrs. Alderwalsey had offered them both a ride home from the village during a sudden downpour. She'd never looked up from her book. She hadn't acknowledged Georgie with a word.

The other day she'd spoken words enough.

Do not come near me ever again.

Georgie was approaching the woodland. Another few minutes and the fishing pond shimmered through the trees.

It made sense as a destination. It made sense to look again for the amulet. As though it were some kind of key.

To what was a question better unanswered.

———

Elfreda stopped on the sweeping carriage drive up to Redmayne Manor. This was her last chance to reconsider. When she turned around, she could see Marsden Hall in the distance, stark and gray on the hill. Papa was huddled in his greatcoat in the frigid library, laboring over descriptions of various disinterred objects for *Ancient Derbyshire*, perhaps at this very moment recalling her disgrace with strong nouns, giving a disgusted shake of his head. He would rail like King Lear on the heath if he knew what she was doing.

And perhaps it was foolery, a mistake that would expose her to Papa's wrath and Georgina's mockery, yielding nothing.

She turned back around. The Redmaynes' park was landscaped with small stands of trees. Yellow flowers—wild irises—brightened the shade cast by the nearest. This wasn't the wild iris patch from the abbey's boundary clause. Silly even to think of it. Charters named features of the landscape familiar at the time, and few endured across the centuries. Even rivers shifted in their beds.

Nonetheless. The irises decided her.

She was closing in on the manor when she heard the giggling.

Instead of knocking on the front door, she followed the sound through the garden.

It was coming from the pergola.

She walked up, stepped between the columns, and . . .

"Jupiter!" she gasped and shut her eyes. The sounds she heard now were in a decidedly different register. Scuffles. Thuds. She spun, prepared to depart posthaste, but her eyes were still closed, and she slammed into something that clasped her in a wild embrace and toppled them both. The something was a someone. The someone was Anne Poskitt. She lay on the stone floor, her face inches from Elfreda's. She was flushed a dewy pink, and her lips looked bee-stung.

"Oh, thank God!" she cried. "I thought you were Mrs. Herridge."

She sat up. Her gown was rumpled, and her bonnet was askew. "We got carried away." She said it confidingly to Elfreda. "Rosalie"—she twisted at the waist—"it's Elf, who we told you about. It's not Mrs. Herridge."

"Shhhhh." This shushing girl was Rosalie, lucky Rosalie, who *hadn't* gotten herself pushed into the pond. She was slight, with glossy black hair and a big-eyed beauty Elfreda associated with portraits from Roman Egypt. She yanked at her emerald-green gown, also rumpled, and knelt on the bench, peering toward the manor through the curtains of wisteria.

"If you say her name too many times, she'll appear."

Elfreda pushed herself to sitting and gripped her elbow. She'd whacked it, hard, the part that sends strange tingles up the arm. But her whacked elbow couldn't explain *all* the tingles. Her whole body shivered into gooseflesh.

Kissing. The girls had been kissing. Not the chaste kisses you might bestow on an elderly relative or a child. The two of them had looked like their bones had melted, like they were fusing at the mouth and the rest of their bodies would follow suit.

"Is that why Elf appeared?" Miss Poskitt giggled. "Because Georgie has said her name so many times?"

Elfreda's tingling intensified and transformed from an inexplicable physical sensation to a familiar emotional one. She was flustered. Georgina and her friends had always flustered her, with their secret smiles and arch looks and social graces that usually seemed to conceal some private joke, often at her expense. Her awkwardness was so amusing.

She climbed stiffly to her feet. "Where *is* Georgina?"

"It's anyone's guess. I haven't introduced myself. I'm Rosalie Mahomed. And very pleased to meet you."

Miss Mahomed had swiveled to smile at her, a warm smile.

"I can guess." Miss Poskitt put a finger to her temple. "The fishing pond! We spent that whole next day searching for your amulet. It's worse than a needle in a haystack, but I doubt Georgie would have stopped, if it weren't for the rain. I'm sure they're there now."

"They?" Elfreda's brow furrowed. "Georgina and Mrs. Herridge?"

"Don't say her name!" Miss Mahomed tried to hide behind her own arms.

"I meant Georgie," explained Miss Poskitt, and then to Miss Mahomed: "It doesn't matter if Mrs. Herridge turns up now. Nobody is getting ravished."

Her blue gaze was suddenly wistful.

Elfreda blushed more hotly than ever before in her life. But she kept her eyes open, and with a strangled *goodbye*, she escaped the pergola without tripping over herself or anyone else.

She raced through the park and plunged into the woodland, because the faster she moved, the harder it was to think about what she'd just witnessed, and what it might mean. She stopped at the edge of the pond, and her last blush became the *second* hottest of her life.

Because Georgina was naked.

7

SHE WENT REDDER and redder, unable to emit a peep. As a result, Georgina kept paddling in the pond, unaware of her presence, limbs stroking lazily through the water, water that seemed suddenly far less turbid, far more transparent, than memory allowed. Every now and then she dove, and Elfreda caught sight of her shining back, her rounded rear, and her two bare legs, kicking powerfully to propel her into the depths. Her head broke the surface, and her bent arms, as she pushed back her hair. Suddenly, she was standing, and the water was only waist deep. Elfreda was staring at her biceps, and then at her clavicles, and then at her nipples, small and tightly budded with cold. A sparkling droplet fell from the one on the left.

"Well met. Or perhaps not in this particular instance."

Elfreda willed herself to expire on the spot. When that didn't happen, she looked up, because the only alternative to conversing with Georgina Redmayne was conversing with Georgina Redmayne's nipples.

Georgina was staring right at her. Her black lashes were spiky with moisture, and her pale irises held a terrible light.

"Per your request, I won't come near you." She slid effortlessly backward, water slipping over her shoulders like a silken cape. After she'd traveled a few yards, she let her legs sink and treaded water to stay in place. "However, I can't stay in here indefinitely. I'm half-frozen as it is. What's the solution?"

Sweat was beading along Elfreda's hairline. Her breathing sawed. It was like a river-crossing problem from a mathematics text. How can the farmer row his goat and his cabbage to the opposite bank without the goat eating the cabbage and a wolf eating the goat?

This was less complicated. Or was it?

If she walked away, Georgina could exit the water, but she wouldn't get to ask for her permission to survey the property. If she didn't walk away, she could ask for permission, but by the time she'd finished begging, Georgina might have turned to ice.

The begging would take a good long while. After all those insults she'd lobbed, Georgina was certain to make her squirm.

She could put her back to the pond. Put her back to it and start the begging now. Georgina could exit the water while she spoke.

Naked.

"I'd swim to the other side," said Georgina, the patience in her voice drawing attention to the length of the pause. "But my clothing is on that log."

Clothing was indeed piled on a nearby log. A white muslin gown. A blue spencer. A chemise. Stockings.

"Here's a solution," said Georgina, her voice slightly less patient. "I swim to the other side, and you carry over my clothing, depositing it somewhere in the vicinity. You return to the willow and read to your heart's content. I dress and leave without disturbing you. Agreed?"

Words emerged, finally, from Elfreda's throat. Not the intended words. "How do you know? About the willow?"

She'd been slipping inside its great green cavern of trailing branches to read since long before Georgina's final departure to London made it entirely safe. If Georgina had known, it meant she'd said nothing, done nothing, left her in peace. But that indicated restraint and consideration. Georgina possessed neither.

"I see you don't have a book." Georgina bobbed, weary perhaps of the relentless motion required to keep her chin above the surface. "Why are you here, if not to read?"

She'd avoided answering the question. It was unsettling, irking, and goaded Elfreda to respond in kind.

"Why are *you* here?" She folded her arms. "Are you really looking for my amulet?"

"Anne." Georgina tilted back her head and skimmed her hand over the water, sending up an arc of spray. "Anne Chatterbox Poskitt. Anne told you. It's always Anne. How did it come about? She's been hoping for a tour of Marsden Hall, but I discouraged her from calling. She didn't attempt to climb the tower?"

"I went to your house."

Georgina laughed, then sputtered as her chin dipped. "You went to my house? The abhorrent house of your abhorrent neighbor whom you abhor? How droll. Elf, for the love of God. I can't feel my toes. Either move my clothing or move yourself. I'm getting out."

Elfreda had failed to cause her own expiry, and now she failed to budge her body an inch. She was trapped by the enormity of another problem some part of her mind had been days at solving without success.

Something *interests you*. Georgina had made that inscrutable claim in the orchard, after Elfreda had gone lightheaded at her touch, looked Georgina up and down, lost her breath, lost her bearings. And not an hour ago, she'd witnessed girls beneath a pergola clinging lip to lip, and the tingles she'd felt then were back now, a confused awareness of her own skin, the fast hot blood beneath.

It was all related, connected by a missing piece.

But no. How could it be?

She wanted to kiss Georgina Redmayne.

"I'm counting to ten!"

At Georgina's shout, she whirled, and the world lagged, as though she'd spun herself out of time and space. She was facing away from the pond, but she could still see Georgina coming toward her, rising from the water.

A moment later, the willow caught up. She was looking at the willow, a mercy. The willow made her heart rate slow. The wind riffled its leaflets and a few showered down. Beautiful willow. *A melody of shade played by the sun's green harp.* That's how Grandmama had described it in a poem.

Kiss Georgina? The desire seemed more distant, more impossible, by the second.

"You *do* have to tell me why you're here." Georgina had reached the log. Elfreda could hear the whisper of fabric as she dressed. "I have a right. This is my land."

The arrogance in Georgina's tone had the same irritating effect as always, and that was a relief. Kiss Georgina? Preposterous.

She succumbed to the irritation, gratefully.

"The land is your brother's. Only he has the right."

It occurred to her that she should write to the Major, beg permission of *him*. He could command Georgina's compliance.

"False," said Georgina. "My father practiced share and share alike. Harry inherited London, and Kent. I inherited Derbyshire."

Elfreda's surprise carried her one hundred and eighty degrees. Thank God Georgina had managed to make herself decent. She was buttoning her spencer, pointed locks of water-darkened hair hanging over her eyes.

"How can he keep you here if you have independent means?" Elfreda glanced at the pond, the ferns, the surrounding trees. She loved this tranquil clearing, and Grandmama had loved it too, and written poems under the willow, back when it wasn't an act of trespass. "You should sell a few acres and settle yourself back in London."

She wondered at the price of a few acres. Could Georgina be persuaded to sell the land back to Papa, piece by piece? Did Papa have the money to buy?

"I can't sell a turnip." Georgina shook back her hair as she did up the final button. "The estate remains in trust until my twenty-fifth birthday. I will rot before then."

"You're four and twenty now. You won't rot in less than a year."

"I'm four and twenty in June."

"You won't rot in thirteen months either."

"Thirteen months doesn't seem long to you, does it?" Georgina smiled thinly. "You measure time in centuries. The rest of us measure time in seasons. It's the Season right now in London. Plays are opening and closing. Dorothy Templeton is usurping my favorite chair at Miss Scarborough's salon. My friends are gossiping about goings-on I know nothing about. And eating pineapple mousse at Gunter's. And watching puppet shows at Bartholomew Fair. And going to the waxworks. And getting their fortunes told. And learning how to ride velocipedes. And I'm here, stuck in amber, like a beetle." She paused. "Like you." Her smile had faded, and her cheekbones had a faint flush.

Elfreda swallowed. "I am not stuck in amber."

Georgina shrugged. "And I don't fritter. I suppose it's a matter of perspective."

Elfreda was in danger of losing all perspective. She'd approached Georgina after forbidding her to do the same, and provoked an argument, instead of smoothing things over. And now, instead of gathering her wits, she was scrutinizing Georgina's face, particularly the shape of her mouth, the peaks of her upper lip and the rounded plushness of the lower.

"I wish I didn't say what I said. About frittering. And you never coming near me ever again." This was scrupulously honest, and as close to an apology as she could get. "I propose a truce." She hesitated. "And ask that you permit me free access to your land. You should, you know, to make amends for the amulet. I won't dig any holes. I'll stay out of your way. You'll hardly notice me."

The scattered sunlight played over Georgina's eyes, creating the illusion of emotion in their depths.

Elfreda braced herself for refusal.

"This is for your father?" Georgina asked. "Druid business?"

"I assume by *druid business* you mean antiquarian investigation." Elfreda worked to school her temper. An angry outburst would hurt her cause. "I am an antiquary too. An archaeologist. This isn't for my father's research. It's for mine. And also for my grandmother's."

"Your grandmother." Georgina fiddled with her dripping hair while Elfreda maintained a tense silence, tracking a bead of water rolling from her hairline down to her cheek to the corner of her mouth.

"Your grandmother," repeated Georgina, and sighed. "My mother held her in high esteem."

This was completely unexpected.

"Did she?" Elfreda gawked. "I had no idea they ever spoke. Grandmama never mentioned her."

She noticed that the skin around Georgina's eyes tightened and that her irises seemed frostier. Had her remark partaken of that superiority Georgina loathed? She hadn't meant to imply that Georgina's mother was beneath mention. She'd simply stated the truth.

Bother.

"They spoke." Georgina's voice was also frosty. "Often. When they met riding."

That sparked a memory, and Elfreda responded without thinking.

"Your mother rode like the goddess of horses! I used to watch for her from the tower. She wore that red habit."

"Horses have a goddess?" Georgina scrunched her brow.

"Epona," Elfreda muttered. She felt silly, but Georgina had tipped her head thoughtfully, the silver frost in her eyes melting into richer blue. Perhaps she was also picturing her mother on horseback. Margaret Redmayne had died young, swept into the North Sea. A tragedy that everyone in the neighborhood had discussed in horrified tones. Unlike her own mother's death, which happened in such slow stages, no one seemed to register the final event.

"They'd ride together," said Georgina, "but only in the woods, where no one would see. And they never spoke elsewhere. A Marsden and a Redmayne. They couldn't *call* on each other."

Georgina's wry smile summoned her own. A Marsden call on a Redmayne. A Redmayne call on a Marsden. Unthinkable.

The discord between their families had never seemed funny. Sharing this bizarrely conspiratorial grin with Georgina suddenly made her want to laugh at all of it.

"My mother always said that the best knowledge is to know yourself." Georgina's eyes became unfathomable. "And she said something similar about your grandmother. That she knew herself."

"Oh." Elfreda lowered her gaze as a lump formed in her throat. She was moved by the fact of Georgina's mother's regard, by the reverberations of her grandmother's presence. A moment later, she shook her head. Georgina's mother had overlooked what made Grandmama so extraordinary, just like everyone else.

"Grandmama knew many other things as well."

Georgina shrugged and bent to pull on her stockings, the motions frank and shameless.

"Knowing yourself doesn't exclude knowing other things." She sounded nonchalant. "But if you *don't* know yourself, the other things you know aren't likely to do you or anyone else any good."

This seemed pointed, aimed at her, or maybe Papa, and rather than begin a fresh argument, Elfreda took a deep breath.

"Will you let me onto your land or not?"

"You're already here." Georgina unbent. "And yes, I will."

Well, that was easy. Shockingly easy.

Georgina continued. "On one condition."

Of course. Elfreda tried to look calm.

"You must fritter." Georgina said it with relish. "That's your term. I prefer *live*. You must *live*, live like it's 1818. Ideally, this would involve a velocipede, or a hot-air balloon, but given the scarcity of velocipedes and hot-air balloons in this godforsaken parish, I will have to come up with something else."

"Anything," she said at once, incautious, caught up in the excitement of winning her objective.

"A theatrical."

"Anything but a theatrical."

Georgina smirked. "About this truce. Am I permitted onto *your* land? May I indulge freely in your mummified apples?"

"My land is Papa's land. So the answer is no." She flushed to the tops of her ears. "And the Major's appearance would be particularly unwelcome."

"I'm sure I can win your father over as Miss Georgina Redmayne." Georgina raised her arms and twirled. She was still barefoot and stumbled on the moss, bumping into Elfreda, then catching her by the elbow to keep herself steady.

"Because I can't marry you," murmured Georgina. The pressure of her hand was firm, and Elfreda's elbow was tender, and the sweet pain of it nearly pressed a moan from her lips. She was unsteady enough herself to curl her fingers in the muslin at Georgina's waist.

They stood like that, holding on to each other, long after the danger of falling had passed. So long that the danger returned.

Elfreda detached herself.

"We have an agreement, then," she said, studiously avoiding Georgina's eyes, afraid to see in them acknowledgment that something significant had just occurred. Or maybe afraid of the opposite. No acknowledgment at all.

Because she wasn't sure what else to do, she gave a nod, then an awkward wave, and started walking through the trees.

Georgina caught up, her shoes in her hands. "I should go too. Mrs. Herridge isn't *my* chaperone, but if I misstep, she'll pack Anne straight off to Halifax. She'd almost recovered from her dyspepsia when she got a glimpse of me in breeches and suffered a fit of apoplexy. Hence my return to muslin."

Elfreda glanced over. Georgina walked with a supple stride, the very picture of grace, even gripping dirty shoes.

Her brain revolved the conversation in the pergola and snagged on a tiny bit of language.

"Miss Poskitt used *they* when referring to you. It's a small thing, but . . ."

"You can't ignore bad grammar." Georgina's brows had a rueful slant. "I know."

"It wasn't bad grammar." Elfreda frowned in concentration. "It was deliberate. Do your close friends say *they* instead of *she* when they talk about you?"

"Mostly." Georgina was looking at Elfreda sidelong. "Not in front of Mrs. Herridge. I can't remember who used it first. But I encouraged it. I like the fit."

"The fit?"

"Sometimes I feel like *she* is a too-tight corset. *He* is nice for a change but chokes after a while, like a cinched cravat. *They* is less constricting. Comfortable even."

"Pronouns aren't comfortable, or uncomfortable." Elfreda halted in her tracks. "Pronouns don't *feel* like anything."

Georgina stopped too. "I just described how they feel to me."

"But pronouns are immaterial. They're parts of speech."

"That follow certain rules." Georgina's voice was dry. "Hence your objection. You disapprove of *they* used in the singular."

"Not at all. Authors were using *they* in the singular back in the fourteenth century. There's a very long precedent."

"I thought the fourteenth century was recent by your standards." Georgina's lips twitched. "It's after 1066."

She was teasing. That was humor in her eyes, not derision. Was she making a special effort? Or had Elfreda sometimes been too quick in the past to assume the worst?

"Actually," said Elfreda, "*they* singular is quite old-fashioned. It was used to indicate a person about whom nothing was known. A stranger in the distance who might be male or female, or someone unspecified. Nowadays we are supposed to default to *he* in such instances. According to Fisher's *New Grammar*, *he* is universal as well as masculine. Like *man* is universal as well as masculine."

Georgina's eyes gleamed. "Propaganda."

"Propaganda." Elfreda was incredulous. "The English language?"

"Codified *by* men *for* men." Georgina focused on her with a sharp gaze. "*Man* is universal? All right. Imagine this. Parliament passes universal manhood suffrage. Would women be allowed to vote? Of course not. But women are hanged and transported for breaking laws that make no mention of women in particular. *Man* is universal then. *He* means *she*, but only when women have nothing to gain by it. For example, you can't claim *he* means *she* to go to Oxford."

Elfreda responded automatically. "I don't want to go to Oxford. Papa went and says it's all drunken stunts and he never read so little in his life."

Georgina laughed. "Too good for Oxford. Noted. But you take my point."

After a moment, Elfreda laughed too. She did take Georgina's point.

"I want to become a Fellow of the Albion Society." She couldn't help her stomach's little plunge. "They don't allow women either. But

I will make such an important contribution to the field, they will have no choice."

Georgina's smile was cynical. "I wish you luck with that."

Elfreda bristled. "I will."

"It's not your ability to contribute that I doubt. It's the other part."

Elfreda bit her lip, mollified and perturbed in equal measure. Everything about this interaction with Georgina had upset her assumptions. She felt halfway dazed.

"Quakers are deliberate about pronouns." Georgina's cynicism had vanished. She looked contemplative. "*You* once marked people as high and low. It was used in the singular only to address one's social superiors. Quakers didn't like that. They insisted on *thee* and *thou* for everyone. Because we're all equal before God."

"You mix with Quakers?"

Georgina registered her incredulity with a faint smile. "My mother held fundraisers in London for women campaigning against West Indian sugar consumption. More of them were Quakers than not. Quaker plain speech is a protest against class division. Why not *they* as a protest against the division of the sexes?" She let this linger a moment in the air, then gave a shake. "In truth, I don't have such lofty ambitions. For me, it's what I said before. The fit."

Elfreda nodded. She was fully dazed. For years, she'd believed that Georgina could only veer between an excess of animal spirits and self-indulgent ennui, due to an empty head and a hollow heart. She'd underestimated her. No, she'd underestimated *them*. It didn't mean they were trustworthy. Her new understanding of their finer qualities, and their powers of fascination, only meant she could trust herself less when she was around them.

She had to stay on guard. Now more than ever.

"Why don't you join us for dinner tonight? No lapdog. Perhaps a game of whist." Georgina gestured in the direction of Redmayne Manor with a shoe. "Have you met Rosalie? Was she with Anne?"

The pergola formed before her, its lavender drapery of wisteria a languid frame for the feverish embraces within.

Elfreda's blush was a screaming red. "A truce is a cessation of hostilities. A *temporary* cessation of hostilities." Johnson's *Dictionary* to the rescue. "A truce isn't peace, or fellowship, or . . ."

Kissing.

"We do not dine," she finished.

"My mistake." Georgina bowed. Elfreda had trouble removing her eyes from the sardonic set of their mouth.

As she hurried away, she felt fairly certain that this was *her* mistake. And that it was entirely too late to correct.

8

I T'S YOUR TURN." Rosalie jammed a ball hard into Georgie's abdomen, which made them double over and drop their quizzing glass. "You dragged us up here for bowls, the least you can do is pretend to play."

Georgie cradled the ball in the crook of one arm and fumbled for the quizzing glass, now dangling from its chain. They lifted it again to their eye. Elf came into focus. She was circling something in a distant field; what they couldn't tell.

"The grass is too long," complained Anne. "And there are too many rocks. When did your family last use this as a bowling green?"

"Never," guessed Rosalie. "Georgie fibbed. Nothing about this spot is suitable for lawn sport. It's the sort of place where sheep get stranded in a storm. There are literal *ledges*."

"There's quite a view, though," said Anne, reflectively. "You can see for miles."

Georgie lowered the quizzing glass and looked at their friends. Anne and Rosalie were physical opposites, but at that moment, they exhibited the same ratio of tiny smirk to overlarge bonnet and resembled each other.

"Yes, quite a view," murmured Rosalie. "Of the park, the farms, the woodlands, the outlying hills." She tapped a finger against her lips, miming thought. "What else?"

"Who else." Anne giggled.

"Stop," Georgie warned them.

"Give me your quizzer." Rosalie beckoned. "I know she's down there."

Georgie fumbled for a better grip on the ball, took a step, and tossed it, without bothering to aim for the jack, which anyway wasn't immediately evident, given its diminutive size and the general overgrown wildness of the terrain. Rosalie was right that the narrow plateau at the southeast corner of the estate didn't lend itself to lawn sport.

The ball bounced once and came to rest in the bracken.

"Your turn," they said, turning to Anne.

"She *is* like us, you know," said Anne, not for the first time that week. "I can tell about these things."

"Can you now?" Georgie tried to sound indifferent.

"In the garden, she was shocked," continued Anne, glancing at Rosalie, who blushed scarlet. "But it was the shock you feel when the world suddenly makes *more* sense, not less. I recognized it."

Georgie opened their mouth, then closed it again, choosing instead to lift the quizzing glass. Green jumped toward them. Grass. Tree. Tree. Cow. *There.* Elf. She was climbing a low stone wall.

"She's not like me," they announced, rather too grandly. "I don't break my word."

"You swore you'd tattoo my name on your ankle," Anne reminded them, "if I brought you the whole Wiltshire cheese at that garden party."

"I received no whole Wiltshire cheese."

"You received and ate the Wiltshire cheese," said Rosalie. "It was after you rolled around in the tulips with that moppy-looking terrier and before you jumped in the fountain."

"Hmm," said Georgie. "I don't break my word sober." They followed Elf with the glass as she cut across a pasture.

"Your engagement?"

"That was a very special case."

The long silence felt like an indictment.

"Fine, we'll tattoo my ankle tonight." They swung around, and Anne's face filled their field of vision. "The fact remains that I am allowing Elf to traipse around my property, in exchange for a bit of fun. Yet four funless days have passed!"

"Funless," murmured Anne.

"Funless," repeated Georgie, in an ominous voice. Anne took a hint and sealed her rosy lips.

"Oh, look at you. You're having plenty of fun spying."

That was Rosalie, so Georgie turned their magnified gaze.

"Irrelevant. I can't let her disregard our agreement. She must *join* in the fun. So far, she has avoided us whenever possible. And refused croquet, shuttlecock and battledore, vingt-et-un, levitation, and now bowls."

Rosalie's long lashes swept up and down. "Who were we going to levitate?"

"Bagshaw. The butler. He's heaviest." Georgie stopped blinking, hypnotized by the dark facets of her iris, and let the quizzing glass slip from their fingers. Rosalie's eyes shrank back down to normal.

"You can't understand." Georgie began to circle Rosalie and Anne. "The two of you are returning to London. And I'll be left behind. I'll probably start keeping a diary where I meditate on my digestion. Oh God." They stopped short, one hand on their stomach, the other on their mouth. "That truly might happen. I'll start voicing opinions on poultry breeding. And waking at the cock's crow." They shuddered.

"It *is* unimaginable," said Rosalie. "Burning every bridge in town then getting sent to one's very own estate to cool one's heels." Rosalie smiled, not a nice smile.

The atmosphere was suddenly icy.

Georgie blinked. A moment later, they got the point.

"I'm rather fortunate, I see that," they said. "How *do* matters stand with your father's restaurant? You had that letter the other day, and I meant to ask."

"Not now," said Rosalie. "You're making it so much worse."

"Inestimably worse," said Anne, moving closer to Rosalie with a head toss that set her ribbons fluttering.

The look Rosalie shot her was noticeably unappreciative.

"I'm going to be left behind too," she said to Georgie. "Just as soon as Anne absconds to Tuscany."

Anne gasped. "What? How can you even think it? You're coming with me!"

"I've told you a hundred times that I'm not."

"Because we haven't finished working out the details."

"Because I'm not."

This fight was ever present, usually at a low smolder, but when it flared it caught on with wildfire swiftness. Georgie was recalled to themself. They often put their foot in it, but they did have a knack for restoring the mood. They swooped to the picnic basket and extracted two bottles.

"Lemonade won't help." Anne was ashen faced, hugging herself. Her desolate expression paired well with the vast, hazy backdrop of checkered countryside and windswept clouds.

"It's champagne." Georgie hefted the bottles higher. "I emptied out the lemonade."

Anne contemplated the bottles. "Champagne might help. I hope you weren't obvious about it. Mrs. Herridge has a suspicious mind."

"Her suspicions are always correct, though. Doesn't that make her mind . . . something else? Formidable? Accurate?"

This musing was obviously not restorative, so Georgie desisted.

"Well," they said, "she suspected nothing. I worked a perfect sleight of hand with these bottles. And I presented this outing to her in the most unobjectionably wholesome terms, while emphasizing the grueling, character-building length of the walk. We're unchaperoned thanks to my magical fingers and silver tongue."

"Lots of girls thank your magical fingers and silver tongue." Anne wrinkled her nose. "I won't add to the number. As much as I appreciate walking about without having to worry if I slouch or perspire or take off my gloves."

"You won't have to worry in Italy either," muttered Rosalie. "No one will be there to dictate your behavior. I hope it's worth it."

Anne faced off with her. "Freedom is always worth it."

"Freedom without love?" Rosalie was staring at Anne so intensely that Georgie had to glance away.

"There's no love without freedom." Anne's voice trembled. "Georgie agrees. That's why they broke things off with Phipps. The compromise was too great."

Georgie felt the weight of two pairs of eyes. The wind was cool on the plateau but sweat formed on their brow as the expectancy thickened.

"If I was in possession of a good fortune," said Rosalie, "I assure you I would have a different relationship to compromise."

Georgie didn't have a hand free to raise the quizzing glass, so they twisted to the north and squinted.

"Let's join Elf," they suggested. "If she won't join us." Neither Rosalie nor Anne made an immediate reply, so they brandished the bottles in the air. "Tallyho!" Without further ado, they bounded toward the slope.

GEORGIE HADN'T MISREPRESENTED the grueling nature of the circuitous, two-mile walk from the manor up to the plateau. The way back—with its detour through the clustered farmsteads in pursuit of

Elf—included more downhill, but also, just *more*. Rosalie had hooked the picnic basket over her right arm and listed to the side with every step. Anne lugged the bowls box like a stevedore, which turned her gait crab-like. Georgie's load was far lighter, only the two bottles. Unburdened, they ranged ahead. Scouting proved necessary, because Georgie's sense of direction was abysmal, and the map they'd tried to fix in their mind as they gazed down from the heights dissolved into the welter of eye-level details on the descent.

They felt like the leader of a raiding party as they crept around barns and reconnoitered fields and footpaths. Rosalie and Anne didn't play along. They moved slowly, argued loudly, and paused at every conspicuous crossing. The sun, too, conspired against stealth, coming out from behind the clouds and lighting the vivid colors of their gowns, Rosalie in eye-catching amethyst, Anne in aggressively bright yellow.

"To the left," said Georgie, sotto voce, slinking back to them after breaking down and begging the help of a bare-chested youth mowing by a pair of cottages. The youth *had* seen a dark-haired young lady go past and pointed the way with his scythe.

"The other left," said Georgie.

Anne and Rosalie changed course again without pausing their conversation.

"Then tell your parents the truth," Anne was saying. "I could never with mine, but yours are different. They'll be happy for you."

"Happy?" Rosalie laughed. "They'll be *happy* if I turn my back on the family, inviting social censure and moral horror in the process?"

"They'll be happy if you follow your heart," said Anne. "After all, they followed their hearts."

"Follow me over this wall," whispered Georgie, demonstrating. Bunch the skirt. Swing the leg. Straddle the stone.

"Pretend you're mounting a horse," they advised. "And dismounting off the other side."

They touched down gracefully.

No one observed the landing.

"I'm tired of explaining myself." Rosalie set her basket on the wall. "What I do reflects on my parents twofold, because of who they are. *Because* they followed their hearts. It's important that my siblings and I appear respectable."

Anne heaved the bowls box over the wall and hoisted herself up. She flopped forward onto the stone, kicked her legs, and wiggled, then slid down into the grass headfirst.

Really not how you'd mount a horse.

"Your parents let you associate with Georgie," she said, wobbling upright, molding her crushed bonnet into shape. "Georgie's not respectable. They're infamous. A walking scandal."

"I'm right here." Georgie frowned. "Let's not get carried away."

Rosalie tried to crawl over the wall, but her knee pinned her dress. The sharp tug of the fabric propelled her into open space with a wild cry. Anne sprang forward, half catching her, half dragging her until her feet hit the ground. The two clung to each other in a controlled stagger, almost like dancers, before separating, both of them pink and breathless.

"Georgie is infamous, but Georgie is also coming into a fortune." Rosalie was panting, but she picked up where Anne had left off, resolutely. "Georgie may have made a cake of themselves in front of the entire ton, but—"

"Right. Here." Georgie waved a bottle back and forth.

"But their rung of the social ladder remains higher than my rung," continued Rosalie. "My parents assume I'll meet *someone* eligible by association. It's that simple."

"And you plan to do so. Meet someone eligible." Anne's eyes shone with tears.

"Eventually. I can draw it out."

"That's not a solution."

"There isn't a solution. But if you don't go to Italy, we can stay ineligibly in each other's lives, and that's something." Rosalie hooked her basket back over her arm and turned to Georgie. "Which way?"

The three of them crossed the field in silence. The next stone wall they encountered was crumbling, so they hopped easily over the rubble.

"It reeks," complained Anne.

"Dung." Georgie nodded wisely. This field had been recently plowed and spread itself before them, all rich brown ridges and furrows.

"It's like an ocean," said Rosalie, as she began to cut across. "But the waves are solid."

"And made of manure," added Anne, wrinkling her nose as her ankle boots sank deep into one of the ridges.

They'd reached the middle of the field when shouts erupted.

"Out! Get out!" A man approached at a trot. He was huge and vibrantly displeased, white teeth bared in his craggy, sunbrowned face, one brawny arm windmilling.

"Oh dear," breathed Rosalie.

"Run!" cried Georgie.

"Stop!" shouted the man, both arms now in the air. "Not through my turnips."

Georgie, Anne, and Rosalie stopped as one. Georgie looked at the man and then back the way they'd come, taking in the trampled ridges. Upon closer inspection, tiny green specks revealed themselves. Realization dawned.

"My mistake," they called. "I should have guessed the field was planted. We were just . . ." They were still standing on a ridge, to the detriment of who knew how many turnips, so they leapt into a furrow. "Terribly sorry! I pray the turnips make a full recovery."

The man was not appeased. He kept charging toward them.

"I'm Georgie Redmayne, actually," called Georgie. "From the manor."

This revelation should have transformed the man from angry ogre to obsequious giant. Instead, he looked angrier. He halted just short of Georgie, two furrows over.

"Redmayne!" He shouted it then spit at the ground. "Haven't you done enough to bring us all to ruin? You had to come and grind with your heels?"

"Be easy, Charles." Another man was approaching. He was much smaller, and smiling, arms at his sides. "We hope we see ye well, Miss Redmayne. We didna know as you were back."

"I'm just recently back." Georgie glanced between the men. "Do you farm this land?"

"Charles farms it," said the smiling man, gesturing. "That's Charles Peach, that is." He said it as though the name meant something.

Georgie nodded, trying to think which Peach. The family was numerous. Was this *big* Charles Peach, who once carried two twenty-stone pigs to market, one under each arm?

Silly question. There couldn't be a *bigger* Peach.

"He's an uncommon fine farmer," said the smiling man. "And he grows a pretty lot o' crops. I feed my milch cows on his cabbages."

"Someone's got to see the beasts don't starve," snarled Peach, glaring at Georgie, his dark eyes hot as coals.

"Do you mean . . . Should that be me?" Georgie cleared their throat, increasingly unsure how to proceed. They'd spent the past hour skulking about their tenants' farms, but they hadn't noticed if the cattle looked thin. They hadn't noticed anything about the state of the animals, or the buildings either. Wasn't Harry seeing to all that? Not literally, of course. No chap, however keen, could count a cow's ribs from France.

"Mr. Tetley!" They snapped their fingers. "I'll let Mr. Tetley know, of course." Mr. Tetley was the steward. He'd always seemed busy, probably because there was a lot to do, and he was doing it. Mr. Tetley would take care of this.

The smiling man's smile wavered. "It's not Mr. Tetley now. It's Mr. Fletcher."

"It's been Fletcher for five years." Peach spoke low and rumbly.

"Whoever it is." Georgie didn't give a fig, so long as the person fattened up the cows. Peach looked ready to feed them Georgie. Did cows eat people? If they were chopped up with the cabbage leaves?

"I'll tell Mr. Fletcher about the cows," they promised. "And that wall there." They glanced at the tumbled stones.

"And my turnips, while you're at it," rumbled Peach, with such menace in his voice that Anne made a squeaking sound.

Georgie added vague, affirmative noises, and the three friends departed the field with as much haste as care for the turnips allowed.

"That was terrifying," gasped Anne, once they were all walking again on a lane. "I feared we'd be ripped limb from limb, and the turnips watered with our blood."

"Was your father ironfisted?" Rosalie gave Georgie a sidelong look. "They're usually ironfisted, the landlords who get ripped limb from limb."

"You're on the ogre's side?" Georgie clutched a bottle to their chest. "Rankest betrayal! He was in a bad mood because the puppies he ate last night for dinner disagreed with him. My father had the opposite of an iron fist. What's the opposite?"

"Silver fist?" suggested Anne. "Silk fist?"

"Open hand," decided Georgie. "He rebuilt the village school. And he always sent a doctor around to the cottagers in winter. There was some talk of improving drainage. Or ditches. Or the drainage had something to do with the ditches. That was all some time ago, but I'm sure . . ." Georgie trailed off. They were sure of nothing. All decisions regarding the management of the estate had been made in absentia for half a decade. Or else left to Mr. Fletcher.

Was everything in rack and ruin?

They applied a bottle to the side of their face. The cool pressure of the glass was reassuring. And reminded them that all they could do at present was watch their step in plowed fields.

And drink.

"I'm thirsty," they announced. "Champagne, anyone?" They lifted the bottle higher and swerved from the lane. "Meet me under yonder oak!"

Anne reached the oak last. Georgie was already filling glasses, and Rosalie was unpacking the salmagundi.

"So many crows," said Anne, dropping the bowls box unceremoniously on the grass. "Aren't they an ill omen?"

"Death," intoned Rosalie, and reached deeper into the basket. "Oh, good. Plum cakes."

"Death."

Something about Anne's tone brought Georgie's head up.

She was gazing out over the meadow, gazing at an irregular patch of darkness amid all the green. Georgie squinted and the patch resolved into a lifeless body.

Anne let out a bloodcurdling scream.

9

THERE *WAS* A body in the meadow, but it wasn't lifeless. Elf didn't move as Georgie's shadow fell across her. She did open her eyes and smile. The smile did something new and beautiful to her mouth. To her face. Her hair fanned around her head, a spill of black silk on the clover.

"What's happened?" Georgie crossed their arms tight over the erratic thumps of their heart. "If you weren't smiling, I'd worry you'd taken ill. But you're smiling at *me*, so I worry you've taken very ill. Did you faint?"

"No." She stretched out her arms, blades of grass peeping between her spread fingers. "But I do feel like I'm dreaming. Can you see it? I'm more or less in the middle."

Georgie didn't know what *it* was. They saw Elf. Elf on her back in a meadow, small, rigid body relaxed in rapture. Like some kind of angel fallen to earth. Or an elfin queen.

They stepped back abruptly and bumped into Anne, who'd rushed up behind.

"What a relief," cried Anne. "I thought you were dead. The crows misled me."

"I see it," said Rosalie, muscling between Anne and Georgie and dropping into a crouch by Elf's feet. "You're lying in a dent."

"A wolf pit." Elf sat up. "A pit to trap wolves. Farmers used to dig them to protect their flocks."

"Deplorable!" Anne clasped her hands. "Oh, woeful pit!"

Georgie looked at her with mild surprise. "You're on the side of wolves?"

"Of course I'm on the side of wolves! I'm on the side of all wild, free, beautiful creatures. Men always try to kill what they can't control."

"Your father's a worsted and woolen manufacturer." Rosalie put her hands on her hips. "The wool trade is *why* wolves were hunted to extinction. The English economy depended on sheep."

"How do you know that?" Anne's forehead puckered.

"Your father," said Rosalie. "He goes on and on."

"I don't listen." Anne lifted her chin. "And now I despise him all the more, for what he did to the wolves."

"To be fair to your father," said Elf, "there haven't been wolves in England since the Tudors, and there weren't many even then. Most wolf pits are far older."

"How old is this one?" asked Georgie.

Elf didn't hesitate. "It was dug before 835."

Georgie blinked at the specificity. "835." They studied the former pit. It was little more than a shallow, circular depression, a few yards in diameter, barely noticeable to a passerby, given the length of the grass. The idea that Elf could read so much meaning into an all but undetectable dip in the ground produced in them a feeling of disconcerted awe.

"Why 835?"

Elf reached for her notebook. She'd been carrying it around all week, a notebook with a mottled pasteboard cover, big as a ledger, stuffed with loose papers and tied shut with string. She picked at the knot. "835 is the date of the land charter establishing the abbey at Twynham. The description of the boundaries of the land parcel relies on landmarks, such as the wolf pit."

"This is what you hoped to find? This . . . ?" They gestured, feeling guiltier than ever for knocking that amulet from her hand. Elf had to content herself instead with a dent. It was lowering, literally lowering.

"Wolf pit. I mapped my perambulations, and . . ." Elf cut herself off. "Never mind. You'd all find it dull."

"Not a bit." Georgie held up a finger. "Hang on, though. I'll bring intoxicants."

They turned and legged it for the oak. They had to repack the basket, and by the time they got back to the wolf dent, Rosalie and Anne were sitting beside Elf, who held the notebook open on her lap.

"Georgie." Anne looked up from the notebook. "Your house was built *on top* of the abbey. Were you aware?"

"There was very little left of the abbey." Georgie sat, flicked off their hat, and arranged the repast on a folded square of linen. Cold meat, salmagundi, plum cakes, cheese, fruit, biscuits, tea, and most important, champagne. "Above ground, anyway." They passed around glasses of champagne. "We turned the crypt into a wine cellar."

Elf made a tiny, judgmental sound in her throat.

"Taste this champagne," Georgie commanded. "Then tell me it wasn't worth it."

Elf hesitated, glancing down at her frothing glass. Finally, she sighed and tightened her fingers around the stem.

"Wassail," she said, and drank.

There were only three glasses, so Georgie splashed champagne into a teacup and polished it off in a single gulp.

Anne downed her own champagne and crawled through the clover toward the plum cakes. "Elf, tell Georgie about Sexburga."

"Sex what?" Georgie refilled Elf's glass. "Yes, please. Person, place, or thing?" They paused. "Or Germanic harvest festival? Pagan feast day?"

"I thought that too!" Anne giggled. "It sounds like a medieval rite of spring that ends with an orgy."

"That's the kind of thought you keep to yourself," said Rosalie, serving herself salmagundi.

"Thank you, Mrs. Herridge." Anne rolled her eyes.

"Person." Elf spoke firmly. "Sexburga was a nun at the abbey, and a scribe. She wrote a chronicle that my grandmother studied and translated. It included the land charter. But it's gone now. Chewed up by rats."

Anne coughed on plum cake. "Did you say *chewed up by rats*?"

"That's my theory. They sometimes come down the chimneys and bite through the leaves of old manuscripts." Elf toyed with her glass. "We've lost several that way. Grendel isn't any help."

"The monster from *Beowulf*?" Rosalie was staring.

"Rats and monsters." Anne looked delighted. "Are there also ghosts and miasmas? May we please pay a call?"

Elf regarded Anne with wary eyes. After a moment, she seemed to decide that Anne was sincere in her excitement, and her face cleared.

"Grendel is a dog," she said. "I can't guarantee ghosts or miasmas, but you will meet my sister Agnes. She spends most of her time playing lute in the tower."

The promise of a lute-playing maiden proved more than satisfactory to Anne. She beamed. And Georgie refilled their teacup, wondering if Elf's tacit invitation had extended to them.

"The wolf pit," they said to Elf, as the foam subsided. "Why is it significant? As a monument to historic gamekeeping practices, it underwhelms. As a boundary, it's defunct. I appreciate it as a picnicker, but you were ecstatic before the picnic arrived."

Elf was smiling that smile again. "The wolf pit." She sounded dreamy and stroked her hand through the grass. "The wolf pit is how I'll catch William Aubin-Aubrey."

As answers went it was the worst.

Georgie poured champagne down their throat then muttered, with obvious bad grace, "It's not a William pit."

"Who is William Aubin-Aubrey?" asked Rosalie, as though this William Aubin-Aubrey hadn't taken up too much of their time already and wasn't best forgotten.

"The Barrow Prince." Elf's eyes sparkled. "Author of *Sepulchral Anecdotes*. He's a Society Fellow."

There was less to like by the second.

"Barrow *Prince*!" Anne gasped.

"He's not a real prince," said Elf. "But he has opened over a hundred barrows, and his method is the finest in Britain. And he's not eight and twenty. No one knows more about Celtic, Saxon, and Roman funeral rites."

"Hmm," said Rosalie, with appropriately diminished enthusiasm.

Elfreda didn't seem to notice. Georgie had never seen *her* show such enthusiasm.

"He is planning a trip to the Peak," she said. "He wrote to Papa about it. But if I can just explain to him the strength of the case for the Northmen's winter camp on the bluff, I'm sure he'll dig here instead. I lack physical evidence." Her avoidance of Georgie's eyes was somehow more damning than a glare. "But there's an entry in our family's copy of *The Anglo-Saxon Chronicle* that records it. And Sexburga's chronicle records it as well."

"And this wolf pit attests to the accuracy and reality of Sexburga's chronicle." Georgie blew out a breath. "Which matters because the original has vanished."

Elf's expression betrayed her surprise.

Georgie enjoyed the feeling of having impressed her with their reasoning, until they remembered her surprise was premised on her thinking them an absolute idiot.

"And Prince William makes all the difference?" they asked, slouching like a child, and feeling like a child, for pettiness.

"He has assistants." Elf was looking at them, brows slightly lower than before. "If William Aubin-Aubrey decides that the bluff is worth excavating, it will be done properly, much more quickly and thoroughly than I could do it myself. And the camp will be uncovered."

"What specifically does one uncover in a camp of Northmen?" asked Rosalie.

"Dice?" guessed Anne. "If they were just sitting around."

Georgie expected Elf to reject this immediately, but instead, she seemed thoughtful. "Perhaps dice. We'll have to see." Excitement flashed across her face. "It will be the very first."

"And so you'll be made a Fellow." Georgie's disbelief was plain in their voice. They dangled their teacup from their pinkie, watching it swing. They felt Elf's gaze, and a blush crawled up their neck. They were acting like an ass, and they weren't even sure why.

"Grand," they said, lifting their head. "Let's drink to it."

Elf shifted a little, the wary look in her eyes again. But Anne poured the champagne, with disarming exuberance, and she settled and accepted the toast with a vaguely suspicious befuddlement that wasn't devoid of pleasure.

For a time, they all ate and drank, warmed by the sun, the low hum of insects creating drowsy music. One bottle of champagne was empty, and two more rounds emptied the second. Elf seemed almost as relaxed as before, smiling as though she enjoyed Anne and Rosalie's convivial chatter. She'd never seemed so at ease when Georgie and the Janes surrounded her at neighborhood parties. She'd exuded disdain and stayed all but mute.

Anne collapsed in the clover, giggling.

"What?" Rosalie raised her brows.

"Nothing." Anne smiled up at the clouds. "It's just . . . Do you think any of the nuns at the abbey fell in love? With each other?"

"Forget I asked," groaned Rosalie. "And stop talking or I'll pelt you with these strawberries."

Georgie tried not to look at Elf.

"I'd like to know is all," said Anne. "Wouldn't you? Not just about nuns. When I go to see the Old Master paintings at the Pall Mall Picture Galleries, I always stare at the women and wonder. Who were you really? What did you want?"

A bee flew around their heads in lazy loops and alighted on a buttercup, buzz fading.

Georgie did look at Elf. They looked at her disheveled hair, and champagne flush, and slightly parted lips.

She turned her eyes to them. Their heart went still.

She didn't want Georgie. She wanted bones and rusty blades and the letters FASA after her name. But her eyes in that moment played tricks with their heart.

"What cheer, sheep." Rosalie's voice broke the spell. "Look, they're coming down the hill."

A large flock was heading toward them at an ambling pace.

Anne went up on her elbows to watch. "Should we pretend we're wolves? Liberate ourselves from the pit?" She stood with another tipsy giggle. "Will they scatter?"

"Don't torment the sheep," scolded Rosalie, popping a strawberry into her mouth.

"Sheep like a bit of sport." Georgie shot to their feet. They grabbed Rosalie's elbow, hauling her up too.

Anne threw back her head and yipped.

"Not bad," said Georgie. They looked down at Elf and extended their arm. She hesitated a long moment before she took their hand. When their palms touched, Georgie's mouth went dry. A spark traveled up their arm.

They pulled Elf upright. They put too much strength into it, pulling her onto her feet, and then nearly off them. She gave a breathless laugh, and for the briefest instant, they felt the press of her body. She half stumbled back.

"Your turn," they said, still holding her hand. "The game is *wolves*. Unless you don't deign to—"

Elf's howl halted their speech. And their breath.

They stared.

"That was *very* good," said Anne. "You have a wild heart. I can hear it."

Elf glanced at her, bright-eyed, and showed her small, white teeth.

Georgie felt a wave of desire so red-hot there was nothing for it but to howl themself.

"The best yet." Rosalie clapped.

"But the sheep aren't scattering." Anne stamped her foot. "They're too bold. I must chase them."

Elf's face changed. "You mustn't."

But Anne was already running.

Georgie howled again and sprang forward, tugging Elf along, racing for the flock.

FOR THE PAST hour, Elfreda hadn't been thinking clearly. Excitement, champagne, the novelty of so much friendly interest—all of it had blurred her mind.

Now she saw everything as clear as day. She wrested her hand from Georgina's and lurched to keep her balance, the horizon tilting. Aggrieved bleating filled the air, punctuated by yips and howls.

"Stop!" She put her hands to her mouth and yelled as loud as she could. Georgina was among the sheep, darting every which way, kicking up their skirts and whirling, auburn hair shining like a flame in the sun. Miss Poskitt kept running then doubling over, out of breath or overcome by fits of giggles. Miss Mahomed loped at the perimeter, yelling something that sounded like *chuckleheads*.

The harassed sheep had begun to mass, climbing each other as they each sought the protection of the center. Georgina let out a particularly earsplitting howl, and all at once, the sheep bolted. A wall of fleece stormed through the meadow.

Elfreda was directly in their path.

So was the wolf pit.

"My notebook!" She sprinted, heart smashing against her ribs. She snatched the notebook seconds before the flock thundered past, splitting around her, a musky odor thick in the air.

She turned, furious, prepared to scream in Georgina's face, but Georgina wasn't chasing the flock like a ravening wolf. They were fifty yards away, chasing Miss Poskitt and Miss Mahomed, all of them laughing too hard to do more than stagger in circles. Behind them, the meadow inclined gradually toward the hill, that slight rise giving Elfreda a perfect sight line to the ram. He was enormous, his hoof pawing the ground.

"Watch out!" This time, Elf's voice carried. Georgina whipped around. They caught her eye, still laughing, brows just beginning to pinch with the presentiment that something was wrong.

The ram backed up. He lowered his horned head.

Georgina half turned. Miss Poskitt and Miss Mahomed followed their lead. The three stood stock-still as scarecrows. Then Miss Poskitt shrieked.

The ram charged.

Miss Poskitt broke left, and Miss Mahomed broke right. Georgina didn't move. The ram rose onto its hind legs as it closed the final yard, and Georgina lunged to the side. The ram's front hooves slammed back down. It bucked and wheeled and charged again. Georgina dodged, and the ram wheeled.

"Over here!" Elfreda waved her notebook at the ram like a flag.

It was no good.

The ram charged. Georgina feinted before diving, and the ram changed directions. He tucked his head and barreled after Miss Mahomed.

"Miss Mahomed!" Elfreda realized she was running.

Miss Mahomed looked over her shoulder and screamed. She zigzagged, but the ram tracked her, bearing down. Georgie was running too, and Miss Poskitt had changed course, swinging her bonnet, trying to attract the ram's attention.

He rose onto his hind legs and butted, missing Miss Mahomed by inches. She screamed more loudly.

Elfreda watched her as she tripped and crumpled, and so she didn't look where she herself was going. She banged into Georgina with jolting force. Her teeth clattered, and she tasted blood. The notebook sailed from her hand. Georgina's arm wrapped her waist, bracing her. Time seemed to stand still. She was pressed against Georgina, head twisted, eyes on the notebook as it hung in the air. Then time restarted.

The notebook swung open. Her grandmother's papers spilled out, the pages catching the wind, fluttering across the meadow.

"Let go of me!" Elfreda kicked Georgina's shins with all her might. "You're like a curse!"

Georgina let go, and Elfreda hit the ground. Hip, elbow, shoulder, head. She howled with pure, lupine rage. "Georgina Redmayne, I swear to God, I will destroy you!"

Georgina wasn't looking down at her. They were staring off, horror stricken. Elfreda looked in time to see it too. The ram driving into Miss Poskitt, sending her flying, her body limp as a rag doll.

10

TWO DAYS LATER, Georgie knocked on Elf's heavily studded, profoundly unwelcoming front door. Rust from the iron knocker left a red smear on their yellow glove. The sight made them feel like Macbeth, or worse, as if they'd uttered the word *Macbeth* inside a theater. Guilt and superstitious dread turned them from the door, just as it creaked open.

"You're not the post boy," came a disappointed voice.

"No." Georgie turned back. "Agnes?"

The last time they'd seen Elf's younger sister, she'd been a scrawny child of nine or ten hugging a pet rabbit with worrisome enthusiasm. She was much taller now, a waterfall of dark hair rippling to her waist, no rabbit immediately apparent.

"Georgina!" Agnes opened the door wider. "Elfreda said you'd returned and that you were twenty times as terrible as she remembered."

Georgie winced. "Lovely. Warms the cockles of my heart. Is she in?"

Agnes regarded them. "Did you cut your hair?"

Georgie touched the cropped locks that peeked out from their plumed French bonnet. "I did. They call this style the Titus."

"Is it fashionable?" asked Agnes. "Beatrice says one *must* be fashionable."

"There are two kinds of fashionable." Georgie stopped fiddling with their hair. "The fashionable everyone agrees on, and the fashionable everyone disagrees on."

"She didn't say which." Agnes looked troubled. "What's the difference?"

"The former guarantees acceptance, and the latter guarantees attention."

"And what is the Titus?"

"The latter."

Agnes pondered with observable vehemence.

"I long for attention," she said, fervently. "I keep my mother's pocket mirror in my bedchamber, and some days I stare into my own eyes for hours."

"Ah." Georgie rubbed the back of their neck, struggling to hold Agnes's gaze, which was decidedly hungry.

"Beatrice and I used to stare into *each other's* eyes." She sagged against the doorframe. "Could she have forgotten me? I haven't received a letter."

"How long has it been?"

"Twenty hours." She thrust out her chin. "It feels longer."

"I'm sure it does," said Georgie, with sympathy. "Twenty hours can feel like a million years. I've felt my heart fossilize while waiting for letters."

"So have I!" Agnes drew a sharp breath. "You understand me. No one understands me." She paused. "Except Beatrice. But she's in London."

"Beatrice Parker?" Georgie had once spent a lovely evening kissing her older sister on one of the dark walks that wound through Vauxhall Gardens.

"Beatrice Eliza Parker. We were both born in February, but she was born on the first, and I was born on leap day."

"I doubt she has forgotten you." Georgie hid a smile. "And I hope the next knock is the post boy."

"Do you know what?" Agnes lowered her voice. "Neither Beatrice nor I have ever thought you were terrible. When Elfreda says you are the worst person who ever lived, I remind her of Richard III and Caligula."

Georgie frowned.

"I appreciate that," they said, their voice a bit too dry.

Agnes nodded. "You fed Rowena rose petals when you came to dinner that time at the Parkers'. That was very kind." She paused. "How did you know that rabbits like roses?"

Georgie tried to peer around her into the house. "Everyone likes roses."

"I mean to eat," she said.

Georgie gave up. "Lucky guess. Is Rowena well? Nibbling spring violets?"

Agnes's eyes filled with tears, and she threw herself into Georgie's arms. She was still a worrisomely enthusiastic hugger. Georgie grunted as the pressure on their ribs increased.

"There, there," they said. "I can come back another day."

"Will you?" Agnes sniffled into Georgie's spencer. "No one ever calls now that Beatrice is gone. I'm ever so lonely. Elfreda is always occupied, and the twins aren't any good for conversation. Yesterday they decided they're spoonicorns and all they do is gallop down the halls and whinny."

"Spoonicorn is like unicorn?" Georgie was beginning to feel damp and out of their depth.

"But with a spoon instead of a horn." Agnes finally ended the hug, stepping back, nose red. "Would you like to attend a concert? If you come up to the music room, I will play my lute."

Her hopeful expression gave Georgie a pang. You could forget the misery of adolescence until a member of that suffering tribe stood before you, spotty, weepy, and a little bit crazed.

"I'd love to," they lied. "But I should speak with Elfreda first."

"Very well." Agnes heaved a resigned sigh. "She's in the library."

Georgie followed her through the granite entrance hall—cold and dark—and through a series of corridors—colder and darker. Dust lay thick on the floor, and shadows welled from every corner. The scent of tallow hung in the air. Georgie's eyes traveled up the great carved staircase as they passed. The finials on the corner posts were probably pine cones or pineapples but looked like squatting demons in the gloom.

"Georgina Redmayne is here," announced Agnes upon entering the library. The room was a maze, too many chairs shoved hugger-mugger between tables, chests, and cabinets, all overflowing with scrolls and relics.

"Hwat?" It was Mr. Marsden's voice. He did not sound hospitable. "The Redmayne girl? Here? Bring her over."

There was a thud. Elf was poised halfway up a bookcase ladder. A book had just fallen from her hand.

They hurried toward it. Elf jumped down from the ladder, determined to beat them there.

"Allow me," they said, but she paid no heed. She spun at the base of the ladder, and as she bent for the book, her elbow struck a clay pot on a stand, bumping it over the edge. She gasped. Georgie lengthened through their torso, dropped their reticule, stretched out their arms—the pot was just out of reach. Their feet left the ground.

"Elfreda!" Mr. Marsden roared.

"I've got it." Georgie was on their knees on a rug worn almost to nothing, the pot cradled in their hands. They could hear the blood crashing in their ears.

"That is the Finglesham urn!" Mr. Marsden had risen from his chair. "Child, how could you be so clumsy?"

Elfreda's face paled.

"I distracted her." Georgie tottered to their feet. The urn was nearly a foot tall, wide around the middle, ornamented with curved lines and indentations. Thank God it had a lid. They shuddered to think what it held. Who it held, rather.

They set the urn back on the stand, picked up their reticule, aimed a smile at Mr. Marsden. He was wrapped in a greatcoat against the chill and did not smile back.

"Miss Redmayne," he said. "I would not have recognized you, except you so closely resemble your brother. Do you intend to stay in the neighborhood?"

"Oh, no, I intend to go back to London as soon as I can."

"London," sighed Agnes. She was communing with a terra-cotta bust and didn't seem to realize she'd spoken aloud.

Georgie cleared their throat. "The Major has already shipped for France."

"Very good." Mr. Marsden made a brief showing of teeth. "I am sure we are safer for it."

"Yes, indeed." Georgie pretended to miss the double meaning. "He's a Waterloo man."

Mr. Marsden's eyes were narrow behind his spectacles. "To what do we owe this visit?"

"I wanted to see that Miss Marsden was well." Georgie's gaze slid to her. She returned their look with an expression many degrees colder than the room. "The ram's attack was such a terrible shock."

It wasn't the ram that had made her pledge to destroy them. It was the sight of her grandmother's papers blowing through the air, like huge white leaves.

Shaken from the tree of knowledge.

By Satan.

Who would be Georgie, in this instance.

"She is not entirely well," said Mr. Marsden. "She nearly shattered the Finglesham urn."

Elfreda clutched her woolen shawl tightly around her neck. "How is Miss Poskitt?"

Georgie looked from her to Mr. Marsden and back to her. "The doctor said her leg would mend by midsummer. Her father insisted she mend at home, and so she and Miss Mahomed left this morning, for Halifax. They asked me to say goodbye. And to thank you. For fetching help."

Elf's face darkened. "All I did was tell a farmer."

She'd run through the fields, toward Charles Peach, while most of the papers blew in the other direction. She'd caught some on the way and gathered more on the return, but many had flown away entirely.

"I caught a few more pages," they told her. "I brought them for you."

"The novel?" Mr. Marsden frowned. "Enough about the novel."

Georgie tipped their head, confused. "Novel?"

"I found the wolf pit." Elf glanced at Georgie, as though for confirmation, and for whatever it was worth, they nodded.

Mr. Marsden snorted. "Yes, the wolf pit. My mother should have titled her romance *The Wolves of Twynham Abbey*."

All at once, Georgie comprehended. The *novel* was the translated chronicle. Mr. Marsden insisted that his mother scribbled fantasy, perhaps because he disbelieved women capable of anything else. Or because other people's accomplishments took attention away from his own. Probably both.

Elf was fighting an uphill battle.

And Georgie had knocked her down, literally and figuratively, at every turn. They hadn't meant to do so, but that didn't matter. What mattered was putting it to rights.

"Is the Barrow Prince still coming?" they asked.

"The Barrow Prince?" Mr. Marsden sounded personally insulted. "Did Elfreda call Aubin-Aubrey the Barrow Prince?"

It was almost sweet, his transparent need for preeminence. He reminded Georgie of a stock character from the commedia, one of the old men who played his miserliness and self-importance for laughs. Except he wasn't acting.

"She said that some do call him that." Georgie brightened their smile. "And she said that *you* are called the Barrow *King*."

"Am I?" Mr. Marsden stroked his beard. "Well, I've opened barrows from Kent to Orkney, and not the piddling grave mounds that satisfy some. The ones mutilated by the plow in a farmer's cabbage patch, and all you get is a handful of flint. No, I am selective about my burial chambers. As you can see, my collections are remarkable." He waved his hand.

"Remarkable," Georgie murmured, smiling around at the clutter, which brought on the urge to sneeze.

"I suppose Barrow Prince isn't far from the mark, for Aubin-Aubrey," conceded Mr. Marsden, with an air of largesse. "He is a bright boy and eager to follow in my footsteps. I shall doubtless pick him, one day, as my successor. Just as Mortimer picked me. He is that talented."

Georgie rounded their eyes. "As talented as you?"

"I would say so, yes. Or thereabouts." Mr. Marsden was growing ever more expansive, and he glanced at Elf with kinder eyes. "He was delayed in Norfolk and decided to travel to the Peak directly. We meet him there on Saturday. Elfreda will assist us. She is not without talent herself. When she isn't behaving like the silliest girl in Derbyshire, taking fairy tales as gospel and knocking over priceless urns." He chuckled. "Well, Miss Redmayne, you are not as deficient in good sense as you might be, and that is to your credit. You are welcome to call again, when next you are in Twynham. Agnes will see you out." He walked back to his chair and pulled it up to a table covered with maps, open notebooks, and assorted fragments, some of which seemed to be bone.

"Elfreda," he said. "Where is the book I asked for?"

Elfreda carefully retrieved the book she'd dropped. She had to pass close to Georgie as she walked to her father, close enough for them to catch the rosemary fragrance of her hair, but she didn't look up.

She set the book before him and pulled her own chair up to the table.

Georgie stared at a point right between her shoulder blades, willing her to turn around.

Five folded pages were burning a hole in their reticule. They had five folded pages, and a plan. But they needed Elf to turn. To rise and follow them from the library. Not forgive them, but at least talk to them, hear them out.

They felt a tug. Agnes had looped her arm through theirs and was looking up at them with those big, voracious eyes. "Instead of a concert, we could go to a banquet. Which do you prefer?"

"One moment." They stared at Elf's back so hard their eyes ached.

"Come with me." Agnes pulled with surprising strength. "We'll go to the banquet. There's a wizard you truly have to meet!"

11

PEACE RESTORED TO the library, Elfreda dipped her pen and began to write—about the leathern cup that stood six and three-quarter inches high in front of her writing pad. It was Saxon, taken from the second of three barrows she'd opened with Papa the previous summer on a rocky hill near Thornton. The leather was decorated with . . .

Elfreda's pen made a distressed noise and released a large blotch of ink.

She had to will her fingers to loosen, to set it down.

There was no peace with Georgina in the house. And Georgina was most definitely still in the house.

Elfreda's nape hadn't stopped prickling, even after the library door clicked. Her body registered Georgina's continued presence, like a barometer registered atmospheric pressure. Georgina did something to the air. Charged it.

"The Barrow King." Papa was chuckling softly beside her. "I'm not at all surprised. Oh, it must turn Clutterbuck green! When did you first hear it spoken? On that trip to the Chilterns? Mortimer himself could scarcely believe the number of Celtic ornaments I carried away. But even before that, the skulls I collected near Parsley Hay made quite a stir. It could have begun then."

Elfreda smiled faintly, all the answer Papa required. He turned happily to his book. His mood had been foul the other day, when she'd limped into the library after the ram attack. He'd just received the letter from William Aubin-Aubrey changing the starting date of their tour, and the meeting place—no small inconvenience. Papa didn't keep a carriage, and what with Aubin-Aubrey driving straight to the Peak, he'd no choice but to ask Sir Graham Tabor to take them in his. Sir Graham was an older friend even than Mr. Clutterbuck— in fact, he was Elfreda's godfather—and Papa had nothing good to say about him. Elfreda listened to all of it, holding her notebook, too few of her grandmother's crumpled papers shut inside. For her, meeting William Aubin-Aubrey in the Peak had been the final blow. She needed him here, in Twynham, where she could show him the note about the winter camp in *The Anglo-Saxon Chronicle*, walk him to the wolf pit, and then to the bluff, to convince him with firsthand demonstrations that her surmise was sound, based in research and an understanding of the landscape.

Fifty miles to the north, she'd have to persuade him with her words alone. She was good with books, with ancient languages, with measurements, with a shovel, but she was bad with people. Not the long-dead ones. The living ones, who were charmed by vivacity, pleasing manners, an agreeable air and address, none of which came to her naturally. Artificial attempts always exacerbated her awkward- ness. And God forbid there were witnesses. One too many and she could as soon speak as fly.

The situation was hopeless. Papa wouldn't come to her aid—he wasn't persuaded himself. Once he'd finished maligning Sir Gra- ham, she'd launched on a halting, not entirely coherent account of recent events on the Redmayne estate, and he'd interrupted, dismiss- ing the wolf pit with a twitch of his brows.

A pock in the earth, he'd said. *From my wishing a pox on the Major. Let this be the last I hear of your setting foot on his side of Holywell Rock. You'll embolden him to set foot on ours.*

As it turned out—as Georgina had predicted—he didn't mind *Georgina's* feet going wherever they liked. All Georgina had to do was smile. Apparently, flattery was an effective substitute for character, if you happened to combine big blue eyes with shamelessness.

Where was Georgina now? Agnes wouldn't have shown them out. Agnes craved company so badly, she waltzed with broomsticks. She wasn't going to let Georgina go without a fight. Had she mentioned something about a banquet?

Papa turned a page of his book, smiling.

"Excuse me a moment," she whispered, and tiptoed from the room. She was nearing the Great Hall when she heard voices.

A banquet was indeed underway.

Agnes and Georgina sat side by side near the head of the long plank table. Twelve places were laid, and every chair was filled, either with a suit of armor or a picture from the gallery. Grandpapa's portrait of King Alfred presided.

"Miss Redmayne." Agnes was speaking in her royal voice, loud and nasal. "His Majesty the King wants to know if you play the lute."

"I wish I did, Your Majesty." Georgina had removed their bonnet, and they inclined their bright head, addressing the portrait of King Alfred with deference. "The lute is my favorite instrument. Listening to its music is my chief pleasure in life."

"Really?" Agnes spoke in her normal voice.

"Oh, not at all." Georgina swirled an empty wineglass. "I was just saying the sort of thing you say in society."

"Untrue things?"

"Courteous things that may or may not be true." Georgina set down the wineglass. "It's best to avoid outright falsehoods if they can be readily exposed as such. Note I didn't claim to play the lute, only that I shared the king's admiration. If I'd said I could play, he might next have asked me for a song."

"This is exceedingly helpful. Now may we practice complimenting soup?" Agnes's expression was so blatantly adoring that Elfreda cringed. Couldn't she see that Georgina was dangerous?

Georgina deposited their reticule in Agnes's empty bowl.

"Soup," they said. "Turtle soup. Sing its praises."

Agnes lifted her spoon. "I have long adored the tortoise!" She announced this to the table at large. "I kept a pet tortoise as a child. His name was Wamba, and I miss him every day." She lowered her spoon, blushing with sudden uncertainty. "I did that wrong, didn't I? I made it too melancholy. I could clarify that Wamba escaped, and that I believe he lives in a log somewhere, with a family of his own? Unless someone has caught him and put him in a soup." Her lower lip started trembling.

"Less is more when it comes to complimenting soup." Georgina sounded gently encouraging. "What you said was very heartfelt, but you could condense it to simply *I adore the soup*."

"I adore the soup," repeated Agnes, perking up.

"Very good." Georgina nodded. "Now let's try artichoke soup."

"Let's not." Elfreda had witnessed enough. Georgina was toying with her sister, and she wouldn't stand for it. She stomped over the stone flags. "Dinner is over."

Agnes saw her and blanched. "We're on the first course."

Elfreda came to a halt at the head of the table, shoulder to shoulder with King Alfred. "I don't care. It's time for Georgina to go."

"You go!" Agnes sank down in her chair. "You're not invited."

"We could speed things up," suggested Georgina, glancing between them. "Skip the soup. The king is missing his spoon."

"Because of the twins." Agnes sank lower. "There's a spoon shortage. I can hear them whinnying now. They're about to interrupt us too."

Indeed, faint whinnies had become audible.

"I'll never learn the proper etiquette," wailed Agnes. "I will disgrace Beatrice in front of her new friends and lose her forever!"

"Oh please, enough." Elfreda's patience snapped. "If Beatrice is so inconstant, you haven't lost much."

"How would you know?" Agnes banged the table. "You don't have any friends!"

The silence that settled was profound. Even the whinnies had faded away.

Elfreda's nose burned, and pressure built behind her eyes. She didn't have friends, but she did have sisters, sisters she loved, whose happiness and comfort she put before her own. She played with them, protected and provided for them as best she could. The only reason Agnes could correspond with Beatrice at all was because Elfreda paid for the postage, out of the money she skimmed from the household budget through such laborious means as refilling Papa's opodeldoc bottle with a liniment she made herself, and repairing certain books he tasked her with sending to the conservator.

The sting of injustice mixed with the deeper pain of rejection. She turned away so Georgina couldn't see her expression.

"Forgive me." Agnes was suddenly beside her, tears trembling on her lashes. "But sometimes it seems that you want to keep me from everything wonderful."

Elfreda sucked in a breath. If that's how it seemed, what use denying it? Besides, her chest was hurting in a way that made speech difficult.

"Do you hear that?" Agnes's face lit up. "It must be the post boy!"

She lifted her skirt and ran, hair streaming behind her.

Elfreda watched her cross the Great Hall, the largest room in the house, and the most austere. Benches against the gray walls. Blackened hearth holding dead fire. Fathoms of dim air between floor and timbered ceiling.

The whinnies resumed, became louder, then faded again as the twins galloped on.

She swallowed, and her throat made a tiny, hurting click.

"They're spoonicorns today," she said, without turning to look at Georgina, so it was almost like speaking to herself. "Hilda and Matilda. They made themselves manes out of Grandpapa's mangy old wigs, and I suspect their heads are crawling with mites. I'm going to have to force them to bathe, and they'll be angrier with me even than Agnes. Usually, they get cake as a reward for a washup, but there's not any cake. I could bake a cake. We're low on butter, though. I could go out for butter. But Papa will want me in the library, to get down more books from the shelves. When his leg is stiff, he can't climb the ladder." She closed her eyes. Last night, she'd dreamed that Marsden Hall was filling with soot-blackened, ice-cold water. It rose from below, and poured down from above, and she'd plugged the holes in a frenzy, but there were too many. The dream came back to her now, that clawing panic, and the desire—just as terrifying—to stop. To let the waters rise, and slip under.

She turned. Georgina was watching her, and she couldn't read the slant of their brows, the set of their mouth. Often, her tongue locked in place. Now, her tongue felt loose, and words poured from her like the dream waters, as though if she kept talking, she could finally breathe. "Aunt Susan, Papa's sister, who stayed with us after Mother died—she recently remarried. In March, her husband wrote to Papa with an offer to bring out Agnes alongside his own daughter the year after next, and to take in the twins as well. He promised to give them every advantage. Aunt Susan's doing, obviously. While she was here, I resented her for her officiousness—all the sermons, all the *ringlets*—but she has a warm and generous heart, and real regard for the girls. The offer was meant as a kindness, not an affront. But it certainly affronted Papa. He tore up the letter, which is the only reason I know of its existence. I found the pieces in the waste bin. He must have written something dreadfully disrespectful in response. No letters have arrived from Aunt Susan or her husband since. I haven't told Agnes. I haven't told anyone."

At this she paused, a bitter half smile on her lips. Of course she hadn't told anyone. She had no friends, no one to whom she could unburden herself. And that was why she was unburdening herself now to Georgina Redmayne.

It was madness.

A crease had formed between their brows.

"Please don't repeat a word of this to Agnes." She met their eyes. "She won't be able to change Papa's mind, and it will only make her miserable. She expects that Aunt Susan *will* invite her at some point to London. I don't want to mislead her, but I don't want to crush her hope. She makes hope into . . . everything wonderful."

She gestured at the table, at the dinner guests. King Alfred, a German knight, an English knight, *Merlin*. The pain she'd felt when Agnes lashed out had abated, and in its place, she felt the usual mix of affectionate exasperation and admiring trepidation. She could appreciate Agnes's resourcefulness, even when she had to tidy up afterward, even when tidying up involved dragging full suits of Greenwich and Gothic armor up the great stair. But what would become of her tempestuous, whimsical sister? How would the world see *her*?

Her gaze had fixed on the painting of Merlin. He was standing with his staff in the mouth of a cave.

She heard the loud scrape of oaken chair legs on stone. And then another.

"Elf." Georgina was standing behind a chair they'd pulled back from the table. "Will you sit?"

She shook her head. "I have things to do." Hadn't they been listening? No, of course not. If they ever listened to her, they wouldn't have come here at all. She'd called them *a curse*. She'd vowed to destroy them.

"You look as though you need to sit down first."

She flushed. They *had* been listening—listening, and studying her too, making determinations about her needs. She wanted to look away from them, but she could read the expression on their face now, and it transfixed her. Sympathy, but not the amused, condescending kind she anticipated, as though she were a pitiably ridiculous curiosity. No, their face held something far simpler, much more frank. Concern. Kindness.

If resistance was beyond her, destruction was too. She felt too defeated to sweep proudly from the room, and so she most definitely wasn't about to charge them like a ram, in a display of vengeful fury. There was no point. In truth, she didn't feel vengeful or furious. That was all gone. She felt tired.

She went to the chair and sat.

12

"I WAS AN ASS," said Georgina, sitting down in the chair beside her. "With you, and with the sheep. I'm sorry for what happened."

She gave a small shrug. Was it really that much more Georgina's fault than her own? She'd howled too. She'd felt for an instant like a wolf, like Miss Poskitt's version of a wolf. A wild, free, beautiful creature. She'd understood, too, for an instant, the glory of the pack, her hand in Georgina's, Miss Poskitt and Miss Mahomed grinning fiercely on either side, their hearts all beating as one.

Her heart was beating now, faster than it should be.

She cleared her throat. "I was glad to hear that Miss Poskitt will make a full recovery."

An understatement. She'd been haunted by the image of Miss Poskitt lying so still in the grass, her face that deathly shade of white. Her face stayed pale and set, and her eyes closed, even as the farmer had hoisted her into his arms. Elfreda hadn't followed him as Georgina and Miss Mahomed had; there was nothing she could do, and she had papers to chase. But the blood crashing in her ears had mimicked Miss Mahomed's agonized cries.

Anne! Oh, please no, Anne!

Yesterday, she'd almost called at Redmayne Manor, but Papa's prohibition, and the thought of facing Georgina, held her back.

Georgina exhaled, their own relief plain. "There's only a small fracture."

"I'm glad." Elfreda repeated herself, and colored slightly at her inanity. "Miss Mahomed feared she'd lose her leg."

"Rosalie is quick to predict amputation. She grew up playing with her father's bone saws. He is the proprietor of the Patna Public House, but he was once a surgeon in the Bengal Army. And also"— Georgina hesitated—"she's in love with Anne. Being in love makes a person go to extremes."

Were they speaking from personal experience? Had Georgina ever been in love?

Maybe she looked at them too searchingly. Their pale eyes seemed to flicker, and they plucked their reticule from the soup bowl and untied the drawstrings.

"For you," they said, withdrawing a wad of folded paper. "Five pages. A little worse for wear." They pushed away their place setting, unfolded the papers, and pressed them flat on the table.

Grandmama's familiar handwriting soothed her like a friendly face.

She reached for the papers. "Thank you."

Georgina slid the papers away. "This one." They rearranged the order. "I am interested in this one here."

She frowned at their long fingers moving capably and possessively through papers that didn't belong to them. When they showed her the page they meant, her frown faded, and she sighed with resignation.

"That's from the section on the heathen men," she said. "Which I told you about."

"You didn't mention treasure."

Of course it was that very page.

"The story of the hoard is relevant in the context of the army making camp in Twynham. The camp is the priority." Not that she hadn't daydreamed about a heavy coffer, lid swung open to reveal a great cache of precious objects.

Georgina nodded. "And you require the assistance of the Barrow Prince to uncover it. Which he will happily provide."

He wouldn't. She'd all but reconciled herself to the missed opportunity. And she knew better than to entertain Georgina's flippant remarks. But she couldn't help but ask. "And why, pray tell, is that?"

"Because I will share my own passionate support for the endeavor." They grinned. "I am irresistible when I choose to be."

She let this pass. *How?* He is bypassing Twynham.

"I'll go with you to the Peak." Georgina said it like it was the most reasonable thing in the world. "Is there room in the carriage?"

There would be, with Papa, Sir Graham, and herself, room for one.

"Not for you," she said. "Papa would never . . ."

Georgina cocked a brow. Their smugness was such that they thought it adequate to say nothing, to let her draw her own conclusion.

She gripped the arms of her chair. "The Barrow *King*? Really? That was an obvious blandishment."

Georgina gave her a knowing smile. "It doesn't matter if it was obvious. It worked."

"You won't sustain his good opinion. He will see your false praise for what it is."

"Your father inflates his ego with self-deception. The last thing he wants is honesty from the people around him."

She opened her mouth, then closed it. She wasn't as flagrant as Georgina, but didn't she adapt herself to Papa daily, smoothing his perennially ruffled feathers in a hundred subtle ways, resorting on occasion to white lies? Didn't he demand it?

Georgina sensed her wavering and pounced. "I will ask him myself."

"Will the Major even allow it?" She stalled, gnawing her lip, uneasy flutters in her stomach.

This was Georgina Redmayne. She should say no. No. A thousand times no.

Georgina Redmayne. They walked into a room and every head turned. They told a story, and people hung on their every word. They were beautiful, lively, appealing—everything she wasn't. When they were sixteen, they'd convinced Lord Fawcett's son to ride his horse into the ballroom—at least, Elfreda felt almost certain it was them. They could convince William Aubin-Aubrey to come to Twynham. She knew it.

She put a hand on her stomach. The flutters were more insistent, more excited.

"The Major doesn't have to know," said Georgina. "I'll go with you, and we'll bring the Barrow Prince back. Unless you'd rather stay here and see if we can't turn up some treasure."

Her spine went so stiff so fast she heard a faint crack. "That's what you're after."

They didn't have the decency to look chagrined. "Is that a sin? Even nuns were after it."

"This conversation is over," she said, but she was too vexed to stop herself there. "If we *did* turn up the hoard, the coroner would hold an inquest. Hidden troves of gold and silver belong to the Crown, not the finder. It would all go to the king."

And probably, eventually, to the British Museum. With her name attached.

Her cheeks warmed.

Georgina seemed unimpressed. "The coroner won't miss a chalice or two. I don't need much, just enough to rent a room for a year in a boardinghouse where I won't get fleas. Plus expenses."

"I would miss the chalices." The warmth drained from her cheeks.

"But you wouldn't miss me." Georgina's eyes sparkled, and they shot her a charming smile. "Just a handful of gold coins, and I'm out of your life. Isn't that worth any price?"

Despite herself, she gave a snorting laugh. "I'm perfectly content to ignore you for the next thirteen months. It doesn't matter where you are."

"Look," said Georgina, "I want loot, yes. I want to get back to London and tread the boards. But I'll go with you to the Peak even if you decline. You're right that I should make amends, and luring your Barrow Prince is the best I can do. So let me do it."

They *were* very nearly irresistible. She could resist them, of course. She could say *no* right now. But this was about William Aubin-Aubrey. Faced with Georgina, he would say *yes*.

"Suit yourself," she said.

"Good." Georgina nodded, pleased. A moment later, they gave their head a shake. "Aren't you intrigued, though? I can't stop thinking about the clues."

She stilled. "Clues?"

Georgina tapped the bottom of the page. "Clues."

"The riddles?"

"Yes. Riddles. Clues."

"The riddles aren't clues." Elfreda's brows pinched. "See this line under the narrative?" She traced the inked line with her finger. "The riddles are beneath. This is a footnote. Grandmama put these riddles there as commentary."

Georgina leaned back in their chair. "Mysterious commentary. Couldn't she have included the riddles because they were there on the page, in the original manuscript? Just not in the main paragraph?"

Notes in the margin. Yes, medieval manuscripts were littered with them.

The possibility hadn't occurred to her. Georgina had arrived at an interpretation that she'd neglected to consider.

The tops of her ears began to burn.

"*Earth-child I was, skulking in ground,*" Georgina read the first riddle aloud, "*Till smelt-flames offered a new name and price: No longer earth, I can purchase the earth.*"

"That's a translation of a famous riddle, by Symphosius." Elfreda paused, pulse leaping. "The answer is gold."

"That's what I thought." Georgina looked at her, and the vindication in their face was mixed with wonder. "It *is* a clue, isn't it? Imagine. The nuns lived in fear of the Northmen, for decades, for lifetimes. The hoard had to stay hidden, its location a secret, so they passed these riddles down for generations. Do nuns have generations? Regardless. They passed the riddles down in the hopes that they'd be solved, and the hoard found, when the time was right."

Imagine. She'd begged Papa to imagine too. *Silliness.* That was his word for imagination—hers at least.

"The first riddle supplies the *what*," said Georgina. "The second supplies the *where.*"

Silly. To race from speculation to speculation. Giddy making. A tickle in her chest threatened to burst into a howl. *Clues.* She could imagine it.

"The second riddle." She swallowed. "It's not Symphosius. Or Aldhelm. I've never seen it in another text."

"*Within my depths, the shadows play. And yet there is light at my mouth and water that brings life.*" Georgina read it aloud, in a quiet voice that somehow carried to every corner of the room. "What's the answer?"

Their eyes were the color of the winter sky. The Northmen might have watched smoke from their fires on the bluff spiral toward exactly that shade of blue.

"I don't know." She slid the papers over, gathered them to herself. "I'd have to think."

"I'm first-rate at charades, but these olden-day riddles are a different beast entirely." Georgina drummed their fingers on the table. "I should practice. Are there any books of them in your library?"

"They are all in Latin, or Saxon."

"That's terrifically inconvenient." They frowned. "None in English? Or very bad French?"

"No." She fought a smile, unsuccessfully.

"Pity." A smile tugged at the corners of their mouth too. "We must at least solve the riddle. We owe it to the nuns. And, of course, to your grandmother."

I know what you're doing, she wanted to say to them. *It's obvious.* Invoking Grandmama, tugging on her heartstrings. Georgina had figured out her formula, as well as Papa's.

"I can translate a riddle, if you want to practice." She tipped back her head, studied the ceiling until she had it. "All right." She felt oddly nervous as she recited. "I create hungry sparks that must be fed, like rubbed against like, warm and then bright."

She turned her gaze on Georgina. Georgina was giving her a very strange look in return.

"What's the answer?" she asked.

"You want me to answer." Georgina seemed vaguely incredulous. "That riddle."

What wasn't she understanding?

"You can take your time," she offered.

"I'll answer." They ran a hand through their hair. "If you're sure."

"I'm sure." My God, this was baffling. "*You* might not be sure."

"I'm sure." A slow smile spread across their face, then faded as they leaned closer.

"The answer is . . ."

Their eyes darkened as their lashes swept down, and then their mouth was on hers. The soft heat of it stopped her breath. Everything stopped. The contact was so light she almost made a noise of frustration, tilted her head to increase the pressure, but she couldn't move a muscle. Sensation tingled over every inch of her skin. The need for touch became an ache. Her lips were burning. They had to do something more, something to quench this spreading fire.

And then they did less.

It was over.

Their mouth was gone, and hers felt scalded, damp and hot.

"Well?" Georgina was draped over the arm of their chair, chin in hand. "Am I right?"

Elfreda exhaled. "You are . . ." She couldn't finish the thought.

"Kiss." Georgina looked pleased. "*Like rubbed against like.* Those are lips."

Kiss? Lips?

"Flints!" Elfreda bestirred herself at last, all the blood that was holding still in her veins coursing now with double the speed. "Rub flints together and they produce sparks. The answer is flints. Or sticks, maybe. Flints or sticks. It's a riddle about making fire."

"Oh." Georgina straightened, skimming a fingertip back and forth over their lower lip. "I thought it was about kissing. And that you wanted me to kiss you."

Mortification made her stomach drop. She barely understood her own desire, but it seemed Georgina had arrived at an interpretation of that as well.

"It wasn't just the *like rubbed against like* that suggested *kiss,*" they continued, their tone defensive. "It was the *hungry sparks.* Kissing does that—sometimes at least. Not literally. The answers to this type of riddle are more literal than metaphorical? Is that the lesson?"

"The lesson is that *I* was right. About you." She wished her voice wasn't trembling. "You should leave."

They collected their bonnet and reticule and stood. She could feel them looking down at her.

"So, just to be clear, you *didn't* want me to kiss you?" The disbelief in the question set her teeth on edge.

The silence stretched until she was on the verge of breaking, blurting *Yes, I didn't*, or *No, I did*, some mixed-up affirmative-negative, negative-affirmative retort that contributed to the unclarity of everything.

"Apologies," they said.

She let a shred of long-held breath escape her.

"Should I talk to your father now about the Peak? Or come back tomorrow?"

"Neither." She kept staring straight ahead at the engraved breastplate of the suit of armor Papa called *the Dudley*. The breastplate had a mortal-looking dent. "You can see yourself out."

After a long moment, she heard Georgina's receding footsteps. When they dwindled to nothing, she slumped and touched her lips, extinguishing any remaining sparks.

13

SHE COULDN'T SLEEP that night. She usually curled herself into a ball in bed, tucked her cold fingers between her legs, and huddled motionless, waiting for her body to warm the sheets, drifting off in the process. Instead, she moved restlessly, sweaty with agitation, kicking her legs as she turned over and over.

"Damn you, Georgina." She muttered it aloud to the dark room. She shivered a feverish shiver, because Miss Poskitt had claimed that fairy tales possessed a kernel of truth, and Miss Mahomed had claimed that repeating someone's name made them appear, and ideas dismissably silly by day gathered weight in the night, and she could almost believe if she said *Georgina* again and again, it would summon them into the room. Into her bedchamber.

And then?

She kicked her legs and heaved herself from her right side to her left. Georgina wasn't going to appear in her bedchamber. Georgina was fast asleep in Redmayne Manor, on a feather bed, smug and smiling. Had they felt *their* lips spark?

Sometimes kissing does that, they'd said.

Sometimes.

She kicked her legs and heaved herself from her left side to her right. What had come over her in the Great Hall? She'd revealed things about herself, about her family, that she shouldn't have. She'd sat beside Georgina voluntarily, let them beguile her, as she had at the wolf pit, and instead of a ram, a *kiss* had brought it all crashing down. In the past five years, they'd gotten worse by getting better, new facets of their personality dazzling her so that she temporarily lost sight of the deeper, ineradicable flaws. This more sensitive, more likeable Georgina, this *Georgie*, made her lose her head. She became the sort of girl who drank too much champagne in the sun, who howled, who forgot her goals, who aired unpleasant family business, who received kisses that kept her up at night, sighing and fantasizing about sparks. What Fellow of the Albion Society was that sort of girl? No Fellow! None! None of them were girls at all, of course, but that only meant she had to try even harder, to show Papa and William Aubin-Aubrey and Sir Graham and whoever else that hers was a scientific mind. She couldn't impress anyone as a learned, well-reasoned individual with Georgina goading her into flights of fancy and fits of temper. Refusing Georgina's offer to accompany her to the Peak was the sensible decision, the correct decision. Or was it?

She kicked her legs and heaved herself from her right side to her left. Was it sensible? Or was it cowardly? She feared Georgina's proximity would prompt her to do something foolish. Didn't that ascribe to them too much power? Wasn't it up to her to exert some self-control? If she allowed the Barrow Prince to slip away because *Georgina Redmayne* had ruffled her feathers, she'd never forgive Georgina, but more crucially, she'd never forgive herself. She wasn't a coward! And she was more than Georgina's match. Suddenly, she knew what to do, and it was so simple, she almost laughed. Take Georgina to the Peak. Accept their help with Aubin-Aubrey. Ignore their provocations. Simple. She'd work with such singular focus, she'd hardly notice they were there. She'd fill her thoughts with urns and calcined bones. She'd keep them at arm's length.

Except each night when they shared the same bed at the coaching inn.

She twisted around and lay on her back, panting as though she'd run a mile. The breathless feeling persisted until she climbed from her bed, exhausted, to begin the morning's chores. Finished at last, she walked the mile to Redmayne Manor in bright sun, flushing with the realization that this was the very mile she'd run over and over in her head through the darkest hours before dawn.

The butler who opened the door wore a beleaguered expression. Her heart went out to him. He too was suffering Georgina's return.

"Have you something in your eye?" he asked, alarmed, by which she understood her expression of solidarity had missed the mark. Her attempts to communicate facially often missed the mark. Once she reassured him that she was perfectly well, he directed her to the garden. She retraced her steps from the week before, walking the serpentine paths around bright flower beds and conical topiaries. She paused by the pergola. The wisteria seemed even more profuse, pouring over the lattices. The morning-glory vines wrapping the columns had put out blooms of vivid blue.

Inside, Georgina was sprawled out on a bench, dappled by the light filtering through the pergola's freight of blossoms, one arm trailing to the ground, the other thrown over their eyes.

She stepped closer and a stray piece of gravel on the pergola's stone floor chirped beneath her shoe.

Georgina sat up, swinging their legs off the bench. They were wearing trousers. A ruffled white shirt. A pink waistcoat. Their cravat was messy, and their jacket was nonexistent. The toe of one shiny black boot rested on the blade of a fencing foil.

"Don't worry," they said, noting her gaze. "I won't put out your eye. I've fenced enough today."

She saw the second foil. "With whom?"

"Robert Peach. Younger brother of Charles Peach, who came to

Rosalie's rescue. He was delivering some cheese, and one thing led to another."

"Did he know he was fencing . . . ?" *A girl* wasn't quite right. But what if Georgina got hurt? They weren't exactly a boy, and their not being one, in this case, would mean hell for poor Robert Peach.

"He assumed I was a roguish Redmayne cousin. With my encouragement." Georgina flicked their foot, and the foil flew up into the air. They caught it by the hilt and jumped into a lunge, arm extended. The foil's blunted tip pointed at Elfreda's throat. Luckily, she was a yard away.

"I say!" Georgina grinned and reversed out of the lunge, looking tall and delighted. "Did you see that?"

"See what?" The tartness of her reply only made their grin widen.

"It doesn't always work," they told her. "I made it look easy, but there's a trick to it. I could teach you."

"You couldn't. Your average box of bone fragments is more coordinated than I am."

Georgina's lips shaped *average box of bone fragments*. Their eyes danced with mirth, but instead of laughing, they gave a shrug.

"If you change your mind," they said breezily, "I'm happy to try. When you're back from the Peak."

This was an opening. She walked closer. They dropped onto the bench and let the foil clatter down. The way they watched her approach, legs stretched out, gaze knowing—they'd given her the opening deliberately. They knew why she'd come. It irked her to behold them casually expecting the outcome she'd struggled toward all night. And suddenly, ignoring their provocations seemed far too much to ask. In fact, a little gloating seemed in order.

"You lost to Robert Peach, didn't you?" she said. "I surprised you in a posture of defeat."

This elicited an amused smirk—even more provoking. "There was no winning or losing. There was only the happy clashing of steel.

Young Peach had never fenced before in his life. Our bout was unorthodox, but nonetheless, highly diverting."

"Diverting and *fatiguing*," she asserted. "It wore you out."

"On the contrary, I'm eager for a new activity. One goes to bed so early in the country. I find it promotes vigor during all the daylight hours. But you—your eyelids are the color of this wisteria." They leaned forward, and that abominable smugness she'd imagined so clearly last night was written all over their face. "Did you sleep a wink?"

The air inside the pergola was drenched with the wisteria's sweet scent. She felt dizzy with it. The delicate purple hues made a backdrop against which Georgina's auburn hair took on the richness of ruby.

They were unfairly, unreasonably attractive, and they knew it.

She wanted to strangle them. She'd have to crawl onto their lap to do it, and slide her hands beneath their high white collar. Their pulse would beat against her palms, and she'd clamp her knees around their hips to keep them still.

"You've gone rather pale," they observed. "Are you all right?"

It required effort to meet their eyes. "I have never been better."

They looked at her a moment, then leaned back with a shrug. "I was thinking about the estate. When you walked up, I was lying here, thinking. Agonizing, really. It's a disaster."

"Disaster?" She gave her surroundings a dubious glance. From the vantage of the pergola, she could see an immaculately kept section of garden, the eclectic mix of plants many-hued and harmonious. The grounds were beautiful. And Redmayne Manor, while not to her taste, had sparkling windows and all its roof tiles.

"The manor's in good order." Georgina shifted their legs, the ankle of one coming up to rest on the knee of the other. "But I got Robert talking, and the farms are not. Every cottage has a rotten floor and a flooded basement. Every barn is overrun with vermin. Every farmer gets broken promises instead of repairs, and a notice to quit when the lease comes around if they complain. I could speak to the steward—I told *Charles* Peach I would—but to what end? I can't sack him. It would have to be Harry. And then we'd need a new steward, and I don't know how to guarantee he wouldn't be just as bad. I'm sure my father didn't pick the current one with the idea that he'd bleed the tenants dry for a few more pounds in profit. My father believed in making fair allowances. And even more so, in making people fond of him. He couldn't have tolerated all this ill will."

Elfreda stared. Georgina's face wasn't smug, but serious, fretful lines bracketing tense lips. She'd longed to get the advantage of them, to see them cut down to size. But this show of vulnerability gave them more power over her, not less. It hooked something tender behind her breastplate.

She hardened herself.

"Out of sight, out of mind," she said. "I doubt your father felt the ill will in London."

"You're implying that he put the steward up to it? And kept away to avoid facing the consequences?" The blue of Georgina's eyes took on an icy cast. "He wasn't like that."

"He did stop coming, though." And so had Georgina. She'd always tried to suppress her curiosity, to appreciate without questioning, but now it spilled out. "Why?"

Georgina looked sardonic. "He died."

"For the two years before that."

They hesitated. "He preferred Kent. We have a hunting lodge there. It was Mother who liked Derbyshire." They reached up and plucked a drooping strand of wisteria blossoms. "I don't want to think about the estate at present. There are far more pleasant things to think about in this floral abode. Anne calls it the *bower of bliss*."

The pause that followed was pointed. Georgina twirled the blossoms by the stem, skewering her with their gaze. Their eyes had grown hot, not the color of ice but of flame's blue heart.

"She told you." Elfreda's pulse spiked. "She told you what happened."

"She did." Georgina let the petals stroke along their cheekbone. "Care to join me?"

Elfreda started. "Join you?" In her mind's eye, she saw Miss Poskitt and Miss Mahomed again, passionately entwined. She all but squeaked her next words. "For kissing?"

"Sitting." They used the blossoms to indicate the empty space next to them. "Care to join me on this bench?" Their voice was dry.

She wished for the ground to open.

"When it comes to kissing, we keep talking at cross-purposes." They regarded her narrowly, one side of their mouth hitched up with amusement. "We should discuss it in plainer English."

"No, we shouldn't." She straightened her shoulders. "We shouldn't talk about kissing."

"We kissed without talking yesterday, and you objected. Would you rather do that after all?"

"No kissing." Her heart was smashing against her ribs. "We shouldn't kiss."

"Ah." They nodded and stroked the blossoms across the bridge of their nose. "Because of the Bible? It would be unnatural?"

She frowned. "No. When Miss Poskitt asked about nuns falling in love, I thought about the Book of Ruth. How Ruth and Naomi refuse to be separated. *For whither thou goest, I will go; and where thou lodgest, I will lodge: thy people shall be my people.* That's what Ruth says to Naomi. It's an ardent declaration of the deepest attachment. There's no exchange between a man and a woman in the Old *or* New Testament half so beautiful."

"Is that so?" Georgina blinked. "I should pay more attention in church." They stood abruptly. "Because I'm a Redmayne, then?"

"No." She swallowed. "That's not it either."

"Because you abhor me personally." They closed the distance between them. "Is that it?" They were staring down at her.

She'd claimed to abhor them. She *did* abhor them. Their smirking, unearned assuredness, their reckless gaiety—it was anathema.

"Because you didn't like it?" they murmured.

Her skin shivered. Her breath caught.

She was still, and after a moment, they lifted their hand, slowly reached out, and tucked the wisteria behind her ear. She felt the little scratch of the stem, the tickle of cool blossoms, and then the tug in her scalp, as their fingers slid into her hair.

Their voice dipped even lower. "Because you did?"

She took a step back, almost stumbling. She'd exerted more energy than she'd needed.

"Georgina," she began, breathless.

"Georgie," they interrupted. "Georgie, please."

"Georgie," she corrected herself. "You offered to come to the Peak, to convince the Barrow Prince to return with us to Twynham. Does the offer stand?"

Their smile was dark. "Yes."

Relief washed through her. She felt steadier on her feet. "Good. Good, then. Pack for a fortnight. Sir Graham Tabor is coming up from Swadlincote. We'll drive with him. He's always impatient to tell new people what he knows of Pompeii, and what he knows goes on for hours, so you should brace yourself. Papa calls him Sir Grand Tour. He hates the turnpike, so you might also get one of his lectures on old Roman roads. Once we arrive, you can sightsee while I assist at the barrows. And you can use your persuasion with Mr. Aubin-Aubrey during dinners. The two of *us* won't have much opportunity or cause to talk."

She gulped air. Thank God, she'd managed to correct her course, to remember that the Peak was the destination, not this *bower of bliss.*

Georgie had tilted their head in thought.

"It is all settled," she said, and added another awkward "Good."

"Frittering." Georgie muttered it under their breath.

"Pardon?"

"Frittering. Kissing." Their gaze sharpened. "You think kissing is frittering. *That's* why not. Kissing is on your list of pointless diversions."

She blanched, and they released a soft, gratified laugh.

"I should have guessed sooner." They folded their arms. "You owe me one, by the way. A diversion."

"No, I don't."

"It was the condition of your coming onto my land. Frittering. *Living.* You said I could pick anything."

"The picnic sufficed."

"Says you. But it's *my* condition. I didn't decide on the picnic."

"The kiss," she bit out. "We already kissed. Let that suffice."

"I couldn't, not in good faith. It was an insufficient kiss. Also, incorrect. The answer was *flints.*"

They were laughing again.

Her jaw clenched, and she stepped up to them, jabbing with her finger.

"I will *not* permit any frittering while we're in the Peak. The trip is too important."

They glanced down at her finger, which had drilled into their shoulder.

"Understood." Their brows had a wicked slant. "I'll behave." They paused. "Until after."

The heat of their body radiated through the thin fabric of their shirt, sending a warm pulse through her fingertip. She could smell their laundry soap, and that light balsam fragrance emanating from their skin.

She retracted herself.

"After," she agreed, voice hoarse. "We can fritter however you like."

Their smile was just as wicked. "My intention is to pick something we both like. Any ideas?"

Even their teeth were unfairly attractive.

She forced her gaze up from their mouth.

"There's nothing we both like," she whispered.

"Liar." An unfamiliar emotion flashed in their eyes.

"It might change," she said, and lifted her chin. "You might develop a partiality for archaeological research."

This time, their laughter burst out sudden and surprised. "So single-minded."

She nodded curtly. "I will see you Saturday morning."

As she whipped around, she felt a fleeting caress, soft on her lips. She froze, heart stuttering, but it was only the strand of wisteria. She blew at the bobbing petals, then plucked the strand from behind her ear. Before she left the garden, she cast it away.

14

LIVING BY A volcano was a very bad idea. Far worse than living by the Marsdens, or by a garden water feature filled with nocturnally singing frogs—although Georgie wouldn't have said so during the wee hours of Saturday morning as sleepless night transitioned into *Bloody hell, I'm late to meet the carriage.* But after the first stage of the journey with Sir Graham, they had a new appreciation for the particular horrors meted out by mountains of flame. Very, *very* bad things had happened to the residents of Pompeii and Herculaneum on the twenty-fourth of August in the year seventy-nine anno Domini. Death by incineration. Death by encasement in choking ash. Death by battery of burning pumice stones. At least one chap's brain had turned to *glass* in the heat. Georgie almost asked Sir Graham how he knew about the glass brain, but then they pictured him cracking a Pompeiian skull like a hard-boiled egg and decided against it. They didn't really want to hear an answer to that question.

"Marsden," said Sir Graham, turning from Georgie at last. "I know you're not asleep."

"I am asleep." Mr. Marsden sat across from Georgie, arms folded, eyes closed.

"I'm driving you to collect your Saxon knickknacks, the least you could do is pay me the courtesy of your attention."

"That's not *the least*," replied Mr. Marsden, eyes still closed. "This is the least."

Georgie glanced at Elf, who was seated next to Mr. Marsden. She'd been staring fixedly out the window for miles.

"And they are *not* knickknacks," added Mr. Marsden, without stirring. "Saxon antiquities have far more relevance to our heritage than whatever classical bric-a-brac you can lug back from the Continent."

"One mustn't neglect the Roman influence." Sir Graham was a silver-haired gentleman with an impressive nose, and he looked down it, impressively, at Mr. Marsden, to no effect.

"This is an Anglo-Saxon nation," said Mr. Marsden, eyes closed. "If we are to trace our forebears beyond Albion's rocky shores, the path leads to the German forest, not the Roman forum."

"See that line across the moor?" Sir Graham smiled and rapped the window. "That's a Roman path right there."

Mr. Marsden did *not* see, but Georgie leaned forward to look, and therefore, received the brunt of Sir Graham's information, more than they could ever retain, about the movements of the Roman legions, and their construction techniques, and the masonry layers of their roadways.

At some point, they nodded off, and woke with a start in an empty carriage.

"Are we there?" they asked, stepping down into a courtyard where Elf, Mr. Marsden, and Sir Graham stood blinking in the sun. It soon became clear that they were *not* there. Sir Graham had decided to stop for refreshment. He continued informing Georgie as he ate and drank—mostly drank—until a squabble with Mr. Marsden diverted his attention, and Georgie was able to slink out of the inn.

Elf climbed into the carriage shortly after them.

"Papa and Sir Graham won't be a moment," she said, taking her seat in the opposite corner. She had a wary look on her face, which made their indignation flare.

"I promised I'd behave," they reminded her. "I'm not about to kiss you."

"Shhh." She shushed them with a scowl.

"I can't even *say* kiss?"

"*Shhh.*" She seized one of the quilted silk sleeping cushions, obviously intending to whack them with it, but the cushion was bound to her seat with a ribbon, so the best she could do was wave it menacingly. The menace conjured by silk cushion waving was not much.

Even so, they relented. "Let's change the subject, then. Why *did* Sir Graham agree to drive?" They glanced around the carriage, upholstered and lined with cloth of Vesuvian red. "He and your father seem to be at odds."

She lowered the cushion. "That's just how they are. They're friends who dislike each other." Her cheeks tinted pink with embarrassment, and they recalled her stricken expression that day at Marsden Hall when Agnes had shouted.

You don't have any friends.

"Or is that a contradiction?" she asked. "They're on intimate but disagreeable terms. They do each other favors to get the upper hand. What would you call that?"

"I don't know. I wouldn't call it friendship exactly."

"Was it friendship, what you had with the Janes?"

They tipped their head, surprised. "The Janes? They're married now, as I'm sure you know."

Jane Slater. Jane Turner. Jane Ratcliff. Jane Tetley. Well, Jane Tetley's real name was Mary. She was an honorary Jane. After Georgie's first full year away from Twynham, they'd slackened as a correspondent, and by the third, they didn't think to feel guilty. Sometimes friendships waned naturally. Friends grew apart, nudged along by geography and the marital imperative.

They sighed. "I called on each of them. Admired the husbands, and the sprats. We don't have much in common these days. But we *were* friends, yes."

She considered. "It strikes me as similar."

They laughed in shock. "My friendship with the Janes, and your father's with Sir Graham? That's ridiculous. There's no similarity at all. No one was trying to get the upper hand."

"You weren't." A line appeared between Elf's brows. "Because you had it. But they all competed for your attention. You paid them so little attention, you didn't notice."

"I didn't realize *you* paid attention to *me*." They scrubbed a hand through their hair, discomfited.

Elf went pinker. "You make it hard not to. You've very . . . obvious."

Georgie's skin felt too tight. The Janes had been inseparable, and easy to excite, always ready for devilry and adventure—albeit of the modest sort available in a country neighborhood—responsive to Georgie's whims and high jinks, trailing them to the pond, if midnight swimming were the thing, or to the gamekeeper's hut, or Lord Fawcett's hedge maze, or Mrs. Pattinson's library.

Rather like a retinue.

"The Janes called themselves the Janes," they pointed out, defensively. "I didn't have a hand in it. The Janes were close. They're still close, I believe, all of them."

"Possibly closer, now that they're not vying for favorite." Elf sounded thoughtful, but Georgie flinched regardless.

"I may have been more careless than I understood at the time," they said, "but I was never manipulative. Perhaps a bit too willing to be fawned over." They remembered Rosalie's unpleasant smile when they'd complained about their exile. Grow up with enough wealth and beauty, and you'll accept anything as your due, until something, or someone, or many someones, teaches you otherwise.

They cleared their throat. "I have things to regret. But I refuse the comparison."

Elf surprised them again by nodding. "I'm not an expert on friends, by any means. I've made observations, but I lack direct experience. I've told myself that sisters are like Latin. And friends are like Italian and French. But I suspect it's more complicated."

"Erm. That's quite complicated enough." They scratched their brow. "You've lost me."

"It's an analogy. If you know sisters, you can figure out friends. Just as, if you know Latin, you can figure out French."

She sounded young, suddenly, and earnest, and more than a little like Agnes.

They knew not to smile.

"I advocate for experience over analogy." They spoke seriously. Their heart picked up speed as they added, with deliberate offhandedness, "Why don't we try it?"

She didn't blink. "Try what?"

"Being friends."

The not blinking continued.

"Friends," she repeated slowly. "Friends who dislike each other?"

"The other kind."

The blinking began, rapid blinks. "That would require *liking* each other."

Her intonation said it all.

Georgie's chest cavity iced over. "And that's impossible." It emerged as a flat statement rather than a question. They tilted up their chin and studied the ceiling. The Vesuvian red didn't reverse the ice spreading through their limbs. "Impossible for you," they clarified to the ceiling. "Not for me."

After a moment of silence, they cleared their throat.

"New subject," they declared, because the rejection stung like a poison dart, and they wanted to move on as quickly as they could. Unfortunately, their mind was blank. They turned their gaze back on Elf. She was blinking normally, but emotions churned in her eyes, all maddeningly indecipherable.

The new subject arrived unbidden.

"What did your father mean," they asked, "this is an Anglo-Saxon nation? The rot about heritage and forebears?"

"Oh." Elf looked nonplussed. "Nothing. He only said that to annoy Sir Graham." She hesitated. "I'm sorry it annoyed you too."

They shrugged.

"Because of your mother?"

They shrugged again. "Because of my mother and the nation's numerous other non-Anglo-Saxons."

Elf leaned forward, eager to explain, or maybe justify. "The Angles and Saxons were two tribes among many. But of course, all sorts of peoples have been living in the British Isles, for millennia."

"Of course," Georgie echoed. "These other peoples just don't matter as much. To the nation. Because only people who do matter get to define what the nation is."

Elf clasped her hands. "Your mother mattered."

"I said it's not just about my mother."

"Papa wasn't—"

"Wasn't *hwat*?" Mr. Marsden loomed.

Elf mumbled something inaudible, scooting over to allow him room.

"You were talking about your excellent mother." Sir Graham settled himself beside Georgie, wafting the odor of bergamot cologne and spirits. His eyes were glassy. "I had the pleasure of meeting her once. Not in Twynham—the grudge between your family and Marsden's prevented any intercourse."

Mr. Marsden grunted.

"I never saw such taste and elegance," continued Sir Graham. "We met quite by happenstance. I was on an archaeological excursion. She was seeing the sights. We ended up dining together, by the sea."

The carriage jerked and began to roll. Mr. Marsden closed his eyes.

"She was indeed elegant," said Georgie, politely, "but I believe you're mistaken. She was never in Italy."

"Did I say Italy? No, this was during the war with Napoleon. It kept me from Italy." From Sir Graham's vibrato, one might suppose this was the war's absolute worst consequence.

Across the compartment, Elf turned her gaze to the window.

Georgie sank back in their seat.

"I spent years going from hillfort to cairn to cist," said Sir Graham. "And I came away with the requisite jet beads and staghorns and silver coins. I collected for myself all the miscellany that overflows the nests of those antiquaries for whom the medieval is an obsession." He squinted at Mr. Marsden's faux-slumbrous face, then back at Georgie. "Sir Grand Tour. That's what Marsden calls me. Did you know that?"

Georgie gave a too-vigorous shake of their head.

"I have a nickname for him as well. Do you want to hear it?"

No answer was safe. Luckily, Sir Graham didn't wait for one.

"Magpie," he said. "Harold Magpie, esquire."

Mr. Marsden, hoping, perhaps, for *Barrow King*, gave an angry thrash, nearly kicking Georgie in the process. They drew back their feet as far as they would go.

"That spring, I traveled to Scotland." Sir Graham picked up his narrative with a sad smile. "That's where I met your mother, while excavating a midden near Lud Castle. She was staying in the village, with Lady Beverly. Both women made such a strong and favorable impression on my mind. It was but a few days before the tragedy."

Georgie's insides had just started to thaw. They were ice again in an instant. Ice and more ice.

"I blame myself." Sir Graham sounded maudlin. "I knew it wasn't wise to walk to the village by the sands. I'd no notion that they would make the attempt, but still, I have often wished I'd thought to warn them about the dangers of a spring tide. The fisherwoman who saw them turn off the high road and failed to call them back—she is a murderess in my eyes." Sir Graham blotted his forehead with a handkerchief, pausing to catch his breath. "I apologize," he said, with genuine feeling. "I should not have spoken so freely. Elfreda, sit by your friend and offer the comfort of your feminine delicacy."

The ensuing rearrangement entailed indelicate bumping and jostling, but Sir Graham managed to cram himself between Mr. Marsden's bulk and the door, and Elf, after tripping and nearly falling into Georgie's lap, perched awkwardly beside them.

Sir Graham pointed with his chin and waggled his brows, until Elf took Georgie's hand in hers.

Georgie looked down at their linked fingers. She hadn't made this contact of her own volition. And Sir Graham's sympathy was misplaced. Only they knew *how* misplaced. But the touch sent a lick of warmth up their arm, and their blood began to flow again. They tightened their grip. Elf gripped back.

Outside the window, the scenery was sublime enough to force all thoughts from their mind. The road followed the sparkling river through the valley, then crested an eminence, so that the green dales dropped far below, dotted with woodlands and bounded by overhanging rocks, the gray hills marching across the horizon.

Those gray, gritstone hills, shadowed by distance—they might have been the dark swells of an angry ocean. The ocean rushed forward, and Georgie's mother was there, galloping a white mare, the white foam of the breaking waves catching up to her until it seemed the horse itself was foam, part of the ocean, and she went as fast as the water would take her, away from Georgie, Lady Beverly clinging to her waist, long pale hair streaming like a comet's tail.

Georgie woke with a start in an empty carriage. They had a crick in their neck and a foul taste in their mouth.

"Are we there?" They half fell from the carriage. It had stopped in a village of slate-roofed stone cottages, hills rising starkly behind. They tottered as they turned a circle, and *there*, there was Elf, hovering on the edge of a group of men, Sir Graham and her father, but also three more, strangers.

One of them was young, tall, golden-haired, and obscenely handsome.

The Barrow Prince.

Georgie took a step toward the little crowd and heard a thump. It was coming from the trunk in the boot of the carriage. Georgie's items had been stowed with Elf's, in one of the imperials on the roof. The trunk had to be Sir Graham's. Did it contain an ash-covered corpse from Pompeii? Had the ash-covered corpse awakened on the journey, eager to wreak vengeance on the man who'd thieved its brain?

Thump. Thump.

Georgie approached, alarm stiffening the fine hairs on the nape of their neck.

Thump.

They jerked their hands back. Nothing. They drew a breath, and reached, and . . . *thump!* The lid of the trunk flew open. Their shout was seconded by a shrill scream. A head popped up, not an ashy, de-brained skull, but a proper head, with mussed hair and flushed cheeks and round eyes and a button nose. A second head appeared, much like the first. Two little girls. Two little giggling girls. One clambered from the trunk with remarkable speed and agility, while the other struggled and flopped.

"Here." Georgie grabbed her, and she clung to them so powerfully it felt like suction.

"Is this the Dark Peak?" she asked. Her hands were sticky, and she smelled like raisins.

"It is," they said, and wondered if they should mention, in their capacity as an adult, that her being in the Dark Peak was the height of naughtiness.

Two little girls hiding in a trunk for a fifty-mile carriage ride was such *spectacular* naughtiness, it filled them with a sense of awe.

"Hilda!" cried Elf. "Matilda!"

The little girl began to wiggle frantically in Georgie's arms. They couldn't *wrestle* a child—what if they damaged her?—so they let go. She dropped, bounced, and was off like a shot.

"Hullo." The Barrow Prince knelt and addressed the other little girl, who'd raced up to the group of men, then frozen in apparent confusion. "What's your name?"

She looked up at him with glowing eyes. "Dorcas the unicorn."

"No! We're wolves now." Her sister ran to her, grabbed her wrist, and pulled. "We've come all this way because we're wolves." She turned and banged smack into Mr. Marsden's legs. There followed the unfortunate, inevitable ricochet. An instant later, both girls lay sobbing on the ground.

Mr. Marsden stared down at them.

"How?" he asked.

"The trunk in the boot," said Georgie, hurrying up as Elf sat and gathered her sisters into her arms.

"I will lock you in a trunk until you are five and thirty." Mr. Marsden addressed his sobbing progeny. "Do you know how many years that is?"

The sobs continued. Hilda and Matilda kept their faces pressed into Elf's bodice, but one of them lifted her hand and spread her fingers.

"Five, five, five, five, five, four," said Mr. Marsden, in time with her movements. "That is correct." He glanced around the circle of men. "They have been this way since their mother died. Willful. Unruly."

"But Mrs. Marsden died during the lying-in," protested Sir Graham. "Do you mean to say since the moment they were born?"

Mr. Marsden gave him a caustic look.

"May I?" The Barrow Prince reached into his coat and produced a lozenge. "Licorice."

He put it in Hilda's hand. Or Matilda's.

"Elfreda," said Mr. Marsden. "Come here, please."

After a plethora of caresses and whispers, Elfreda disentangled herself and rose.

"You will take the twins back tomorrow, by the very first coach." Elfreda went pale.

"I'll take them," offered Georgie, before they could think it through.

Mr. Marsden nodded. "You will go as well." He turned away. "Where were we? Aubin-Aubrey."

The man who inclined his head was short and broad-shouldered, with a bright white scar splitting one black brow, and a face like a rock. He was leaning on a shovel.

Ah. The Barrow Prince.

"You were describing the barrow by Nine Stones Close," said Mr. Marsden. "Mortimer and I opened that barrow in 1806. Upward of thirty yards diameter, if I recall."

"Not twenty." The Barrow Prince's voice was also like rock, like rock grating on rock.

"Excuse me," said the princely-looking man. "But those sweet little unicorns, or wolves, rather, Hilda and Melinda—"

"Matilda," interrupted Mr. Marsden.

"Yes," said the man. "Hilda and Matilda. They're gone."

15

THE TWINS WERE indeed gone. Vanished. Elfreda surveyed the street, panic gripping the back of her skull.

"They can't have gone far," said Sir Graham, wrongly. He didn't understand anything about the twins. Hilda and Matilda had uncanny abilities. They'd reach the North Pole by midnight.

"Best check the cottages." William Aubin-Aubrey turned to do just that. The group fanned out, calling to the girls by name, circling into back gardens.

But wolves didn't answer to girls' names, and they didn't play in back gardens like cosseted family spaniels. In recent memory, Elfreda had been a wolf herself, with a wolf's wildness.

A shadowed alleyway caught her eye, angling between cottages. She took it. Beyond the cottages, the alleyway turned into an uneven path, sloping up onto the moor through stone outcroppings.

She began to run, clumsily.

"Careful." It was Georgie, catching her elbow as she slid on the loose rocks.

She jerked away, ankle twisting, and tripped. This time, they caught her hand. She let them. They'd let *her*, in the carriage, after

Sir Graham spoke about their mother, every word draining more color from their face.

"I'm sure they went this way," she said. "It's the wildest, most rugged, dangerous, desolate direction. They *are* unruly. Mrs. Pegg can't keep up with them, and Agnes won't be bothered. But this—this is my fault." She gasped for air. "I put the idea in their heads, making up stories about wolves in the Dark Peak. This is why Papa discourages make-believe, and plays, and novels, and poetry. He says it all leads to heightened feelings, and women are too emotional in the first place. I'm supposed to rise above the limitations of my sex, and use my intellectual faculties properly. But I'm not rational, or objective. I lapse constantly into folly. I embarrassed him, and I embarrassed myself, and spoiled the excursion, and my chance with William Aubin-Aubrey, and my sisters are going to fall off a cliff. And now, my God, now—now I might cry." She broke off in horror, eyes stinging, throat clogged. She hardly ever cried.

"Cry on my shoulder," offered Georgie, stopping, tugging her toward them. "I know you don't want to lose too much time, but storms of violent weeping are usually brief, and you'll feel much better. I always do."

She shook her head and ran, but slower than before, because the ground sloped more steeply, and the pressure in her chest made it difficult to breathe. Georgie seemed to jog with no exertion at all, speaking easily as they bounded through the heather.

"I don't see how feeling is a limitation," they mused. "Heightened feelings prompt people to transcend limitations. That's not always a good thing, of course. We shouldn't just succumb to impulse. We should think. But thinking isn't something abstract that happens in the ether. It's a physical process that happens in the body. Doesn't that mean that objectivity is always subjective? And that no one can really separate thinking and feeling? You're not a glass brain, and if you were, someone like Sir Graham would stick you in a cabinet."

"Don't be absurd," she said, stopped, and burst into tears. Georgie folded her into a tight embrace. She muffled her wet face on their shoulder, clinging to them, the release of pent-up fear and misery and shame so ferocious she didn't care that she was making a fool of herself.

The storm of violent weeping passed quickly.

She stepped back, wiping her eyes. "I'm sorry." She meant for dripping all over them, and also for Sir Graham bringing up their mother's tragic death, for their mother's tragic death itself, for Papa and the Anglo-Saxons, for everything, and most of all, for allowing them to believe that she thought friendship with them impossible because she couldn't like them, when really, she was frightened that she could. Too much. Ever since they'd kissed her, she'd been possessed by the urge to feel their mouth on hers. She felt it now, standing before them, wrung out, with the taste of salt on her lips.

"No need." They shook their head.

She set off, the wind cooling her cheeks, drying them. The moor kept rising, rucked up here and there by strangely shaped boulders. She climbed, and climbed, and when the ground leveled, she turned, scanning the hills.

The village lay below, in the tree-scattered valley.

She looked over as Georgie approached, then away.

"Can we still try?" she asked. "Being friends."

"Friends who like each other?" They were suddenly beside her.

"You said it wasn't impossible." Bilberry bushes grew at her feet, flowering pink. A bird's warble was the only reply.

She lifted her gaze. They were looking back at her, narrowly, the black of their lashes startling against those crystalline irises.

"No," they said. "It's not impossible."

She drew in a breath, some strange force thrumming through her. It took all her strength to turn from them, to turn north.

The North Pole. Hilda and Matilda. Her sisters were disappearing more irrevocably every moment.

She came around a boulder, and there, like magic, in the near distance, gray heaps of stone resolved into ruins. Ragged bailey. Square tower.

It was a castle. Norman, but it might as well have been timeless, a fairy-tale figment.

She went weak with relief. Was there a more tempting destination on earth for wayward children?

She hurried forward, Georgie falling into step with her.

"We're friends, then," they said, with evident satisfaction. "Should we apologize for past offenses? So we can start afresh? I'm sorry I pestered you. It was because I wanted you to play, and thought I could badger you into it. And then it was comeuppance for your unbearable haughtiness."

"That's your apology?" She hit upon a wide footpath, perhaps a coffin road, which meant fewer spiny plants tearing at her skirts, and sped up, putting distance between them.

They closed it quickly. "There's more."

"Spare me the rest, please."

They didn't. "You aren't unbearably haughty. I misjudged you. You're a bit uppish, it's true—"

She glared.

"But you're also a bit impish," they went on, undeterred, "and that makes up for it. Impish, or maybe Elf-ish. Either way, I'm incredibly glad your father hasn't succeeded in stamping it out. I've mocked your devotion to old books and old bones. But you're just as devoted to your sisters—admirably so. If I get the French to their Latin, I'll feel lucky indeed."

Gratification unfurled inside her. She had to fight a very silly smile.

"Oui," she managed. The sudden brightness of her mood was two parts twins—she was *certain* they were at that castle—and one part Georgie.

Her friend, Georgie Redmayne.

"And I like the way you howl," they added. "You're magnificent at a picnic. And—"

She grabbed their arm, shocking them into silence.

Wolves didn't answer to girls' names. But all at once, she knew what they would answer to. Of course. It should have occurred to her before.

A tickle built in her chest, a laugh, but not exactly a laugh. She tipped up her chin, opened her mouth, and howled. It echoed back from the hills. Georgie looked bemused.

"You don't have to howl on my account," they told her. "Just because I like it."

She howled again, louder.

The answering howl was so thin and faint that, at first, she couldn't distinguish it from the echo of her own. But another howl sounded, and another. And then she saw two small figures detach from the long shadow at the base of the castle tower.

"Oh," said Georgie, looking impressed. "Well done."

"I'm going to kill them," she vowed, but once she'd reunited with her sweaty, rumpled little sisters, both frisking through the heather and yipping excitedly, the remnants of her fear and anger dissipated in a rush of endearments. Her mood darkened, though, on the walk down to the village.

She didn't blame Hilda and Matilda—what was the point? But to have come all this way, only to be sent immediately home again—it was a cruel disappointment.

Georgie seemed to sense her thoughts.

"There's still tonight," they said, consolingly, hoisting Matilda higher on their back. "We can talk to the Barrow Prince at dinner."

"*You* can talk." Such dinners for her were always a trial. She wouldn't manage a word.

"I will focus on cajolery." Georgie stopped to reel Hilda out of the gorse. "You will furnish the details."

Why press the issue when they knew it brought her pain? Would a friend do such a thing?

"I won't furnish any details." Elfreda stopped too.

"Why not?" They seemed perplexed.

"Because I get tongue-tied in groups. I lose my capacity for speech. Completely." She frowned. "Don't pretend you're unaware."

"I'm aware that you're reserved in company. Too fastidious for drawing room conversation. Icy enough to freeze the tea if anyone persists in a pleasantry." Georgie's voice changed. "*Oh.*"

"You didn't know." Unbelievable. "You thought I was silent out of contempt and self-consequence." Maybe social agony wasn't so easy to distinguish from unbearable haughtiness. Mortified, she clutched Hilda's hand and started walking again, picking her way through the gorse.

"I'm not *fastidious* in drawing rooms," she said at last, without turning to Georgie, who'd come up on her left. "I'm not there. People look at me, and I become a hum. Everything goes out of my head but a kind of humming."

"You become a hum." Georgie repeated it slowly.

Instantly, she regretted her confession. She shouldn't have revealed even *more*.

"All right, then," they said. "Leave it all to me."

She glanced over. They gave her an easy grin and hoisted Matilda with a bouncing step that made her squeal. "The Barrow Prince will pledge to you his shovel before the waiter serves the chops. Trust me." They winked. "I won't let you down."

By eight that evening, the waiter had served the chops, and Georgie was well on their way to letting Elf down. Thus far, the Barrow Prince had ignored them. He sat by Mr. Marsden, chewing gristly mouthfuls of meat with expressionless resolve. The princely chap, on the other hand, kept up an amiable stream of chatter. His name was, ridiculously, Nicholas Fluff, and he seemed a very good sort. The other fellow, Simon Sykes, seemed less so. He was recently back from Egypt and his talk was all mummies, dozens of which he'd brought to London.

"Visit, and I'll unwrap one for you," he said to Georgie, a loathsome proposition uttered in a tone so unsavory, and so salacious, it put them off their meal.

Elf sat between her father and Sir Graham with downcast eyes, moving peas around her plate. The dining room was loud and crowded, a mix of holidaymakers and villagers. A dog barked incessantly. Should they start *yelling* about the Great Heathen Army?

"Bloody dogs everywhere!" Sykes thumped back his chair, scowling. "Under the table, even."

Fluff bent over and looked.

"They just want affection," he said, placidly, as he straightened. "And sweets."

Sykes harrumphed and seized his pewter tankard of ale. While he drank, Fluff reached into his pocket, slipped out a licorice, and passed it under the table. He grinned at Georgie and handed off another.

Not dogs, then. Wolves. They were supposed to be in bed, not crawling around the filthy stone floor.

Georgie didn't look. They didn't want to draw attention to this latest fiasco. The Barrow Prince was at the other end of the table, looking as personable as granite, and they needed to figure out an approach.

Suddenly, he leaned forward and spoke. His gravelly voice carried surprisingly well.

"Miss Marsden," he said. "You are left-handed."

Elf stopped moving her fork.

"So am I." The Barrow Prince raised his left hand. His palm had a yellow cast and looked hard as horn. "When I make diagrams of a tumulus's interments, I draw the skeletons facing right more readily, and faithfully, than the skeletons facing left. I noticed the same pattern in your father's *Two Dissertations on the Saxon Grave Hills of the Peak District*."

Mr. Marsden was holding his wineglass in his right hand and lowered it with a clink.

"Did you make those diagrams?" asked the Barrow Prince, black eyes fixed on Elf.

She went rigid. Sir Graham was looking at her too, and Fluff, and Sykes, and Georgie, and her father. He wore a disgruntled expression.

"She assisted," he said. "She is the eldest, and happily, the least silly of my daughters. You met the youngest, so *least silly* may seem faint praise. But I do believe she will, someday, under my guidance, develop into that rarity, a truly *rational* dame."

The Barrow Prince's smile was a crooked slash.

"Miss Marsden?" he repeated.

How wonderful. The Barrow Prince wanted to hear directly from Elf. He'd identified her work and demanded its acknowledgment. How wonderful. How terrible.

Elf was staring into space, cheeks pale, mouth tense. Georgie tried to catch her eye, to nod encouragement. *Yes.* All she had to say was *yes*, to start. *Yes, I made the diagrams.* She had, hadn't she? She must have. If Mr. Marsden was willing to admit she'd *assisted*, she'd done it all.

One word to start. Less than a word. A sound.

"Are you humming?" Fluff turned to Georgie.

"Lovely," murmured Sykes, his gaze hot.

"No." Georgie shook their head. "I wasn't."

"You *were* humming, and it did sound lovely." Fluff turned gallant. "You have the voice of an angel."

Sykes leered. "You must give us a song."

"What's this?" Sir Graham glanced over. "A song?"

"I can't sing at the table," protested Georgie.

"There's a pianoforte." Fluff rose excitedly. "I adore music, and I've been a week listening to that." He pulled a face at the Barrow Prince. "You've heard how he rasps. My ears are rubbed raw. The balm of melody is required."

Georgie stood. Now all eyes were on them. Could Elf speak to the Barrow Prince if the table were distracted?

They walked with Fluff to the pianoforte, drawing more eyes as they passed by the bar. A music book lay open on the stand, and they took their seat, turning over a few pages before flipping the book closed. They'd already decided on a song their mother used to sing, in Welsh, simple and sweet and sad, about a sailor's lost love. At the first stroke of the keys, the roar of conversation gentled. When they began to sing, the room fell silent. Even the dog stopped barking.

Georgie did have the voice of an angel, thank you very much.

They pronounced the Welsh without fully understanding it, shaping their mother's syllables, understanding them by color more than sense. They let the language and the tune wash through them, wash away everything but the present moment, one silver note, and then the next.

After the last, the hush was profound. Thunderous applause followed, and shouted requests for another, which Georgie indulged, a ballad this time, known to all. Other voices joined in, Fluff's included, his baritone smooth as silk. The zeal and adoration of the crowd—it felt like a warm bath, dissolving the weariness and aches of the day's travel and misadventure.

Until Georgie swiveled enough to glimpse their table, Elf sitting motionless, the Barrow Prince sitting . . . nowhere.

"I SHOULD HAVE guessed he hated jollity," said Georgie, later, in the dark. Elf lay on one side of the bed, they on the other. "That face. If he smiled, it would cause an avalanche. His nose would break off."

Elf had changed and crawled beneath the covers with deadly quiet. Her deadly quiet persisted. In fact, it seemed deadlier.

"I didn't expect he'd run from the room," they continued, more apologetically. "Please believe me. I was shocked."

"And yet," Elf responded at last. "And yet, you kept singing."

"Well, yes." They cleared their throat. "Nothing else I could do at that point."

"The point at which you were already leading the room in song."

"Yes." They had a sinking feeling in their chest. "Can't stop in the middle. I'm relieved you understand."

"Georgie." *Understanding* wasn't the word for her tone. "You promised to talk to him. Instead, you put on a performance for the whole village."

"Not for my own sake. I was trying to—"

"You're a show-off." She said it with unmistakable disgust. "You were showing off. It's what you do."

"That Fluff fellow begged me to sing."

"Because you started to hum!" Elf's voice rose. "Why *did* you start to hum?"

"Because I was thinking of what you said."

"What I said?" She spoke more softly now, with more than a touch of apprehension.

"What you said about becoming a hum."

She inhaled sharply, a wounded gasp, as if from a blow.

"No. Drat. Elfreda." They went up on an elbow. "I wasn't poking fun. A hum is a sound. And a sound is nearly a word. And it occurred to me, if you *hummed* the hum in your head, maybe you could keep going from there. So, I hummed, and I hoped *you* might hum, and we could both hum, and then you could, you know, *hum* at the Barrow Prince."

"Hum at him. You hoped I'd *hum* at him?"

"I hoped it would break the ice. Sometimes we hum to get going at the theater. Or vocalize nonsense syllables. It limbers the tongue and lowers the inhibitions. I really was trying to help." They rolled onto their back, defeated. "I miscalculated. I'm sorry. I'm a twit."

"Oh, stop," she muttered.

"Stop being a twit? It's not so easy."

"Stop calling yourself a twit."

"You disagree?" They lifted their head in hope.

"Not necessarily." The pause lengthened. "But I don't let people talk that way about my friends."

It took a moment for this to sink in. When it did, they lowered their head to the pillow and grinned. "We're still friends, then?"

Her grudging sigh was affirmation.

"I haven't given up," they vowed. "With the Barrow Prince."

She sighed again. "Go to sleep."

"Impossible." They grunted. "Matilda is walking up my ribs." It was true. Matilda was fast asleep but was rotating herself perpendicular, and her heels pummeled Georgie's side.

They inched away, closer to the mattress's edge.

Contented snores sawed the air.

"Elf," they whispered. "Is that you?"

"That's Hilda," she murmured. The blanket tugged off Georgie's body completely, a sign that she'd rolled over.

When they'd imagined sharing a bed with Elf, they hadn't imagined snoring six-year-olds turning somersaults between them.

"You drew those diagrams," they whispered. "Your father should have admitted it." They listened to the bed creak, more soft snores. "I'll tell the Barrow Prince. I'll tell him that and everything else. I'll rise at dawn. Depend on it."

Rising at dawn was not their forte. But they did so. Groggily. Dependably.

Unfortunately, the Barrow Prince had risen even earlier, to walk on the moors. Georgie, Elf, and the twins were loaded into the stagecoach and rolling south in disgrace before he returned.

16

THE STAGECOACH PASSED through Thornton, not Twynham. A hack post chaise waited outside the Yellow Lion, ready for hire, and Georgie stood with the luggage, and Hilda and Matilda, while Elf talked with the postillion.

She hadn't talked with Georgie on the drive. She'd read continuously from *Sepulchral Anecdotes*. Nothing but books in her portmanteau, as it turned out. They'd watched her read out of the corner of their eye, considering the way forward.

There *was* a way forward. A way shadowy, watery, and as yet obscure.

They were considering it still.

"Let's be off," called Elf, walking briskly back to them. She wore the same brown dress as yesterday, more wrinkled, and her eyes were tired. She opened her portmanteau. Besides the books, she *had* packed a few articles of clothing, and when Mr. Marsden had handed her a small coin purse at breakfast, she'd stuffed that inside too. She dug out the purse and shook the contents into her palm.

"Oh." The syllable was small and dismayed.

Georgie stepped closer and peered. One shilling, two thrupenny bits, five metal buttons, and a tooth.

"That isn't human?" they asked. "No," they answered their own question, because Elf seemed frozen. "Stag, maybe."

"He didn't give me enough." She lifted her blanched face. "He put us on a stagecoach, and he didn't give me enough to hire a carriage home. If it were only me, but . . ." She looked at the twins, who were sitting now on Georgie's valise, oblivious.

"Even if it were only you," said Georgie, "it's wicked."

"He forgot to check." She slid the coins and buttons, and the tooth, back into the purse and tested its weight. "It feels full."

"It *is* full. Full of buttons."

"He thought it was money."

"There's no one here but us. You don't have to defend him."

Elf returned the purse to the portmanteau mechanically, not meeting their gaze. But of course. She'd been defending her Papa to herself.

His actions weren't defensible. Mr. Marsden had stayed in the Peak, with his cronies, because he'd rather poke around for Saxon skulls than see his daughters safely home.

They felt a tug. Matilda had grabbed onto their skirt.

"May I sit on your lap in the carriage?"

"Erm." Georgie caught Elf's eye. "No?"

For a split second, she looked even more tired, shoulders bowed, but she straightened and smiled, and said, in a deceptively cheery voice, "We're going to walk."

"May I sit on your lap?" Matilda kept tugging.

"My lap will be vertical, I'm afraid," said Georgie. "Is it even a lap, if it's vertical?"

Matilda turned to Elf. "I want to ride in the carriage. And sit on Miss Georgie's lap."

Elf bent down, still smiling, and tapped Matilda's nose with a fingertip. "Next time."

"This time."

"This time we're walking."

"I hate walking."

"You love walking." Elf's smile began to fray. "Yesterday you would have walked to the moon."

Matilda crossed her arms. "Today I want to ride in the carriage."

"I'm hungry," Hilda complained from her seat on the valise. "I am ravenous."

Elf gazed longingly at the postillion. He'd realized something was amiss with their party and was taking payment from another.

"Look there." Georgie pointed. "That's the high street."

The twins looked.

"There's a bun-house on the high street," said Georgie. "The buns are hot and buttery and scrumptious, but no one riding in a carriage is allowed to buy them. The buns are only for walkers."

"Why?" asked Matilda.

"It's a rule," said Georgie. "Set by the bakers guild."

"I want a bun!" Hilda stood up.

"To the bun-house, then." Georgie grabbed the handle of their valise and twirled as they lifted it, feeling light-heeled with self-congratulation. Which was a good thing, because it was easily six miles to Twynham.

The twins went skipping for the high street. Georgie followed. Elf struggled along beside them, looking less than pleased.

"We can switch," they offered, extending their valise. "I didn't pack any books."

"It's not heavy." She gripped her portmanteau with both hands, her grunt belying her words.

Georgie didn't insist. "How many buns should we buy? I say a half dozen. We bribe them with one per mile, split between them."

"We shouldn't buy any," said Elf. "We've too little money."

"Too little money for the post chaise." Georgie's heels came to earth. "Plenty of money for buns."

"The post chaise is what we need, though."

"Yes, but we can't afford it. Whether or not we buy buns."

This was inarguably correct, but Elf's jaw exhibited a stubborn tightness. "If we buy the buns, we're further from affording it."

"If we don't buy the buns, we're not driving *or* walking. Or do you have another incentive? Do you think you can bribe them with buttons?"

"I can reason with them." Elf was breathing hard. "And save the shilling. It might come in more use later."

"That attitude is why coins turn up in graves."

Elf frowned. "No, it's not."

"Ask the next skeleton. Ask them what good it did, holding on to that last shilling."

They caught up to the twins on the high street.

"Here it is!" declared Matilda, craning her neck at the sign. "The bun-house! Established 1668." Hilda had her hands on the window and was staring through the glass at the buns, expression worshipful.

Georgie opened the door for Elf. "After you."

Matilda and Hilda squealed as one and darted inside.

Elf sighed. A moment later, she was sliding her shilling across the counter.

Georgie waited outside a little longer. Thornton had very good shops, considering it wasn't London, or Bath, or even Derby. They used to visit them with the Janes, and eat buns at this bun-house, and fritter the days, lounging and parading, showing off, as Elf would have it, for everyone and no one.

They were about to turn, to enter the bun-house, when they glimpsed, across the street, an enormous bonnet laden with artificial fruits. Its owner was just disappearing into the milliner's.

They recognized that bonnet.

Or not that particular bonnet. Five years had gone by, after all. Rather, they recognized the ratio of berries to buckram.

"Mrs. Alderwalsey!" They dashed after her, between the passing carts and horsemen.

Within the hour, Mrs. Alderwalsey's carriage was crammed with wayfarers, Matilda on Georgie's lap, Hilda on Elf's, each twin piled in turn with Mrs. Alderwalsey's parcels.

"I was sorry to hear that your father died," Mrs. Alderwalsey said to Georgie, as the carriage bumped out of Thornton. "It's inevitable, of course, but one always hopes to put it off. For oneself, at least."

"Yes, ma'am," said Georgie, politely.

"On occasion," she continued, "one does wish to hasten the demise of another."

Georgie hesitated. "Yes, ma'am."

"Mrs. Roberts bought the last of the fine spotted muslin." It might have been a non sequitur, but then again, perhaps not. You never knew with Mrs. Alderwalsey. She was in her upper seventies, wealthy, ubiquitous, and slightly terrifying. "I was forced to get the jaconet." She unwrapped a parcel. "Try the texture."

Georgie stretched around Matilda and touched the fabric. "Perfect for a gown."

"Do you think so?" Mrs. Alderwalsey thinned her lips. "I don't. It won't wash well. I'm going to cut it into handkerchiefs." She addressed Elf. "*You* are in need of a new gown, in a better style. Tell Harold I said so. I won't speak to him myself. I haven't spoken to him since he shouted those scurrilous insults. How did he describe that incident to you, I wonder?"

"There are so many." Elf sounded regretful. "I wouldn't know which."

"It was the year before last. At Sir Hugh's. A meeting of the St. Alcmund's restoration committee."

"Oh, yes. That one." Elf nodded. "He has strong feelings about the preservation of historic buildings."

"I await his apology."

"I'm sorry," said Elf.

"*His* apology. He owes an apology to Susan as well. She wrote that he severed *their* connection in the least civil terms."

Elf covered Hilda's ears, so Georgie did the same to Matilda.

"Aunt Susan wrote to you?"

"Of course she wrote to me. I am her godmother. She asks about your hair. Straight as a pin, I see. And your hands. Show me." Mrs. Alderwalsey leaned forward and seized one of the requested appendages, tugging off Elf's glove. Instead of exclaiming in horror at the calluses, she thumbed Elf's palm with surprising gentleness.

"You are very like Caroline." Her voice was gentler too. "Hers is a demise I would have deferred if I could, even if it meant compacting with the devil." She returned Elf's hand and glove. Her eyes had a damp sheen.

Georgie removed their hands from Matilda's ears. They hadn't realized Mrs. Alderwalsey and Elf's grandmother were so close.

"Write to your aunt." Mrs. Alderwalsey commanded it. "You neglect her. And pay me a call. I will give you a pot of salve for those corns. And some blue satin. You'd look well in blue satin. You haven't called since Susan brought you. Promise you will."

"I promise," said Elf.

"And how is Agnes? I saw her at the Parkers' last August. She was blowing on an odd-looking horn and was quite red in the face. I hope her face isn't always so red."

"It's not usually red, no."

"Does she still play that odd-looking horn?"

"More so the lute."

"She should play the pianoforte. Why doesn't she?"

Nothing Elf said was to Mrs. Alderwalsey's satisfaction. The interrogation went on and on. The carriage turned onto the road to Twynham, and eventually the lane to Redmayne Manor and Marsden Hall.

Georgie began to consider it again: the way forward.

Within my depths, the shadows play. And yet there is light at my mouth and water that brings life.

One answer would solve many problems.

"What is wrong with the gentleman?" asked Matilda.

Georgie shifted her to the side and looked out the carriage window. Their fist shot up and banged the roof.

"Stop!" they cried.

The carriage stopped abruptly. Georgie tumbled out. There was Marsden Hall, gray and grim on the hill. And there, stuck sideways in the hedge, squirming, his plum-colored coat snagged on broken twigs and thorns, was Lord Phillip Winston.

"Phipps." They hissed it. What was wrong with him was obvious. He was half-sprung and fully embedded in a very prickly shrub.

"Do you know this man?" Mrs. Alderwalsey called from the carriage.

"No." The denial dropped from their lips like a stone. "I feared some mishap, but he's one of those devotees of nature, the sort that's always climbing into hedges for solace and inspiration. We should drive on."

"Don't go," slurred Phipps, squirming more vigorously. "I came all this way to see you."

"Shh." Georgie tried to shush him and simultaneously tried to appear as though they were doing nothing of the kind.

"Can't hear you," slurred Phipps. "Can't find my topper."

"You're drunk." Georgie linked their hands, standing decorously on the verge of the lane, posture upright, voice a furious whisper. "How did you get here? And get drunk?"

"Arrived yesterday. Spent the night at yours. There was a decanter in the study, and . . ."

"Spent the night!" Georgie yelped, then twisted around to wave at the onlookers. "Just one moment. Mr. . . . Mr. *Hawthorne* is a stranger to these parts and inquires after the nearest inn." They moved closer to the hedge and resumed their furious whispering. "You can't set foot in my house. Harry will have us both killed."

"He won't find out." Phipps ripped himself free of the hedge with a curse, white blossoms and green leaflets showering down. Georgie danced backward.

"Yes, Mr. Hawthorne," they said loudly. "A clean, well-run establishment, to be sure." Back to furious whispering: "He will find out! He told me he asked the housekeeper to write him a tattling letter if I stepped out of line."

Phipps was shaking the hedge now, trying to dislodge his top hat. It had the merciful effect of muffling his voice.

"The housekeeper won't give herself the trouble. Housekeepers have too much else to do. Also, I tipped liberally."

"You *bribed* her?"

"Tipped. Bribed." Phipps gave the hedge a final shake. "Whichever it was, I'm completely out at the pocket. And my father's about to disown me. We had an awful row. He insists I marry at once." Phipps retrieved his hat and spun to face Georgie, overshooting and swaying back to center, much like a devotee of the bottle. "Your fault. There's more gossip about me than ever. Our marriage was meant to *quell* gossip."

"Shhh." Georgie twisted toward the carriage. Mrs. Alderwalsey, Elf, the twins, the coachman, and the horses were all staring. "One more moment! He needs directions." They snapped back around. "Phipps. I can't help you."

"You have to help me." Phipps stuffed his hat on his head. The hedge had poked various holes in his coat. Georgie had never seen him look so seedy. Typically, he put Nicholas Fluff to shame. He had the face not of a prince but an archangel. Now stubble roughed his jaw, and his eyes were bloodshot.

"It's Lady Cecelia." At least he was whispering. "That's who my father picked as my bride. Cecy, who clings like a limpet. She's been in love with me since she was a child. I can't do it. It would feel like drowning a sack of kittens. Not to mention she'll cry about my indifference to her mother, and her mother will complain to my mother, and I'll never know a day's peace in my life."

"A horrid predicament," acknowledged Georgie, with more sympathy. "But there's nothing I can do. I'm sorry."

"What is happening?" called Mrs. Alderwalsey. "I have not the patience. Introduce me to Mr. Hawthorne."

"There's nothing I can do," repeated Georgie, meeting Phipps's red-threaded eyes but briefly before looking away. The whole business felt shabby. But the last time they and Phipps had been together, three people had nearly died. Enough was enough.

"There is something," muttered Phipps, but Georgie was already turning, hurrying back to the carriage.

That's why Phipps had to yell.

"Marry me!"

17

Later that day, Elfreda found herself wandering between the standing stones in the garden. She'd slipped off her shoes and stockings, and the grass alternately warmed and cooled her bare feet as she crossed through the shadows cast by the stones. Around and around.

She would listen to Mrs. Alderwalsey. She would write to Aunt Susan. Tell her she knew what her husband had offered, how Papa had responded. Thank her. Swallow her pride and admit that Agnes was lonely and languishing. That Hilda and Matilda had journeyed fifty miles *in a trunk*. That Papa had paid the fare for a stagecoach and left them with buttons to get the rest of the way home. That her hair was straight as a pin, and the house was a shambles, and she didn't know how to go on.

But what then? Aunt Susan couldn't take in her sisters, not if Papa didn't relent. And she couldn't fix the situation with curling tongs and castor oil. It was beyond repair.

Around and around.

No, she wouldn't write to Aunt Susan. She would write to Papa at the inn. Let him know they'd arrived home safely. She would write to William Aubin-Aubrey as well. About her work on *Two Disserta-*

tions, about the bluff, the camp, all of it. He'd show Papa, though, wouldn't he? And Papa would feel betrayed—rightly so. He supported her, and it was wrong to circumvent him. But didn't he limit her as well? What if it wasn't her sex, her emotions, but *him* allowing her to go so far, and no farther?

Around and around.

When she heard footsteps approaching, she didn't pause, didn't look toward the sound.

"Hwat?" she demanded, exploding the initial *h*, like Papa, a warning. If her sisters could refrain from disturbing her for another quarter hour, the night would go better for everyone.

"I hoped we could talk."

She stopped short and looked. Georgie was coming toward her. They were first in shadow, then in the slanting light.

They'd donned a gown of spotted muslin, a tribute, perhaps, to Mrs. Alderwalsey, sky blue, trimmed with black ribbon to match the black dots. Their hair was burnished by the setting sun. They caught her eye and smiled. The smile caught her heart.

She was glad the shadow hid her expression. "I thought you'd be on your way to Gretna Green by now."

Back on the lane, they'd scrambled into the carriage, exclaiming in shock at the sudden proposal, calling Mr. Hawthorne a rattle, a cad, and a libertine. As acting went, it had seemed fairly good. But then again, it had seemed like acting, which defeated the purpose. She hadn't believed them for a second.

"That was Lord Phillip," she said. "Your betrothed."

"How did—" they began, then laughed, and shook their head. "Anne. Anne told you. Yes, Lord Phillip. Phipps. But he's not my betrothed."

"He was, though. And he wants to be again. And you want to return to London. So . . ." She trailed off with a vague gesture in the direction of Scotland.

"There are a few more elements weighing in the balance." Georgie was studying her now, with an uncomposed look on their face that seemed very much *not* like acting. "Did you really think I'd leave without saying goodbye?"

She'd been trying *not* to think of it. "Is that what this is? You're saying goodbye?"

"No." They joined her in the shadow. "I do want to go, but not with Phipps, not like that."

They wanted to go. They were going. It was important to keep it front of mind. And difficult when they were in front of her, smiling that Sphinx-like smile, as though they were the keeper of some marvelous secret. She used to feel excluded by that smile. Now she was inside it, or the smile was inside her. She was sharing its conspiracy.

They'd taken her hand. "I have other ideas."

"Like what?"

The wind blew, flattening their hair on their brow, and they shivered. The sun was sinking, and the shadow anticipated the evening's chill, but their hand felt warm. It wasn't the cold that made them quake.

"Shall we leave the stones?" They glanced about, fingers tightening on hers. "This is the site, isn't it? Where your grandfather burned the wicker man."

Her turn to laugh. "You're frightened."

"So what if I am?" They frowned at her. "Who wouldn't be?"

"Despite rumors to the contrary, I can assure you that my family doesn't practice human sacrifice."

"You're barefoot." They were staring at her feet, white and stark in the dim grass. "Like a druid priestess."

"Indeed." She curled her toes. "And behind my back I hold a ceremonial dagger."

"You don't." Georgie's eyes widened. She'd folded her arm, hidden her free hand behind her. "Let me see."

She bent backward as they tried to reach for it.

"Sacrificed by a druid priestess," they muttered, tugging her forward. "What did I do to deserve such a fate?"

"Everything." She was giggling now, which made her easier to subdue. They had her pinned against them in an instant, and it took only an instant longer for them to wrench her arm around.

"No dagger," they confirmed. They were gripping both her wrists, grinning down at her, eyes darkened by the shadow of the stone.

"The wicker man was filled with straw." Her pulse was thundering, beating in her wrists, under their thumbs. "But I've looked at Grandpapa's sketches. It was enormous. People saw it burning from Thornton. I understand how they might have jumped to conclusions."

"Mm," said Georgie, amusement in their voice. "As far as outlandish rumors go, it has a surprisingly solid basis in reality."

"And the ones about you?" Her breath hitched. A broken engagement. A duel. A curricle crash.

"Also." They nodded and released her.

She walked out of the circle of stones, as they'd suggested, but mostly to clear her own head, to exist again in ordinary daylight. The unkempt lawn prickled the soles of her feet. She sat on the nearest bench and gazed over the grounds. When Grandmama was still alive, before the gardener was sacked, the garden hadn't been smothered with weeds and vines. Now the fountains were dry, the camellia walk impassable. The statues had been swallowed whole by the shrubberies. Stray tulips provided pops of color here and there, but green and brown predominated. The wind made a whisking, rattling sound as dried stalks and pods rubbed together.

Georgie sat beside her for a time in silence. Finally, they spoke, quiet as a sigh. "*Within my depths, the shadows play.*"

It turned her toward them. She'd lain awake last night with the riddle running through her head. She supplied the second line. "*And yet there is light at my mouth and water that brings life.*"

They smiled. "I know the answer."

"I doubt it." The words slipped out.

Their smile became a laugh. "Of course you do."

She rolled her eyes, a warm glow in her chest.

Strange thought: Georgina Redmayne was poking fun at her, at both of them, and she *liked* it.

"Go on," she said. "I have a guess of my own, but I want to hear yours. What's the answer?"

"I can't tell you. Not until I know we're looking together."

"I don't know that we *are* looking together."

"You'd rather we compete?"

"You would look for it, without me." Her throat tightened. "A hoard you learned about from *my* grandmother's papers."

They put up their palms. "I'd tell you if I found it. I'm not trying to run away with all your gold, or even a fraction of your glory."

Yes, she remembered clearly. "You want a chalice or two. A handful of coins. To sell."

"Exactly."

"No." She shook her head. "We're not talking about robbing a stagecoach. We're talking about delving into the past. The hoard's value is the story it tells, not what it can buy."

"And you'll tell its story." Georgie sounded certain, so certain her heart gave a leap. "I won't get in the way of that. But you can't control what happens to the objects. You said yourself they'll all go to the Crown in the end. Well, minus the odd chalice."

She swallowed. The hoard would draw antiquaries from every corner of Britain. And she would tell its story. She'd write a book of her own, and include Grandmama's notes. As a Fellow of the Albion Society, she'd request patronage to dig next in Orkney, where Papa had never taken her.

"You doubt my use to you," said Georgie. "But I'll prove myself. Let's count to three and give our answer at the same time. One."

She met their eyes. "Two."

She could feel something gathering in the space between them, as though the air were crowded with all the things yet unsaid.

Were friendships always like this? Crowded? Haunted even? Or was this friendship different, because the two of them had known each other for so long without really knowing each other at all?

She pressed closer.

"Three," they whispered, as her hands settled on their shoulders. She kissed them, their soft lips parting in surprise, their hand curving around the back of her neck. She could almost smell the wisteria, although *this* garden contained no such blooms. Bliss beat through her like butterfly wings, a delicate sensation tremoring over her skin. And then their tongue slid inside her mouth, and they were tipping back her head, and she pushed with her own tongue, and moaned, because she hadn't known, but of course. It was so obvious. So right.

"Wrong," murmured Georgie, easing back. Their hand was still on her nape. She realized again that the bench was cold and hard. Her toes were digging into the chamomile.

"Not the answer." She was blushing. "*Kiss* is never the answer. Not of any riddle I know. And we shouldn't. Never again. That was more sufficient than last time, I think. We're finished now. Anything else might distract us."

Their lashes lowered, and a gleam entered their narrow gaze. "Distract us?"

"From our search," she said. "For the Viking gold."

18

THE ANSWER WAS *cave*. That was her guess, and Georgie's too. A cave by the river. Dark and deep, limestone mouth open to the sun-dappled water.

Amazed by her own daring, she shut herself up in the library after dinner, built a small fire, drank a finger of Canary sack from the green goblet, and began taking books down from the shelves.

She found mention of four caves along the River Thorn. One was upstream, north of Thornton, near the Roman ruins, boulder-choked and inhabited by badgers, explored by the author of *Sketches Toward a Topographical History of the County of Derbyshire* in 1753. A certain Reverend Cruttwell, in *Walks Through the East Midlands*, described another, a "bats' cave" located in a "steep ridge" even farther north. The other two he'd chanced upon during walks around the village of Twynham.

None were promising prospects, already discovered, already searched. But perhaps they opened onto neglected chambers, or branched into narrowing tunnels, inaccessible to male invaders and explorers. Accessible only to someone small. A medieval nun.

Elfreda Marsden.

It was somewhere to start at least.

The next morning, she met Georgie as planned at Holywell Rock.

She'd come alone. Agnes was punishing Hilda and Matilda for running away, giving her and Mrs. Pegg such a terrible fright. The punishment was a game of Princes in the Tower, which pleased all parties. Papa always objected to Princes in the Tower—Agnes made her Richard III sound too much like him—but there it was, another benefit to Papa's being gone. He couldn't accuse anyone of pertness.

Georgie had not come alone. Elfreda's eyes lit on them first. Purple silk jockey cap. Cocky grin. Lilac walking dress.

She sped up, drawn to them like a bee to a bloom. She'd almost closed the distance entirely before she saw the man from the hedge.

Lord Phillip. Georgie's former betrothed.

He was perched atop the boulder.

"Ahoy!" he called. "I understand you're the captain of this outing."

He jumped down, demonstrating significantly more dexterity than he had the previous day and managing to hold on to his hat.

"I offer myself as boatswain. Harpooner? Yeoman of the sheets!" He was clean-shaven and gave her a lopsided, unconscionably charming smile.

"Yeoman of . . . ?" She blinked at him, then turned to Georgie. "A word." She dragged them by the elbow several yards down the path toward the woodland.

She stopped, still holding their elbow. Sometimes she held Agnes by the elbow, or one of the twins. This was different. Georgie's elbow attached to Georgie's arm, and their shoulder, and neck, and chin, and mouth. Their mouth—it seemed very close.

She let go. "What's he *doing* here?"

"He's staying with me for the time being. Hiding out." Georgie cupped their elbow absently, their palm where her palm had been, and watched as Lord Phillip climbed back up Holywell Rock. He posed, hands on his hips. Anyone driving down the lane would see his head and shoulders rising above the hedges.

"Hiding from his father," Georgie amended. "Lord Hartcliffe. If you're going to cross a viscount, it shouldn't be him. A swan once had the temerity to defecate near his foot at a garden party and he wrung its neck with his bare hands."

"That's horrible." She tried not to picture it. "But what is he doing *here*—right now? You didn't tell him?"

"About the hoard?"

"Shhhh." She glared.

Georgie lowered their voice. "All I said was that you were keen on historical remains and wanted to take me along on a ramble. I thought *historical remains* would deter him from joining, but he's also keen on the stuff. Has an arrowhead collection and everything. I should have remembered that."

"What a view!" Lord Phillip jumped once more to earth and jogged over. "That pile on the hill—it's deliciously dilapidated. No one *lives* there?"

She stiffened.

"Phipps." Georgie was wincing, on her behalf, which was either mollifying or mortifying, she couldn't quite tell. "We'd better part ways. You go see about the pile, and we'll go see about . . . something else."

"Something else?" Lord Phillip raised a quizzical brow.

"Something of interest only to us."

Lord Phillip chuckled. "So! That's how it is."

"How it is?" Elfreda inquired. "How is it?"

"You're in love," he announced, his index finger waggling from her to Georgie and back to her. "*Historical remains*, my foot! You want to ramble to some secluded dell so you can have your wicked way with each other in the roses."

Elfreda went hot from head to toe. She couldn't look at Georgie. She heard their low laugh.

"I'd never," they said. "Roses have spikes."

"Posies, then," said Lord Phillip.

"Buttercups," suggested Georgie.

"Violets," countered Lord Phillip.

Elfreda cleared her throat. "We are not in love."

Her voice had a strange pitch.

She could feel Georgie's gaze heating the side of her face.

Lord Phillip shook his head. "You don't have to lie."

"I'm not—" she began, but he interrupted with another knowing chuckle.

"There's no scandalizing *me*. I've tumbled half the House of Commons. Oh, no." He paused, wearing an expression of concern. "Did I scandalize *you*? When I say *tumbled half the House of Commons*, I don't mean all at once. It was one by one, for the most part. The work of several years."

He said it modestly.

She couldn't think how to respond. "Congratulations?"

"Thank you." He bowed. With his square jaw and mop of curls, he looked a bit like Antinous, the handsome young lover of Emperor Hadrian. But perhaps she was imposing a family resemblance on men who desired men. She'd never met one in the flesh. Or she had and hadn't known. People didn't speak of such things. People rarely wrote of such things, not directly.

Years ago, she'd read the story of Ruth and Naomi and felt a thrill. *Whither thou goest, I will go.* The poetry of it had moved her. But until she'd glimpsed Miss Poskitt and Miss Mahomed entwined in the bower of bliss, she hadn't fathomed all the possibilities. All the ways devotion between women might manifest.

You're in love, Lord Phillip had said, pointing at her, at Georgie.

And Georgie hadn't contradicted him.

She risked a glance. Georgie stood with their arms crossed, looking at her. The morning was cloudless, and their eyes should have shone, but instead, they smoldered, dark with emotion.

Because she *had* contradicted him?

But she wasn't in love. Georgie wasn't in love. Someone had needed to correct the misapprehension.

"Miss Marsden—it's Marsden, isn't it?" Lord Phillip interrupted her thoughts. "Let's elope."

Her head whipped around. "Pardon?"

He was smiling even more charmingly than before. "Separate bedrooms. No relations. No relations with each other, that is. Anyone else is fair game. Unfortunately, Georgie can't pose as your lady's maid. Everyone knows them in town." He tapped his chin. "If *Georgie* would elope, you could pose as *their* lady's maid. That would simplify things."

"Georgie will not elope," said Georgie. "Georgie could have married you at St. James but decided death first."

"I know I was bossing you." Lord Phillip looked contrite. "I promise, as my wife, you can dress however you want—in private. You can go about the house in trousers. You can go about *naked*. Just draw the curtains. You can even act. Not in England, because my father might catch wind of it. On holiday, though. We can spend the winter in Italy! They must want English actors. It's so hard to understand Italian."

"No." Georgie's arms remained firmly crossed. "Be grateful I haven't turned you out of my home. I will, if you bring this up again. And don't pester Elf about eloping either. Unless . . ." They tipped their head. "Elf, do *you* want to marry Phipps? It's not for me to decline on your behalf."

Elfreda's ears were ringing. Nothing in her life had prepared her for a proposal from a stranger, let alone a future viscount with a swan-murdering father and male paramours in Parliament.

She didn't feel scandalized so much as saturated. She couldn't absorb anything else.

"I want to take a walk," she said, and hurtled down the path. By the time she'd reached the river, she'd slowed her pace, and Georgie and Lord Phillip had drawn up alongside her, bickering.

She passed out of the woodland, into the sun, and followed the gleaming river through the meadows.

"Blast!" Georgie gripped her arm. By Lord Phillip's yelp, they'd gripped his too. "Did he see us?"

Elfreda looked. The enormous farmer with the cart, who'd come to Miss Poskitt's aid—he was cutting across the pasture toward the river.

The two trajectories—hers and the farmer's—were going to intersect by the packhorse bridge.

"La!" Lord Phillip craned his neck. "He's strapping."

"He's my tenant." Georgie's hand was still tight around Elfreda's arm, and they were walking faster. "He wants to feed me to his cows."

"Why? Are you beastly to the tenantry?" Lord Phillip tutted. "I wouldn't have suspected."

"I didn't know I was."

"Oh, you're one of *those*."

"Maybe." Georgie's hand released. "What defines one of *those*?"

"You own the land. But blame the mismanagement on the steward."

"Yes, I'm one of those." Georgie kicked at the hem of their skirt. "But the steward *is* to blame."

"Sack him!" Lord Phillip sang it out. "Get a different steward."

"Harry would have to sack him." Georgie frowned. "Is that what your father would do? Sack the steward?"

"Of course not." Lord Phillip laughed. "My father is the other kind. Beastly to the tenantry. It's what *I* would do. Farmers have had a bloody time of it, ever since the war ended. Plummeting prices. That goes for grain, cheese, mutton, beef, wool. Everything. And last year the spring was cold and wet, catastrophic for the harvest. They need rent abatement. But that means *us* taking in less. The landlords. Worth it in the long run. I'm not talking in terms of the soul, although

I don't discount that aspect. I mean, economically. *Good morning.*" His voice dropped a register.

The farmer was upon them.

"Fine day," offered Georgie, as everyone came to an awkward halt.

"Fine," agreed the farmer, shortly. "But foul's blowing in."

Elfreda had forgotten just how tall and broad he was. His face was weather-beaten, but he couldn't have been so very many years older than the rest of them.

"How are the turnips?" asked Georgie, too heartily.

He grunted. "I had to sow my field all over again on account of them sheep running amok."

Elfreda met Georgie's eyes. No blaming a steward for *that*.

The farmer tugged on his blue neckerchief. "How's the young missis?" His tone was grudging, but his gaze grew intent as he waited for Georgie's reply.

"Recovering well," said Georgie. "Thanks to your timely intervention."

The farmer grunted, with a fraction less animosity.

"Are you going that way?" Lord Phillip pointed at the bridge. "So am I. Lord Phillip Winston. And your name?"

The two men crossed the bridge and took the turning that would lead into the village. Lord Phillip was talking animatedly, and the farmer kept shaking his head, as though beset by a mosquito.

"Hmm," said Georgie, staring after them. After a long moment, they glanced at her, eyes bright, brows arched.

She could hear the low rush of the river as it slipped along between its banks. The sun was climbing in the sky. The warming air smelled of honeysuckle.

And Georgie. Georgie looked like spring itself. Beautiful, and new, and familiar, all at the same time.

You're in love.

"This way." She forced her feet forward, perpendicular to the bridge, cleaving to the river's western bank.

No distractions. No secluded dells. Or yes, secluded dells, if caves figured among the topographical features. No roses, posies, buttercups, violets. Those were to be avoided.

As she walked, briskly, she explained to Georgie about her evening's research. Reverend Cruttwell had identified one cave on a walk through the parish that led him past a lime kiln.

She was heading now to the only lime kiln in the vicinity.

Georgie's stride was longer than hers, and so they gave the impression of strolling in a leisurely fashion, even as she began to puff and sweat.

It was always so cold *inside* Marsden Hall that she wrapped herself in shawls and wore her warmest woolen garments, and sometimes she went out overdressed. Like this morning.

She stopped abruptly and unbuttoned her pelisse.

"Are we stripping off our clothes?" Georgie had stopped too and was leaning against an oak, that cocky grin splitting their face. "To swim? Or to do something wickeder?"

She shrugged out of the pelisse and hung it carefully on a branch. Sweat was still collecting near her hairline. Georgie's grin, and the idea of doing *something wickeder*, had sent heat pouring through her, and it quite negated any relief she might have derived from shedding layers.

What did having one's wicked way entail exactly?

She wasn't sure. And it seemed a dangerous line of questioning. She took learning seriously, and to understand fully she would need a demonstration. And where was the line between demonstrating, for educational purposes, and simply *doing*?

Doing because she wanted to. Because the long grasses on the riverbank looked deeply green and inviting, and threaded between the grasses, buttercups glowed like the softest gold.

Georgie's narrow gaze was traveling over her.

"Does Lord Phillip hope to find a girl with whom to elope in the village?" She blurted a different question, resuming her hurried walk.

"I doubt that's on his mind at present." Georgie fell into step with her. "He was too taken with Charles Peach."

"It should be easy, though. He's a lord." More trees closed in around the bank, and finally, the air was cooling her. "Can't he elope with almost anyone?"

"Not anyone he'd actually want to marry" was Georgie's dry response.

It made her blush. Of course.

"He wants to marry a man," she said. Did Georgie want to marry a woman? She kept her eyes on the ground, necessary given all the tree roots.

"Maybe I shouldn't have generalized." Georgie sighed. "Everyone feels so much pressure to perform according to expectations, who can even imagine what they'd want? What they'd *really* want, if it were up to them alone? Given that Phipps must marry, and can't marry a man, I do know that he wants to marry someone who, like him, wants a marriage in name only. And it's nothing easy to negotiate such a thing."

"Doesn't he require an heir?" She avoided a clump of nettles. "And doesn't the production of heirs require . . ."

A memory of rabbits in the garden transitioned into a mental image from *The Canterbury Tales*, a young woman meeting her lover in a pear tree. The bit she'd found most interesting concluded thus: *He pulled up her smock, and in he thrust.*

"Consummation," provided Georgie. "Indeed. But Phipps has a younger brother liable to spawn. That's good enough, so long as Phipps can appear to play his part."

"But you won't play a part beside him." She gave them a sidelong look. Shadows sifted over their face as a breeze tossed the leaves on the treetops.

They returned her look, more shadows pooling in their eyes. "I agreed to the betrothal impulsively. Harry wouldn't let me live alone in London. I had to share the town house with my cousin, Mrs. Morris. She tried to make me drink vinegar at breakfast to improve my complexion and swore she'd see me married to a duke. I was at my wit's end. She stopped with the vinegar—and the dukes—when I got engaged. It was a blessed relief. Marriage to Phipps seemed like the shortest road to the broadest freedom. But he's under his father's thumb, and I realized I would have been too. That I was hazarding my whole life for want of patience."

Elfreda bit her lip. Georgie would inherit this estate at five and twenty. She had no such guarantee. A vague sense that Papa would never send her away, that she'd live on at Marsden Hall after he was *truly* gone, and discover then how much, or how little, money remained—that was her security. He did mutter darkly on occasions that he would donate the house and the collections to the nation, so it could all be preserved as a museum dedicated to his legacy. But he muttered all sorts of things.

Was she hazarding her whole life, and her sisters', by refusing Lord Phillip's proposal? Had he even been serious? His father didn't sound as though he'd approve of a woman archaeologist.

"So." Georgie shrugged. "I broke things off."

"And then there was a duel." She blinked against the sun as the trees thinned. The river was meandering through meadows again, and the banks were low and well grazed. Several cows stood knee-deep in the river. One was drinking. Elfreda watched her flick away flies with her tail.

"A duel," she repeated, although it was hard to imagine anything so dramatic in such placid environs. "A curricle crash."

"Anne Chatterbox Poskitt." Georgie sounded amused. "I suppose you heard the whole story."

"None of the details. And we've at least a mile to go."

It was an invitation, and they took it.

"Where to start?" They looked at the blue sky, theatrically. "All right. To set the scene. I break the engagement. Phipps is miffed. Hartcliffe is murderous. Harry comes heroically home, to shake some sense into me. One maudlin night, I try to patch the situation. I was sleepless, sitting up in my bedchamber, feeling I'd really thrown a rub in Phipps's way, and he didn't deserve it. I had the idea to atone with a gift, something he'd coveted: my father's gold snuff box, with Apollo and Adonis on the lid. I couldn't rest—my brain wouldn't stop spinning. I changed into trousers, put the snuff box in my pocket, and went out the window. I *had* to wear trousers—Phipps resides at the Albany. Bachelors only. I hailed a hackney in my bachelor garb, and I was off. So far, so good. But unbeknownst to me, Harry was on the street, and he'd caught sight of my exit, or rather, an unknown bachelor's exit. Of course, he gave chase. When I arrived at the Albany, I went around to the Rope Walk, because Phipps's set is in the back. Harry mustn't have arrived in time to note my exact route. He marched in the front door, and Phipps happened to be in the entrance hall. Which rather confirmed Harry's suspicion. By the time I heard the shouting and doubled back, the entrance hall was packed with onlookers. Harry was storming off, and Phipps was shouting after him, and pistols at dawn was on everyone's lips."

Elfreda's mouth had dropped open.

"Your brother thought Phipps had been leaving your bedchamber, but it was *you* leaving your bedchamber?"

"That's it, yes."

"Why didn't Phipps deny it? Or say he'd marry you? Isn't marrying you what he wanted?"

"Phipps didn't grasp the charge. Harry isn't very articulate when his blood is up, and Phipps was taken by surprise and more than a bit bosky. Everything he shouted was terrifically slurred, although I could make out very clearly the phrase *backbiting hyena* as applied to myself. I think he wanted to shoot Harry as a proxy for me. And Harry wanted to shoot him also as a proxy for me, but in a different sense. It was like a farce, but with the very real threat of bloodshed. Not anyone's finest hour."

"You didn't try to explain?"

"I *tried*." Georgie made a face. "But I was surprised too. It took me several minutes to piece it all together. Harry was already gone, and Phipps was thronged with volunteer seconds. I couldn't get near him, and then *he* was gone. A bevy of bachelors hustled him through the courtyard and into a coach. I spent all night between the town house, the Albany, and every other establishment I could imagine either of them frequenting. I found neither. Just before sunrise, I returned to the Albany to beg a ride to the duel itself. A fellow drove me in his curricle, drove far too slowly, and to the wrong spot. He jumped down to poke among the trees, but we were alone, I could tell. Dawn was breaking. The sudden light in the sky pulled a trigger inside me. I seized the reins and drove wildly across the heath, and I finally spotted them, my brother and Phipps. They were halfway through their twenty paces. I urged the horses to a gallop, aiming right between them, but a wheel hit a rock, and I flew the final yards. I saw Harry's face as he turned, and that was the last thing I saw for several hours."

Elfreda shook her head. "And he sent you here? I can't believe he didn't pack you off to St. Helena, with Napoleon."

"Where's your fellow feeling?" Georgie shot her a look of mock offense. "I could have been killed."

"My fellow feeling is for your brother, and the horses."

"The horses were fine. I inquired."

She was still shaking her head. "It must have been terrifying."

"It was."

"I mean for the people who care about you." She imagined Georgie crumpled on the ground, face blanched, body broken. Her heart clenched.

Georgie was observing her closely and raised an intrigued brow.

"Would *you* have been terrified?"

She looked away. There was smoke in the air.

"The lime kiln is over there." She gestured. "We should search in earnest now."

Not far from the kiln, the river flowed around a bend, and the banks rose in brambly hillocks. Georgie insisted on wading across so they could search the other side.

Elfreda focused all her attention on the bank before her. She crawled up and down the sloping terrain, parting ferns, patting the moss, feeling around the edges of every large stone.

At last, she came to a shelf of rock in the hillside, and as she pushed aside the vegetation, she saw the void beneath. A cave. A den. A lair. From the dark came a hoarse cry.

"Stand and deliver! Your money or your life!"

Her pulse exploded. She sprang forward, crashed into the bandit charging out of the cave, and went down, hard. The breath left her lungs. She was sprawled across the bandit's wet body, struggling for the pistol, a vibration beneath her transforming, unmistakably, into laughter.

A laughing bandit.

A laughing, wet bandit.

She lifted up. Through the murk, she saw blue eyes sparkling with mirth, a wedge of luminous white teeth.

"My God, you're bold." Georgie's voice was appreciative. "*I* wouldn't attack a bandit."

Her hips were flush against theirs, and her thighs, and the wet was seeping into her skirt, the cold shocking against her overheated skin. She wouldn't have been surprised if steam billowed up. She'd already begun to go foggy, her heart beating everywhere, her eyes on their smile.

"That wasn't funny." Her breathing was unsteady.

"No," they agreed, mirth fading. They had hold of her hips.

"We must search the cave," she whispered.

"I already did. It only goes back a few feet."

"We must search elsewhere, then."

"Right now?"

Slowly, she nodded, which had the unfortunate effect of bringing their faces into closer proximity. She stilled, every muscle in her body locked.

"Aye aye, captain," they murmured, and tightening their hold on her hips, tipped her off them.

For the rest of the day's fruitless search, she worried that, if it had been up to her alone, she'd still lie pressed against them at the mouth of the wrong cave. And what would that mean, for her, for them, for the days to come?

19

I SAW HIM CARRY a horse! On his back. A full-grown horse. Sixteen hands." Phipps was waving emphatically with his fork.

Georgie sat at the other end of the breakfast table, failing to glean something about agriculture from *The Derby Mercury*. "You told me last night. I still don't understand the circumstances."

Phipps began to explain. A few minutes into it, Georgie realized the problem was them. They'd stopped listening. Yesterday afternoon, Charles Peach had, for some inexplicable reason, performed the impossible feat of horse portage—a truly remarkable exploit upon which Georgie couldn't focus for half a second.

They were counting down to their rendezvous with Elf.

"He's going to show me the threshing machines," Phipps was saying when Georgie stood up. "I take an interest in threshing machines."

"Grand," responded Georgie, meaning it. If Phipps didn't intend to leave, at least he didn't intend either to be always underfoot. They wouldn't worry about the trouble he could cause for Charles Peach. Peach could drop a horse on him.

The clouds were low and drizzly. As Georgie reached Holywell Rock, the clouds dropped lower still and opened. Elf had a lantern, and a trowel, and no umbrella. Georgie had a flask, and some chocolate, and no umbrella. Both of them were soaked to the skin within minutes, and raced through the soggy park up to Marsden Hall. Elf took them straight to the library, left them dripping by the Finglesham urn, and returned promptly, with linens, Agnes, the twins, and a fat, friendly beagle. While they dried off, Elf built a fire in the fireplace, a novelty and a defiance, to gauge by her sisters' awed excitement. As soon as it was crackling, everyone piled in front of it. Georgie realized they'd rather missed Matilda's wiggles and kicks, and surrendered as well to the beagle, who draped herself over their legs. The twins wanted to hear a story, and Elf obliged, and then Agnes wanted to dress her hair, and Georgie obliged, extracting carefully from children and dog, and following her to her bedchamber. She wanted the Titus, in fact. Georgie demurred, but she grabbed one of her waist-length tresses and snipped it so close to the scalp that they had no choice but to finish the job.

"It wasn't my idea," whispered Georgie to Elf afterward, when Agnes was back by the fire, the twins rubbing her shorn hair with chocolatey fingers. "I tried to stop her."

Elf was stretched out, propped on her palms, feet toward the hearth, and Georgie assumed the same position, right next to her, pinkies overlapping.

"My sisters have ideas," she sighed. "It's very hard to stop them." She sounded sleepy, and fond, and before long, her head was in Georgie's lap, and they were stroking her silky hair, surrounded by napping Marsdens, listening to the grunts of the beagle and the soft patter of the rain.

The next day was fair, and the next, and the next. Reverend Cruttwell's second cave proved recalcitrant, and they tramped with Elf upstream and downstream and back, again and again.

"Perhaps the intrepid vicar mistook a hollow log for a cave," Georgie suggested on the afternoon of the fourth day. "No lack of hollow logs around here."

That was the day Elf found it, the second cave, as shallow and underwhelming as the first.

"We'll head north, to the Roman ruins," she said, so determined, they didn't lodge the obvious objection. What two defenseless nuns would have dared to travel so far with stolen gold?

Instead, they agreed, and proposed they go by boat.

The following morning, they rowed upstream, facing Elf, who sat stiffly on her bench.

"I've never been in a boat before." She gasped and gripped the hull as it pitched in the current.

"We Redmaynes made our fortune on boats." They grinned. "Watermen all the way back. Transported cargo and passengers on the Thames. Until my grandfather got a foothold in the Docklands and became a go-between for suppliers and wholesalers."

"That's why Papa refers to him as . . ." She bit her lip.

"Pray continue. Is it scurrilous?"

"Fishmonger," she said, with obvious chagrin.

"Nothing wrong with fishmongering. And it's not too wide of the mark. I'm sure Grandfather mongered a few fish, among other things."

Elf rarely took the path of least resistance, not if it involved letting an error pass. They knew this about her. They liked it about her. They could see the thoughts moving behind her eyes as she conducted a rapid self-interrogation.

"Be that as it may," she said, "in my family, it's used as an insult. Because of our appalling prejudice."

"You understand your family's treatment of my family as deriving from . . . appalling prejudice?" They raised their brows.

She nodded. "And I am endeavoring to examine more closely my own assumptions."

"According to your newly examined view, tell me: Is being in trade a blot on one's character?"

She shook her head.

"Good." They laughed. "I should do more to examine my own assumptions as well."

Her lips twitched, then she sobered once more.

"Your grandfather *did* level a historically invaluable Saxon abbey," she said. "So my unprejudiced opinion of him remains very low."

"Noted." They paused. "You could have left it, you know. At examining assumptions."

She looked at them, uncomprehending.

They smiled widely and focused on the oars.

The day was already warm and hazy, and the air had a sweet, summery sluggishness. Clouds of insects hovered over the water.

Elf's posture gradually relaxed, and her complexion improved. She wasn't green around the gills and seemed more at home on the water.

"The Northmen's boats looked like dragons," she said, leaning over to dip her finger in the water. "They had heads carved on the stems and tails on the sterns."

"Dragon boats." Georgie kept rowing, slow, even strokes. "Terrifying. I'd rather face a seventy-four-gun French ship of the line."

She shivered. "Seeing those ships racing up the river—it must have felt like a bad dream."

This. This felt like a good dream. Afloat with Elf, the boat bobbing gently, the sunlight painting her with gold, a reminder to treasure *this*, now, this moment, worth as much as whatever cache of cold metal waited in the dark. Worth more.

Why such urgency to get back to London? Their haste seemed increasingly misguided. Life wasn't *there*, passing them by. Life was here too.

They rowed on, between low hills quilted with pasture and tillage, green checkers interrupted by the occasional copse of trees or quadrangle of farm buildings.

It was early afternoon when the stone cottages of Thornton appeared on the banks.

"Shall we stop for buns?" They maneuvered the boat under the stone arch of the bridge, fully aware that Elf would brook no delay. They'd packed a basket with jam puffs, strawberries, cheese, bread, butter, and lemonade with her doggedness in mind.

"No," she said. "Unless—do you need to rest?" She gave them an unexpectedly protective look, concern for their welfare written plainly on her face. Their chest felt tight, not from the exercise, from an emotion that strained their breath.

"Rest?" they scoffed. "I can row all day."

Their arms were screaming by the time they reached their destination. *Roman ruins* conjured visions of the Colosseum, but what Georgie confronted was a few low stone walls in a field.

Why all the fuss? was the question that sprang to mind.

They didn't ask.

They searched with Elf, rowing from bank to bank, then combing through the vegetation, zigzagging farther and farther upstream, even as the river narrowed on its course through a high valley, and they had to take increasing care with the boat to avoid scraping rock.

The bat cave was visible from the boat, near the top of a hill, and they carried up the lantern, clambering behind Elf, who went into the cave first—thank God. This cave was taller, thinner, and longer than the other two, with sharp turnings, and Georgie didn't like the experience of shuffling blind around corners, and liked less the idea that sleeping bats dangled all around them, that any moment they might feel the impact of furry bodies, tiny claws tangling in their hair, leathery wings brushing their cheeks.

They were so relieved to exit, they didn't care that the cave had been empty. Elf bore that disappointment alone.

She insisted on searching the banks again, after they'd turned the boat around, and on this pass, she spied the badger cave—maybe. It didn't match the description she'd cited, but it *was* a cave, albeit the smallest yet, and it did smell a bit like badger, or at any rate, like animal, a rangy, musty stench, with a tang of ammonia.

No gold.

This time, they insisted.

"Enough for today," they said. "Or it will get dark while we're still on the water."

The trip downstream was relatively swift. When the river widened and smoothed, they stowed the oars and gobbled a jam puff.

Elf ate her own jam puff in neat bites. She seemed thoughtful, rather than deflated, and was watching them with an expression they couldn't interpret.

They swallowed the last of the pastry. "What?"

"I owe you something," she said.

They didn't let their gaze drop to her mouth. Their heart began to pound, and they tried to sound offhand as they drawled in response.

"Another kiss? I thought we were finished."

"Something else." Her smile was a bewitchment. "Come closer."

They scooted forward on the bench. "Should I shut my eyes?"

"If you like."

Her sugary tone set off warning bells. They lowered their lashes, not all the way, and saw her hand flash out.

An instant later, cold water slapped the side of their face.

"That's hardly sporting," they began, but *sporting* became a sputter, as more river water splashed into their mouth.

"You threw me into a pond!" She splashed them again, expression delightedly righteous. "This is your just deserts."

"A half measure, really." They wiped their face with their sleeve. "Just deserts is throwing me in the river." They bared their teeth. "If you dare."

She looked at them warily.

"You don't," they observed. "Well, that's for the best. It would be unwise."

She pounced, seizing them around the waist. The boat rocked. They felt absurdly joyous as they wrestled her down to the boat's floor.

"Do you give up?" They were half on top of her, their legs and hers in a tangle, jammed beneath a thwart. The boat was hard, and various objects poked at them, but Elf was soft and warm, and they'd swear on their life she smelled like rainbows. Red was strawberry. Orange was orange. Yellow was a lovely lemon custard.

"I don't give up." She tried to twist.

"Ow," they said mildly. "Easy there."

She twisted again, this time managing to flip onto her side. This maneuver had the inadvertent effect of trapping their arm between them. Their palm came flush against her breast.

She froze, her face inches from theirs. They froze too. Their gaze traced her brows, the slope of her nose, the curve of her lips, the freckles below her right eye. Her eyes themselves were midnight dark, glowing with midnight's magic. They could feel her heart beating into their hand. If they curled their fingers, they could tug down her bodice. Their other hand was free to slide up her skirt, to skate over her stockings, over the bare skin of her thigh.

"You win." They bolted to sitting, squirming away from her, voice hoarse. "*I* give up. I will throw *myself* into the river."

"Don't." She fumbled upright, raking back her hair. "You need to steer the boat."

They collapsed onto their bench, grabbing for the oars. "Another time, then. At your convenience." They rowed, without looking at her, because if they did, they might wrestle her down again, and lick her neck, eat her in bites.

Shipwreck the boat.

Spoil the friendship.

Their eyes roamed the landscape. It appeared aroused in its own right, every budded blossom on the verge of bursting open, every open flower sticky and swollen, petals ready to drop. The sap coursed audibly through the trees. And the birds! Had birds ever twittered so excitedly?

I will destroy you.

She'd vowed it in that pasture. She was small but strangely powerful. They should have known then to fear for their body and soul.

"Tell me something about the ninth century," they demanded. Boredom was the solution. Boredom was ardor cooling.

In the pause that followed, they listened to the birds, the sap, the plash of the oars.

"How about the seventh?" she asked.

"Better still."

"I can tell you more about the *olden-day* riddles," she said, and did, and it didn't bore them, but at least it diverted blood back to their head. There were different types of riddles, and people had riddled them all over medieval England, and *kiss* was never the answer, although some riddles mentioned kissing: *Courtly men and women kiss me!* Answer: *Cup*. The best Saxon riddle writer, Aldhelm, was imitating an earlier riddle writer, Symphosius, who lived in North Africa.

"And this Aldhelm, you said he was taught by the archbishop of Canterbury, who was also from Africa?" They lifted the oars from the water, so their mind could churn on its own. "The archbishop of *Canterbury*? Chap who heads the entire Church of England and crowns the king? Doesn't that mean we should trace our forebears to Carthage?" They shook their head and started rowing again. "Funny how some debts never get acknowledged. Do you know what I've noticed, about your Fellows of the Albion Society of Antiquaries? They're all using the past to substantiate a particular version of the present—the version they think most favorable to men like themselves. I don't trust it. What they say the world was. What they say the world is."

They lifted the oars and looked at her. A line formed between her brows.

They waited for her to argue.

"I don't either," she said.

"But you hope to join them?"

She crossed her arms. "I hope to say things about the past as well."

"What do *you* want from it? The past?"

They waited, and when it seemed they'd waited too long, asked a question to which she had no response, they dipped the oars.

Her lips parted. "Connection."

"Connection," they repeated, and paused rowing, waiting for more.

"A single life is such a little thing. It's barely anything, in the succession of generations. The generations go on and on, but individuals vanish like foam." She broke their gaze, watched the river instead. "When I touch a jet bead that a girl wore around her neck five centuries before I was born, I feel as though we're part of something continuous, she and I, for all our smallness. When I dig, I feel as though my grandmother is with me. I want that contact. It's silly."

"No," they said, and she lifted her gaze. "It's not silly."

Her brown irises were starred with deeper, darker brown, as though the black had leaked from her pupils. She had eyes like portals.

They were staring into them, no, falling into them.

She *was* going to destroy them. After this ended, whatever this was, they would never be the same.

Shadow swallowed the boat. They tipped their head. There was the bluff, rising from the earth like a shrugged shoulder, blocking the sun. Home lay just around the bend.

Elf stood abruptly. The boat seesawed. They lunged and grabbed her legs before she was ejected into the river.

She staggered, laughing, bouncing even.

"Here!" she cried. "It's here!"

20

"WHERE?" ASKED GEORGIE, standing beside Elf on the ferny riverbank. Viewed from this angle, the bluff daunted, with its stark face of exposed rock ledges and clinging shrubs, its high crest of trees black against the sky. At its base, a few light-starved saplings clustered amid clumps of moss, more ferns, some white flowers on long stalks, nodding.

Georgie rummaged in the undergrowth. "Where's the cave?" Elf didn't answer. They looked up. "Where are you going?"

They ran after her.

She was going up to the top of the bluff, which required circling around to a path that ascended a gentler slope.

"I left a shovel under a beech tree," she told them.

"We need a shovel why?" They yanked their skirts from a thorn bush, cursing under their breath.

"To dig."

"That bit I inferred."

Her face was flushed. She'd left her straw hat in the boat, and her hair was loose, flying in the sudden wind.

"Do you remember that spring the river flooded? It ran over the lane. It made lakes in the park. Imagine how many times it must have flooded over the past thousand years." She stopped and turned to them, eyes radiant. "If there's a cave, the river buried it in settlings, mud and sand."

"*If.*" Georgie's fatigue hit them all at once. They couldn't prevent a doubtful sigh.

Elf's gaze darkened. She hurried again uphill.

They called after her. "So, the plan is to dig through a thousand years of mud and sand?" They rubbed their forehead with the heel of their hand.

Of course. Of course that was the plan.

They enlisted their longer legs to catch up.

"It makes sense that the nuns would have hidden the gold as quickly as possible, which means near to where they found it. But a cave open to the river, right where the Northmen would have landed those dragon boats . . ." They shook their head. "That makes less sense."

She gave an impatient shrug. "They would have disguised the entrance. With large rocks, perhaps."

"The plan is to dig through a thousand years of mud and sand, and also large rocks?"

Of course. Of course it was.

An eternity later, Georgie was collapsed on the cool ground, wheezing next to a modestly sized pit.

"I'll continue," they promised. "As soon as I reattach my arms."

They listened for a time to Elf digging, the rhythmic thunk of the shovel, the thud of the displaced earth. Clouds had stacked in the sky.

The next thunk thinned into a raspy screech. Metal on rock.

They sat up.

Elf scraped sideways with the shovel, clearing dirt from a perpendicular surface.

"Limestone." She pushed back her hair with a trembling hand

and left a muddy streak above her brow. "It's all limestone, a wall of it."

She scraped, and dug, and scraped, and dug, and scraped.

"I hear that with my molars," remarked Georgie, through gritted teeth.

She didn't seem to hear anything, not the horrible scraping noise, not their voice. Her concentration was absolute. Admirable. A bit frightening.

She'd dig to the center of the Earth.

"My turn," they said when her arms began to wobble with each upward swing.

They pulled the shovel from her hands and took her place in the pit.

They dug, and then she dug again, and then they dug. The shovel's blade skittered off something unyielding, reverberations traveling up to their elbow. It wasn't a protuberance of the limestone wall itself, but a separate rock. They worked at it with the shovel until they could wiggle it like a loose tooth.

Slowly, they pried the rock free, tipped it toward them, slid it out of the way.

Behind the rock—nothing.

A black gap.

They extended their hand, felt the cold air rush over them, and yanked their hand back, whooping. Elf tumbled into the pit, bumping them, *hugging* them, and she was laughing, and so were they, hilarious with exhaustion.

"Is anything in there?" they asked, breathless. "Watch out for bats, and badgers." They giggled. "And bandits."

Her elbow connected with their ribs. "Get the lantern."

They scrambled from the pit, staggered through the ferns to the boat. Leaves whipped past. Wind was bending the trees. A raindrop

splashed the corner of their mouth. They had to hunch with the tinderbox to light the candle.

When they passed it down to Elf, she looked at them, and it
seemed candles were lit, too, behind the dark panes of her eyes.

She swung back to the fissure, holding out the lantern. "It keeps
going." She sounded muted. She was sending her voice down the
tunnel, sending it after the lantern's wan rays.

"Tomorrow," they said. "Tomorrow we'll . . ."

They were addressing her skirts, the soles of her shoes.

Their heart stopped. Time stopped.

But of course. Of course.

She vanished into the mountainside.

"Elf!" Their shout was drowned by a crash of thunder. They felt
another raindrop, and another, and tilted up their face. The sky was
livid.

"Blast," they muttered. "Blast, blast, blast."

They dropped into the pit, stuck their head gingerly through the
jagged crack. The blackness within dizzied them. Their palms were
sweating as they inched forward.

"Elf, it's raining. It's dark. Come out." The back of their skull
grazed stone. They had to lower onto their belly, slither like a snake.
The stone hemmed them in on every side. It didn't matter anymore
if their eyes were open or closed. Irregularities in the floor, the ceiling, the walls, jabbed them in tender places, grated on their bones.
Their breath sawed in their ears. One moment, they felt certain
they'd be crushed, pressed flat by the weight of the bluff itself. The
next, they felt certain they'd plummet, that they were sliding to the
edge of an abyss. They stopped moving, every muscle cramped with
horror. This was the third possibility. They'd remain trapped, just so,
immobile, unable to force their body forward or back. Something
tiny and frantic inside them began to run in wild circles. They

couldn't breathe. They couldn't breathe. Something tiny and frantic inside them was screaming, and there was no way to cut off that scream, no way to inhale.

"Georgie?"

"Elf?" They gave a convulsive gasp, sucked in a clammy mouthful of air.

"Georgie?"

They squirmed, dragging themselves onward with their elbows.

"It ends here." Elf's voice was muffled but normal, a lifeline. "You can almost stand. It's a chamber, a small one though. Not quite two arm spans across. I couldn't keep the lantern upright, so the candle went out. Do you have the tinderbox?"

"No," they grunted. The walls had pulled away. The ceiling had lifted. They were breathing more easily, but chills rippled their flesh. "Wouldn't fire eat up the air? *Is* there any air in here? God, it's stagnant." Their chest bucked. "Let's leave. This isn't the place."

"I suppose not." Elf was notably reluctant.

They'd already rotated, crawling, then again slithering, for the opening. They needed to stretch out, to feel the wind moving over their skin.

They strained to see, eyes wide open, eager for the first glimpse of faded daylight.

There it was. A gray glimmer.

And then a wave of black came down.

And there was none.

ELFREDA'S FOREHEAD STRUCK a shoe. Georgie was blocking the tunnel.

"You're standing on my face." She wiggled backward. "Well, you're not *standing*, but . . . Go on. Why have you stopped?"

Georgie uttered a string of profanities.

"What is it?" She shoved their foot. "I'm in the narrowest part. Please, go."

"I'm trying."

"Trying?"

Georgie kicked.

She wiggled back farther. "What are you doing?"

The oppressive little cranny filled with a scuffling sound, punctuated by kicks and grunts. Foreboding sent her stomach rising toward her throat. She rested the point of her chin on the chill stone, an attempt to ease the painful crick in her neck.

"Hurry," she urged.

"I can't." Their voice was tight. "There's mud, where *outside* should be. I saw it. It just slid off the mountain. Because of the shoveling, or the rain—I don't know. I'm trying to dig through it. But I can't do anything more than scratch with my fingers." They were kicking, she realized, in time with the scratching. "It's so bloody dense. And there's so much of it. I can't get into a decent position to—gah!"

There was a sickeningly sharp rap, like an iron knocker against a door, and then silence.

She lifted up, the one possible inch. "Was that your head?"

A groan was the response.

"Are you all right?"

Another groan.

They'd only just recovered from the curricle crash. Their skull might not have healed. What if they'd cracked it open? What if they lost consciousness?

Fear crooked a finger around her windpipe.

She reached out blindly and grasped their ankle. "We should get you sitting up." She towed them, reversing slowly, using her elbows, and her hips, the brass lantern rasping and shrieking on the stone, as though in pain.

After the first tugs, Georgie groaned louder and began to move under their own power. Once she'd backed into the chamber, she cast aside the useless lantern and knelt. Moments later, she was struck by Georgie's feet, and then she was tangled with them, each arranging their limbs with difficulty, given the confines of the space. When it seemed she was facing them, she groped for their head.

"Hold still." She slid her fingers into their slippery hair. Their indrawn hiss coincided with her discovery of a nasty lump. She skimmed over it and continued probing their skull. "Everything is intact at least. How do you feel?"

"Like I've been buried alive, with a migraine." They sounded sardonic. It was oddly reassuring.

Her fingers were still stroking through their hair.

"I'll dig us out." She withdrew. Her heartbeat felt jerky. "Stupid," she whispered, and sat, shuffling backward until her spine hit the wall. "Stupid. This was so stupid of me."

"Zealous," Georgie offered, settling next to her.

"Overzealous."

They didn't disagree.

She flexed her hands. They ached. What if she couldn't dig through the mud? What if neither of them could?

"You're shaking." Georgie's shoulder touched hers.

"It's cold." She hesitated. "And ever so slightly horrifying."

"Being buried alive?"

"Don't call it that."

"Being below ground with no egress, probably forever?"

She laughed unwillingly. "Much better."

"At least we're together. I'd rather I was with you than anyone else. Except Charles Peach."

"The farmer?" She drew up her legs. Every inch of her felt grimy and raw.

"From a practical standpoint. He could punch through the mud."

"I don't think he'd have fit into the tunnel."

"You're probably right. Did I tell you that he carried a horse on his back?"

A tired smile curved her lips. "I don't believe you."

"It's true. Phipps watched him do it. A full-grown horse."

"Why?"

"I think anyone would watch something like that."

She bumped their shoulder. "Why carry a horse?"

"Unclear." There was a pause. "Why not? If you can?"

She exhaled on another laugh. Her heart was beating more steadily. "This helps."

"I've taken your mind off our being buried alive?"

She bumped them harder.

They laughed, and their laughter warmed the darkness.

A little more, and she'd stop shaking. She'd summon the last of her strength, and she'd do what had to be done.

"Tell me something else," she said.

"I told you a man carried a horse. What else is there?"

She giggled. It was utterly bizarre, how *much* this helped. How blithely she could confront the fact that she was trapped in a horrible, dank hole, thanks to Georgie attempting so transparently to bolster her. Usually, *she* did the bolstering. Soothed and cuddled. Dried the eyes.

"A secret." She leaned into them. "Tell me a secret."

She'd said the wrong thing. She was pressed to their side, and she felt their resistance, their limbs still but suddenly unyielding. She might have been leaning on stone.

"Not your deepest, darkest secret." She pulled away clumsily, embarrassed to have overstepped. But she hadn't known that Georgie harbored a deep, dark secret.

And they did, didn't they? What else could their reaction signify?

"A small secret." She swallowed. "Something comical."

"Comical?" They shifted closer, restoring contact. The odd moment had passed. "Give me an example."

She hadn't prepared one of her own. But there it was—blaring in her brain. Her embarrassment increased. She tried to think of anything else, failed, and proceeded.

"Well, then." She hesitated. "It's about that riddle, with the hungry sparks."

"Good Lord. The answer *was* kiss?"

"No, but I wanted you to." Now that she'd confessed, she prickled all over. "I wanted you to kiss me. I'd no idea you would, in that exact moment. It was more of a general condition."

"You had a general condition." There was a new note in their voice. "Of wanting me to kiss you."

"Comical." She gave a weak laugh. "Your turn."

"How is it comical?"

"Because. Because *you*. And *me*. We were enemies. Enemies don't kiss. Now we're friends, and friends don't kiss either."

"Who kisses, then? People with purely neutral feelings?"

She felt cornered and tried to hide it with a dismissive snort. "We're not debating this."

"The condition." They said it delicately. "Does it afflict you still?"

"Not in the present circumstances. Obviously." Was it obvious? Maybe the present circumstances called for kissing. Their surroundings felt like a tomb, but she was alive, and Georgie was alive, and she wanted *more* aliveness, wanted to touch it and taste it.

She touched the floor. "We need an implement, for digging. Do you feel any loose rocks?"

She began to crawl, feeling her way.

"It still afflicts you, though." They'd begun to crawl too. "Generally?"

She stopped. "There's no generally if we don't unbury ourselves."

"My God." They barked a laugh. "That's a bracing thought."

The cave floor was covered with smooth clay in some places, rough grit in others. None of the loose rocks were sized or shaped remotely like chisels.

She crawled straight into Georgie.

"Was that your head again?" She sat up, gripping her shoulder.

"It was my nose that time." Georgie's voice was right by her ear. "Elf, I was thinking. The last time we saw each other, before I went to London—"

"Mrs. Pattinson's?" Surprise and displeasure sharpened her voice. "You're bringing up Mrs. Pattinson's? *Now?*"

"I didn't follow you to the library."

"Honesty. Please." She hunched, instinctively guarding her middle. "We're friends. You don't have to lie about how things were back then."

"I'm not lying."

Why did they persist? Why return at all to that night?

The ball had been a torment from beginning to end. Aunt Susan had dragged her in front of every bachelor in the neighborhood. She could still feel the crisp ringlets twinging her scalp, and the flood of relief when she'd managed to sneak up the stairs. She'd stolen into the quiet library, tucked herself behind the curtain in the window seat, opened a book on her lap, and escaped into the pages—an escape that proved temporary.

"I went to the library to hide." Wallflowers did such things during dances. Georgie didn't. "You and your friends followed, to entertain yourselves at my expense. Otherwise, how do you explain your presence? Did you come to read?" Her tone jeered at the very possibility.

"Erm. Yes, in fact."

A scoffing laugh burst from her. "Conduct manuals? Religious tracts?"

"Bawdy pamphlets. With pictures, we hoped." Georgie muttered it, sheepishly. "Supposedly, Mr. Pattinson kept a secret shelf of them."

She shut her eyes. The memory was crystal clear: Georgie yanking back the curtain and staring down at her, exultant. Their brows had tilted with wicked amusement, and a moment later, the Janes appeared behind them, and two or three others, everyone rosy from dancing and equally hilarious.

"All of you laughed," she whispered.

"I wish we hadn't."

She could hear the sincerity in their voice.

"The laughing was a kind of fit that came over us. It had less to do with you than our surprise at discovering a witness to our foolery. You ran off before I could say anything. I couldn't chase you down the stairs without giving us all away. So, I let you go."

She opened her eyes and had the strange sensation that she was meeting theirs through the darkness. "That's your comical secret? I wasn't your quarry, but rather *bawdy pamphlets*?"

She could tell they were shaking their head.

"No," they said. "I mean, yes, but that's not why I brought it up. I thought of Mrs. Pattinson's for another reason. A more general reason. That is—" They hesitated. "The reason of my own general condition."

"Your own . . ." Her voice trailed away as her throat constricted.

"I wanted to kiss you," they said, "then, there, in the window seat. I wanted to make you forget your book, and remember me, when I was away in London. As I remembered you."

The cave was silent.

"For I did remember you," they said. "Always."

She felt shaky and sank down slowly, sitting on her heels. Georgie Redmayne, remembering *her*, in London, remembering *her*, as they cavorted in the parks, spun around the ballrooms, spouted on the stage, every movement followed by eager eyes. Remembering that night at Mrs. Pattinson's, with longing.

Her restless hand brushed something hard, and she started. It was only the lantern.

Only the lantern.

She snatched it up with a cry.

Georgie was the one who snapped the door from its hinges and broke the rest apart, smashing and flattening, until Elf had something like enough to the blade of a shovel.

Even so, the digging was miserable. Slow. Laborious. There was no way to get leverage. She had to rely on her wrists, which burned like fire.

When she finally broke through, she couldn't force herself forward. Her joints had locked, and her hands and feet felt like foreign objects. They didn't obey her commands. Georgie ended up propelling her from behind.

She emerged from the cave coughing, on her belly. She came up on her knees, swaying, too stunned, for those first few ragged breaths, to think. The world was almost as dark above as below. Rain lashed, and thunder shook the trees. The pit was a pond, surface boiling.

Georgie tried to tug her to standing, but she slipped and brought them down on top of her. Their weight knocked the air from her lungs. She was on her back in sucking mud, liquid seeping up around her, face burrowed into their neck. Their body was solid and hot, covering hers completely. Their body was absorbing the rain. It was absorbing the thunder. She could hear the low rumble in their chest. A long moment passed before she realized they were laughing.

"Move." She wiggled beneath them, parting their legs with her thigh, bucking her hips. Their laughter hitched, and they pushed up, hands plunged in the mud. They gazed at her, rain dripping from their hair.

The leaden sky flashed.

Their eyes were the only color. Storm-lit blue against all the streaming dark. Dancing with mirth and mayhem.

"Elf," they began, and wobbled. Suddenly, they were on top of her again.

"Sorry." Their smile burned into her cheek. "Moving is more difficult than I remember."

Her heart thumped in her ears. "You're heavy as a horse."

"Maybe that's why. I definitely can't carry a horse."

"I can assist you."

She couldn't. She was pinned. Georgie touched her along every inch. Her brief struggle pressed her even more snugly against them, creating delicious licks of friction, speeding her pulse.

"Do you want me to kiss you?" Their head raised a fraction.

"Generally?" she asked, but the thunder rolled, and she had to slide her mouth toward their ear. "In general?"

They laughed, shaking their head, flinging more droplets. Lightning arced across the sky, and she gasped. It drew their eyes to her lips.

"I was thinking right now," they said.

"I'm not sure," she breathed. "I'm not sure if my feelings are neutral enough for kissing."

They lowered their face until there was just a whisper of separation. "Are you teasing me?"

"Yes," she said, and tilted up her chin.

Their mouth was wet with rain and carried the warmth of a thousand suns. It made sense when the velvety black behind her eyes went wine dark and then berry red. Georgie kissed her and kissed her, and everything made sense, every mad thing ever done for love, or lust, or whatever this was that braided hot ribbons inside her, that pulled the silk tight, so that a stroke of their tongue shivered all the way down to her belly.

Red was glowing there, in her belly, and between her legs, and behind her eyes, especially behind her eyes. Smears of red, changing shape.

Her lids flew open. Georgie's mouth dragged over her jaw, her throat, and she was blinking against the rain at a flaming treetop.

Hungry sparks.

"My God."

Smoke twisted as it rose, far blacker than the clouds, and the flames bathed Georgie in demonic light as they turned.

"Is that branch . . . ?"

They didn't complete the thought. The branch crashed down, trailing streamers of light. Sparks burst into the air as it hit the ground with a boom and a crackle. Elfreda felt the shudder of the impact and the rush of heat. Fiery leaves writhed less than a yard from her face.

Georgie was on their feet. She shot up, slammed into them, and clung. Their arm came around her waist. Another bolt forked from the clouds. She saw jagged gold reflected in their eyes, and sparks whirling overhead, and she could see them seeing her, every dark region of her body and soul lit with ecstatic terror. She pushed up, and electricity seemed to snap between her mouth and theirs. Both of them gasped into the kiss. The next thunderclap might have been an earthquake. Everything shook. She staggered, and then she was running, blinded by rain, slapped by brambles, holding tight to Georgie's hand.

21

MRS. PEGG SCREAMED when Elfreda led Georgie into the kitchen.

In the firelight, Elfreda could see why. They were caked with mud from head to toe, and she was too.

"I'll mop up these puddles," she promised, looking down at the dirty water gathering by her ruined shoes. Georgie sidled up to the hearth, extending their arms.

"Who's this?" demanded Mrs. Pegg. "A boggart from the rotten fens?"

"Georgie Redmayne." Elfreda blotted her face with a rag, then stepped on it and swiped it back and forth on the floor. "From across the park."

"How do you do," said Georgie, through chattering teeth.

"Hmph." Mrs. Pegg made a doubting noise.

"May I trouble you for a cup of tea?" they asked.

Still muttering about boggarts, Mrs. Pegg put the kettle on the hob and laid the tea things on the table.

"Not with those dirty hands," she said when Elfreda reached for the milk jug. "You're as sorry a sight as that one. What am I to do with you duckies? Always running into trouble. I was about to send Billy out to find you."

"Billy?" Elfreda rounded the table and looked toward the larder. Mrs. Pegg's grandnephew was sitting on the cabbage crate, nibbling a pickled egg.

"Off home with you, Billy." Mrs. Pegg made a shooing motion. "Stop by the manor on the way. Tell them Miss Redmayne is staying the night."

"Staying the night?" echoed Elfreda, just as Georgie said, "I can go, surely."

Mrs. Pegg shot them her quelling look. "And belike catch your death. I'll not hear it. A bath and then bed."

Elfreda bathed first. She was dozing under the covers in her bed when Georgie opened the door to her chamber.

A creak. The glimmer of a candle.

She became fully alert. She became so alert she couldn't move. She became a scientific instrument designed to measure the effects and properties of Georgie Redmayne. She was a barometer registering the precise degree to which Georgie's presence changed the weight of the air in the room, and a telescope focusing on the galaxies hidden behind the sky blue of their eyes, and a thermometer with its sealed liquid expanding and contracting as Georgie . . . hesitated uncomfortably on the threshold.

"Um," they said. "Maybe I shouldn't have . . ."

"Come in." She sat up so quickly her vision sparkled at the edges.

Georgie was still hesitating. "Mrs. Pegg said there aren't any rooms made up for guests."

"There aren't." Her voice was unnaturally high. "We haven't had a guest since Aunt Susan. Her room won't do. Birds are roosting in the rafters." Did this necessitate explanation? "Broken window. Agnes. Papa's armillary sphere." She was leaving out the connections,

but there was no need to *belabor* the explanation. Not when everything she said emerged with such an awkward squeak.

"It won't do," she repeated.

"Mrs. Pegg said I should sleep here. But if you'd prefer, I could go
roost."

Elfreda huffed a laugh, relaxing. "You're too tired to climb up to
the rafters. And sleeping *below* roosting birds is revolting."

Georgie stepped into the room, glancing about with curiosity.
There wasn't much to see. The room was dim even by day, with dark
oak-paneled walls, dark oak floors, bulky oak furniture casting per-
petual shadows.

"Is that Mrs. Pegg's?" she asked, and they looked down at their
nightgown, too short and too wide.

"Yes," they said. "She insisted. It was very generous, and also very
intimidating. I'm relieved she no longer thinks I'm a swamp demon."

They didn't take another step.

Elfreda swallowed. "You'll catch cold if you stand there." She
twitched the counterpane, flipping a corner back.

Their gaze filled with light. They crossed the room in three bounds,
deposited the wildly flickering candle on the table, and swung themself
up onto the bed.

They slid under the covers.

"Are those your feet?" Elfreda gasped. "You're an *ice* demon. Is this
what ice demons do? Drain their victims' warmth with their toes?"

"With their fangs, please. A demon can't attack with their toes.
No one would take them seriously." Georgie attacked. She felt their
mouth on the crook of her neck, then the edges of their teeth.

"Your hair still smells like smoke," she whispered. She'd scrubbed
herself in the tub, washed her hair and wrung it out, and Georgie had
too, but beneath the scent of soap, the scent of smoke lingered, the
strange hot smoke of lightning strikes, and lightning too, and even
thunder.

They lifted their head and lowered their mouth onto hers.

Warmth flowed into her.

"You wanted to do this," she whispered, between kisses, "for years?"

They eased back, hands cradling her face. "Years." They kissed her, one perfect, perfectly self-contained kiss, parted lips, warm glide of tongue. "And years." They kissed her again, gossamer light, a kiss that was mostly heat and breath and made her ache for more. "And years."

"How did you know?" She kissed them.

"It was something I felt. And hoped would go away."

She withdrew far enough to peer into their eyes. "Why?"

"You didn't feel the same. The more I thought of you, the less you seemed to think of me, and the worse. Call it self-preservation."

Her skin rippled with gooseflesh. "That's not why you stopped coming to Twynham?" As soon as she said it, she blushed, waiting for them to mock her presumption.

"In part."

Their toes weren't cold anymore. Her feet were between their feet, her knee between their knees. Their hand moved lazily through her damp hair, then drifted down, stroking from her temple to her jaw.

"But how did you know that you could kiss girls at all?" She was blushing so hotly Georgie could probably detect it with their finger, which was now tracing small circles high on her cheekbone. "I'd never read or heard or seen anything to make me think that kissing wasn't just for . . ."

"Princes and princesses?" They sounded droll. "Husbands and wives? I didn't know. But I knew myself. I knew that certain girls made me feel certain things. So I gave it a try."

"With whom?"

"Jane."

"Which? Never mind." She ducked her head, nestling her face against their throat. "Did you have your wicked way with her?"

"No." They laughed. "It was only kissing. We were twelve."

"But since then?"

"Nothing with Jane."

There had been others, then, in London. She wondered if it was jealousy, this ache in her chest, or simply longing.

"Have you ever been in love?" She whispered it into their skin.

Their throat moved.

"I'm sorry." She rolled away, onto her back. "It seems I'm trying to pry out all your secrets today."

They gathered her to them, settling her head on their shoulder, hooking her leg beneath the knee and drawing it across their thighs.

"If I *were* to fall in love with someone, I'd rather not keep it secret." Their hand was stroking again through her hair.

The gentle, rhythmic touch made her hazy and limp. She curved her arm around them, curled fingers tucked below their ear, knuckles grazing the lobe.

I can't marry you.

She could hear Georgie saying it, by the fishing pond, and remembered how, even then, she'd gone dizzy and hot when they came near to her, when they slanted her that look from beneath their lashes.

She buried her face in their shoulder's hollow. "Neither could you announce it with a banns."

"True enough." They were sardonic. "But if you're wealthy, and landed, and no one has a prick, you and your love can do most anything else."

She suspected her face was red. She was very aware, suddenly, of what she had between her own thighs, the sensitive flesh spread to accommodate the press of their hip.

"I see," she said faintly.

"You can retire to the same bed, every night. There's not a thief-taker who can drag you out, like at the molly house. However wicked your ways." There was a smile in their voice as they said this last.

"The Ladies." She was squeaking again and had to clear her throat. "The Ladies in Llangollen. The ones Miss Poskitt mentioned. You want to live like them."

"When I'm that old, perhaps." They gave a shrug. "I'm in no rush to rusticate. I envision a life of variety, occasion and adventure, big crowds, long voyages."

Her face was cooling. The coarse fabric bunched beneath her cheek had begun to itch. "And your love is along with you?"

"Or I'm along with her."

She tried not to imagine Georgie rowing a boat on a loch in the Orkneys, chattering gaily as they ferried her between cairns. They had something else in mind, of course.

Rain tapped on the roof tiles.

It was late. She was sore, beyond exhausted, incapable of teasing out her emotions. Her muscles hurt, but the feel of Georgie under her, and against her, was like a coating of honey on the nerves, dulling discomfort, tempting her with sweet urges.

"We should sleep," she mumbled, alarmed into wakefulness by the alternate suggestion that had nearly escaped her lips. A plea for something wickeder.

"Mm." Their chest rose and fell on a deep breath. A hand settled heavily on her leg.

She was on the brink of drifting off, draped over them, when they spoke again, their voice soft.

"My mother and father were among the visitors to the Ladies' cottage, before I was born. Mother said they rode very well and showed her particular favor." The hand lazing through Elfreda's hair paused and cupped her head more tightly. "I've often wondered if that visit planted the seed of doubt, for her, about her decision to marry."

Elfreda's eyes opened.

Their heart was beating hard beneath her.

"There *is* a secret," they murmured. "It's not dark, rather the opposite. But it casts a strange shadow on my life all the same."

"Georgie," she whispered, in case they thought she was asleep, in case they were drowsing, unguarded, confessing to something in the night they'd regret in the morning. "You don't have to say anything else."

"I know." Their arms locked around her. "I want to say it. I'll just . . . say it, then. I'll say it. She's alive." Their heart was beating faster. "My mother is alive."

GEORGIE HAD SAID it. The words floated free. *My mother is alive.* There was no taking them back.

"It's not true, the story about the spring tide, that she was swept out to sea. I believed it, though, like everyone. I mourned her. I would sit under the willow by the fishing pond and sob. When you weren't there, that is." They sensed rather than felt Elf's movement, it was so infinitesimal.

"That's how you came upon me reading? You were going to the willow yourself, to . . ."

"I always loved that tree." It had felt odd, and oddly fated, seeing her there, bent over her book. Each time, they'd back away, silently, letting the fronds fall into place.

"Your mother . . ." There was confusion in Elf's voice, a hesitant hope, an undercurrent of apprehension. But how was anyone to greet such news, the details as yet obscure? And even then.

"She might *not* be alive, I suppose." Anything could have happened in the decade since she'd disappeared. "All I know is that she didn't die in Scotland that day. She wrote my father a letter, afterward, saying she was sorry. Saying goodbye. I found it in his study, in London, but not until *he'd* died. I couldn't ask him to explain."

Ask him to explain. How reasonable it sounded. How measured. They'd wanted to scream in their father's mild-eyed, sweet-tempered face.

"Most of the letter's illegible," they said, when they were sure none of that shattered fury would poison their tone. "He must have held it over the candle, then changed his mind and waved out the flame. But I could read enough."

Elf was caressing them, fingers moving lightly, soothingly, along their collarbone. It felt better than good. It felt like a miracle, her tender touch, the way she fit against them. "There was only the one letter?"

"Only one." They stared up blankly at the bed's carved tester, shadow-formed faces leering down in the struggling candlelight. "I tore his study apart. That one letter—I found it by accident." They exhaled shakily, aiming for self-deprecatory humor but landing instead on something bitter: "I can't find a damn thing on purpose."

"You can," said Elf at once. "What about those pages of my grandmother's manuscript?"

"I knocked those pages from your hands during an attack by a disgruntled ungulate, which I caused." They laughed and were grateful for the easing of pressure in their chest. "I don't deserve credit for finding things I made go missing in the first place." They thought of her amulet and grimaced. They thought of their mother and shut their eyes.

They hadn't made *her* go missing. She'd spent her days, and nights, mostly with her friends, with Lady Beverly, but she'd enjoyed their company in bursts. She'd liked to ride with them, fast, taking fences. She'd applauded with unfeigned enthusiasm when they acted out their favorite scenes from *The Busie Body* in the drawing room. They hadn't driven her off. But they hadn't given her reason enough to stay.

"What about the hoard?" asked Elf. "The hoard of the Great Heathen Army? That's a damn thing."

"We haven't found it yet." They opened their eyes.

"We will, though."

"You believe that? Despite this past week?" Of course she did. Once she committed herself, she was tenacious. They sighed.

"Yes," they said. "We will find the hoard of the Great Heathen Army."

Elf's fingers stilled. "You want to find *her*. That's what you meant."

They rocked their head slowly from side to side. "I want her to find *me*. And nothing could be easier, if *she* wanted. I'm right where she left me."

Elf hugged them, her grip so sudden and so fierce, they lost their breath. She was far too small to have any right to be so strong.

"I'm sorry," she said.

"No reason to be sorry." They grunted. "She's alive. It's reason to rejoice."

"Yes," said Elf. "But it can hurt too." She hesitated. "Her leaving."

For an instant, the hurt was there, tearing through them. They were glad she couldn't see their face.

"Shall I tell you why she left? It's all right." They arrested her quick gesture of demurral with a squeeze to the shoulder. "I started down this road." They could hardly believe they had. But they'd taken the first step in the cave, another in the lightning, and here in the dark with Elf, safe in her arms, continuing felt imperative.

"It was love," they said. "She paid the fisherwoman for her lies and absconded with Lady Beverly. How can I grudge her that happiness?" They cleared sudden hoarseness from their throat. "My father never grudged her anything. He was classical himself. Theirs was the sort of marriage I thought to have with Phipps, only they saw fit to reproduce."

"They told you all this?" Elf lifted her head.

"There wasn't any need. I kissed Jane, and the scales fell from my eyes."

Her eyes had a faint shine, reflecting the light of that dying candle. "But why would your mother abscond, if she could see Lady Beverly within the confines of your home?"

Anne's claim marched through their mind.

"The compromise was too great," they said. "That's how I felt as well, with Phipps. I realized sooner than she did."

She lowered her head slowly. "Does the Major know?"

"No one does. I'm afraid to tell Harry. What if he tried to track her down? I thank God I found the letter before he did. My father built model ships. His study was filled with them. The *King George* was my favorite, a cutter. When I was eight or nine, I painted over the lettering. Made it the *King Georgie*. He never noticed." A laugh caught in their chest. "I was moving the ship to my bedchamber, and the letter slipped out. He'd tucked it into the mainsail."

"King Georgie." Elf surprised them by kissing their cheek. A moment later, she was snuggling into their side. "You cried under the willow tree because your mother was dead. Did you cry when you discovered she wasn't?"

"No," they said, too sharply. "I regret the circumstances. I regret the method. But I respect her choice."

Elf made a small sighing sound of acknowledgment, if not affirmation.

When they spoke again, their voice was thin as smoke. "I don't wish that she stayed. I only wish that she'd trusted me. Or that my father had trusted me. I'd imagined they understood that *I* understood, about them. And that they understood what that understanding signified, about me."

"Maybe they did trust you." Elf's speech was slow and almost too soft to hear. "Maybe he was waiting for the right time to tell you. Maybe she still is."

Before they could respond, she was asleep.

They lay awake, listening to Elf as she breathed. The tenderness ballooning in their heart made its wall too thin and fragile. They half hoped the feeling would vanish at dawn like fairy orbs and field dew. They half hoped it was a spell. That the spell would break before their heart did.

22

D AWN CAME AND went. When Georgie woke, the room was gray with dingy light, less to do with residual cloudiness than with the grime on the windowpanes.

They were alone. Elf had set a pair of house slippers by the door—her father's, or grandfather's, perhaps. This thoughtfulness did nothing to shrink or toughen their too large, too tender heart.

They stepped into the slippers, big and worn to holes at the heels, and shuffled to the staircase. The number of steps seemed to have trebled overnight. All their joints felt like rusty hinges, and they descended haltingly, legs moving, not automatically, but by argument.

They couldn't remember the way to the kitchen and hobbled along a series of unpromising corridors. Tapestries puffed dust. Strands of spider silk trailed from the webbed ceiling. The air was stubbornly cold. It would take a great retinue of servants working around the clock to reverse Marsden Hall's long-unchecked natural tendency toward disintegration. Mr. Marsden didn't seem to worry that his daughters risked constant sneezing fits, fevers, chilblains, flea infestations, and spider bites, but there'd come a point at which this neglect jeopardized his collections. Would he act then? Maybe not, given that the books were already getting chewed up by rats.

They turned a corner into the kitchen.

"Ha," they said. "What do you know."

"There you are!" Agnes greeted them excitedly. "Will you join me for breakfast?" She was sitting at the end of the table, a large strawberry positioned at the center of her otherwise empty plate. As Georgie stared, she picked up her knife and fork and began to slice it like a sirloin. She forked a red sliver daintily into her mouth. It was no larger than her pinkie nail, but she chewed and chewed, lips sealed in a half smile.

She seemed to be savoring her self-conscious refinement as much as the strawberry, so they pressed their lips together as well, mirroring her smile, lest they laugh.

Finally, she swallowed. "Beatrice breakfasts each day at noon, on a single strawberry. She says it is a graceful repast."

"It's not a repast at all." They couldn't restrain themself. "It's a strawberry. Is there any bacon? My God, is it noon?"

"Noon," nodded Agnes. "Mrs. Pegg took the twins to market in the village, and Elfreda is in the blue room, and I've been waiting here for you, but I'm feeling—I'm feeling awfully faint." She wavered, fingertips to her temple.

"Stay right where you are." Georgie clattered around the kitchen, managing, after several more ambitious efforts, to transform half a loaf of bread into toast.

"Do you know what happened to my gown?" they asked, when the toast had done its work and Agnes was crunching with restored animation. "Was it laundered?"

"Cut up for rags." Agnes studied them, looking big-eyed and winsome with her shorn hair. "Is Elfreda your friend now?"

"She is." Georgie nodded matter-of-factly, as though it were merely that, a matter of fact, and not also a matter of dreams and fancies, of yearnings that enchanted reality itself.

Agnes's genuine smile showed charmingly crooked teeth. "Will you write to her from London?"

"I will." Georgie considered the crumbs on their plate, suddenly bereft. They took another piece of toast.

"Will you invite her to go with you?"

"No." Georgie stuffed too much toast into their mouth. Invite Elf? To share a shabby room in a boardinghouse inhabited by singers and dancers, artists and radicals? Perhaps if there was a desk, a place to put her books . . .

"Beatrice hasn't invited *me*." Agnes drooped. "My clothing isn't right for London."

Georgie washed down the toast with a swig of lukewarm tea. "Your gown is lovely. You look like an orchid."

"Do I?" Agnes held up her arms, showing off the pale purple sleeves, which boasted three tiers of flounces. "It *is* lovely. But I wore it to dinner once at Beatrice's and overhead her mother telling Mrs. Alderwalsey that I looked like I'd escaped from a lesser Gainsborough."

Thomas Gainsborough *had* painted ladies in similar attire, in the mid-1700s. All those lace fichus peeping over the low necklines. All those embellished stomachers.

Georgie coughed. "No one who wasn't trying too hard to be witty could ever compare you to a *lesser* Gainsborough."

"Thank you." Agnes lowered her arms. "I don't believe the Parkers want *any* Gainsborough with them in London. I hope Aunt Susan sends me some pretty muslin soon, so I can have a gown made. She promised she would, once I turned fourteen, and I *am* fourteen, but perhaps she's confused, because I was born on leap day."

Aunt Susan's well-meant meddling had been rebuffed. No muslin was forthcoming. Knowing the truth, and looking into Agnes's big, guileless eyes, made Georgie squirm in their seat and mentally review the items in their own wardrobe for something that might suit. They hadn't a Season's worth of gowns to donate, and even if they had, the girl would need a modiste. They *could* help her, much more substantially, in a year's time. If they stayed in Twynham themself, learned the ins and outs of the estate, read some agricultural journals, they might come to understand how to manage the land in nonbeastly fashion, to increase profit and prosperity for everyone. They'd turn *five* and twenty in the best possible circumstances. They could let something less shabby in London for the Season and invite Elfreda *and* Agnes, and Rosalie and Anne, and ask along, too, as chaperone, an older woman who'd shop and gamble and drive about and largely ignore the goings-on. Mrs. Alderwalsey?

Clearly, they'd gone staring mad.

They were staring, they realized, at Agnes, who didn't seem disconcerted in the least.

"I do have something for *you* to wear," she said, and hopped up. "Follow me."

She flew before them, along corridors and passageways, and up a spiral stair to the room at the top of the tower.

"This is my music room," she said. "And my dressing room."

The room was cluttered with trunks and musical instruments, most of which Georgie couldn't identify, except as oddly shaped guitars and trumpets. They blew into a trumpet until it produced a passably trumpetlike noise, akin to that of a sonorous goose. Meanwhile, Agnes tore through a trunk, heaping the floor with garments.

The garments did not, at first glance, bode well. Rigid, tightly structured gowns sized to a smaller frame. At least nothing crawled visibly with mites.

"This one will fit," said Agnes, holding it up. "Grandpapa's druidic vestment. There are antlers to wear with it."

"The robe will do nicely." Georgie took it. "I'll pass on the antlers."

As they changed, awkwardly, behind a unicorn wall hanging, Agnes strummed upon her lute.

"I don't know any songs," she said. "So I compose my own. This one is called 'Beatrice.'"

Georgie emerged, druidically clad.

The song was melancholy, beautiful, and very, very long. Endless even.

"Bravo." They began clapping.

Agnes stilled her fingers, blushing. "Thank you."

"I should go down to—"

Before they finished speaking, she began to play. "This one is called 'I Have Not Forgot—Has She?'"

"Bravo," they said weakly. "Bravo."

"Thank you. This one is called . . ."

"Would you tell me how to get to the blue room?" they interrupted.

"This one is called 'How to Get to the Blue Room.'" The plaintive strains of the lute once again drifted through the tower room. The melody sounded a great deal like "Beatrice."

Agnes turned to the window, and Georgie backed slowly toward the stairs.

Eventually, they found the blue room. Furniture lined the hall outside, and through the open door, they could see blue walls, and then Elf, dragging an elaborately carved oak armchair across the checkerboard floor.

"What are you doing?" they asked, although it quickly became obvious, what with all the wet rags mounded about. Elf had been mopping. Mopping and moving furniture out of the way of . . .

They looked at the ceiling. "That's not good. Will it stay up like that?"

Thunk.

Elf had let the legs of the chair bang down. She stood beside it, gazing at them with those bottomless eyes, seemingly at a loss for words.

Because of all that had passed between them last night?

Her brows met. "You're wearing Grandpapa's druidic vestment."

Ah. That.

"Yes." They flapped the heavy folds of roughly textured fabric, which flowed over their arms like ungainly wings. "Druids wore pink?"

"Pliny the Elder said they wore white. Something went awry with the laundry." Her smile flashed at them, the smile they'd glimpsed more frequently over these past weeks and wanted to spend forever summoning forth.

Not that they were thinking in those terms. Forever.

The smile had already vanished. "Papa wouldn't want anyone wearing it."

"I'm not just anyone." They stood tall. "I am Georginion, the archdruid, keeper of the sacred oak chair." Her smile returned as they flung their aching body into said sacred chair, pulling her onto their lap, and a moment later, that smile was pressed to their mouth, as her arms circled their neck. She was kissing them through her smile, kissing and kissing them. All at once, Georgie's heart burst. There was pressure in their chest, a sudden release, and they laughed. What had they been afraid of? Too-big feelings sweeping them away. But why fight it? Why not tumble and explode? Elf's kisses were remaking them anyhow. If they weren't smothered in an absurdly voluminous robe, and she weren't buttoned up to the neck in a wool pelisse, and the door wasn't open to the hall, they'd be slotting their mouth over other regions of her body, the very thought of which made them light in the head and heavy between the thighs.

They tilted her face up and kissed her harder. She made the most encouraging sound—a gasping, surprised, excited sort of moan—and their glee was as uncontainable as the other emotions swirling and swelling within. They softened their mouth, moved their tongue with slow, languorous strokes, and felt their heart burst again as she whimpered. They fanned their fingers over her cheekbones and jaw and eased her back. Her eyes were heavy lidded, and her lips were swollen, and she was still smiling—no, *newly* smiling. It was a smile they'd never seen before. Lovely and debauched.

"Just wait," they murmured darkly, without realizing they'd spoken aloud, and watched a blush tinge the crests of her cheeks, and a hint of uncertainty creep into her gaze.

"So." They cleared their throat. "Next task. Should I mop?"

They mopped. They mopped, moved furniture, and helped Elf empty the bookcase. They noted poetry volumes and novels mixed in with the lethally dull atlases and histories.

"Grandmama's," explained Elf. "This was her favorite room." She turned a circle, frowning at its gutted and precarious state. "This is where she wrote, and read, and took her tea. I don't think she felt welcome in the library. Grandpapa made it his domain, and then Papa. Her desk was right there."

"You miss her," they observed, hands tucked into the gaping sleeves of the robe.

"Many years have gone by." Elf looked down, but not before they glimpsed the tears in her eyes. She took a few steps. "The sofa was here. She encouraged me to sit beside her and read too, even though I always interrupted with questions. Sometimes she'd read aloud, or we'd play Game of the Goose. Just us, the two of us." She glanced at Georgie, then back at where the sofa wasn't. "My mother kept to her bedchamber. And I kept away from it. Noise disturbed her."

That Mrs. Marsden had been, for over a decade before she died, afflicted with ill health was a fact bruited about the neighborhood.

"It was rheumatic fever?" they asked carefully.

"Is that what everyone says?" Elf pressed her interlaced fingers to her chin, eyes still fixed on the floor. "It might have been. We didn't talk about it. Papa didn't." She corrected herself. "Grandmama said once that Mother felt low, but not like I did when something made me sad. That it was different. There was a weight on her, an invisible weight, so it required all her strength even to breathe. She was kind to me when she did come down, but . . . distant."

Elf had never spoken of her mother in Georgie's presence.

She seemed suddenly distant herself, so they put an arm around her and drew her close. She pressed her face to their neck.

"I wish I'd tried harder."

Georgie stroked her hair. "To do what?"

"I don't know. To bear some of the weight."

"How could you have? If it was invisible, like your grandmother said?"

Elf inhaled and drew away. She'd spent all morning trying as hard as she could to mitigate the damage to this well-loved room. Clearly, she'd bear the collapsing ceiling on her shoulders, if such a thing were possible.

Did she see the irony? Asking for more weight, when what she carried already was enough to crush?

"I've been wondering," she said, before they could figure out the way to put their thoughts into words. "Do you have your mother's letter with you, in Twynham? Would you show it to me?"

They tensed. They'd been aware, of course, that she'd return, at some point, to the subject of *their* mother. It was inevitable after their dramatic disclosure. Regardless, her request caught them unprepared. They'd had time to get used to the idea that their mother was alive. But they hadn't had time to get used to the idea that someone else knew, that *Elf* knew, and was forming her own opinions, charting a course of action. In the light of day, they felt exposed, guilty even, for betraying their mother, or perhaps, paradoxically, on their mother's behalf.

This was all too fresh.

"Show it to you," they said gruffly. "Why?"

A crease in her forehead acknowledged this gruffness, but her gaze didn't waver. "You told me the letter was barely legible. I have experience reading all sorts of barely legible texts. Perhaps I can fill in the gaps."

Instead of shaking their head, they lowered it and rested their brow on Elf's brow. She curled her fingers in the robe. Slowly, their spine relaxed, and they folded over her more naturally.

"Thank you," they said. "But you won't ascertain where she went from the letter."

They could feel the flutter of her lashes. "Maybe there's more about *why* she went."

"I know why." Their mother had chosen Lady Beverly over everyone and everything else, without any compromise whatsoever. "I know all there is to know."

Her fingers clutched at the robe. She wanted to argue, but instead, she exhaled and released her grip.

They straightened. "And now?" They aimed for a lighter tone. "Shall we go get a carpenter to patch up the roof?"

Her beautiful mouth had that downward turn. "Papa won't allow Mr. Hibbert through the door."

Their mouth twisted too. Mr. Marsden had scattered his petty rules all over Elf's life like pins, making every step hazardous as she staggered under burdens that were his by right. But all they said, mildly, was "Your father's not here."

Elf hugged herself. "He won't want to pay for it. Once he returns, he'll yell about not getting blood from a stone and rip up the bill, and . . ."

"Does he want the ceiling to come down with the next rain?" Georgie interjected, less mildly. "He *has* to pay. And what's his quibble with Hibbert?" The man was a master builder and a model of rectitude.

Elf twisted a dark lock that snaked down her neck, fallen loose from her messy chignon. "It's to do with St. Alcmund's."

Again with St. Alcmund's. "Why such scurrilousness associated with a bloody old church?" No one even went to services at St.

Alcmund's. It was less a church than a ruin. All Souls was newer, bigger, the *church* church. A moment later, they remembered who they were talking to.

"Oh." They frowned. "Of course. It's *old*. That's why."

Elf nodded. "St. Alcmund's was founded in the year seven hundred. It's one of the few Saxon churches to have survived the conquest unaltered. For centuries, it served as an ossuary, but the bones were removed in . . ."

Seven hundred. Saxon church. Elf was going on about bones, but Georgie wasn't listening. They wanted to shout, to dance.

Elf fell silent. Her look was quizzical.

"Georgie?"

They kissed her. Any excuse. And this was more than an excuse. This was a cause for celebration.

"Georgie?" She was breathless now, as well as quizzical, but she took the hand they offered and went willingly, with light steps, as they pulled her, cackling, from the room.

23

ST. ALCMUND'S?" ELFREDA had missed something crucial. She turned to Georgie, who was giving her a significant look, arching their dark brows. She turned back to the church, bloody old, yes, and small, and unprepossessing. To the uninitiated, it appeared an unlikely focal point for a village war, albeit a war that consisted primarily of *damn your eyes* and spittle. As Georgie's destination, it bewildered in the extreme.

While walking with them, arm in arm, over the springy meadow grass, she'd begun to suspect they were leading her to a field of buttercups in a secluded dell. They'd grinned mysteriously every time she'd asked where they were bound and peppered her with questions of their own, questions about druid lore. Grandpapa hadn't raised a dragon, but, according to Papa, he *had* raised a snow-white pig that marched with him through the standing stones, garlanded with anemones. With Georgie laughing and goading her on, she'd revealed that the pig also told fortunes, at which point Georgie had to hold her up, she was laughing so hard herself. *And your grandmother was the fanciful one?* The honeysuckle was blooming profusely, perfuming the air. The storm had blown by, and the sun felt delicious. She'd slammed the door in her mind on the blue room, on her worries, on everything but the day. When they'd reached Redmayne Manor, she'd wondered if the bower of bliss was journey's end, but Georgie had gone inside, swapped the druidic vestment for a walking dress, and then driven her to the village in a gig. They drove at least as well as they rowed, and bowling along the muddy lane was a pleasure.

The inn? The green? Where?

"St. Alcmund's?" she repeated now. "I don't understand."

Georgie passed into the churchyard, with its sprawling yews and tilted gravestones, and stood in the deep green shade. She followed, tingles moving up and down her spine as her eyes roamed the stones. Georgie grasped her hands.

"*Within my depths,*" they recited, "*the shadows play. And yet there is light at my mouth and water that brings life.*"

Her stomach fluttered at their touch, and her brain rebelled.

Kiss. Wasn't it always *kiss* when it came to Georgie and riddles?

She glanced around. St. Alcmund's stood in the heart of the village, just off the high street, but the curved walls enclosing the grounds, and the large churchyard, and the ancient trees made it feel remote. No one would see.

She stepped toward them, pressed up through her toes. The look of surprise that crossed their face halted her forward motion.

"Kiss," she muttered, heels coming back to earth.

Their laugh shook their shoulders.

"Font," they said, and backed her up against the nearest tree, planted their hands on either side of her head, and kissed her, mouth moving hot on hers. Too soon, they broke away, and twirled. "Font! Baptismal font. It's a riddle written by nuns, after all. When babies are baptized in the waters of a font, they're given new life in Christ. And Christ is the light. The nuns hid the hoard beneath a font."

She shook her head, kiss befogged, dizzy, the tree's trunk keeping her upright. "I'm not so sure." She wasn't sure of anything, truth be told. Georgie had come up with a new possibility, a location, plausible if not probable, but the urge to drag them off into the buttercups was still rolling through her in waves. *Tomorrow for the hoard.*

Appalled, she focused on the reasonable objection. "The Northmen looted churches. Hiding a hoard of items looted *from* churches *in* a church—it's . . ."

"Ingenious," supplied Georgie. "Why look beyond the cross on the altar?" Their sparkling eyes searched her face and clouded. "Don't tell me there's no font."

Obviously, her face was communicating distress. Distress she absolutely shouldn't feel. "There's certainly a font."

"Hooray." Georgie strode down the path that wound toward the church's keyhole-shaped door. She watched them walk away. Mortifying, that she'd hoped to linger, among buttercups, while they'd kept their attention fixed on their goal. Treasure. London.

"I've never been inside," they said when she caught up to them. "It looks more solid than I remember."

"And less Saxon." Her response was instantaneous. "The north porticus was reinforced with buttresses."

"Oh, no," Georgie teased. "Not buttresses. The horror."

She wrinkled her nose at them. "The buttresses are innocent. But they don't belong on a Saxon church."

"That's what you think? Or what your father thinks?"

"We agree on the buttresses. However, I'm unconvinced that Sir Hugh and Mrs. Alderwalsey are vandals, or that Mr. Hibbert merits rat torture."

"Rat torture. I should hope you're unconvinced." They linked her elbow, fitted her snugly to their side. "What *should* happen, in your opinion, to a church like this? Should it crumble?"

"Ideally, no." Elfreda looked up at it. "I'd rather someone stabilize the church than let it fall to pieces. But not through so many insertions of new materials and styles that the building dies."

How strangely easy it was to speak with Georgie about what

mattered to her. In their presence, she said things she'd never gotten the chance to say, things she'd barely articulated to herself.

"A building can die," they said, musingly, "when it loses its connection to what it was?"

She met their eyes. "The stains of age on a stone, the divots worn by centuries of feet or fingers—they create something like a voice."

They were smiling at her, not a dazzling smile, a vague smile, a little misty. A lump formed in her throat. Were they feeling nostalgic already? This golden day already behind them? They'd always remembered her. They *would* remember her. From miles and miles away.

"Will you do the honors?" They said it with an odd formality.

She tore her gaze from them, separated their arms, and pushed open the church door.

The nave was empty, narrow, with high, blank walls. The only light slanted from two tiny windows set high overhead.

Georgie moved into it, blanched face floating in darkness, and then out again, footsteps muted, whispering on the stone.

She said nothing as they wandered into the chancel. Finally, she shook herself, and called out.

"It's over here." She crossed to the font, set just inside the main entrance, badly decayed and recently blocked off. The basin was about three feet deep, devoid of ornament, the pedestal knee-high, carved with a simple geometric design.

She peered into the basin—dry, of course—and her skin tightened at the imagined cold, the phantom cries. How many lives now over had begun right here?

The thick air stirred as Georgie came to stand beside her. They laid their hands on the font's stone lip.

"So this is it," they said, voice low. "A thousand years ago, a baby was born in Twynham, and dipped in this font. And some Saxon girl, his older sister, felt dull during the service, and cut off another girl's braid—with a knife, probably. I doubt Saxons had grape scissors."

Elf's laugh was also low. She put her hands on the font. Georgie was joking, and yet she could detect the note of wonderment.

"Vanished like foam," they whispered, and with a start she recognized her own words. "Those Saxon girls have vanished. And yet the generations go on."

Her fingers bumped theirs.

They looked at her through the shadows. "These walls heard them, and us too, and who knows who else, years from now, if they're still standing."

She nodded. Only their fingers touched, and the light from their eyes. It was a kind of touch, that blue shining into her.

"I'm going to slide the font over." They adjusted their position. "To see if there's anything beneath."

She nodded again, anticipation prickling down her spine. The floor was stone, but it could have been dug out, the font positioned over the hole, lidding the precious contents.

Georgie drew a breath and pulled, fingers flattening inside the basin. The font didn't budge. She gripped as best she could and tugged with them. Something audible happened, stone grating on stone.

"Nearly there," they said, and pulled harder, leaning back.

"No." She let go, but it was too late. The basin was moving but not the pedestal. They hadn't been carved as one piece, and stupid, stupid of her not to have thought.

And not to push. She needed to push. To counter gravity, which had begun to do its work. She flung her weight against the basin, her pulse gone wiry, her underarms slicked by sudden sweat. Muscles she'd strained yesterday began instantly to scream, and a sound escaped her, not unlike a scream itself. Something hooked her around the waist—hard—and she went over sideways, the blow of her body against the floor cushioned by Georgie, who sprawled beneath her.

The next noise was a crack as loud as a cannon.

Her insides flinched. She extricated her limbs, crawled from Georgie onto unforgiving stone.

"It's not broken!" She patted the basin everywhere in time with her erratic heartbeats, all but sobbing with relief. "It's not broken."

Further noises turned her head.

A thump, a rattle, a creak, a booming voice . . .

"What's going on in there?"

Georgie bolted across the nave, shoulder smacking the door just in time to prevent it flying open.

"Thank heavens," they grunted. "We thought no one would ever find us. The door is stuck."

"Who is that?"

Elfreda recognized the voice. She stumbled over to Georgie.

"Georgie Redmayne," they said, and before she could stop them: "Elfreda Marsden."

"Miss Marsden." The voice at the door was perceptibly colder.

"Sir Hugh." Elfreda cast a wild glance at the toppled font. *She* was now the vandal. Papa would judge this as harshly as marriage to the Major.

I have no such daughter.

"The door is stuck," she confirmed, adding her shoulder to it, although the lie only forestalled the inevitable.

"Did your father put you up to this?" asked Sir Hugh. "The committee has voted to move ahead with the repairs to the chancel arch. We will not be delayed."

"My father is opening barrows in the Peak." This was the truth, but her false brightness made it sound like a lie.

"I asked Miss Marsden to show me the church." Georgie piped up. "I'm only lately returned to the neighborhood and was keen to admire all that had previously been lost to decay."

"There is much to admire." Sir Hugh spoke like a man who'd just inflated his chest.

"Indeed," said Georgie.

"I was sorry to hear about your father."

"Thank you," said Georgie.

"And when should we expect your brother's return?"

Elfreda crept to the font and dropped into a crouch. She grabbed onto the basin. Hopeless. It was utterly hopeless. She and Georgie couldn't *lift* the thing, not with all the time in the world.

". . . sometimes swells after a rain," Sir Hugh was saying. "I believe it has jammed. Stand back, my dear."

Elfreda scurried to the door, bracing herself alongside Georgie. The door jolted and began to leap in its frame.

"Sir Hugh!" A shrill salutation made the leaping cease. "You're behaving like a March hare. What's come over you?"

"Mrs. Alderwalsey." Sir Hugh's voice became muffled. Presumably, he'd moved away from the church to address her.

Elfreda sagged. Was the entire restoration committee convening? Would the vicar turn up next? Lord Fawcett? Her forehead felt damp.

"Can you hear what they're saying?" whispered Georgie, ear pressed to the door.

She shook her head.

"We can tell them we found it like that."

She shook her head.

"Should we try to move the pedestal too? Seeing as we're in a pickle regardless."

She shook her head. "The pedestal isn't Saxon. If the hoard was beneath the font, someone else discovered it centuries ago."

"I'm sorry." They looked pained. "I've gotten us into a scrape."

"I got us into one too," she admitted. "Let's consider it even."

"*Even?* You think this compares with live burial?"

There came a sharp rap on the door.

"Sir Hugh has gone for help," announced Mrs. Alderwalsey. "I gave him explicit instructions, so there is every probability of success.

Left to his own devices, he is indecisive and dawdles. It is very vexatious. Never play chess with Sir Hugh. You might as well watch the grass grow." A pause. Then another sharp rap. "Say 'How do you do, Mrs. Alderwalsey,' so I know I am not speaking to a door."

"How do you do, Mrs. Alderwalsey," chorused Elfreda and Georgie.

"How do you do," said Mrs. Alderwalsey.

"What sort of help is coming?" asked Georgie.

"Charles Peach," said Mrs. Alderwalsey. "I passed him on my drive. He was pulling that rascally Mr. Hawthorne out of the ferns by the packhorse bridge. I believe they'd had an altercation. Both were disordered in their dress, red in the face, and panting furiously."

Georgie made a strangled sound.

"You would rather not hear of him," said Mrs. Alderwalsey, sagely. "But see the consolation: our Peach is the doughtiest fellow in the parish. Mr. Hawthorne won't be making quite so bold after the encounter."

"Mmm," managed Georgie.

"What's keeping Sir Hugh?" Mrs. Alderwalsey rapped a third time. "I should drive after him. If Mrs. Roberts arrives before I've returned, tell her to go home, there's been an emergency, but you're not privy to the details."

"Aren't *we* the emergency?" asked Georgie, but Mrs. Alderwalsey's chuckle had already faded.

Elfreda stepped away from the door.

"In the ferns," murmured Georgie. "I say, Phipps."

Elfreda blushed. "Are you sure? It might have been an altercation."

"Sometimes love is war." Their grin was wicked. "Hearts are breaking in the House of Commons."

She shook herself. "Quickly."

The moment she knelt again at the basin the futility struck her anew. She and Georgie grappled with it, panting. It lay on its side, and they managed to tip it upright, but that was all.

"We can't lift it." She put her face in her hands.

"We can't," agreed Georgie. "But perhaps . . ."

"What?" She looked up.

"Perhaps we can *levitate* it."

"Are you joking?"

"I once saw four debutantes levitate a drunk duke to the ceiling using just their pinkies. He wasn't a small duke either."

"You are joking." She gnawed at her lip with frustrated hurt. This wasn't a joke to her. "My father won't see the humor. He'll see that I've done something detrimental, to the church, and to his reputation with the committee, and that I'm foolish, unfit for a fellowship. It's bad enough when I seem like a silly daughter, but one day he might not own me as his daughter at all."

"What a loss that would be," said Georgie softly, hands palm up on their knees. "For him."

Her laugh was short and depreciatory.

"All these conditions on his love and aid," continued Georgie, "they're not fair to you. I recognize that you depend on him for many things. I hope your self-worth isn't one of those things. Your sense of who you are. And what you deserve."

She inhaled and realized she'd unwittingly mimicked their posture, hands palm up on her knees. Suddenly, gazing at them, in the dim church, she felt peace welling in her chest, clear and refreshing as water.

"And I'm not joking," they said. "Will you try?"

Levitation. She looked at the basin, a heavy tub of gray stone, immovable.

"I will try," she said.

Georgie sidled over so they were crouching directly opposite, the basin between. "Lay your palms on the side, like so."

She laid her palms on the stone.

"Light as a spirit," they began, holding her gaze. "Light as the air. Light as a spirit. Light as the air."

"Truly?" She removed her hands.

"It's a chant."

"I could tell."

"Chants are powerful. We have to chant in unison."

She laid her palms on the font. "Do you think this is going to work?"

Their gaze was steady.

"Light as a spirit," they said. "Light as the air."

She joined the chant. "Light as a spirit. Light as the air."

It didn't seem that something powerful was happening, but rather the reverse. Her muscles relaxed, and her voice and her breathing found a slow rhythm, a rhythm that blended with Georgie's rhythm. Their voice was in her ears, in her head, in her lungs, in her mouth. *Light as a spirit. Light as the air.* She was chanting, and so were they, and then she was exhaling, and so were they, and they were both of them lifting—levitating—the font, up and up and up, with no effort at all, guiding it as it sailed onto the pedestal.

The crunch it made as it landed belied the featherlight transit.

"By Jove, he's strong," said Sir Hugh as the door swung open, Charles Peach blocking the daylight. "Barely laid a finger on it!"

"*DID* YOU THINK it would work?" asked Elfreda when she and Georgie were rolling along the lane again, the bay horse at a gentle trot.

"No." Georgie laughed. "Absolutely not."

Elfreda leaned into their side, enjoying the feel of them and the way the wind played with her hair.

"Charles Peach seemed happy," she said.

Georgie tipped back their head, sending their laughter up into the air like birdsong. "Happy? My God, he has *dimples*. Who would have imagined?" A few moments later, they sobered. "His present happiness doesn't absolve me of my responsibility, of course. As a landowner."

She angled them a look. "Maybe it's not all bad, that you don't have your chalices yet and can't race back to London."

They nodded. "There are things I should attend to here."

She nodded.

They looked at her full-on. "And things I want to attend to."

The glint in their eyes made her stomach flip.

They could tell. A smirk edged their lips as they turned back to the lane. "Not all bad. Not bad at all."

24

RESPONSIBILITY. GEORGIE HAD always tried to evade it. Circumstance had doled them far fewer small responsibilities than was the norm. They didn't have to build their own fire, or sweep their own ashes, launder their own linens, or boil their own eggs. But the big responsibilities—every class had its version, and for all classes, so far as Georgie could tell, the responsibilities were starkly divided.

Masculine. Feminine.

You were a man, and so you perpetuated the family name, and added to its glory through your endeavors in the public sphere. You were a woman, and so you created sweet order within the household your husband ruled, and tended to the children whose moral development was your special charge.

That division—the circumscribed choices implied—made Georgie feel queasy, viscerally unwell. Man or woman. Husband or wife. Father or mother. They felt well, felt *full*, when they imagined themself between and beyond. But in practice, those options didn't exist. Not wanting to choose required a constant dance, a light-footed way of living premised on constant escapes from assumption, convention, obligation. And responsibility, which was composed of all of these.

The morning after St. Alcmund's, they drank their coffee in the breakfast room, looking out the window at the garden. Phipps hadn't come down. They were completely alone. Once, their father would have sat to their right and dawdled smilingly over a plate of kippered herring, their mother across from him, talking horses. Harry would have sat to their left, dripping egg on whatever chapbook he was reading, inevitably one that recounted the exploits of a highwayman. And they would have been bouncing in their chair, interrupting everyone with cheerful prattle. Showing off. Earning chuckles from their father, ripostes from their mother, eye rolls from Harry. A united family, and a jolly one. A family that, behind closed doors, flouted society's rules. And maybe, when it came to their mother, even its own rules.

Which rules would *they* break in their life, and which would they follow? Being responsible to the people they loved, to the principle of love more broadly—they didn't balk at that. But what would it entail?

Maybe they'd taken evasion too far.

Maybe it was time to think.

Thinking, they finished their coffee. Still thinking, they walked to the steward's house to pay an unannounced visit to Mr. Fletcher.

Mr. Fletcher wasn't at home.

Elf was.

The rest of the day unspooled in a treasure hunt that looked indistinguishable from kissing on a slow stroll through the woods.

During the week that followed, the routine was thus:

Georgie woke, breakfasted while paging through Arthur Young's *Course of Experimental Agriculture*, then met Elf at Holywell Rock to commence the slow kissing and slower strolling. When the pretense of progress toward the hoard couldn't be maintained a minute longer, Elf went off to Marsden Hall. Georgie walked or rode around the estate, talking to tenants, whose complaints turned over and over afterward in their head, like milk in a churn. Sometimes Phipps accompanied them, because Charles Peach had only so much daylight to spare for illicit rendezvous.

In the evenings, they drove the gig to Marsden Hall, usually with cheesecakes, and passed an hour in the library with Elf, and Agnes, Hilda, Matilda, and Grendel, until Elf sent everyone to bed, which only rarely succeeded without her having to transport twins and dog bodily to the nursery.

On this particular night, Agnes floated up to bed early to finish a letter to Beatrice, and the twins fell asleep in front of the fire.

"I finally spoke with the steward, Fletcher," reported Georgie, wedged with Elf in Mr. Marsden's throne-like reading chair. "Caught him as he was going out his front door."

"And?" Elf sat sideways, mostly on top of them, legs tucked beneath her. The position of her shoulder made it difficult to breathe, or their swollen heart was to blame, bigger by the day.

"He's a Kentishman. He's got this *chin*, this memorable chin." Georgie thrust theirs out. "I remembered it."

"You'd met him before?"

"Once before," they said. "In Kent. My father had a dear friend, Mr. Owlett." They paused. *Darling of my heart* was what their father had called Mr. Owlett in private, but it didn't seem right to share an eavesdropped endearment. "Mr. Owlett had a nephew," they continued, "a scapegrace. He was studying to be a solicitor but got sent down. He went to live with Mr. Owlett, and it came to light that he'd fled from enormous gaming debts. Mr. Owlett settled them. He started playing cards again, with much greater luck. Suspicious luck. Someone went so far as to call him a cheat, and then no one in Higham would receive him. Mr. Owlett brought him to see my father—that's when we met—and afterward, I stopped hearing about him."

Elf stirred. "Because your father made him steward *here*."

"A favor for Mr. Owlett." They sighed. "Father was an optimist. Probably he told himself young Fletcher just needed the right opportunity. Probably he intended to keep a close eye on the accounts and records. None of us expected . . . It was sudden, you know. I wasn't there. But Mr. Owlett, he told me one moment my father was standing on the lawn, and the next, he was on the ground. And it was over. He didn't suffer. That was the same week as Waterloo."

As the pause drew out, Elf's fingers threaded through theirs.

They lifted their intertwined hands and brushed them against their lips.

"Harry can't keep a close eye on anything he's not trying to shoot. He's a soldier, a sportsman, a *hero*. No interest in humdrum details. And he's been away from England so long. I'm sure he doesn't ask questions, especially given that the news is always good. For us. Fletcher assured me that the income from the land is increasing. But I *have* been asking questions, of the farmers, and their lives are only getting harder."

If anything, the picture Robert Peach had painted was too rosy. Fletcher demanded that tenants bear the entire cost of repairs, labor *and* materials. And invested nothing in improvements. He raised rents whenever possible. He'd discontinued their father's drainage project.

During his brief conversation with Georgie, he'd spoken in a soft, servile voice and humbly deflected every query. It was less a conversation than an exercise in trying to pin down a cloud.

Begging your pardon, he'd murmured after only a few minutes, looking sadly at his watch. *As much as I sincerely wish it were otherwise, I must be off.*

"What are you going to do?" Elf twisted to look at them.

Slowly, they lifted their gaze to the ceiling. Write to Harry, already at his wit's end with them? Write to Mr. Owlett, well rid of his charge?

"I don't know yet." They started as a vise closed around their ankle. "What in the . . . ?" It was only Matilda.

"Is there more cheesecake?" she asked.

After the twins had finished the cheesecake, and been deposited in the nursery, right before Georgie turned at the base of the stairs to depart for the night, Elf shook her head, as though she'd arrived at a hard reckoning.

"What?" they asked.

"The hoard," she said, with palpable reluctance. "We're wasting our time."

A sinking feeling threatened to pull Georgie's stomach down into their feet.

"We've been a bit remiss." They couldn't help but look at her lips.

"That's not the main issue." Her cheeks were turning pink. "There's too much guesswork. Conjecture nested within conjecture. We might as well search for a pot of gold at the end of a rainbow. I had to try. But now I have to remember my priorities."

They frowned in confusion.

"The bluff. I'm going to start digging on the bluff again." She reached for their hand and squeezed it, apologetically. "I received a response from Papa. The only workman he'll sanction in the blue room is the original workman."

"Who is . . . ?" Their brows went up.

"Dead," she said, wryly. "This is a medieval hall."

"Right."

She released their hand and gripped her own elbows. "And he's extending the tour another week. I *know* the Northmen camped on the bluff. I found one artifact. Perhaps I'll find another while he's still with the Barrow Prince. If I dig."

The glance she gave them was apprehensive. "I'm sorry. I understand if—"

"I'll dig too," they interrupted, grinning with relief. She didn't want to stop spending time with them. She wanted to shift her efforts from the hoard to the camp. "I'm a dab at shoveling. Remember?"

"There's nothing in it for you," she protested. Her eyes, though, had begun to shine. "If we're lucky, we'll find some nails or buckles."

We. She'd said *we.* It was decided.

They drew her toward them and kissed her mouth. "Wonderful. Nails and buckles."

And this. More of this.

They could feel her smile, and a thrill curved their lips in answer as they pulled her nearer still. She wanted *this* as much as they did, at least as much as she wanted those nails and buckles, and that knowledge flooded them with a triumph so intense it felt perilously close to surrender.

THE NEXT MORNING, *The Derby Mercury* was on the table.

"The fourth of June?" They snatched it up. "How is it the fourth of June?"

Bagshaw was just leaving the breakfast room and paused at the door. "It is the fifth of June. The paper arrived yesterday afternoon."

They sat down hard. "It is my birthday."

"Many happy returns," said Bagshaw.

"Do I have any letters?" they asked.

"No," said Bagshaw.

"Will you tell Cook I'm having two guests for dinner?"

"Including Lord Phillip?" asked Bagshaw.

Georgie frowned. Phipps. Was he even a guest at this point? He was just . . . *here.* For better or worse. "Two in addition to Lord Phillip."

Bagshaw inclined his head. The door shut behind him.

"I am four and twenty years old," Georgie told the empty room, experimentally. The clock ticked back at them. They ate their eggs and went up to the bluff.

"Will you come to dinner?" they asked Elf when she'd decided it was time to break for the day, both of them more tired from repeatedly chasing the twins out of the trench they'd been digging than by the digging itself. "You and Agnes?"

She had dirt on her forehead, from swiping at her hair, and they wanted to grab her with their dirty hands, and make her filthier, everywhere. But: twins.

Georgie behaved.

"Depends," said Elf. "Is lapdog still on the menu?"

She was twinkling at them. The fact that they weren't naked with her this very moment in a fern brake seemed a crime.

"Seven o'clock," they said. "You'll see."

When they arrived home, they discovered that letters had too. Letters wishing them joy on their birthday from Rosalie and Anne, and Harry as well. His letter was the shortest, but it wasn't short on affection, and ended with him sending his *best love*. Georgie rubbed a finger over the inked phrase, sudden tears pricking their eyes. Harry's last few letters had struck a colder note. But to be fair, he'd been answering Georgie's aggressively petulant missives, a mix of pleas and insults, which, all at once, seemed shameful.

They'd made a cake of themself before the entire ton, it was true, and they'd infuriated, and possibly, yes, as Elf had suggested, *terrified*, their brother.

When they'd woken up from the crash, head throbbing, Harry had been sitting at their bedside, white to the lips, his chair surrounded by a mess of threads, because men didn't have knitting or needlepoint to absorb their nervous energy. Henry had spent the long hours of his vigil picking apart his handkerchiefs. He'd yelled. The moment Georgie's eyes focused, he'd yelled. And Georgie had latched onto the yelling, instead of the fretting, which, in retrospect, was just as obvious.

This banishment had struck them as vindictive, controlling, harsh. But maybe Harry was as fearful as he was furious. Maybe he hadn't been able to think of any other way to force Georgie to slow down. Reflect on their stupidity.

Spiting Harry by learning nothing from this experience was childish. It was spiting themself.

They weren't a child. They were four and twenty.

They dressed in a black tailcoat and breeches for dinner. Maturity didn't mean conformity, after all.

Elf and Agnes had both dressed out of the trunks in the tower— that is to say, like Gainsboroughs—Elf in blue striped silk, Agnes in the pale purple. Georgie tried to ignore just how much of Elf's bosom her gown left *un*dressed.

Agnes gaped when they bowed in greeting.

"Are breeches fashionable for women to wear in London?" she asked.

"Assuredly not." They winked at her. "But at least they're legal. You can get arrested in Paris."

At the table, Agnes did a very creditable job of adoring the soup. It was excellent soup. Everything was excellent. The wine, the fish, the golden pies, the roast. The company. Even Phipps. Hartcliffe— and marriage—aside, they liked having Phipps knocking about.

Life is here.

It ran through their head, as it had that golden day on the river. Life wasn't something happening somewhere else, at some bigger, better party. It was here, now, wherever and whenever they allowed themself to feel it, to feel this beautifully, joyfully alive.

"Is it the fifth?" asked Phipps during a lull in conversation. He slashed with his fork. "Georgie, it's your birthday."

"Oh," said Georgie, and took a sip of wine. "So it is."

"You didn't mention it." Elf was staring.

"Joy!" Agnes clapped her hands.

"You do seem gay," observed Phipps, leaning back in his chair. "For all your moaning, the country agrees with you. You realize we missed the Epsom Derby? My God, I didn't think of it until just now. I was meant to go with Cecy. She couldn't wait to show me her hat. From Milan." He leaned forward abruptly and emptied his wineglass.

"I won't have a birthday until 1820," said Agnes. "I'm glad there's a leap day in 1820 because I'll be sixteen, and that's the most important birthday."

"I wish you'd told me." Elf was still staring, rotating her glass. "I'd have tied ribbons on your shovel." She blushed and set her glass down. "Or you could have done something else, something more celebratory."

They loved the idea of her tying ribbons on their shovel.

"I wanted to dig," they said.

"Usually Georgie wants to see fireworks," said Phipps, wagging his brows. "Vauxhall." He gave Georgie a speculative look. "The country doesn't deliver by way of fireworks. Or rope dancers. That *is* regrettable." He turned to Agnes and Elf. "Last year on Georgie's birthday, a large party of us went to Vauxhall and saw Madame Saqui dance on a rope strung high above our heads. She danced, plumed and spangled, at the very stroke of midnight, rockets exploding in the air. Hard to beat *that*."

Elf had lowered her eyes to her plate.

Agnes's were wide as saucers. "Beatrice hasn't written a word about rope dancing."

"It's not the be-all and end-all." Georgie shrugged. But memories crowded their mind, shimmering with different-colored lamps strung from the trees of Vauxhall. With cut-glass lusters surrounded by gilt theater boxes. And when Elf glanced up, she seemed aware that distant lights had summoned them away.

After dinner, everyone repaired to the drawing room to drape on the softest furniture and drink champagne.

Agnes draped adjacent to Phipps.

"Let's play rhymes!" she said to him.

Elf draped adjacent to Georgie. "Why *didn't* you tell me it was your birthday?"

"I forgot it myself, until this morning. I spent the day getting used to it. Four and twenty."

"Antique," she murmured. "I could almost collect you."

They grinned. Her humor still surprised them. And so did her presence beside them. Elfreda Marsden. Eternally aloof, infinitely scornful, with those sharp eyes and that sad mouth. They'd wanted her, and wanted not to want her, and wanted her regardless for so very long. The idea they'd first formed of her was a stark sketch, a few strokes, black and white. The reality was messier, contradictory, complex, not otherworldly at all, but human, and that much more irresistible.

"I need something that rhymes with *Beatrice*." Phipps spoke loudly and skeptically.

Georgie glanced over.

Agnes was giggling with anticipation. She drained her champagne and poured herself more.

Georgie's glance slid past, around the room, still decorated to their mother's taste. It fell back on Elf.

"These past three years, I've wondered," they said, in a low voice, "if *she* forgets. On this day, of all days, she probably can't help but remember."

That meant somewhere, at some time today, their mother had been thinking of them.

Elf's eyes were soft. She pressed closer.

"I forfeit," said Phipps.

"You can't forfeit," cried Agnes. "Think harder."

"Georgie, help."

Georgie glanced over again. Phipps was scratching his brow.

"Forfeit," said Georgie.

"*So* many things rhyme with *Beatrice*." Agnes gulped her champagne. "Flea circus! Tea service!"

Georgie raised their brows.

"Ah." Phipps nodded agreeably. "I am humbled."

"Have you ever had fleas?" asked Agnes.

"I fear Agnes has had too much wine." Elf whispered it in their ear. They examined Agnes more closely. She was sliding down the sofa, like a spill of syrup, slowly heading for the floor.

A quarter hour later, Georgie and Elf had climbed into the gig, and Phipps was lifting Agnes onto Elf's lap. She wrapped an arm around Elf's neck, waving goodbye to Phipps with the other.

"Adieu, my lord!" she cried. "Adieu!"

As the gig rolled down the drive, she kept swinging that arm, pointing out imaginary sights, and twice knocking the reins from Georgie's hands. At least she was a happy drunk.

"Behold the shapely knolls!" she exclaimed. And then: "At last, Lake Windermere!"

Georgie could hardly drive for laughing.

"Will you wait?" asked Elf, when all three had stumbled into the entrance hall. She was holding Agnes around the waist. "I'll see her to her room, and then . . ." She bit her lip, and her gaze seemed unaccountably shy. "Will you wait?"

They waited. They waited in the dark entrance hall a surprisingly long time.

"Everything all right?" they asked, as Elf finally approached, holding a lantern, its glow sliding through her hair. She'd taken it down, her hair, all of it, long locks flowing over her shoulders, framing the milky skin above her gown's low neckline, which they'd done their best to ignore all evening and absolutely couldn't now.

She stopped in front of them, and when they moved in to kiss her, she stepped back, a smile tilting her lips. It wasn't no. It was *not yet*.

Excitement laced through their veins as she led them along black corridors, up the winding tower stair. When she reached the top, she crossed the room to a door Georgie hadn't noticed on their prior visit. A narrow door, between tapestries.

At Elf's touch, it swung open.

25

ELFREDA STEPPED OUTSIDE and felt breathless.

Georgie came up and stood beside her, silent. By day, the tower roof afforded giddy views of the countryside. She used to dare herself to go up on her tiptoes at the parapet, to lean out, stare straight down, and imagine leaping into space, not because she wanted to fall, because she wanted to fly.

She hadn't thought of that little ritual for years and years.

By night, the countryside was invisible. The black, black sky swept out in all directions, pierced by the pinpoints of the stars. The moon was thinner than a sickle.

None of that robbed her breath.

It was the thought of Georgie seeing the makeshift bed she'd created, a pile of quilts and pillows, lanterns on either side.

"Elf." There was amazement in their voice. "What is this?"

"Vauxhall." She swallowed. "Only, Marsden Hall. It's silly but—"

They grasped her arm, spun her toward them, and kissed her. She almost stumbled, but they caught her, laughing against her mouth.

"There's no rope dancer," she breathed, when they broke the kiss. "But I thought . . ."

She looked up.

"I thought the stars might do." She looked back at Georgie.

"Do for what?" The light from the lantern played over their eyes, the blue bright and strange, noon in the dead of night.

"Fireworks."

Those eyes turned back to the pallet. "This is for stargazing?"

She was suddenly too tense to answer directly.

She looked again at the sky. It was so beautiful, and so ordinary. Taking Georgie up here most likely made them regret Vauxhall even more.

"Stars aren't thrilling like rockets. Once in a great while, one shoots across the sky, but mostly, they stay in one place and shine." She wiped her clammy palm on her skirt, willing a star to shoot. But the stars were motionless. "They don't explode. They don't make noise. They don't give off smoke, or the stimulating smell of gunpowder. Or if they do, they're so far away you can't tell." All of her second thoughts were knotting together in her stomach, making a heavy ball. "I should have realized this would seem dull, after the spangles and plumes. We can go back down."

Georgie had already dropped onto the linens. They were stretching out their long legs and settling their head on a pillow. "How far are the stars, really?"

She set down her lantern, then stood with her arms hanging awkwardly, overwhelmed by hesitation.

"They look impossibly close," they said. "Come see."

Heart thundering in her ears, she lay down beside them. Wind streamed over the parapet, gentle and warm. The night was mild, balmy and summer sweet. The knot in her stomach loosened.

"They look close," she agreed. "But only if they're truly that small." She lifted a fanciful finger to touch one of the tiny, twinkling lights.

Georgie trapped her wrist on the way down and brought her knuckles to their lips.

"Thank you," they said, breath seeping through her fingers.

"I know you'd rather be there," she whispered. "In Vauxhall. In London."

"That's the thing." They rolled onto their side, propped themself on an elbow, and peered down at her. Their face was shadowed, the lantern light touching one cheekbone with flickering gold. "I'd rather be where I am, with you."

She almost shook her head. Because she was hearing *always*. She was hearing *anywhere, together*. And surely, they meant something more specific. They meant this particular moment. They meant it would do. Country fireworks. The two of them, beneath the stars, for this one birthday night.

She didn't know the hour. She couldn't mark midnight with a dazzling show. But she knew what she wanted to do instead.

"My plan," she said softly, "is to make you smile like Charles Peach was smiling at St. Alcmund's."

They'd been smiling. But now their smile faded. The way they looked at her . . .

Her pulse raced faster.

"I want to do something to you," she continued, "like Lord Phillip did to him, in the ferns."

The corner of their mouth tipped up. "What do you think they did?"

"I almost asked Lord Phillip," she confessed, "as we were leaving, but I couldn't figure out how to get him alone."

Georgie's laugh rang out, and they flopped on their back, hands pressed to their eyes. "My God."

"I like to gather information."

"You do." Georgie's murmur was richly amused. "I know."

"I *have* thought about it. I expect there was thrusting, based on reading, observation, and extrapolation. We could *thrust*. Fingers must work as well as pricks."

"I might die," said Georgie. "You're killing me."

She raised up on an elbow. "You don't like my plan?"

They folded their arms beneath their head. "I love it. I love everything about it. Keep talking." There was something more than amusement in their voice. "Thrusting, and what else?"

"Kissing. Of course."

"Of course."

"It's so lovely. To kiss." She was blushing. "I'm sure it's lovely on places other than the mouth."

"And on other mouths," Georgie drawled, and she gave her head a dizzy shake, confused into a resurgence of awkwardness.

"And perhaps licking?" she asked. "They might have licked each other."

"Very possibly licking," said Georgie. "Licking and sucking."

"Have you?" she asked, heart skipping. Imagining Lord Phillip and Charles Peach in the ferns was one thing. Imagining Georgie . . . it was something else entirely. "Have you . . . thrust?"

"A few times."

"Licked?" She got to her knees.

"Also. I've engaged, too, in a bit of sucking. And rubbing."

"And you like doing it? Or having it done to you?"

"Both."

"May I?" She touched the top button of their coat.

"Please." They stretched their arms above their head.

She straddled their waist and undid the buttons with trembling fingers. They sat up to shrug out of the sleeves, their face an inch from hers, eyes dark with shadow. The bodice of her gown whispered lacily against their silk waistcoat, and her breath caught.

"Your plan," they said, hoarsely, "it's for my sake, my birthday. If you don't want it for your sake too . . . we should stop."

She swallowed. It wasn't only her fingers trembling.

They were watching her intently.

Deliberately, she set to work on their waistcoat, pushing the cool buttons through the narrow holes. They slid out one arm and, with a jerk of the other, sent it flapping into the dark.

Their braces went next, shoved over their shoulders, and their shirt, which they tugged from their breeches. She lifted up as they wiggled out of those, and when she settled back down, they were naked beneath her.

She was breathing hard.

What now? She wasn't sure. Sometimes you tried first, though. You tried before you were sure.

"May I lick your nipples?" It was a question she couldn't have imagined asking last year, last month. Even now, her face burned.

But ever since she'd seen those nipples sparkling with water as Georgie splashed in the fishing pond, she'd wanted them under her tongue.

"Lick anything at all," they said.

She wanted their nipples between her teeth too—she discovered that soon enough. The soft gasp she elicited from Georgie as she bit at them made moisture gather between her thighs.

"How do you feel about breasts?" she asked, sitting up, stroking their collarbones, trailing her fingers down the center of their chest, over their warm, smooth skin. Their breasts were much smaller than hers, tipped with those tiny, jaunty nipples. Rakish breasts. She'd like to devour them.

"I want to feel yours," they said.

Their abdomen tightened as they curled to sitting, hair falling over their eyes as they unpinned her stomacher. She wiggled her arms from her sleeves, shivering.

They were unlacing her petticoat, her stays, and then it was only her shift, her drawers, and stockings. She pulled her shift over her head.

Their hands closed on her breasts. "Your breasts feel wonderful," they told her, and she gave a shaky laugh.

"I meant how do you feel about yours, not mine."

"Hmm?" They were caressing her, attention trained.

"Your breasts."

"Oh." They tossed their head, flicking back their hair, looking at her with a smirk. "I like them well enough. I liked when you had your mouth on them. Sometimes I'd as soon do without them. When they're *signifying* something to someone that I don't want them to signify. That's the only problem, really, for me. I like all my bits. Just not the meanings people give to them. And you?" Their hands stilled, cupping her. "How do you feel about your breasts?"

"The opposite. I've never thought about breasts signifying anything. But they get in the way, so I don't much care for them."

"Do you mind if I care for them?" Their hands started moving again. They had calluses on their palms, from digging. The calluses scratched at her nipples, and a cry shivered out of her. "I do care for them." Their lips were at her ears. "Very much."

She grabbed their head and turned it, fastened her mouth to theirs. Her kiss was greedy, her tongue gliding deep. She locked her hands behind their neck. Her breasts were slippery now as the two of them pressed together, skin to skin. She felt the poke of their nipples, jaunty and taunting.

"I don't want your nipples to mean anything," she whispered between kisses. "I just want to bite them again."

She pushed their shoulders hard, pushed them down, the rush of air tingling over her belly. She could see the gleam of their smile, and then she was curved over them, curtained by her hair, kissing and licking and sucking and biting, and the noises Georgie made began to throb inside her. She didn't realize she was moving her hips, until she felt their hands clamp around them.

Panting, she straightened her spine, looking down at herself, the dark jut of her breasts, her pale, stockinged knees on either side of them.

"Am I doing this right?"

Their thumbs pressed her hip bones, and their fingers dug into the soft flesh of her backside, nudging her back into motion. "Do you like it?"

She was rocking over them, pleasure building with every stroke. Her *yes* was barely audible, lost between a hitch and a hiss of breath.

She tried again. "Yes."

"I do too," they murmured. "So it's right. And this? What about this?" Their hand slid forward, down her belly, fingers opening the slit in her drawers, spreading her damp curls. With their other hand, they were spreading theirs, and then, *God*, then the slippery center of her sensation was rubbing delicate skin equally slick. She gasped and arched her back, dragging that needy wet center in slow circles, which only wound her need tighter. Their flesh was wet and soft beneath her, but also firm, with a tightly budded tip she drove herself onto, again and again.

"Oh God." Georgie canted their hips, straining upward, and she parted her knees, moaning at the stretch in her inner thighs, sinking down.

Their head tipped back, and they yelled, hoarse and exuberant, shuddering under her, their breath gusting into a moaning laugh.

"You have killed me," they said, rolling their head from side to side, hands sliding down her legs, the skin of her thighs, the silk of her stocking. "Now prepare to meet your fate."

Their hands skated back up, one clamping again around her hip, the other . . . the other . . .

"Lift up." It was a dark command. She obeyed, thigh muscles so taut they tremored. Their fingers were rubbing her now, targeting the pulse of tension at the apex of all her slick, swollen, clutching inner flesh. She fell forward, hands slapping down flat on either side of them.

"Georgie," she gasped, or pleaded. Her body was a vessel for waves of feeling, waves that rolled on and on, from her belly down to her toes, and back, rolling without breaking. "I need you to—"

She wasn't sure. She wanted to try anything, no, everything. Maybe everything was right. Kiss. Lick. Rub. Suck. *Thrust.*

Their fingers thrust inside her and began to churn, the rhythm slow and inexorable. Her heart stuttered to a stop. Her blood wasn't moving in her veins. Everything concentrated into a single point. They thrust higher, and she burst. She burst open, liquid trickling down her thighs, a scream tearing from her throat. Her eyes were closed. Against the velvet dark, stars shot in all directions. She rolled off of them and lay on her back, stunned for several ages.

Before she could think again, the candles in the lantern had gone out.

"I can't see if I've achieved the correct smile," she complained, flinging out a hand, feeling for their face.

"You've given me dimples," they said, yanking her hand from their nose, and guiding it down until . . .

She shrieked as their teeth closed on her fingertip and whacked them with a pillow.

"Do you think it's still my birthday?" they asked, tucking her against them.

"You can have until dawn," she said, head on their shoulder.

"Let's stay up." Their arm cradled her closer. "I want to see a shooting star."

I already did. She almost said it, except she was beyond saying anything. Their heart was beating against her palm, and she was asleep before she understood what was happening.

26

THE MORNING LIGHT washed the color from Elfreda's dreams. Her eyes fluttered open. Sky, pale blue behind a lacework pattern of cloud. She was on the tower roof, warm under a quilt she vaguely remembered Georgie pulling over her when she'd woken earlier, in darkness, shivering. *Georgie.* She sat up. They stood at the parapet, wrapped in a sheet, gazing toward the horizon.

She was still wearing only her stockings and drawers. As quietly as she could, she crawled for her shift.

"Good morning."

Georgie's sleep-roughened voice stopped her midcrawl. She knelt, arms crossed over her breasts.

"Good morning."

They'd turned, one fist holding the sheet closed at their throat. Their hair was tousled, lips hitched in a half smile. And their gaze. Their gaze pinned her, bright with the starlit remembrance of pleasures given and received.

A silvery tingle moved over her skin.

She felt more than naked, shockingly excited by the feel of her own breasts pushing against her inner arms, by the breeze teasing her bare skin, by the slight bite of her garters.

She didn't move.

Georgie didn't blink. The moment stretched, and at last, they gave themself a slight shake.

"Pardon my . . . You were about to . . ." They put their back to her.

She pulled her shift rapidly over her head.

"I can see the manor from here," they remarked. "And the village. That's the spire of All Souls."

She went to stand beside them, leaning into an adjacent notch in the battlement. The meadows fanned below, green upon green, all gentle undulations to the southeast, higher hills blued by distance to the northwest.

She let her gaze snag on the church spire, and on Redmayne Manor, and then on the bluff, the light green of the treetops mixed with velvet shadows.

Georgie followed her gaze. "We'll dig?"

She nodded, although the thought of digging didn't summon visions of swords and amulets but rather the memory of their calluses scratching lightly on her nipples.

It should alarm her. But she was too well pleased, and warm at her core, for anything but complacency.

"Look," they whispered in a changed voice. "The moon."

There it was, still overhead, a near transparent crescent floating ethereally in the blue.

She regarded it, and realized *they* were regarding her.

She met their heavy-lidded eyes.

"It's not *quite* morning, is it?" Their brows had a suggestive slant. "If the moon's still up."

"You're claiming it's still last night?" She tried to scoff, but her heart betrayed her, jumping up and down in her chest, undignified and eager.

"Something in between." They shrugged, the sheet slipping down from their shoulder.

She swallowed. "And that means?"

Their eyes flashed. "Anything we want."

The curve of their mouth was unholy.

But they only watched her, and she had the distinct impression that they were waiting, that they'd let the air thicken unbearably, make her pant with anticipation, and even then, they'd wait with that unhurried, nearly evil smile.

She reached for their fist, inserting her thumb, prying their fingers open.

They grinned wider as they let the sheet fall.

She stared, then shut her eyes, terrified by their beauty, by how badly she wanted to touch their skin, by the thought that she *needed* them to kiss her, now.

Those curls she'd touched last night between their thighs—they were orange as flame.

She felt their fingers graze her throat.

"Elf." Their breath was hot against her lips.

"Kiss me," she said.

Their open mouth moved on hers with torturous slowness. She made an angry, needy sound, and they laughed with an unbridled delight that once would have made her bristle with its smugness. But she was beyond caring. And she could feel their own need in the convulsive flex of their fingers on her jaw, could hear it in their laughter's ragged edge.

She put her hand between their thighs.

They inhaled sharply. She didn't move a muscle. They held her face an inch from theirs and peered at her.

She peered back.

"You really are a menace," they murmured. "What to do with you?"

She shook her head, unable to speak, belly aching, thighs already flooded.

Slowly, they lowered their mouth until it brushed her ear.

"Don't worry," they whispered. "I have ideas."

They bent their knees, wrapped their arms around her, just beneath her bottom, and lifted. She squealed, hugging their neck, her breasts very much in their face.

"You can't see," she gasped as they began to walk.

They mumbled happily. "Tell me if we're going to fall off the tower."

Fly. Fly, not fall. If she and Georgie went over the parapet like so, they would definitely fly.

A few moments later, they tripped on the pallet. She bumped down onto her heels then toppled backward, dragging them with her. Luckily, the quilts were thick. She thudded, painlessly, Georgie managing to slap their palms out in time to brace themself. They hovered over her.

"Whoops," they breathed.

"Whoops," she echoed, more sardonically.

"Do my pride a favor." They gave her an overly beseeching look. "Forget that ever happened."

"Never." She taunted them.

They lowered down an inch, eyes narrowing.

"I'll make you forget," they promised.

"Unlikely."

Their darkened gaze glittered a challenge. "I will make you forget everything."

They pushed up, grinning, and crawled down her body. They shoved her shift up to her waist and knocked open her knees. Propping herself on her elbows, she intercepted their jubilant look as it sharpened with purpose.

"What are you—" she began but got no further.

They pressed forward and latched their mouth to the part of her already wet with desire for exactly that.

Her arms collapsed. Her head fell back onto the pillow. Her knees splayed, legs going boneless. Their tongue turned more of her to liquid with each hot swipe. This time, they didn't thrust. Their fingers glided inside her, and their tongue glided too, stroking languidly. It was the suction that made her babble and beg. The hard pull of their mouth. She winched tighter, and relaxed, winched tighter, and relaxed, as they alternated tactics, obliterating her will, her memory, her mind.

"Don't stop," she pleaded as they eased off, and they took pity on her, giving it all to her, all at once, and harder, the stroking and the suction constant now.

"Ah," she cried. "Ah."

Their calloused hand closed roughly on her breast. She broke apart, the rippling sensation of relief, of freedom, so profound and all-encompassing it felt like flight.

"Come closer," she demanded, when she could speak, and as they obliged, mouth glistening, she kissed them once, and pushed under their arms, attempting to heave them up farther.

"What are you trying to do?" they asked, bemused.

She wasn't exactly sure. "I want you . . . up here."

Bemusement shifted. They were almost somber, nearly reverent, as they settled their knees above her head, slender thighs parted. They hovered. Her vision went fire bright.

"This belongs in a cathedral," she whispered.

They laughed that ragged-edged laugh. "There's no way *any* archbishop of Canterbury would ever agree."

"I mean the color. It's like stained glass. It's like the fruit in Eve's hand on the Great East Window at York Minster."

She fondled them with her thumb.

"Elf." Their voice was hoarse. "This is wickeder than I imagined."

Exultation crashed through her.

"Should I . . . ?" They sounded desperate.

She guided them down onto her mouth, and it *was* wicked, the most deliciously wicked thing she'd ever experienced, Georgie's wet heat smothering her face, their urgent gasps, the way they pumped their hips helplessly, and then froze, as though struck by a bolt, while a tiny part of them pulsed and pulsed against her tongue.

Afterward, she was damp everywhere, sweaty and sated, and they joined her in making a sticky heap, tangling their legs with hers. The two of them lazed in the sun. At some point, she fell asleep. She came to consciousness parched and hungry as a ravens bear. Georgie was at the parapet again, fully dressed, bent over a telescope. Their hind end looked magnificent in breeches. But the sunlight winking on the brass brought her eyes back to the telescope.

"Agnes isn't supposed to leave that up here," she said. "Papa would—" She cut herself off. Yes, Papa would roar about his telescope, out of its case, exposed to the elements, and she knew *what* he would roar, and why rehearse it? His voice was louder than hers in reality, but perhaps she could quiet that voice, at least in her own head.

"There's some commotion on the green." Georgie kept their eye to the eyepiece. "I can't quite make it out."

"Don't get your hopes up." She leaned back on her palms, straight-armed, legs stretched out, swishing her feet back and forth. "Remember, Twynham is invariably dull."

"I'm offended." They swiveled. "*Dull?*" They prowled to the edge of the pallet and loomed, hands on hips. "*Dull?*" They flung down beside her. "I'll double my efforts."

Smiling, she shook her head.

"Triple? Quadruple? My God, you're demanding." They beamed at her, and their blatant enthusiasm gratified little vanities she hadn't known she possessed and stoked her desire for little intimacies. Heated looks. Coded words. Casual touches. And now they were nuzzling her like a giant cat, silky waves of auburn tickling beneath her chin. She laughed.

This thing between them charged the air.

But it didn't change the facts of village life.

"You said being here was like being stuck in amber." She pushed their head away, and they sat back, obedient, adopting her same posture. "Like being a *beetle* stuck in amber," she recalled. "And Twynham is still amber."

They frowned. "I said *beetle*? Not butterfly?"

She shot them a look.

They winced. "I was angry at Harry. He rattles off to fight old Boney for *years*—doesn't even come home when father dies, was never there when I needed him—and then he shows up when I don't need him, makes bollocks of everything, nearly shoots poor Phipps, and expects me to respect his authority? Ha!" They winced again and continued in a less heated voice. "The point is that I'd pretty much determined to hate everything about being back here before I'd even arrived." They paused, gaze narrowing in thought. "Which may have led to my exaggerating the ceaselessly thrilling wonderfulness of my life in town just a bit—to myself, and to you. I didn't want Harry to win by being even the teensiest bit remotely correct about any of it." They tipped back their head and sighed. "To be fair, he didn't come home when father died because of Waterloo. I'm aware of that. He did come eventually. Not for long, but he came."

"Love." Elfreda murmured it. Georgie's head came back to center. Their eyes held the whole sky.

"Death." She swallowed. "War. Your mother, your father, and your brother all had their reasons. For not being there. But you still had to go through what you went through without them, and that isn't easy. Or fair."

Georgie was quiet for a time. Their smile seemed a little broken.

"I wish we'd found the hoard," they finally said. "So you could have dazzled the Fellows with gold and gained immediate admission into their Society, and posthumous honors for your grandmother."

She shrugged a shoulder. She wished many things. And she tried simultaneously to reconcile herself to the way things were. Flying was a wonderful dream, a fleeting sensation. In life, you moved forward slow step by slow step, if that.

Their frown lines reappeared. "For my part, the whole idea of racing off to town, with chalices, to live in a boardinghouse and act—it was rash. Harebrained. If anyone in society found out, they'd call it something significantly worse."

"And that's reason not to do it?" she asked, genuinely curious. Georgie courted scandal, didn't they? Their plan, though—it overshot scandal, and then some. Actresses were a breed apart. Usually born into acting families. Sometimes famed as courtesans. Even the few whose personal lives were considered respectable retained a whiff of dubious repute. For Georgie to make a career on the stage, they'd have to take an irrevocable step from one world into another.

They seemed to read her thoughts. "It's crossing the Rubicon. Harry might well disown me. My society friends would cut me, necessarily, or I'd tarnish their reputations." Their gaze was brooding. "And what if I made the sacrifice for nothing? I don't have much experience. I can't guarantee I'm any good."

"Of course you're good." She had no doubt.

"Hmm." They considered her. "You're usually right." Their lips twitched, and then flattened into a line. "Maybe not in this instance. Last year, I started performing in the lesser-known minor theaters. Breeches roles. But none of the managers kept me long."

"Why? You're so natural in breeches. The way you . . . *strut*."

"I strut, do I?"

"Like a dandy. Sometimes like a sportsman. You did a fair job at seeming soldierly as well."

Their lips were twitching again. "Well, that's the problem. The managers all said I was too *convincing*."

"Isn't that the job?"

"Not in a breeches role. You're meant to sway your hips to suggest femininity even as you swagger to suggest masculinity. You don't assume the character. You flirt with him. I enjoyed the challenge, but I didn't care for all the men gawking at my bum."

She went pink faced with guilt. She could feel it. And they could see it. Their eyes gleamed.

"Don't tell me *you* were gawking at my bum," they drawled.

She began to sputter. Mercifully, they cut her off by laughing. "Gawk anytime."

She pressed her flushed cheek into her shoulder. "Aren't there other roles you could play?"

"I'd have to try for the patent theaters, where it's doubtful I'd get engaged at all. And if I did tread the boards, say, at Drury Lane, well—the whole *ton* would know by morning. In the minor theaters, at least, I run less risk of being recognized."

"What role do you most *want* to play? If you could play any?"

"Macheath." They didn't hesitate. "The highwayman from *The Beggar's Opera*. Or a handsome youth from Shakespeare. But first and foremost, Macheath." Now they hesitated, but only for an instant. "My mother loves *The Beggar's Opera*. I use her maiden name as my stage name. I'm Georgie Bowen. That's what I wrote down when I applied for theatrical engagement at Russell Court. I had the sudden thought that maybe someday, somewhere, she'd pass a playbill, and she'd see that name, and that role, and put it all together. And we'd hold a clandestine reunion in the green room." They shifted their gaze away from her, self-mockery too thin a veneer on the hope that blazed beneath.

Elfreda's heart gave a painful knock.

And then her stomach growled.

"My thoughts exactly." Georgie bounced to their feet. "Breakfast. Then bluff." They extended a hand.

She took it.

Georgie meant breakfast at the manor, so they could change out of their evening kit, and spare Mrs. Pegg the shock of it. Elfreda de-toured to her bedchamber, washed up at the basin, and pulled on her oldest muslin, gray and ideal for digging. She checked the nursery—the twins were absorbed in Game of the Goose—and met Georgie in the courtyard.

"What would Mrs. Pegg have said about my breeches?" they won-dered on the walk.

Elfreda shook her head, unsure. "She knows who you are, which means she wouldn't have taken you for a stray libertine or feared for my virtue. So. Probably nothing? As you once noted, Marsdens are peculiar. She has been in service at the hall for decades upon decades, bearing witness to any number of druidic vestments."

"And that oracular pig," laughed Georgie.

When Holywell Rock heaved into view, they ran to it lightly, scrambling up to the top, grinning in the direction of Marsden Hall, and then toward Redmayne Manor. They hopped down on the Red-mayne Manor side.

"The Ladies of Llangollen wear riding habits exclusively," they told her, as she drew up to them. "With top hats and powdered hair. Dressing as you please on your own demesne—that is a distinct ad-vantage of the country. For those advantaged with a demesne, of course." They inhaled the sweet air. "And June smells like bouquets." They plucked a scarlet poppy and passed it to her. "That's another advantage. Although," they reflected, brows lowering as a breeze wafted from the fields, "sometimes it smells like cows."

At Redmayne Manor, in the breakfast room, Elfreda gobbled inde-cently and drank coffee, tea, and chocolate in such quick succession her head began to swim. She lingered over the meal, while Georgie skipped upstairs to change. It was one in the afternoon, hardly the hour for breakfast. Yet she continued unalarmed, no inkling of her habitual anxiety. This decadent languor would dispel once she had her shovel in hand and set to work. For now, she'd revel in the last of the chocolate, in the airiness of the lovely room, so very modern, with its large windows, and its pink-papered walls, decorated with convex mirrors and an oil painting of mares and foals under a spreading oak.

It was almost impossible to connect the manor with Sexburga's abbey, to remember that the abbey had stood on this very spot.

This very spot.

The moment Georgie reappeared, whistling, she sprang at them.

"The crypt." She clung to their neck, laughing. "The crypt!"

"The crypt," they agreed readily, and locked their arms around her waist.

"I should have thought of it before."

"You certainly should have," they agreed, squeezing her tightly.

"Do you have the faintest idea what I'm talking about?" She drew back.

They shook their head, unabashed. "No, not the faintest. But I appreciate the passion."

She tried to frown but couldn't. They were too adorable. She was too excited. "*Within my depths, the shadows play.*"

"The riddle, yes." They nodded.

"The crypt!" She started waving her hands. "Pilgrims descended to see the relics. There was light—a shrine surrounded by candles. And water—holy water. The hoard!" She bounced on her toes. "Crypt! It's the answer."

Georgie's smile grew brighter, until it blazed.

"I've never been happier to say this." They headed for the door. "Follow me to the wine cellar!"

AN HOUR LATER, she admitted defeat. She and Georgie had searched the wine cellar and found . . . wine. Also, a sarcophagus. A lidless sarcophagus. A lidless sarcophagus that contained a chest of bottled claret.

She dragged her feet on the narrow stair.

"Not crypt," she muttered. "Not cave. Not font."

"Crypt was a good guess," said Georgie, turning their head to look back at her from the step above. "They were all good guesses."

She nodded, chin heavy with disappointment. She ground her teeth to keep it from wobbling. She was reacting too strongly. This morning she'd been content to dig.

Once she had a shovel in her hand . . .

As she exited Redmayne Manor into the afternoon sun, she blinked. The light was glaring, and she'd been straining her eyes in that dim cellar.

She blinked again.

Three gaily clad young women stood on the drive.

Georgie had stopped dead in their tracks, goggling.

"It *is* your house!" cried the one in the middle, in a rich, carrying voice. "Charlotte and Louisa were afraid to knock."

"I didn't hear *you* knocking." The woman to her right tossed her head, the feathers on her high-crowned bonnet swaying in emphasis. She was a tall and slender blonde. So was the woman to the left. The woman in the middle was far shorter, but no less imposing, full-figured, with strong features and lustrous eyes. Chestnut curls made a cloud around her heart-shaped face.

"How is this happening?" Georgie's gaze moved back and forth. Their stunned expression had bloomed into pure delight. "Elf, these are my friends, Charlotte and Louisa Quiddington, and Sally Linley. We met at the Cabinet Theater. And this is Elfreda Marsden. My neighbor."

Elfreda dipped her head, neck suddenly stiff. *Neighbor.* That was . . . accurate.

The three women curtseyed as one, as though to resounding applause.

"You're actresses?" Elfreda's question sounded toneless. Her speaking voice wasn't melodic like Miss Linley's, or flexible like Georgie's. Shyness made it flat. Her stomach began to squirm. What if these women interpreted her shyness as scorn?

"Ostriches," laughed Miss Quiddington. "Just the other day we were ostriches in the pantomime."

"Sometimes we are ostriches." The other Miss Quiddington extended her elegant neck. "Sometimes we are opera dancers." She kicked up her heels.

"We're strollers, presently," said Miss Linley. "The manager at the Cabinet dismissed us! He dismissed *me*, rather, but he was so vile about it, Charlotte and Louisa left too." Miss Linley's eyes fixed on Georgie. "We went on the road with Mr. Arbuthnot's Company of Players right after I received your letter. That's why I didn't write back."

"We were to play for the month at a theater in Daventry," interjected Miss Quiddington. "But it burned to the ground the second day, and now we're true itinerants, acting in barns and stables."

The other Miss Quiddington frowned. "Only until our summer season starts in Manchester."

"We're headed to Thornton now," said Miss Linley, "but when I realized we were passing through Twynham I begged Arbuthnot to stop."

"Just to see me?" Georgie grinned. "I saw you. The lot of you. On the green, with your wagon. I didn't know at the time."

The time. The time they were on the roof, with Elfreda, and the world belonged to the two of them alone.

"Yes, to see you." Miss Linley swept Georgie with her gaze. Did Georgie mind that they were wearing what had to be *their* oldest muslin, their excavation costume, selected for shabbiness? It was stained from the previous days of digging.

They didn't seem to mind. They were returning Miss Linley's gaze just as deliberately.

"And to ask if you'd bespeak the night's performance," Miss Linley continued smoothly. "Buy up our tickets, and we'll stay here and put on any play you choose."

"I can't," said Georgie at once.

The actresses exchanged glances. Miss Linley lifted her gaze and looked well above Georgie's head. Elfreda didn't have to turn to know she was inspecting Redmayne Manor, and that the red bricks and tall windows were resplendent in the sun.

"You're not a *Bowen*," said Miss Linley. "You're a Redmayne. The Redmaynes are among the local worthies. I had it confirmed by the blacksmith."

"I'm a Redmayne who currently lacks ready money." They sighed. "Believe me, I'd bespeak every night between now and Manchester if I could."

"And your neighbor?" Miss Linley moved her gaze to Elfreda.

Elfreda shook her head.

The actresses seemed to shrink with disappointment. Their bright silks looked suddenly tattered and garish.

"I do *know* every worthy in the neighborhood," said Georgie. "I'm sure I can help you find someone to bespeak the performance."

Miss Linley beamed, once again inhabiting her gown like a queen. "Do you have a carriage? The quicker the better."

"I can drive one of you in the gig."

"They'll walk." Miss Linley waved her hand at the Miss Quiddingtons and gazed again at Elfreda.

"I'll walk as well." Her eyes slid to Georgie. "To where we were going."

"Elf." Georgie looked stricken. But she hadn't intended the *we* as a reproach. It had simply slipped out. Clumsily. She was always so clumsy. Her stomach kicked.

"Good luck," she managed, and this she *did* mean. Georgie responding generously to an unexpected plea, driving off with Miss Linley—their behavior befitted the exigency of the situation. She wouldn't want them to forsake friends in need. And choosing those friends in this moment didn't mean they were forsaking her in any larger sense.

Her. Their neighbor.

"I'll meet you on the bluff." Georgie claimed her hand. "Just as soon as I secure a patron for these children of Thespis."

She looked them full in the face. There was still starlight in their eyes. And she was still flying into love with them. And someday soon, they were going to shake the amber from their wings and fly away altogether.

"Ask Mrs. Alderwalsey to buy the tickets," she said. "Be sure to tell her that you're asking Mrs. Roberts next."

Georgie's grin was wolfish. They leaned closer, their voice dipping into its lowest register. "You *are* a menace."

And it was as though she was back on the tower roof. Everything fell away but their look, their touch.

They pulled back slightly. "Tonight, I will take you to the theater."

"Barn," interjected Miss Quiddington. "Or a room at the inn, if we're lucky."

Elfreda pressed Georgie's fingers before letting go, and smiled at the actresses, less awkwardly.

"In any case," she said, "a night to remember."

It was a promise she made to herself. However few or many nights she had with Georgie, she would treasure them all.

27

THE NIGHT WAS lucky. The strollers played at the inn, on a stage demarcated by a green curtain and paper screens. Wire contraptions of hoops and nails had been hung from the ceiling, a candle stuck on each spike. Benches arranged at the front of the house served for boxes, and the standing audience jostled behind, stamping their feet and sloshing their pints, sending up roars of mirth well before the kettle drum beat the preamble to the opening entertainments.

"I should have brought my lute!" squealed Agnes when she saw the orchestra pit, three chairs at stage right set up erratically to avoid drips of wax from the crude chandeliers. In the chairs sat farmers with fiddles, hired on for the evening. Georgie recognized Robert Peach. The youth was much better with a bow than a fencing foil.

Crammed to capacity, the room was close, smoky, odorous, and suffocatingly hot. Mr. Arbuthnot's company lacked elaborate properties, varied scenery, and celebrated talents. But the specially written prologue—spoken with wonderful naturalness by the theater manager himself—painted the village of Twynham as a wellspring of gentility and taste, and throughout his delivery, Georgie sensed an upswelling of beneficence from the Quality seated around them on the benches. The next moment, the pantomime commenced, with such an explosion of antic buffoonery even the most genteel spectators could be excused a few uncouth bellows and guffaws. The majority needed no excuse and shook the house.

Mr. Arbuthnot's strollers had been lucky, but beyond that, they possessed whatever alchemy transforms the ordinary into something more, that guides an audience into waking dreams. The room was no longer a room but a series of worlds.

Elf was nearly crying with laughter, gripping Georgie's hand, utterly focused on Harlequin, who whacked at nothing with a mop stick. Here was everything Georgie loved combined: the noise, the heat, the motley crowd, the spectacle, the feeling of aliveness too big for one body to hold. And Elf, holding on to them. The two of them holding on to each other, sharing it all.

She let go of their hand to applaud wildly when Charlotte and Louisa sang and danced between the acts. But she gripped them again during the play, which Mrs. Alderwalsey had requested from the repertoire—*Macbeth*. Georgie would have chosen something less grisly and tragic. *Much Ado. All's Well. A Midsummer Night's Dream.* The performance, however, riveted completely. Sally had complained about the actors who'd deserted after the fire, over half of the company's men, and all its male principals. This loss proved a boon, making for exhilarating casting. Women played Banquo, Donalbain, and Macduff. A gentleman of color played Macbeth, his expansive interpretation of that noble villain the most perfect Georgie had ever witnessed. Mrs. Arbuthnot played Lady Macbeth with a fiendish intensity. It mattered not at all that the dagger derived obviously from a drawer in the inn's kitchen. Or that the witches appeared to the sound of thunder made by mortar and pestle.

When the afterpiece ended, and the cheers of approbation died down, illusion faded, and the revelers found themselves back in a beery public room. The innkeeper rapidly reclaimed his tables, and members of the company sat and ate a hearty supper, joined by Sir Hugh and other notables, while the rest of the audience poured rowdily out the door, or lingered in groups, conversing, laughing, and, in some cases, drinking additional pints.

Mrs. Alderwalsey received compliments on behalf of the strollers, enthroned on one of the fiddler's chairs between the chandeliers. Georgie, Elf, and Agnes went to her to express their gratitude for their tickets, which she'd bestowed upon them free of charge. Mrs. Roberts, standing nearby with Jane Ratcliff's mother, looked over with a sour expression, and Georgie guessed the price of *her* ticket had been set rather higher. Jane Ratcliff herself wasn't in attendance, but Jane Slater was, only she was Jane Worrell now. She met Georgie's eyes from across the room, then turned away as she was greeted by a second Jane—Jane Tetley, now Jane Avery. The two Janes put their heads together, whispering. Georgie gazed at them, an odd little pull in their chest, not exactly longing for the good old days, when every village gathering provided an occasion for mischief, but rather wistfulness. Their former accomplices were all but strangers, and there was no crossing the gulf between then and now.

Except both Janes suddenly returned their gaze and smiled. Their smiles were not the vapid, wifely smiles Georgie expected, but the familiar smiles, lively, and a little bit sly. And Jane Slater—no, Worrell—glanced at Elf and then at Georgie, and her smile shifted, became a tad more meaningful, and Georgie laughed aloud.

Before they could approach, the Janes were departing on their husbands' arms, but even as the physical distance increased, the gulf seemed smaller. Georgie faced the uncomfortable thought that, perhaps, when they'd called on the Janes, *they* had been the one whose behavior made confidences impossible. They'd sat awkwardly with a teacup, imagining the Janes not so much busy with marriage as essentially altered by it. That *was* the law of the land. Marriage legally dissolved a woman's personhood. But the law was just a story. Its claims were enforceable, not true. The Janes weren't *wives*, or rather, they weren't *only* wives. Maybe Georgie would have understood that more readily if they hadn't thought of the Janes as *the Janes* in the first place. Each Jane had always been and was still living her particular life.

They wanted to rush after Jane Worrell and Jane Avery and apologize, but it wasn't the time or the place, and what would such an apology do anyway?

They'd call again soon. They wouldn't spend the visits apologizing. They'd spend the visits paying attention.

The claws of self-recrimination retracted, and hope unfolded its wings.

"It was Jane Worrell, wasn't it?"

Georgie blinked. "What do you mean?" Elf was studying them with a slight smile. "What about Jane Worrell?"

Elf raised her brows . . . and puckered her lips.

They stared, speechless, caught entirely off guard.

"You're blushing," she informed them.

They recovered and leaned in, lowering their voice. "Because what you're doing with your mouth makes me think about where your mouth has been." They straightened, noting the result of their words with satisfaction. "Now who's blushing?"

Elf scowled, pinkly. "I'm right, though." She peered after Jane Worrell with intrigue. "She's the one you kissed. And she knows, doesn't she?" Elf whispered it. "How does she know?"

"About us?" They matched Elf's whisper, even though nobody was listening. They liked whispering in her ear. They especially liked whispering *us*. "Some things are glaringly obvious once you know how to look."

They raised their eyes, and over there, the two men in the corner. Case in point.

"Charles Peach," they whispered, pointing with their chin. "Should I go thank his dimples for last night?"

Elf's elbow connected with their ribs, and they laughed and tucked her arm under theirs. With their other hand, they waved at Phipps, close by his lover, lounging with his shoulder on the wall. Phipps lifted a brow in answer, his smile pleased as punch.

All at once, Mrs. Alderwalsey's authoritative voice rang out. The low rumble of conversation ceased. Every head turned. She had risen from her chair, the trimmings on her hat flirting worrisomely with the candle flames above.

"Mr. Arbuthnot," she said, and gestured to the manager, still at his table. He laid down his cutlery and somehow, without moving another muscle, increased his dignity of bearing. "In days of yore," continued Mrs. Alderwalsey, "back when even *I* was but a child, strolling companies strolled right by our hamlet, bound for more populous towns. When rarely companies did beg leave to play for us, the magistrates rightly denied them licenses. Too often country actors are nothing but unscrupulous mountebanks. You will not disagree."

Mr. Arbuthnot's tufted eyebrows commiserated with her assertion.

"This has been our first ever theatrical evening here in Twynham," she went on. "I am gratified that *your* players are so well-conducted. And I trust that you have felt well-received. I bespoke your performance thinking it a charity, and I now retire feeling I am in your debt. Thank you, and adieu."

"Thank *you*, good lady," cried Mr. Arbuthnot, standing and raising his glass. Every glass in the room rose with it. Mr. Arbuthnot hefted his higher. "He that dies pays all debts. And mine to thee expires only then."

He drank, for rather longer than a toast required.

Mrs. Roberts's face had turned such a ghastly shade that Georgie angled away from her.

Meanwhile, Mrs. Alderwalsey had addressed herself to Agnes and Elf.

"I will drive you home," she announced. "It is late."

It was ten o'clock. Georgie was wide awake. They were ready to climb mountains, to skip from star to star.

"I will drive Miss Marsden myself," they said. "In my gig."

"To bed," moaned Agnes, rubbing her hands. "To bed." She'd been unusually quiet since the performance ended, and she hadn't once stopped worrying her fingers. Georgie understood why with a sudden jolt, and wished again that Mrs. Alderwalsey had picked a comedy.

"Out, damned spot!" moaned Agnes.

"Language!" barked Mrs. Alderwalsey.

"Out, dratted spot," moaned Agnes.

"That reminds me." Mrs. Alderwalsey swung around to smile victoriously at Mrs. Roberts. "The dratted spotted muslin. You may bring it to my house tomorrow morning."

So that was the price of admission.

Georgie bowed their head in deference.

"Come along." Mrs. Alderwalsey beckoned to Agnes then sailed for the door.

Elf watched her sister go with an expression of mild concern. "She won't imagine herself as Lady Macbeth forever," she said, as though hoping to be convinced.

"*Fair is foul*," sang Charlotte, materializing at Georgie's elbow.

"*And foul is fair*," sang Louisa, right beside her.

"You were bewitching witches," Georgie told them.

"I feel like a fillet of a fenny snake," complained Sally, the third witch, face shining with sweat and speckled with soot from the candles. "It's hot as a cauldron in here."

"There's a fishing pond near my house." Georgie looked around the little circle, inspired. "We could bathe under the moon. I wouldn't be able to fit you all in the gig, but it's only a mile, and . . ."

"Stop right there!" cried Sally. "I'll ask Mr. Arbuthnot. He never says no to a lark."

Mr. Arbuthnot didn't say no. He said, "Fetch me another bottle and we'll go in the wagon."

28

WITHIN THE HOUR, a theater troupe, two farmers, and a fugitive lord were bathing under the crescent moon. And Georgie, of course, floating on their back, looking up at the stars. Elf was wading in the shallows. When they rolled over and paddled for shore, they could just distinguish her moving shape from the solid blackness behind.

She couldn't hope to find her amulet, not now, in the pitch dark, but she was haunting the pond's edge all the same, as though tethered to its possibility. Their feet touched the muddy bottom, and they stumbled to her through air that felt warm against their dripping skin.

"Are you naked?" she gasped, as they threw their arms around her.

"No one can see."

"Is *everyone* naked?"

"Dunno." They turned their head, wet cheek against her hair, and squinted at the pond, which didn't so much as glimmer back at them. A full moon would have flooded the clearing with light, silvering the rippled water, outlining the crowns of the surrounding trees against the midnight-blue sky. The crescent moon conspired with the dark. From around the pond's invisible circumference came shrieks and splashes, laughter. Phipps was calling to Charles Peach to get in the water, and Charles Peach was calling to Robert Peach to get *out* of the water.

Georgie pressed Elf closer, until she began to wiggle and push them away, with an accusatory huff.

"You're using me as a towel!"

"Towel?" someone called. "Who has towels?"

Georgie recognized Mr. Arbuthnot's voice, rising above the rest. "Roscoe," he shouted. "Get the Roman habits!"

A short while later, everyone was sitting on the grass in a ragged circle, huddled under togas in various states of semidress, passing around Mr. Arbuthnot's bottle. Mr. Arbuthnot sat in the middle, by a lantern, smoking a pipe. Georgie sat so near to the pond they could dip their fingers in the water and drag them through the silt. Every time they encountered a stone, they dislodged it and checked covertly for signs of ancient craftsmanship before tossing it into the depths.

Eventually, Robert Peach, smiling shyly, obliged repeated requests for a tune, and the woman who'd played Banquo danced a hornpipe, and then more people danced, to warm up, or because they couldn't resist once the music began. Georgie grabbed Elf's hands and hauled her to standing, each of them leaning back to swing around and around, until Georgie's grip slipped, and Elf flew into Sally, and Georgie careened into the pond, just managing to keep their feet. They splashed back to the bank, balling up their shift to wring out the soaking hem. Elf was dancing with Sally now, and Charles Peach was dancing with Phipps, and Macbeth and Lady Macbeth were whirling together, and the old man who'd played the old man in the panto-mime was leaping balletically between side shuffles left and side shuffles right. Mr. Arbuthnot chuckled and clapped his hands. Georgie danced a hopping dance all their own, toes in the moss and arms in the air, the stars spinning overhead. Robert Peach fiddled louder and louder, and faster and faster. The whole world tilted and blurred. The dancers dropped one by one and two by two, until even Charlotte and

Louisa were flopped on the ground, gasping for breath, at which point the woman who'd played Macduff caught hers enough to sing. The fiddling quieted and slowed, supporting her sweet voice with harmonies that filled out the sprightly sound. Georgie didn't recognize the song. The melody wandered, light and merry, and seemed to shine, sparkling in the dark night. They felt sparkles in their blood. They pushed up to sitting, and looked for Elf, to see if she felt it too.

Yes, they thought, the moment their gaze landed upon her, forgetting the question, even as the answer beat through them, propelled by their heart. *Yes, yes. Yes.*

The bottle came their way, and they gulped. They turned to pass it off and froze when Charles Peach's massive hand enveloped the glass. The farmer's eyes locked Georgie's, his muzzy, happy look hardening into something guarded and watchful. Georgie gave him a slight nod, and a very large smile. Charles Peach's expression didn't change, which Georgie had to admit was fair. They'd yet to make good on any of their nonbeastly intentions. Charles Peach looked away and passed the bottle without drinking, as though suddenly suspicious he'd stumbled into fairyland, where all offerings were magical traps. The moment the song ended he stood.

"Come, Bob, lad," he said. "That's enough."

Robert grumbled, but his brother was unmoved, and a giant, and so he lowered his fiddle and followed him down the path, his slumped shoulders straightening when he heard the applause that attended his departure. He glanced back, saw Charlotte and Louisa blowing kisses, and almost walked into a tree.

After that, there was relative quiet in the clearing. Mr. Arbuthnot turned the talk to business.

"Another lady has granted us the favor of a bespeak," he informed his company, to mixed cheers and groans.

"Not again in that heinous hot inn," sighed Sally.

"It was a mean little room," agreed Banquo.

"A hayloft would have smelled sweeter," said Macduff.

"I'd also have preferred a barn," agreed Charlotte, wonderingly. "And I hate playing barns, at least when they're nasty."

"Now, now." Mr. Arbuthnot waved his pipe, the smoke curling up through the lantern light, vanishing as it rose. "My histrionic ones. You won't have to peddle your poetry in cowsheds much longer. Manchester awaits."

"I told Mrs. Roberts we would play for her," said Mrs. Arbuthnot, and paused for dramatic effect. "But not in Twynham—in Thornton."

"Where there is a playhouse?" Macbeth's query was full of optimism.

"The nearest playhouse is in Derby." Georgie inserted themself into the proceedings, compelled to defend Twynham, or at least make it clear that Thornton wasn't *so* much the better option. Would tonight mark the first *and* last theatrical evening in the village? Because the inn was paltry, and the barns were nasty, and the neighborhood was small?

"You could play on the village green," they suggested. "People would come *here* from Thornton, if you advertised."

Mrs. Arbuthnot was staring at them. "In Thornton, there are assembly rooms." She looked far less haggard and murderous now that she wasn't channeling evil spirits as a would-be Scottish queen, but her gaze was steely. "We can raise the price of the tickets."

Her husband concurred with a nod.

"Our benefactress agreed to Thornton," he said. "It is settled. She requests *Romeo and Juliet*, in its entirety. So. Double parts. You." He pointed his pipe at Georgie. "I saw you on the boards, at the Cabinet. You can sing. But can you speak?"

Georgie sat bolt upright. "*But soft! what light through yonder window breaks?*"

"*I* am Romeo," objected Banquo, whose name, Georgie had gleaned, was Letitia Blanchard.

"*I* am Romeo," objected the fellow called Roscoe. He'd played Harlequin, and the drunk porter at Macbeth's castle, and both the Arbuthnots were already shaking their heads at him.

"You know you're our Balthasar," said Mrs. Arbuthnot. "And Sampson. And one of the friars. Let's make it both of the friars."

"Mr. Garnet will play Mercutio and Montague," said Mr. Arbuthnot. Macbeth—Mr. Garnet—inclined his head. Mr. Arbuthnot went on. "Miss Blanchard will play Romeo and Capulet." Miss Blanchard tossed her head in Georgie's direction. "Miss Campbell will play Benvolio and Paris." Macduff—Miss Campbell—inclined her head.

Georgie stopped listening. They crawled to the dark, mossy spot where Elf sat cross-legged, watching them approach.

"I thought for a moment he wanted me for his troupe," they whispered.

"You spoke well," she whispered back.

"You think so? Tell me how I sigh. That's the real test, with Romeo. He's such a mope." They sighed a lover's sigh. Despite her distance from the lantern, and the thinness of the moon, Elf's eyes illuminated her whole face as she laughed.

"It needs practice. You're not used to sighing."

"I'm not?"

"You're used to getting what you want."

"I am." Their laugh felt bittersweet. "But then, I'm usually wrong about what I want."

She studied them, with that sharp, intelligent, utterly concentrated look in her eyes, and they felt true longing, helpless longing. They sighed.

Her look turned wry, and then it turned into something else, something that made their heart thump hard in their chest.

"O Romeo, Romeo," she said.

"Who?" Light wheeled as Mr. Arbuthnot lifted the lantern.

"Who was that? You?" He walked forward on his knees and thrust his arm toward Elf, so the light lapped over her. "By Jove, a girl with the face of tragedienne. Go on. From *O Romeo, Romeo*. Speak."

"*I* am Juliet," objected Donalbain. "I am always Juliet. And you just said I am Juliet."

"Shh." Mr. Arbuthnot waved his pipe at her. "We are in Capulet's orchard." He pointed the pipe at Elf. "You have appeared at a window. Now, speak."

"She's not an actress." Georgie jumped in to preempt Elf's misery as the players arranged themselves into an audience on the grass.

"*Wherefore art thou Romeo*," prompted Arbuthnot.

The expectancy thickened. Elf was blinking unnaturally, eyes darting. And then her gaze settled back on Georgie.

Their throat vibrated. Because—*oh no, oh no*—they were humming. Again. Like a twit. By God, they were a twit for the ages. Aghast, they cut it off, hoping she hadn't heard, that no one had heard.

A smile ghosted her lips.

She hummed, quietly at first, and then louder. It was tuneless humming, and the players shifted, exchanging looks. Mr. Arbuthnot frowned.

She shut her eyes, humming. And then:

"*Wherefore art thou Romeo!*" She ran the words together in one triumphant shout and opened her eyes.

Charlotte tittered. Sally coughed.

"Butchery!" Mr. Arbuthnot reared back. "I have heard the bard abused, mangled, put on the rack, but you, my child, *you* have disemboweled him with a truncheon."

Elf was pressing her fingers to her throat, a smile spilling off her face.

"I know the bard will recover." Her voice shook but only slightly. "You and your company give him new life every night." She gazed at Mr. Arbuthnot, and then out at the dozen players, all staring back at her. She was shaking visibly now, but she continued. "So would Georgie Bowen there. If you need a new player to help you captivate the public, look no further."

Every pair of eyes swung to Georgie.

There was only one pair that they saw. Deep as the sea. Deep as their love.

Help.

"I can even fence," they said, forcing themself to focus on Mr. Arbuthnot.

"In that case"—the manager pinched the bridge of his nose—"Tybalt. And if you prove yourself tolerable, I'll engage you for Manchester."

Georgie grunted as Sally, Charlotte, and Louisa rocketed into them. They went down under a giggling pile of congratulations.

"Zounds," they breathed, as they struggled upright, grinning in all directions. "I am peppered."

"That's my line," said Mr. Garnet, mildly.

"We'll rehearse in the morning." Mr. Arbuthnot lumbered to his feet. "Is that a sea monster?"

It was Roscoe, back in the pond. Georgie charged after him, and so did Sally, Charlotte, and Louisa, shrieking, and Phipps, with a mighty yawp. Georgie's steps slowed as the water pushed on their legs and pulled on their shift, and they dove. When they surfaced, they could hear Mr. Arbuthnot's distant voice. He was singing a ballad about Robin in the greenwood, *derry derry down*s floating on the air, growing fainter as the wagon creaked away through the trees.

Georgie emerged from the pond, all chattering teeth and racing thoughts. There was no one on the bank. They wrapped themself in their discarded Roman habit and padded to the willow.

"I've never been here at night," said Elf, as though in explanation, as they ducked through the fronds, relief coursing through them to find her there.

"Me either." They sat next to her, resting their damp head on her shoulder. The air was warmer in this curtained place and smelled of green growing things. A breeze whispered through the leaflets.

"I think I'd like being anywhere with you," they said. "Even that cave was delightful, in retrospect."

She laughed. "No, it wasn't."

"This is *more* delightful." They sighed. "You were wonderful to-night."

"You forgive me my crime against Shakespeare?"

"You spoke in front of a whole crowd of strangers. It was as bold as when you attacked the bandit, who turned out to be me, but never mind. It was bolder even."

"You hummed."

"I know. I'm a twit."

"*I* hummed." She said this with all the surprise she must have felt still there in her voice. "I *knew* I was embarrassing myself, so I didn't dread embarrassing myself. Somehow that helped. And my vocal cords weren't waiting for my brain anymore. That helped too."

"It's the twit's creed. Speak first. Think never."

Her shoulder made a small, exasperated movement. "You're not a twit."

They lifted their head. "You wouldn't give me so much credit last time. Have I risen in your esteem?" They couldn't determine anything about her expression, only that her face was turned toward them.

"Thank you," she said, after a pause. "For humming."

"Thank *you*." They reached out slowly, until their fingers touched her jaw. "For what you said about me. I'm not going with them, of course. But thank you."

"Not going." Her tone was as unreadable as her face.

"I can't play in Thornton. Mrs. Roberts will invite the neighborhood. It's worse than Drury Lane when it comes to discretion."

She didn't move. They didn't move either, but they felt their heart teeter, waiting for something, unsure what it was.

"But that's easily resolved," she said, and now she sounded confused, perhaps even disappointed, that they'd let themself be stopped by such a trifle. "You could start *after* Thornton, couldn't you?"

They swallowed. "Maybe." They'd thought of that. They could at least inquire. They'd thought, too, of the letter they'd write to Harry. It would say that Anne had invited them to Halifax for a long visit. And meanwhile, they'd tour north, a strolling player, acting the parts they'd dreamed of acting, in locales where no one would know who they really were. Their first *real* opportunity. Was that what gave them pause? They preferred fantasy to reality? Preferred to leave potential unrealized, keeping every door open, passing through none?

"You think I should go," they said, fingers drinking in the feel of her skin. Their very *fingertips* thirsted. "Why?"

Delicate muscles tensed as she swallowed. "Because you want to go."

They were glad she couldn't see their smile, its ugly edge. Elf had never doubted her purpose in life, only the best method for attaining her goals. But they had no goals as such. They were uncommitted even to their frittering, always chasing new interests and pleasures like will-o'-the-wisps.

I'm madly in love with you. They could say it to her now. But wouldn't it seem no more than their latest diversion? And what if it was?

Elf was braver than they were. And truer. And responsible already for so much. They couldn't ask her to take responsibility for *their* decisions on top of everything else.

They asked anyway. "Tell me what to do."

"Georgie!" There was a world beyond the willow, and Sally Linley was calling. "Where have you gone? You haven't left us?"

"We'll get the worst rooms if we go back to the inn now." That was Charlotte. "May we stay the night with you? Just the three of us. And Roscoe, but he won't mind sleeping in your stables."

"I'm fagged to death," said Louisa. "I could sleep right here."

"I have to . . ." Georgie began, and Elf nodded, not meaning, probably, to shake off their fingers, but that was the result.

They spread the fronds. "You're all welcome to stay the night." They turned back to Elf. "Will you come too?" they asked in a softer voice.

When she nodded, they released their breath.

It was an odd procession up to the manor, Georgie driving slowly in the gig, with Elf at their side, Phipps and the players trailing after, in Roman habits, looking both silly and solemn. The present in the garb of the past always looked silly and solemn. And the future? Georgie didn't have the least idea what the future looked like, but they drove on regardless.

29

ELFREDA HAD NEVER been in Georgie's bedchamber. It was like every other room in the house, colorful and plush, hung with brightly patterned wallpapers. Only the fencing foil on the upholstered bench at the foot of the bed, and a periodical—*The Farmers' Magazine*—carelessly splayed on the elbow chair, announced anything about the individual occupant.

Georgie had been away for years, after all, and was poised to go away again. Their personality hadn't seeped into the décor.

"The *King Georgie*." She spotted the model ship on the mantel and went to it, gathering up the excess fabric of her borrowed night-gown, one of Georgie's, much too long.

"I brought it with me from London."

Something in their voice cautioned against questions. She bit her tongue instead of asking about the letter—if they'd brought it too. They hadn't answered her the first time, except to close the subject. Why would they answer now, at two in the morning, as the bond they'd formed across these weeks unraveled? Georgie flying off, and she . . . staying right where she was, stuck.

The ship had gunports fitted with tiny gold cannons. Her eyes got lost as she tried to trace the threads of the elaborate rigging. Many of the sails were set, as though drawing wind. Square topgallant and topsail. Larger triangular sails fore and aft. Georgie's mother's letter had been hidden among those spans of cloth.

Her eyes fell to the painted name on the stern.

The *i* in *Georgie* had been added clumsily, and obviously. She could picture them painting it, could summon an image of that headstrong child, eyes too blue, brazen red hair not yet mellowed to auburn. Provoking in every way.

Her heart skipped a beat. Georgie had been under her skin from the beginning, jangling her nerves, rankling her mind, stinging her pride, and she'd shied away from the intensity of her reaction. Tried not to look at it too hard, to recognize it as infatuation. And now she understood the wisdom of that ignorance.

She couldn't return to her old life. She'd been kissed in starlight, kissed *by* starlight. She knew how it felt. Everything was different.

She hovered her pointer finger over the *i*. "Your father really didn't notice?" The disfigurement of an object in his collection was the only sort of thing *her* father ever did notice.

"If so, he didn't let on."

She turned and met Georgie's gaze. Their hair had dried in errant waves, and the candle they held made their eyes glisten like melting ice.

"We should sleep." She crossed to the bed. "You have to meet Mr. Arbuthnot at the inn by ten."

Their gaze tracked her movement. "So early?"

"That's what Miss Linley said." The bed was narrower than hers, and lovelier, and fresher, the mint-green blanket swirled with pale pink florals, the sheets sweet smelling and butter soft as she slipped inside.

They snuffed their candle, and then the two on the bedside table. The room turned black.

The mattress dipped beneath their weight. She rolled onto her side, her face next to theirs.

"I'll be there at ten, then." Their statement had a nearly imperceptible lilt.

Tell me what to do.

They'd begged her permission to leave. As though permission were hers to give, as though they'd listen if she responded *Stay*. But it wasn't, and they wouldn't. She might have been angry at their emotional deceit. Indeed, beneath the willow, she'd almost screeched like some taloned bird of night. The next moment, understanding blunted her anger, dulling it to an ache.

They had been abandoned, and it had hurt them deeply, more deeply than they'd admit. Now they worried they were abandoning *her* and needed to convince themself they'd considered her wishes. But they didn't owe her such consideration. They'd never made her any promises. She'd always known they were leaving. If she'd failed to protect her heart, that was her own concern. This pretense of reluctance—it was the only thing for which she could fault them. It forced her to pretend too.

"I'll come to see you perform in Manchester," she lied.

"Your father will permit it?" they asked, and her throat relaxed. Their skepticism invited honesty.

"No." She exhaled. Papa would return soon, with baskets of artifacts for her to sketch and describe. They'd fall back into a rhythm of working on *Ancient Derbyshire*, and soon it would be time to prepare his presentation for the next Society meeting. The weeks and months would pass. She'd dig on the bluff, during her few spare moments. She'd do what she could to keep the twins from climbing out windows and into trunks. She'd call on Mrs. Alderwalsey. She'd take that good lady's blue satin and see if she couldn't sew it into a prettily trimmed spencer for Agnes.

Georgie's breath warmed her cheek. "I didn't think so." They slung their arm over her waist and curled her closer.

"I'd like to," she said honestly. "Maybe someday." When the twins were grown. When she made Fellow and had the resources to travel.

Maybe someday. Maybe never.

"I won't be gone long," they said, and she kissed them, urgently, to stop their words before they could say anything else reassuring and untrue. They kissed her back, their hand sliding up to her nape, their tongue in her mouth, matching her urgency.

They thought *never* too.

Their kiss tasted like the end, the final sip of summer cordial, in which all the crushed berries had settled, a sweetness that scorched.

She wiggled to work the nightgown up her thighs, wrestling up Georgie's as well, with an impatience that would have shocked her if she had time for it. Their bare legs threaded hers, and she gasped against their lips. She tore at the ruffles interfering with her access to their breasts, fumbling for an opening. They heaved up, wrenching their nightgown over their head, and she did the same, buttons snagging in her hair. She hadn't learned finesse from previous encounters. It was the opposite. She was rougher now, but so were they, dropping down on her, pressing her flat beneath them, pinning her wrists.

"Elf." They gulped air. "I—"

She pushed up, fusing their mouths. Kissing instead of speaking. Kissing instead of thinking, instead of breathing. A world of lips and tongues and teeth.

Abruptly, they rolled them both onto their sides. She groped for their breast, and they grabbed her bottom, kneading it, reaching around, and . . . she cried out as their fingers slid into her from behind. She gripped their breast convulsively, too hard, but they arched their back, and their moan meant *not enough*. She struggled to wedge her other arm between their bellies, panting, and finally, her finger struck that springy, jewel-toned hair, which gave gloriously onto their sopping wet cleft. Her wrist burned from the angle, but when she moved her fingers, the sounds she pulled from Georgie's throat made a different fire go everywhere. She cinched her legs around their thigh, trembling, her fingers stuttering out of rhythm, because the way they plunged *their* fingers up inside her, again and again—she couldn't control herself. Her mouth was open on their neck, and she screamed as she climaxed, shaking into delirious pieces. Georgie thrashed and shook with her, and then they sighed—not a Romeo sigh, a richly satisfied sigh, pure contentment stroking her over like velvet. They held all the pieces of her in their arms. She slept so soundly that she awoke in the same position, their arms still around her.

For several blissful minutes, she didn't move a muscle, committing everything to memory, the feel of their body tangled with hers, heavy with sleep. And then she extricated herself carefully, dressed, and tiptoed from the room.

It was eight in the morning. Mrs. Pegg would be making breakfast, wondering what delayed her. She descended the stairs and bumped into a housemaid hurrying out of the drawing room. She was round faced and young, with a feather broom and a friendly smile, and she agreed readily to waking Georgie in another half hour.

Another minute, and Elf was outside in the cool morning light, the dewiness of the air soothing her sandy eyes.

She was tired. She was simultaneously hollow as a reed and spilling over from fullness. She was running away, perhaps, from goodbye.

When she reached Holywell Rock, she paused to put her hand on it, the lichen slightly damp, itching under her palm. It seemed more significant than usual, the idea of passing by the boundary stone.

The pause extended.

She found a toehold, a handhold, and she was atop the rock. She didn't stand long to gaze between the two houses. She sat cross-legged to think.

GEORGIE RESISTED BEING roused. They could hear the maid, Jenny, rustling about, thumping chairs unnecessarily, rattling the fire iron in the grate, although no fire had been laid. They pulled the covers over their head when she opened the curtains and the windows, light and fresh air galloping into the room.

"Have mercy," they muttered.

"It's almost nine," came Jenny's chirping voice. "And the lady said as she was leaving that you had to rise."

Elf was gone. They'd been struggling against that awareness, and now the sense of loss paradoxically weighed them down.

"All right," they said at last. They kicked free of the bedclothes and prepared to confront the day.

Downstairs, the house reverberated with the sounds of a merry brawl. The drawing room door stood open. Georgie peeked inside to investigate the racket.

Sally, Charlotte, Louisa, and Roscoe were putting on a pantomime for the servants. Roscoe was in the midst of a tumbling routine that involved flipping from his feet to his hands to his feet to his hands, over and over. Sally stood on the tea table, singing, as Charlotte pirouetted by the fireplace, a half dozen petticoats flaring out from her waist. Louisa stomped here and there, hatted, in a long coat and breeches. Last night, Georgie had established the Quiddington sisters in their parents' unaired but commodious bedchamber, where they'd clearly ransacked the wardrobes.

No one in the audience seemed worried about the pilferage, or about the fact that Roscoe's left foot had just kicked the petals off a tulip in a vase. Mrs. Smedley, the housekeeper, bounced on the edge of the love seat, face wreathed with smiles. Bagshaw sat ramrod straight beside her, steel-gray hair clashing with his expression of childlike wonder. Bess, the other maid, was kneeling in an armchair, shouting encouragements.

"We weren't any of us able to see yesterday's performance." Jenny had come to hover behind them in the hallway. "And they offered to give us an entertainment, and it didn't seem any harm, so—"

"Of course," said Georgie, clearing their throat. "No harm." They felt like a louse. They'd canvassed the gentry on behalf of the company, helping to spread the word and fill the boxes. They'd forgotten about the manor staff completely. They should have given everyone the evening off.

"No harm," they repeated. "Why don't you . . ." They made a gesture, and Jenny beamed at them as she skipped through the door to claim a chair.

Georgie stalked to the breakfast room. Phipps was seated at the table, staring meditatively into his teacup.

"Your theatrical comrades already ate," he said, lifting his gaze. "They're juggling plates in the drawing room."

Georgie grunted. There was no one to bring them their eggs, so they loaded up with double toast.

"Are you really going on the road?" asked Phipps.

Georgie heard a faint crash from the drawing room.

Were they really going on the road?

Elf had all but ushered them along. And it wasn't because she despised them. Perversely, it was because they'd risen in her esteem. She'd come to assume they were like *her*, staunch and decisive, persevering toward one all-consuming aspiration. They'd whined for more excitement, claimed they'd *rot* if they stayed in the country. How vacillating and frivolous it would seem if they spontaneously reversed their position. They'd end up with more of Elf's time and less of her respect.

You want to go, she'd said to them, but they wanted one thing, and then another, flipping over and over, like a bloody clown in a harlequinade, and their inconstancy recommended them for precisely nothing.

Phipps frowned, seeming to take their silence for assent.

"It's not at all sensible." He filled a second teacup and pushed it toward them. "But I shouldn't talk. Sensible is kissing my father's ring and marrying Cecy."

Georgie accepted the teacup. Confound it, they'd even miss Phipps.

"Do you think Hartcliffe is looking for you?" They took a swallow of tea. Usually, tea swept away the mental fog. Today, they'd need to drink a gallon. "Not personally," they added. Hartcliffe himself wouldn't stoop. "I mean, hired some Bow Street Runners."

"No." Phipps hesitated. "Because I wrote him."

"You *wrote* him." Georgie set their teacup down on its saucer. It clinked.

"Said I was sailing for Switzerland." Phipps tipped back his head. "*There comes a time in a young man's life when he must, before taking any other steps, reconcile himself with nature on the summit of Mont Blanc . . .*"

"Mont Blanc." Georgie blinked. "Golly. Is that where you'd go? The Alps? If you got together the blunt?"

"I don't suppose I'd go anywhere." A line of crimson decorated Phipps's fine, high cheekbones, and he sipped at his tea without meeting Georgie's eyes.

"I see." Georgie tried to sound innocent. "You have found a pastoral pastime."

"He's a person, not a pastime." Now Phipps looked at them, offended. This from a man who'd tumbled half the House of Commons.

The prickliness. The blush. *Phipps* was in love.

"You have found a person." Georgie leaned forward, relentless. "With whom you share a pastime."

"We share several pastimes." Phipps sniffed. "There's one, of course, that's extremely agreeable. But we also talk about seed drills."

"Seed drills." Georgie fell back. It was too good. "*Seed drills.*"

Phipps glared. "Just so. But we haven't much cause to pass any time together, so it's all a bit too furtive for my taste. And I can hardly lodge at his cottage when you jingle off. In fact, I'm hard-pressed for what to do."

"Stay on here." Georgie waved their hand.

"Without you? Just stay on, at your house? Bagshaw enjoys my flirting, but I hardly think—"

A sound interrupted him. This time it wasn't a crash. It was pounding footsteps.

They pushed back their chair, were already rising, when Elf pelted into the room. Blades of wet grass stuck to her skirt, and all her hair had come loose. She smelled like wind and electricity and came at them like a storm.

"The answer!" She had to grab their arms to arrest her forward momentum, and even then, her damp skirt slapped their shins. "I have it." She sobbed for breath. "I have the answer."

So do I, they almost said, but didn't, because she was running again, and they had to chase her down the hall.

30

SOON GEORGIE WAS also sobbing for breath. Last night, the trees had swarmed in darkness like denizens of a mythical greenwood, party to the revelry of outlaws, vagabonds, and witches. They'd seemed animate, ready to march to Dunsinane under their own power. Now Georgie leapt their stubborn roots and wove between their expressionless trunks.

The trees were once again typical trees, filled not with spirit but timber.

The morning was a typical country morning.

Why, then, did Georgie still feel sorcery, darkling bright, flowing in their blood? Why this buzzing in their ears?

Elf ran quick as a hare through the woodland, and they followed, heart tumbling loose in their chest. She passed between two oaks at the woodland's edge. The sun spilled over her. She was racing into an ocean of clear morning light, her long shadow black on the vivid green grass.

Georgie slowed, sun dazzled, watching Elf open the distance between them. She'd almost reached Holywell Rock. Was she heading for the bluff?

She spun toward them. "Holywell Rock!"

They'd barely slept. They'd spent the previous hours cycling through emotions, stirring up the sediment of all their hopes and fears even as they strained for clarity. Then Elf had flown through the doorway, and their body and soul had made the same decision. But they'd yet to turn that decision over fully in their mind, to examine the angles. It was still revolving, occupying every thought. And now she wanted them to think about something else.

They rallied their forces.

"What about it?" They trotted on until they reached her. "You're not saying the answer to the riddle is Holywell Rock."

"Holywell Rock," she repeated. "Why is it called Holywell Rock?"

"All I know is we could call it by another name, and it would smell as sweet. Or weigh as much. Feel as hard? What's the most rocklike quality of a rock?"

She pushed her hair over her shoulders, face flushed with eagerness, and exasperation. They loved that look. But maybe they were about to earn a kick instead of a kiss.

"It's in the Domesday Book." They hurried to redeem themself. "It has been Holywell Rock for a very long time."

She nodded. "Holy. Well. Rock."

They turned their gaze from her face to the rock. Their pulse had been returning to normal, but it tripped, then began to sprint.

"There's a well?" they attempted. "The rock was rolled over it?"

"More conjecture." Her voice was suddenly hesitant. "But imagine, yes, there was a well, a sacred spring, known to the nuns of the abbey. They hid the hoard inside. Sexburga solved the riddle, but there was still great danger from the Northmen, raids and the like, so she had a rock moved over the well. And by the time of William the Conqueror and the Domesday Book, the well itself was forgotten, and the rock was a landmark, with a name that was just a name."

They were still gazing at it, Holywell Rock. It had always loomed large, this boulder sitting on the line between two properties contentiously divided. Even as a child, if they stood on top of it, they could see over the hedges, into the forbidden realm of the enemy. They'd often climbed up with their wooden sword, to glare at Marsden Hall, at the tower, guarded by a dragon that they longed to fight, vanquish, and befriend, assuming the vanquishment wasn't mortal. They'd passed embarrassing lengths of time atop the boulder, waiting for glimpses of the dragon, and for glimpses of the haughty girl who'd refused to introduce them to said dragon when they'd asked.

And beneath the boulder, all this time, a treasure had been waiting for *them*, for them and for Elf.

"It's here." They turned their gaze back to her. They had no doubt. She nodded again. "We have to lift the rock."

They laughed. There was no other fit response. She'd run to them with the knowledge of the hoard's location flaming in her brain, and then she'd run back, too excited to waste a single second. And now what?

"We can't lift it." They stated the obvious.

She knew. But she tilted up her chin in refusal. And they weren't about to let her down.

"That leaves us one option," they said. "We must levitate it."

This time, she didn't need convincing. She sifted through her hair, searching for stray pins, and twisted the dark locks into a messy knot. Her eyes fixed on the rock with such dauntlessness and determination, they almost expected it to roll itself out of her way.

It did not.

"Ready?" She circled behind it. They paced closer and crouched, pawing at the grass to see if they could wedge their fingertips beneath.

No. Emphatically, no.

"Are your hands on it?" They put their palms on the rock, shifting their weight from foot to foot, settling themself. The rock was cool and scabrous, with luridly colored lichens and tufts of moss.

"Yes," called Elf.

"Ready, then."

She sent up the chant. "Light as a spirit. Light as the air."

"Light as a spirit," they chanted with her. "Light as the air."

Their nose itched, and their thighs burned, and some bird was calling them a twit, repeatedly.

"Um," they said at last. "Maybe it doesn't work when we can't see each other."

And when the thing to be levitated weighed over a ton.

Moving this rock would take an army.

Unless . . .

They sidled backward and gave the rock a narrow-eyed look. "How would you quantify its weight in horses? Two? Two and a half?"

They stood, shaking out their skirt. "One more option."

CHARLES PEACH WAS in a field, pulling weeds from a row of robust-looking plants. Georgie approached, mindful this time of how they stepped.

Peach looked up and startled. His tanned face turned white as lime.

"Those aren't turnips," observed Georgie, upon closer inspection of the plants. "You've planted mangel-wurzel."

"Aye." Peach straightened abruptly.

Georgie tried not to look too impressed with themself. They'd but recently fallen asleep over "An Account of the Mangel Wurzel, or Root of Scarcity" in *Annals of Agriculture*, volume XI.

"A vigorous crop," they declared. "Very healthy."

"Aye." Peach was squeezing a weed in his fist. He seemed strangely skittish. Shouldn't their shared revelry have brought them closer? Or was the shared revelry precisely what ailed him? He and Georgie had rubbed shoulders on an occasion quite beyond the bounds of propriety. Midnight memories of scantily clad swimming, laughing, singing, and dancing suddenly filled the space between landowner and tenant.

Oh dear. That *was* awkward. And Peach and Phipps had danced rather lustily, hadn't they? In full view?

No wonder the gigantic farmer looked one heartbeat away from bolting.

Georgie thought what they might say to put him at ease.

While they thought, Peach spoke.

"Last night were a bit of a frenzy," he said, gaze shifting to the left. "Everybody jumping about like grasshoppers."

"Jolly good fun." Georgie tried to sound as jovial as possible. "Everybody deserves some."

"Aye." Peach's gaze shifted back. "You won't go making any big fuss, then, out of what was a trifle?"

His tone wasn't wheedling, or threatening, but wary.

"I wouldn't dream of making a fuss," said Georgie, and paused. "If it wasn't a trifle, even better." A longer pause, as they debated their next words. What the hell?

"I don't think it's a trifle to him," they said.

Peach's mouth opened but no sound came out. The weed fell to earth. He looked down at it. And then—Georgie's sinking heart rose up again—a dimple flickered in his cheek.

It seemed the right moment to hasten on.

"I came to ask your help," they declared. "There's a boulder I need moved."

Peach lifted his eyes. The dimple was gone. He looked like the old Peach, not apprehensive, not besotted—annoyed. Powerfully annoyed.

"I know." Georgie winced. "I haven't been any help to *you*, not as yet. But I've been reading about husbandry and listening to whoever will tell me more. I'm learning all I can, because I want to invest in the land productively and beneficially." They gave Peach a winning smile. "I recognized the mangel-wurzel."

Peach grunted.

"And I plan to dismiss Mr. Fletcher," they continued, with all the credibility they could muster. "There are complicating factors, but I *am* going to do it. And then I'll fatten the cattle, splendidly. I'll bring a portion of the park under cultivation and buy spent brewer's grains to supplement the hay and cabbages and turnips. I'll see to repairs. I'll bring in new manures. I've learned a shocking amount about manures. There's dung, of course, and coal ash, and lime, but I am most interested currently in gypsum. It's used extensively in Germany. Raw, not calcined. Six hundredweight to the acre. I have an idea to—"

"Botheration," muttered Peach. "That's enough."

He'd said the same to his brother last night, in the same voice. It was firm and yet fundamentally benign. It was not the voice of an ogre.

Georgie grinned, encouraged. "You don't doubt me, then?"

"I don't doubt your tongue will keep running like an overwound clock." But there was a glimmer of amusement in Peach's resigned expression. He looked across the field to where Elf was waiting by the ruins of the wall.

He brushed the dirt from his hands. "Where's this boulder?"

GEORGIE AND ELF had led him halfway there when he stopped short.

"The boulder," he said, glancing about at his surroundings, suspicious. "It's never Holywell Rock?"

Georgie hesitated. "Let's see, shall we?"

When Peach saw, he shot Georgie a glare. "It is Holywell Rock."

"You hoped for something smaller." Georgie could understand. "But you're Charles Peach! You carried a horse."

Peach pointed at the rock. "That's three horses."

"Three?" Georgie frowned. "Ponies, maybe."

Peach twitched his head, as though this didn't merit a verbal rebuttal.

"You'll try, though." Georgie smiled a hopeful smile.

"You'll tell me what's the reason?" Peach retorted.

"There's something under it," said Elf, and Peach flicked his glare to her. The expression on her face made him turn his eyes up to the heavens and mutter under his breath.

It seemed the opposite of prayerful, but also, promising.

"You'll try," said Georgie, more confidently.

Peach loosened his neckerchief, rolled his head on his shoulders, cracked his knuckles, and tried.

He tried, and he failed. He couldn't get his arms around the boulder, or budge it with his shoulder, even as his boots slid and gouged the earth like a plow.

After a quarter hour of bone-cracking effort, he stepped away, red in the face and steaming. He didn't so much as look at Georgie or Elf. He turned and strode down the path.

Georgie sagged as he disappeared into the woodland. Elf was biting her lip, arms tightly folded.

That cheeky, sarcastic, intolerable bird was still twit, twit, twitting.

And then Peach reappeared, a Christmas goose–sized rock under one arm. He was dragging a tree branch.

With the Christmas goose as a fulcrum, and the branch as a lever, he tried again. The branch snapped with a sound like a gunshot.

Peach didn't flinch. He repositioned the shortened length.

Georgie watched him work with bated breath and didn't realize Elf was gone, until she was back, dragging a second branch.

Peach directed its placement, and together, she and Peach levered

Holywell Rock up by inches, and then Georgie braced Peach's branch, while he set his shoulder to the rock once more. His neck bulged. A vein throbbed on his forehead. And Holywell Rock began to tilt.

Peach made a noise like a bull.

Holywell Rock flipped over. Georgie and Elf fell backward. Every bird that hadn't fluttered off at that first crack of wood flapped into the air.

There was silence in the meadow. Peach was doubled up, hands on his thighs, heaving for breath.

Elf crawled forward. Georgie crawled too.

The recess in the earth was circular, perhaps a yard in diameter, embanked with masonry, its crumbled gray rim scratched white.

Georgie expected to confront their own face, and Elf's, reflecting up from the surface of an ancient pool.

The well held only river stones. Stones those two Saxon nuns had thrown down on top of the sunken treasure, to conceal it.

Georgie's gaze locked on Elf's. She was thinking the same thing.

Together, the two of them stretched their arms down into the well. The stones were smooth and cold, bigger than muffins, for the most part, smaller than loaves of bread.

Georgie dropped them one by one on the grass, rapidly, carelessly. They clattered off each other. Some of the stones were gray, others paler. The one in Georgie's hands was streaked with dark brown and darker red.

"Blood?" Georgie dropped it, wiping their fingers frantically on the grass. Visions of murdered nuns danced before their eyes.

"Metal." Elf lifted a stone similarly smeared with gore. "Any iron would have rusted in the water."

Iron nails connecting the planks of a chest. Iron straps reinforcing the wood.

"And oak?" asked Georgie, grabbing another stone. "Would an oak chest have rotted?"

Elf didn't respond. The stone in her hands thudded to the ground beside her.

"Oh," said Georgie. Because they were looking down at the answer, looking into the gap between stones at the dark grain of preserved wood.

"Oh," they said again, heart swooping. "Oh."

The last stones were the most difficult to pull out, given their depth, about the length of Georgie's arm.

"I'll do it," said Charles Peach. He knelt and removed them, and then, as easily as Georgie might have lifted a hatbox, he lifted out the chest. The chest was the size of two hatboxes, but clearly much weightier. It looked intact until he set it down, and then the sides collapsed. The lid balanced on the contents, some of which spilled onto the grass.

Georgie's gaze followed a ball of dirt as it bounced, only it wasn't dirt. It was fragments of tarnished silver stuck together with rust. They looked at Elf. Her eyes were huge, her knuckles white, fists crossed at the wrists against her chest.

"What is this?" asked Peach, voice soft with wonder.

Elf unfroze. She crawled to the chest and picked up the lid. Georgie and Peach leaned closer. A mass of metal, gleaming in the morning sun. Coins, rings, bracelets, their warm yellow undimmed by the centuries.

"That's gold," said Peach.

It was gold. Silver too. Georgie glanced from a lidded silver vessel to a large silver cross. They started to laugh. The bird had returned, twitting away, and they whistled along, then gave up, to laugh some more.

A two-handled silver cup had tipped when the chest broke apart, scattering glass beads and other small ornaments. The cup had a gold lip, gold bands and enamel studs around the bowl, a short stem and a flared foot.

A chalice.

Georgie felt a jolt when their fingers closed around the stem. *Connection.* Not only with the metal but with the other hands that had touched it before them. They sought Elf's eyes, which she raised now from the treasure to meet theirs.

"To Sexburga." They raised the chalice. "And to your grandmother," they went on. "And to you, Elfreda Marsden, archaeologist."

The holy well itself had gone dry, but Elf's dark eyes welled with tears and with light. They could fall into her eyes, and keep falling, for another thousand years.

She turned away, turned at the waist to lay down the lid, and turned back, accepting the chalice. She rotated it every which way, studying it hungrily, then shook herself.

"It's yours," she said. "We had an agreement." She held it out to them. They didn't take it. "Give me something less unique."

Her smile was relieved. "There are chopped ingots. Little hunks of hack gold and silver."

"I want three," they said. "Three pieces to sell. I'll divide the proceeds between the three of us, the finders."

"Me?" asked Peach.

"Of course you," said Georgie. "We all found it together."

Elf was hesitating, and they wondered for a moment if she'd reject the proposition, to preserve a sense of herself as disinterested in anything but the hoard's historical import. She needed money, though. Besides, money *was* the hoard's historical import.

"These objects were twice plundered already," they pointed out. "Don't you antiquaries like to uphold tradition?"

She looked nettled, but she returned the chalice and selected three hunks of gold.

"Your plunder," she said as she dropped them into their hand.

"Our plunder." They grinned. A good thing they'd dressed in a gown styled like a riding habit, with buttoned pockets. They slipped the gold inside.

"And the rest of it?" Peach seemed dazed.

"By law, all of it belongs to the king," said Elf. "Once we report it to the coroner, he'll take possession and hold an inquest. But first I'll catalog and describe and draw every piece." Her face was lighting up at the thought.

Peach's face had darkened. "The Crown owns what's buried?"

"Only if it's gold or silver, and deliberately hidden," replied Elf, almost absently. She was somewhere else, winging away in her mind, toward the Peak was Georgie's guess.

"So not something as was dropped?" persisted Peach. "Or made of bronze or iron?"

Georgie was about to ask him why he wondered, but Elf was rising, and they forgot Peach as they sprang to their feet.

"I must go to the Peak at once," she said. "I must tell Papa, and the Barrow Prince."

"I'll drive you," offered Georgie, but she was staring at them like a woman newly woken from a dream.

"What time is it?" she gasped. "After ten? The theater company! If I've spoiled your chance, I won't forgive myself. Perhaps it's not too late. Hurry."

She made a frantic, flapping gesture with her hands.

She wouldn't believe them if they told her now that they'd already chosen to stay, so they didn't bother.

They shook their head. "You need me to drive you. How else will you get there?"

"Mrs. Alderwalsey. She'll let me take her carriage, I know it. Papa last wrote from Incledon Hall, in a village near Youlgreave. It's not so far." Her flapping hands pressed their arm in an urgent little shove. "Hurry."

They let her move them away a step. And because a plan had been forming in their mind all morning, and they *did* have cause to chase down the strollers, they took another step away.

"All right," they said. "I'll hurry." They glanced at Peach. The farmer cut his eyes at Elf, then cocked a brow at them.

"Don't mind me," he murmured. The dimple was back in his cheek.

Georgie didn't mind him. They didn't mind anything. They bounded the two steps back to Elf, and before they hurried off, they gave her a thorough kiss goodbye.

31

MRS. ALDERWALSEY DID not let Elfreda take her carriage, not exactly. She insisted on accompanying her.

"Treasure!" She cackled gleefully. "This news will certainly overshadow Mrs. Roberts's theatrical evening. I have never been so eager to send my excuses."

The carriage rolled up into the Peak, through steep-sided dales, and finally, just beyond a pretty village of limestone cottages, it rolled to a stop in front of Incledon Hall. The hour was half past four. Teatime. And Papa was, in fact, sipping tea in the drawing room.

"Elfreda!" He choked at the sight of her, and then he choked again. "Mrs. Alderwalsey!"

"Harold," replied Mrs. Alderwalsey. "There is only one thing I will permit you to say to me."

"What are you doing here?" asked Papa.

Mrs. Alderwalsey sniffed. "That is not the thing."

"Madam." Frederic Incledon nodded, with severe courtesy. "Miss Marsden." He was a severe man, whose published papers focused on trial by ordeal, particularly the medieval Frankish practice of trial by cauldron. He was once among Papa's most regular correspondents and most frequent visitors. Then he became the Albion Society secretary, under Mr. Clutterbuck, and the letters and visits fell off.

"What of the little ones?" Nicholas Fluff spoke much more warmly. "Have they come too?"

"Egad." Papa's face was turning red. "They had better not have come. What is the meaning of this? I trust no one is ill."

"No one is ill," said Mrs. Alderwalsey, gleefully. "But *you* might require my smelling salts." She fixed her sharp eyes on Elfreda. "Well? We rushed all this way. Will you make them wait?"

"Wait for *what*?" Papa's face was completely red.

The moisture wicked from Elfreda's mouth. Her stomach roiled.

"*What?*" repeated Papa.

The drawing room was filled with antiquities, and also antiquaries. In fact, the antiquaries had doubled in number. Ten men sat in bishop's chairs arranged loosely around the tea table. The tea things were shoved to one end, and trays of grave goods occupied the majority of its surface.

Elfreda's gaze moved from Papa to Sir Graham. Then to Nicholas Fluff. Simon Sykes. Mr. Incledon. Hudson Roach was there. Hudson Roach, the Albion Society treasurer. He always wore around his neck the Albion Society money-horn, a stag's horn mounted with silver, from the reign of Emperor Louis I. She looked at the horn, and then briefly at Craven Braybrooke, author of *Observations on the Body-Armour Anciently Worn in England*. He sat beside Stephen Pettigrew, the engraver who made the plates for the Society's annual publication, *Antique Monuments*.

Finally, she looked at the Barrow Prince. His chair was angled away from the table. He'd been sketching a bronze casket set on a flower stand, but now he closed his notebook. His eyes bored into her. Everyone's eyes bored into her.

"Miss Marsden?" The Barrow Prince's low, rough voice scraped upward at the end, interrogatively.

"A little suspense is well and good," observed Mrs. Alderwalsey, smirking around at the assembled men, before fixing again on El-freda. "But you should get on with it."

Ants were marching down Elfreda's spine. Her tongue was stuck to the roof of her mouth. Her head filled with noise.

"While I still have my teeth," said Papa.

She tried to press the hum down into her throat. Sound buzzed behind her lips.

"For God's sake." Papa slammed down his teacup.

A word flew out. It wasn't a suitable word, alas.

"Romeo!" she cried. The room went completely silent. She wished desperately that the floor would open. Could she have said anything more foolish? Georgie. It was Georgie's fault. Georgie, who'd teased and kissed and laughed and listened their way into her life. And out of it. They were the reason she'd managed to speak at all, and the rea-son she'd spoken like a woman about to swoon, not from nerves, from love. She couldn't think of Georgie without a million feelings flood-ing through her, making her less rational, and maybe . . . more herself. Not because women couldn't be rational. Because rationality without the emotions, without the senses—it was cold and incomplete.

Her back straightened. She met Papa's eyes.

"Did you say *Romeo*?" He looked flabbergasted.

"Of course she didn't," Sir Graham assured him. "She said *Rome*. I believe she found a Roman antiquity."

"Did you find a Roman antiquity?" Papa was obviously relieved by Sir Graham's suggestion. He looked better disposed already, face expressive of a readiness to welcome her back into his good graces. He glanced at the reticule she was holding and held out his hand.

She swallowed. "I found antiquities verifying the location of the Great Heathen Army's winter camp." She could barely hear herself over the nervous hum in her skull, the wild roar of blood in her ears, but she was saying words, suitable words.

"I found their hoard," she was saying. "I haven't yet counted the objects, but there are easily two hundred, including coins. I brought a few of the coins." Her fingers fumbled at the drawstring of her reticule. She shook the gold and silver into her palm.

A collective intake of breath greeted the sight.

"By Caesar's ghost!" exclaimed Sir Graham.

"Where? Where did you find it?" Many voices went up in unison. "Where is the camp?"

"Show me the coins." Papa had rounded the table and was nearly upon her. She remembered, suddenly, the lighter weight of the buttons in her palm that day in Thornton. How she'd gone, for a moment, hollow like a bell, ringing with panic in the afternoon light.

She shouldn't feel panicked now. Papa was smiling broadly, beaming with the fondness of a father who wouldn't dream of putting his unaccompanied daughters on a public coach, all but penniless.

"You've done well, youngling," he murmured. But even that—the approval she craved—didn't make her stomach unclench.

She could tell he was about to embrace her and stiffened. Only she'd mistaken his movement. His arm swung out, but it was so he could sweep the coins from her hand into his. He strode back to his seat at the table.

"Gentlemen," he said, sitting. "I shall not withhold a moment longer." He paused, for two moments, posture regal, while the antiquaries leaned toward him. "The Great Heathen Army overwintered on the bluff at the edge of my park."

"You old slyboots." Sir Graham scowled. "You never said."

"I began digging months ago." Papa's smile was sly indeed. "Guided by a Mercian annal. And assisted by my brilliant daughter, who has carried me the first fruits of my endeavor." He beckoned to Elfreda. She walked to him on legs that did not feel like her own.

Nicholas Fluff had ceded his own chair to Mrs. Alderwalsey, and now he carried over another, for her. There wasn't space at the table to accommodate it. Or rather, no one made any space.

Elfreda gave him a grateful glance but remained standing.

"As for the fruits themselves," said Papa, and laid the coins down one by one on the table. "Frankish. Islamic. Frankish. Byzantine. Islamic. Anglo-Saxon." He held up the last coin. "This is a penny of Ceolwulf the Second."

"It's not," Elfreda responded instantly. "It's a penny of his father, Burgred. The annal says the Great Heathen Army encamped in Twynham in 868, and the penny supports that chronology. Ceolwulf the Second ruled later."

There was a sound like gravel crunching under carriage wheels.

The Barrow Prince was laughing.

"Let me see." Hudson Roach stretched across the table and snatched the penny from Papa's hand. "Burgred Rex," he confirmed. "There are a few perforations on the obverse, but you can still read the letters."

"I thought it was Burgred," said Papa. "But the *B* looked like a *C*, because I am not wearing my spectacles."

"Oh, pish," said Mrs. Alderwalsey. "Spectacles aren't the problem. Harold, you have always been blinded by your own conceit."

Papa's head whipped around. "How dare you!"

"How dare I?" Mrs. Alderwalsey had taken over Mr. Fluff's tea as well as his seat. She sipped delicately. "I was at your breeching ceremony. I dare anything."

"Miss Marsden," rasped the Barrow Prince, "was the hoard on the bluff?" Her gaze skittered away from his almost at once. She studied her interlaced fingers where they pressed into her belly.

"No," she said, drawing a breath, then lifting her eyes, looking at him directly. "The army encamped on the bluff, but the hoard was in a well. It's fascinating how it ended up there. My grandmother was a scholar—"

Papa emitted a rude noise.

Mrs. Alderwalsey pointed a spoon at him, and remarkably, he quailed.

"My grandmother was a scholar," continued Elfreda. "She prepared a translation of a nun's chronicle, a nun from Twynham Abbey. That's what led me to the hoard. The chronicle recounted—"

Mr. Incledon interrupted.

"Your well is from the Dark Ages?" He addressed the question to Papa.

Papa gave an uncomfortable shrug. "It is much older than the hall, yes."

It was not, but Elfreda avoided correcting the factual error.

"I didn't find it in our well," she said, "but in a well beneath Holywell Rock."

"Holywell Rock!" Papa couldn't hide his surprise. "How the devil did you move Holywell Rock?"

"Fire setting," suggested the Barrow Prince. "Heat the rock, then add cold water, so it cracks. That's what I'd have done."

"That's what the Romans did." Sir Graham nodded.

"A farmer moved it," said Elfreda. "He's very strong and used a lever."

She hadn't thought of fire setting, but even if she had, she would have dismissed the technique. Too slow. She'd been in such a rush to tell Papa, to tell the Barrow Prince, to make her discovery *real*. But it had already been real. By rushing to Incledon Hall, she'd made her discovery Papa's.

She wadded the empty reticule in her hand.

"The hoard isn't still in the well?" he asked.

"It's in the library," she said. Mr. Peach had helped with that too.

"Good." Papa exchanged a look with Sir Graham. "We'll return directly."

"Not without the rest of us," protested Craven Braybrooke. "It's the object of the Society to investigate all the remains of antiquity, and this is our very first chance to explore a heathen camp." His pale eyes burned. "Think of the armor."

"As secretary, I must record the excavation," said Mr. Incledon.

"You'll need illustrations and engravings," said Stephen Pettigrew.

"We should convene a special meeting of the council at Marsden Hall," said Hudson Roach. "With your permission, Marsden, of course."

"You forget I am not *on* the council." Papa's voice was waspish.

"Easily remedied." Hudson Roach smiled, unperturbed. "We'll take a ballot. Who would say *nay*? My God, a Danish camp!"

Elfreda cleared her throat. Her heart thudded in her ears. "And myself?"

"You wish to attend the meeting?" Now Roach was less certain. "It's unprecedented, but . . ." He blinked rapidly, tapping his money-horn in time, then nodded. "Just this once, given that it's a special meeting, convened under special circumstances, in which you played a special role . . . I don't foresee any objections."

He hadn't even understood what she'd been asking. It was inconceivable—*her* name on a ballot.

"I will not attend." The Barrow Prince shrugged his broad shoulders. "As I told you all this morning, I've been called away."

"Deuced mysterious," grumbled Simon Sykes. "You could tell us the reason."

The Barrow Prince ignored him. "If you have ever an interest in joining one of my excursions," he said, turning his hard gaze on Elfreda, "know that I am honored to receive you."

"My thanks." Papa tipped his head with amused condescension, intercepting both gaze and invitation. "But I will be some time occupied with my own findings. Speaking of which—" He glanced at the coins on the table, and then up at Elfreda.

"Child," he said, "bring me my spectacles. I must have left them in my other coat. A maid will show you to my chamber." He put his finger on a coin and slid it toward Mr. Incledon. "What do you make of this one?"

Elfreda walked out of the drawing room. She walked out of the house. She walked across the lawn to the nearest tree and put her hand on it.

Was she going to cry? Laugh? Something was building in her chest. And she did laugh because the something felt very much like a howl.

All her life, she'd wanted to belong to the Albion Society, badly, for the practical benefits. As a Fellow, she could attend meetings, see exhibitions, hear lectures, participate in excavations, send her own papers to be printed in *Antique Monuments*.

She'd wanted membership, too, for what it signified. As a Fellow, she would exist, finally, as an archaeologist, on paper, and in the eyes of the world.

That dream had died back there in the drawing room.

She wasn't a Fellow. She wasn't ever going to *be* a Fellow.

Oddly, she didn't feel devastated. She felt . . . unfettered. Her new dream would have nothing to do with those men. None of them got to define her, not even Papa.

Georgie had said as much that day at St. Alcmund's.

Georgie believed in her.

Her sisters believed in her.

Her grandmother believed in her.

She believed in her.

She was laughing, *and* she was crying. She pushed off the tree and went farther from the house, into the sun. The fresh air filled her lungs, more and more of it. Laughing, crying—it wasn't enough. She was going to howl. There was nothing else for it. The ground seemed to shake beneath her feet.

It took her a moment to realize.

Hoofbeats.

Hoofbeats were drumming the earth. A rider was galloping toward her up the drive, a rider astride a black hunter, skirts hiked up, slim legs gripping the horse's sides.

Scandalous. Impossible.

Instead of a howl, their name tore from her throat.

32

EORGIE!" SHE RAN to them. They swung off the horse before it came to a full stop. An instant later, she was crushed to their chest, their arms around her, their momentum carrying her off her feet.

"You're soaked," she gasped. "Is that sweat?"

"Partially. I've been riding for hours. Through spots of very dirty weather. The downpours account for some of it." Their face was pressed to the top of her head. She could feel their heart pounding into her. They smelled like rain, and like horse, and she never wanted to let them go.

"What happened?" they asked. "What did your father say? Is the Barrow Prince coming to dig?"

"You first." She mustered her resolve and stepped back from them. "What happened? What did Mr. Arbuthnot say? Did he rescind his offer?"

Georgie stepped forward, eyes on her lips. She touched their arm in warning, and they flicked their gaze up to hers, and then over her shoulder. She watched their face turn rueful as they took note of the bay windows of Incledon Hall.

They were alone with her on the lawn but not necessarily unwitnessed.

They moved away, a few reluctant inches. "Mr. Arbuthnot did not rescind his offer." They said it carefully. "I declined it."

She looked at them without comprehension.

"I declined it," they repeated. "Then I attended to some pressing business. And then I tried to catch up with you." They'd lost their hat during the wild dismount. They glanced at it, upside down on the grass, and ran their fingers through their flattened hair. "I wanted to be here," they explained, "in case you required a spokesman."

"I didn't." Because she'd been crying, her smile tasted like salt. "I acquitted myself well, in fact." Leaving to the side the *Romeo*. "I said what I had to say. There was much excitement."

They tipped their head, peering at her intently.

"These are the traces of happy tears?" They lifted a hand, hovered their finger by her cheek.

She didn't want to talk about it yet.

"You're staying?" she asked. "In Twynham, I mean."

Their eyes were like diamonds. How could anyone have eyes like that?

She wished she were nearer the tree. She wanted to lean on something. She wanted to lean on Georgie, but she was too aware of Incledon Hall looming behind her. Any moment, the front door would open and disgorge the men within.

"I'm staying," said Georgie. They tilted up their chin, studied the sky. When they looked at her again, their eyes had absorbed some of its blue, and their face was tense.

"I seem fickle, don't I?" They stated it like a fact. "Frittering. And *flittering*. Dithering." Their laugh was strained. "I've always admired your conviction. At times, I was jealous of it, and offended by it, and until this summer, I didn't understand it one jot. But I admired it. I *lack* conviction. I haven't dedicated my life to anything, not like you have. I realized I couldn't dedicate it to the stage. I'm not sure if the stage is the problem, or the dedication."

She bit her lip at the echo of her past accusation. "You don't seem fickle to me."

"How's that?" They sounded cynical, but she glimpsed something vulnerable in their expression.

"You might not have centered all your energy on a single enterprise," she said, "and you might not ever—but it doesn't follow that you aren't dedicated. You're dedicated to . . ." She thought of the way to put it. "*Enlivening* life. You enliven life for the people around you, as much as for yourself. You make bonhomie contagious. No matter the situation, you try, always, to make it better. You're a show-off." They frowned at that, and her lips twitched. "You're an incorrigible show-off. You attract so much attention to your own person, it's easy to miss the fact that what you're doing is often in service of someone else. You've helped *me* immeasurably."

The tense lines bracketing their mouth softened. "We found the gold."

"We had fun doing it." Her voice was hoarse. "I've never had such fun."

They shot a glance at Incledon Hall and edged closer to her, forward and sideways, so the side of their hand brushed hers.

"I'm staying for you," they said quietly. "Not *only* for you. It's just—everything else I want connects to you, to how I feel about you, to how I feel about myself when I'm with you. I suppose I could say I'm staying for everything. Or that you're everything. You're everything." They sucked in their breath, and their eyes weren't diamonds, they were stars. "May we *please* go behind that tree so I can kiss you?"

She tried to walk back to the tree casually, but her legs trembled, and she ended up stumbling, then skipping, and she might as well have been swooning—her every motion was so, so obvious. To any-one who could see and knew how to look.

For their part, Georgie was sauntering as though they hadn't a care in the world. But the moment the tree stood between the two of them and the house, they kissed her, pressing her into the trunk, holding her face, their touch light, their mouth barely there. A kiss like their very first. It was a beginning. The first of many more. Fire licked through her. It was eating all her oxygen. She felt lightheaded.

"I asked Roscoe to act the part of my brother." They separated from her but took her hands, squeezing them tight. "He dressed in a naval uniform and sacked Mr. Fletcher using the most martial terms."

"Isn't Major Redmayne in the army?"

"Roscoe would have made a better Admiral Nelson, in truth." They shrugged. "But it worked."

"That was your pressing business? Sacking Mr. Fletcher?"

They grinned. "And persuading Phipps and Peach to accept the positions of chief steward and resident steward. They'll have to work together closely. Late hours in the steward's house."

She laughed. "You're very persuasive. But I doubt persuasion was necessary."

"They seemed keen." Georgie's grin widened. "Harry will find out eventually. He'll shout about the subterfuge. But once he sees that the ends justify the means, he'll come around." They paused. "I think." They gave their head a shake. "Anyway, too late now. At least he'll appreciate that I'm staying out of trouble."

She raised her brows. "Staying out of trouble?"

"Staying out of London, at least. And when I'm five and twenty, you and I can go together. You should experience Vauxhall at least once. We won't stop at London, though. We'll travel the whole world. Provided I've got my estate in order, and your dig has con-cluded."

Her dig.

She gripped their hands tighter.

"We could go to Denmark," they suggested. "Or Norway. Whichever was the home of the Northmen. You'll be an authority on their nails and buckles by then, and their taste in pillage. You can hobnob with the modern Northmen and get them to take you to *their* archaeological sites. Meanwhile, I'll learn how to build one of those dragon boats, so we can sail it back to England. At the very least, we should—"

"I love you." She kissed them.

"You do?" They looked as dizzy as she felt. "How manifestly unreasonable of you." They pulled her into another kiss. "It happens I love you too."

She was on the verge of confessing more, that she had no dig, that it was Papa's, that it was the Albion Society's, that she'd travel the world with them right now, if it weren't for her sisters, and their estate, and Papa's voice.

She started. Papa's voice. He was calling her.

Further confessions would have to wait.

But so would Papa. Because Georgie was kissing her again behind the tree, and she preferred to take her time.

PAPA WAS SO confused by Georgie's sudden appearance, he forgot to scold Elfreda for her disappearance. And he was so pleased in general, his usually stamping footfalls barely whispered on the ground as he led them both into the house. He was practically floating.

The house was a flurry of activity, antiquaries preparing for the journey south, except for Mr. Incledon, who'd opted to drive to Twynham in the morning, and the Barrow Prince, who wasn't going south at all. After speaking with Georgie, Nicholas Fluff decided to delay his own departure by a day and ride Georgie's horse, thereby allowing the animal to rest, and Georgie to join Elfreda and Mrs. Alderwalsey in the carriage.

The return took longer than Elfreda expected. Those spots of dirty weather had grouped together into something filthy, and the night grew filthier near Twynham. It was midnight when they arrived at Marsden Hall, Sir Graham's carriage a minute behind.

Agnes was awake and must have been listening for the sound of wheels, for she threw open the door before anyone reached it. Mrs. Pegg was also awake, and the twins. Awake and too uproarious to make the reason for the uproar immediately known.

"Talk sense, someone," demanded Papa, standing in the entranceway, rain dripping from his hat.

Soon, though, it was Mrs. Alderwalsey making demands, and denouncing Papa's senseless negligence.

Because the ceiling of the blue room had completely collapsed.

33

OVER THE NEXT week, a great deal happened very quickly. Antiquaries flocked to Twynham from all over England to pore over the hoard and jockey for position vis-à-vis the impending excavation. And Mrs. Alderwalsey drove back up to Marsden Hall, this time with visitors from Surrey: Aunt Susan and her ringleted stepdaughter, Cassandra.

"It *does* have to be seen to be believed," said Aunt Susan, pale with horror, as Mrs. Alderwalsey toured her past the wreckage of the blue room, Elfreda and Cassandra trailing behind.

"And your hair," moaned Aunt Susan once the little party had reached the tower, where Agnes stood at the window, strumming her lute.

"I adore it!" cried Cassandra. "You look like Joan of Arc."

Agnes curtseyed to Mrs. Alderwalsey, kissed Aunt Susan, and smiled delightedly at her new cousin.

"I will write a song for you," she declared. "How would you describe the essence of your being?"

"D major," answered Cassandra. "Or G-flat major. And yours?"

Aunt Susan was the one who looked like Joan of Arc, not the hair, of course, something about the facial expression, both martyred and defiant.

She turned to Elfreda. "Take me to the nursery."

Agnes and Cassandra stayed in the tower, conferring and composing in the most rapturous tones, and Elfreda took Aunt Susan and Mrs. Alderwalsey to the nursery, or part of the way. They'd just started up the staircase when Hilda and Matilda came sledding toward them on a mattress. Luckily, Mrs. Alderwalsey led an alacritous retreat down the steps, or the collision might have involved casualties.

"They almost never do that," said Elfreda, but Aunt Susan was now marching toward the library.

"Papa won't receive you," called Elfreda, racing after. It wasn't only that Aunt Susan had offended him—these past days his time had been entirely occupied, and the present moment was no exception. "He's meeting with the coroner."

"How convenient," cackled Mrs. Alderwalsey.

Aunt Susan flung open the library door.

To Elfreda's surprise, Papa didn't respond to the interruption with wrath, even when he realized it was his estranged sister descending upon him. He smiled, introduced her to the coroner, and with a casual sweep of his hand, drew her attention at last to the glittering gold and silver on the table.

Aunt Susan gawked. But only for a moment.

"Harold," she said, "I do not advocate spoiling young people with excessive indulgences, but a house must have, over its entire area, a roof. Do you intend to use *that*"—she pointed at the precious metal—"to shelter your children from the elements?"

The coroner straightened. "That would be a crime, madam."

Aunt Susan stamped her foot and waved her arms, rather magnificently. "*This* is a crime. All of this."

In the end, Papa agreed to let her take the twins for the summer. The twins didn't protest, not after Aunt Susan said Grendel could come too. By that point, she probably considered dogs in the nursery the least of all possible evils. And Agnes was so enamored of Cassandra, she invited herself along. All three girls burst into tears when they realized Elfreda was *not* inclined to quit Twynham, but she promised to write, and Cassandra promised they could ride her pony, and everyone seemed cheered.

Her sisters' departure made Marsden Hall feel different—emptier, colder; however, it was, in fact, more peopled than ever. Antiquaries filed in and out of the library, cataloging the coins and objects in advance of the inquest. Elfreda worked on her own catalog, unnoticed except when a Fellow found himself in want of more tea or biscuits.

Mr. Clutterbuck arrived, and the special meeting was held, during which Papa was duly elected to the council, and Elfreda was praised for her cleverness in solving the riddle that led to the hoard's recovery. Attention shifted quickly to the hoard itself, and to the camp, and then splintered as the men formed factions, arguing over who should be in charge of what.

No one asked to read Caroline Marsden's papers. Nor did anyone seem interested in contemplating the significance of the riddle's transmission from woman to woman, down through the centuries.

Once her bitterness subsided, Elfreda felt relieved. The disinterest meant her grandmother's papers wouldn't be taken from her.

When the excavation began, bitterness surged anew. The bluff became busy as a beehive, Fellows cutting turf, shoveling, clustering around the finds—slag metal one day, a charcoal-stained stone hearth the next, then iron ship fastenings. She had no place in it. She was relegated to bystander, or more accurately, by*sitter*, as Nicholas Fluff made sure to usher her time and again to a camp chair in the shade.

"Georgie Redmayne has solicited my company," she told Papa, upon encountering him alone in the library, as the excavation entered its second week. "I'm going to visit at Redmayne Manor—to stay there, I mean."

"Is the Major back?" Papa narrowed his eyes.

"No," said Elfreda, shortly.

"Even so, child." Papa was shaking his head.

Elfreda was shaking hers. "I am not a child. And I am going. It's just across the park." She didn't add: *and even if it weren't.*

"This isn't because of the blue room?" asked Papa. "I should think you understand my position."

"I do, Papa," she said. "I have come to understand your position perfectly."

He considered her for a moment. "Good. You have always been my great favorite. You will come if I call for you." He turned back to the coins on his desk, confident of her nod.

She stood very still. Then she turned away. She packed, in a basket, her grandmother's writings, her own notebooks, *Sepulchral Anecdotes*, and such clothes as fit on top, and she walked to Redmayne Manor. Despite the weight of the basket, she felt lighter with each step.

Holywell Rock was still on its side, the empty well too exposed, vulnerable, the river stones heaped haphazardly on the grass. She stopped and selected a stone, a small one. She added it to her basket and returned the rest to the well. That night, she asked Georgie to see if Mr. Peach would move Holywell Rock back into place.

"Why?" They cocked a brow. "Don't want me gaining the few extra feet of land?" But that wasn't it, and they knew it. "Of course I will," they said. "But first, perhaps *we* should hide something, for future Elfreda Marsdens to discover."

She debated with them about what to hide, a long desultory debate that continued from the dining room to the drawing room to the bedchamber, with many digressions along the way. And later, when they fell asleep, she lay curled into them, and she thought about the future, so much less certain than the past, essentially unknowable. And yet, the past wasn't knowable either, was it? The past was more than objects and events. It was made, too, of unrealized possibilities. It was made of memories, of hopes and dreams. It was made of the future. Those two Saxon nuns had changed her life when they'd buried the hoard, and now that she was changed, she wondered differently about *their* lives. She wondered if they'd fallen in love with each other, if they'd stayed at the abbey or struck out into the world, chalices hidden in their sleeves. She wondered what had become of them, and what would become of her, and what might be possible for a woman who wanted to live and love as she did, in fifty years, in a hundred years, in a thousand. What she herself might help *make* possible, by living and loving now.

By howling in meadows. By kissing in starlight. By reading the dirt. By recording its stories. By imagining more.

The following day, Georgie carried a mahogany tea caddy to Holywell Rock and situated it in the well, layering the stones on top.

"You didn't tell me what you put in it," she complained, watching them with folded arms. Georgie grinned and stood, turning to face her. "I figured *you* are the future Elfreda Marsden who should recover the Great Octagonal Tea Caddy of 1818." They grabbed her by the hips and drew her close, eyes brilliant with summer sun. She felt their mouth and their laughter against her neck. "You know where it is. So it's no fun if you also know what's inside."

"How long must I wait?"

"Fifty years."

"Fifty?"

"Not a day less. Mark it on your calendar."

She kissed them, the darkness behind her lowered lids sparkling with traces of light.

That afternoon, Mr. Peach heaved Holywell Rock back into place, the process quicker and even more impressively vigorous than the last time, perhaps because Lord Phillip was watching.

"I could impersonate Napoleon, ride up there, and scare them all off," murmured Georgie, and she realized that her gaze had strayed to the bluff, green treetops swaying against the blue sky.

She gave her head a slight shake. They were looking at *her*, a worry line between their brows.

"I have a saber," they added.

This merited another shake of her head, and a smile. Because they were outrageous enough, and dear enough, to make good on their offer. They'd slap on a bicorne, mount their steed, and charge the Fellows of the Albion Society, rattling their saber and shouting in very bad French.

Georgie's Napoleonic charge wouldn't win her back the bluff. But even the ridiculous idea of it swelled her heart. It told her the battle wasn't hers alone. She'd fight with her pen—continuing her grandmother's researches—and someday, she'd fight again with her shovel, as an archaeologist in the field. And Georgie would stand beside her, with a metaphorical, or maybe literal, saber, and a wicked smile, lending her their strength and charm and spirit.

"I'm glad the Society is excavating," she said, dashing away sudden tears. "It would have taken me another year to accomplish what took them weeks."

"Yes, of course, many hands make light work." Georgie shot the bluff a leaf-singeing glare. "But in this case, they're ghastly, acquisitive, antiquarian hands, and they should have leave to dig only under *your* direction. At the very least, they shouldn't obstruct you."

She rubbed her calloused palms together. She itched to dig. But on the bluff there was a chair set up for her, away from the trenches, near the refreshment table. She did *not* itch to sit, serving coffee to Simon Sykes, watching Nicholas Fluff shake her sieve with all the skill and intention of a puppy with a stick. She wouldn't.

She put her back to the bluff. A breeze was rustling the nearer leaves of the woodland. Mr. Peach and Lord Phillip had disappeared into its fragrant, sun-dappled depths.

"The only gold I want to find today is buttercups." She started along the path, casting a wickedly mischievous glance over her shoulder that caused Georgie's face to blank with shock. But they were more than equal to the suggestion. One moment later, their eyes kindled, and they bounded up to her, wrapping an arm around her waist and growling in her ear.

"Onward to the secluded dell."

THE ITCH TO dig didn't subside completely, but as midsummer approached, it ceased to irritate. The days were long and diverting, the nights warm, the secluded dells plentiful, and so too the meadow-sweet and lady's bedstraw. She went whole hours without lamenting her removal from the winter camp of the Great Heathen Army.

And then, a Northman burst into the Redmayne library.

She was sitting at the desk, ostensibly working on her manuscript, and yet her eyes kept wandering to the windows. This library was cheerful, furnished with relatively few books and antiquities, and relatively numerous sofas and soft reading chairs, and the windows were tall, fitted with panes of clean glass that displayed the fineness of the day. It was almost too cheerful. It recommended walks and frolics as much as study and conversation.

She had just put down her pen. She had just succumbed to an urge for more sun. The door flinging open snapped her head around. And the axe—the axe rooted her in place. She might have been a Saxon nun, staring down her doom.

The Northman held the axe aloft, the blade red with rust, contours jumping out against the leaf green of the library paneling. Not a wood-cutter's axe. A weapon. An axe that had chopped bone. The blade was bearded, the long hook ideal for catching and yanking an enemy's shield. The Northman was ducked behind a shield of their own, or rather a round serving tray, strapped to their forearm by a cravat tied to the two brass handles. They wore a fur cape, an untucked shirt that hung like a tunic, buckskin breeches, and riding boots.

"To Valhalla!" they roared, and leapt forward, swinging the axe in a figure eight.

"Georgie." She stood. "Is this an attack?"

"A display." They lowered their shield. "I thought it would feel more exciting if you saw the axe in action."

"Where did you find it?" She rushed to them, seizing the axe by its wooden handle. She could smell cold iron on the air, taste it as a tang at the back of her throat.

"Hibbert found it. Repairing the wall in Peach's field."

She turned until light from the windows struck the blade. The metal didn't glow. Runic markings didn't appear beneath the rust. The axe was ancient, though, irrefutably ancient, and it had once been deadly—to whom? She touched the blunted edge, nicked from repeated impacts, and shivered.

"You *do* think it's exciting?" asked Georgie.

Exciting? It required significant effort to remain calm. She could only nod, rotating the axe, unable to tear her eyes from it.

"And you think it belonged to a Northman?"

She nodded again.

"Peach said he's found all sorts of things plowing by that wall. He has a whole collection, a cabinet of curiosities, except it's a refurbished chicken coop. Elf, there's a large piece of granite incorporated into the wall."

Her gaze flew to their face. They'd roughed up their hair to wildness—their notion of a Northman's coiffure—and lined their eyes with lampblack. The effect was a beauty so ferocious her knees went wobbly.

"Hibbert pointed it out," they said. "And I thought . . ."

"A grave marker," she whispered. The Northmen had camped on the bluff, but they'd buried their warriors down below. She realized she'd forgotten to breathe. "Can I dig? Will Peach allow it?"

"He will." Georgie was smiling. "Now that I've given him a better piece of land in exchange. Also, he's as keen on historical remains as Phipps. Another thing those two have in common." They gave a bemused shake of their head. "Phipps is already talking about the day they merge their arrowhead collections."

She pushed the papers on the desk to one side and laid the axe down. She needed both hands free to push on her chest, to keep her heart from beating through it.

"Notify your father. The Barrow Prince. Whoever you please. This is *my* property." Georgie's chuckle was evil. "No one can wrest away control. If some Fellow wants to participate, he must beg my permission, which I will grant only if you want assistance, and only if he submits to instruction. It's your dig."

Her heartbeats filled her hands.

They were grinning at her, face flushed, tousled hair sweaty at the temples—they were draped in fur, for heaven's sake.

She filled her hands with *them*, their damp, satiny face, then their fur-draped shoulders, and then she slipped her arms inside the cape, over the lawn on their shirt, hugging them fiercely.

"Shall we go right now?" Georgie gave her a wry and tender look as she released them. "You're eager to begin, I can tell."

"I've begun," she said, thickly. "It's begun."

They inclined their head in puzzlement.

"My life," she explained, everything blurring, because she was crying again. When had she ever cried so much, or laughed so hard? Never. The answer was never. She felt so raw these days, so open, so new, so needy. *Needing* Georgie frightened her, and simultaneously overflowed her with glee. It felt delicious to acknowledge a need, to allow them to meet it, with all of their being. She was going to keep needing, willfully, needing and receiving, offering everything in turn, a giddy cycle without beginning or end.

"My life." She swallowed hard. "*Our* life."

It felt like stepping off a cliff.

Georgie was immobile. Except for their eyes. Those pale, bright, black-lined eyes widened. "Our life?" Their grin returned, and they leaned toward her. "Are you saying there's more to it than digging for the bones of long-dead Danes?"

She kissed them, because yes, there was, there was more to it. And then she dragged them out the door in quest of the bones of long-dead Danes.

34

THERE WAS AN immediate, positive result to discovering the burial site of the Great Heathen Army.

Leverage. The kind that moved boulders, and mountains, and intractable men.

The Albion Society was forced to parley with her as an equal. If any of the Fellows wanted access to *her* dig, she had to form an avowed part of *their* dig. The camp and the grave together shed light on the nature of the Great Heathen Army, on life and death in ninth-century England, and beyond. Cooperation benefited all. That is, if the true goal was the investigation of the remains of antiquity rather than the self-aggrandizement of the Society and its members.

Truly, it didn't seem to be. But when pressed, everyone had to pretend.

Elfreda wasn't much good in a parley, even if she went into it humming "God Save the King." Georgie, however, was brilliant in a parley, not to mention the fact that, as landowner, they held all the cards. Their easy charm in combination with that hard fact had Mr. Clutterbuck submitting a supplemental charter for Elfreda's admission to the Society within half an hour.

She'd almost refused. Almost. She'd rather start her own society.

But the one didn't preclude the other. And she vowed to make good use of her fellowship.

Now it was midsummer's day, and she was walking back to Redmayne Manor after digging, not in Mr. Peach's field but on the bluff. Of the items turned up and sorted, her mind kept circling an amber bead with two concentric grooves. *Was* it a bead? Or a spindle whorl? And if a spindle whorl, did that indicate *women* had camped alongside the men? Did whole families travel with the army? Gradually, raiders from the north had become settlers. That very transition was spelled out here, in the dirt of Derbyshire.

As she cut across the woodland clearing, skirting the pond, she realized she wasn't heading to Redmayne Manor, not quite yet. The willow summoned her like harp song. Lines of her grandmother's poetry seemed to float on the breeze.

A few minutes of communion.

She parted the fronds, slipped inside the shivering cascade of leaflets, and sucked in her breath.

"I'm all right," said Georgie, looking up from where they sat, in trousers and shirtsleeves, back against the trunk, arms around their knees. Tears glittered on their lashes. They wiped them away. "Just a storm of violent weeping."

She dropped down beside them. "Did something terrible happen?"

"No." They gave a choked laugh. "Yes. Perhaps. I was thinking about my mother. I don't do this anymore. *This.*" They waved their hand, indicating their wet cheeks and swollen eyes, expression frustrated, hurt, and so guilty, she pulled them into her.

"You don't do this anymore," she murmured, resting her cheek on their head, remembering their reasoning, "because your mother is alive."

They grew heavy in the circle of her arms. "And because she did what she did for love."

Love. Elfreda shut her eyes. She understood it more and less than ever before. Love wasn't something you found, or fell into—it was the whole path and the process of seeking. You had to look where you were going and learn from where you'd been. You had to treat your wounds, or you wouldn't get very far.

"Your mother made a choice." Elfreda opened her eyes. "You respect that choice, I know. Perhaps it was the right choice, for her." She shifted, settling them more firmly against her. "It wasn't the right choice for you. Admitting that you're sad, or even angry—it doesn't mean you grudge her any happiness."

They inhaled deeply, but for a long moment, they didn't speak.

"What if I do, though?" Their voice was clogged with pain.

It made her ache. She wanted to take all their pain from them, to tell them that nothing and no one would hurt them ever again. But she wanted most of all to be true, true to Georgie, and to love's promise, which was joy, *real* joy, joy that befriended even sorrow, even grief.

"Then you do," she said. "You're sad, and angry, and you grudge her."

"That's not who I want to be."

"You could forgive her." She hesitated. "You'd have to forgive yourself first."

All was quiet within the lucent green bell of willow fronds.

They stirred, breaking free, turning from her. "Her letter." They turned back, a folded paper in their hand. "I was thinking I should destroy it."

She had to struggle not to snatch it away. "Why today?"

"Phipps brought me this morning to my estate's most miserable little farm. Northeast of here, near the village. Untenanted, due to the condition of the buildings. It gave me an idea." Something began to bloom in their face. "The barn is large, two stories, stone built. I want to turn it into a theater, with boxes and a pit, a stage with pulleys and trapdoors for flying and sinking, painted scenes, all the modern machinery. I'll invite companies to play. They can stay in the farmhouse. In between, I'll mount my own private productions. A small audience of intimates—my staff, of course, and the Janes, Phipps, all the Peaches—they're rather a numerous family, in fact—and Mrs. Alderwalsey, although I most want to see her on the stage, along with Agnes, and Anne and Rosalie, and, well, there's time to sort out the cast, and all of it, really." They caught their breath. "What do you think?"

"I think it's perfect." Her heart soared. "A perfect idea."

They were rotating the paper lengthwise. "My mother will never watch me perform. Twynham is the last place on Earth she could ever show her face. I can have the theater. But I can't have her." They stopped rotating the paper, pinching it so tightly, their fingertips went white. "Today, I realized I needed to let go of that fantasy—my mother in the audience, not just watching, *seeing*. It's too late anyway. I needed her to see me years and years ago, not now." They frowned down at the paper. But when they glanced up at her, their eyes were aglow. "I do feel seen. *You* see me. That makes it easier."

She held their gaze, a lump in her throat. "May I?"

They handed her the paper. It wasn't the letter itself but rather an envelope protecting it. The letter was a fragile, ruined thing, smoke stained and charred. She needed more light. She went out from beneath the willow and sat cross-legged in the sun near the water, examining the words that were there, pondering the words that weren't.

After a time, Georgie joined her. "Any discoveries?" They were teasing. And also, not.

"Your mother called Lady Beverly by her Christian name."

"Penelope. That's hardly a discovery."

"It means the *Beverly* lower down can only refer to her husband."

"Where does it say *Beverly*?"

She showed them, the distinctive capital *B* evident in a soot-darkened sentence that terminated early, bitten off by the flame.

They scrunched their brow, trying to make it out, then gave a defeated shrug. "I have difficulty deciphering everything after the first paragraph."

She nodded. The first paragraph was unscathed. The apology, the revelation, the farewell—all there, in a hurried but elegant hand. Reading the rest required eye strain and inference.

"Tell me about Lord Beverly."

They snorted. "My mother usually referred to him in Welsh. I forget the phrase. It translated to sheep's fart. As good a description as you'll ever get."

"So he wasn't like your father, aware and accepting of his wife's entanglement?"

"*Lord Beverly?*" They were incredulous. "He was the unwitting cuckold par excellence. A horned sheep's fart, you could say."

"What does this mean to you?" She squinted. "*Beverly was for Auch* . . . It's too burnt."

"Auchmithie," they supplied. "The village where Mother and Lady Beverly were staying."

"Was it widely known that Lord Beverly also went to Scotland that spring?"

"I've never heard that he did. Parliament was in session. He wouldn't have traveled for pleasure."

"Not pleasure," she mused. "Dominance. Revenge."

Georgie stared. "You suggest he learned of the infidelity? And pursued them? To do what? Drag his wife home? Slay my mother?" Their mouth had a sarcastic twist. "How very Gothic."

"It's not any more Gothic than his lady wife and her lover faking their demise."

Georgie's features gentled as they studied her. "You offer me a villain, to make my mother's actions more forgivable. Thank you. But it's not necessary."

"I don't think it's necessary. Only possible."

They loosed a breath and gazed moodily over the fishing pond.

"Beverly is dead now. Maybe he did pursue my mother and Lady Beverly with evil purpose. I can't know for certain. I'm not sure how much it would change things if I did."

"There's something else." She pointed at the letter's ragged black bottom, the very last semilegible line. "Something your mother wanted your father to tell the king when . . ."

"The king?" Their gaze swung back to her. "When . . . when what?"

"That part of the sentence is cinders."

"The *king*." They frowned. "Could she have wanted my father to denounce Lord Beverly? I can't really picture him banging on the door of Kew Palace."

"Georgie." She was almost afraid to say it. "Could *you* be the king?"

Their face was suddenly naked. "Me? How could it be me?"

"I saw that model ship." She gave them a wry look. "Your handiwork wasn't at all subtle. Your father never mentioned it to you, but what if it became a little joke between him and your mother? And their pet name for you?" She could imagine Mr. and Mrs. Redmayne laughing about the youthful vandalism, amused, exasperated, and fond, and so proud of their child, for whom the name *Georgina* didn't quite fit, along with the too-tight pronouns *he* and *she*.

She could see that Georgie was also imagining it. Tears stood in their eyes.

"King Georgie?" Their throat worked. "You think they called me the king? That my mother wanted my father to tell me. That he would have done it, if he hadn't . . ." They bit their trembling lip. Another instant and they were shaking their head. "I can't know *that* for certain either."

"You can't." She tucked the letter back inside its envelope. "But you know it's possible."

They narrowed their eyes, tears brimming. "Isn't this the same as your father believing he's the *Barrow King*? Am I deluding myself? If I believe?"

"With Papa, it's egotism. With you, it's openness." She hoped her face was open and showed them the truth in her heart. "You're allowing that your parents saw more than you'd come to assume. Your kingship isn't about wielding power. It's about mutual recognition, and care. You and Papa aren't the same kind of king."

"King Georgie," they whispered, still shaking their head. Their smile was as wide as possibility itself, as wide as the whole world. And then they sighed. "I wish I were king of the fairies. I'd use my magic to get back your amulet."

A fish jumped in the pond. Elfreda started, and Georgie laughed. "Maybe a fish *did* swallow it."

"Is that your excuse? To stop looking?"

"I'll never stop," they said, looking at her. "I hope it takes forever."

And when she pushed their shoulder, they obliged her by tumbling right into the water. And when she splashed in after them, they kissed her. And when she floated on her back, she gazed up at the sky, and it might have been any day in any century since the origin of love, or all of them, and she sent her laughter into the infinite blue.

HISTORICAL NOTE

ISTORICAL ROMANCE, HOW do I love thee? Let me count the ways.

I love historical romance because it's the subgenre of romance I found first, at an impressionable age. The local library held a used book sale every summer, and I'd stock up on ten-cent paperbacks that promised to transport me to the Highlands, or the high seas.

I love historical romance because it *is* so transporting, so unabashedly escapist. The adventures depicted are thrillingly different from any I could ever hope to have. I'm in it for the pistols at dawn, the curricle races, the bare-knuckle boxing matches, the train robberies, the undercover spies, the orphans, the governesses, the scandalous gambling hells, and the extravagant house parties.

I love historical romance because all that escapism is actually holding up a mirror. The versions of the "long ago and far away" that we create reveal so much about our here and now. The great Beverly Jenkins describes her meticulously researched historical romance novels as "edutainment." It's fun to learn about the past through, for example, a love story between a banker and an outlaw set in Philadelphia, in 1895, and to see types of characters at the center of the narratives who don't usually star in the history textbooks. It's fun to project present-day values back onto a different social context, to watch struggles for emotional justice unfold against even greater odds, and with perhaps unexpected opportunities. How we think about the past can change how we think about the future, and vice versa.

I love historical romance because it emphasizes joy, pleasure, agency, and interdependence, and can challenge assumptions that certain things are new. Women enjoying sex. People flourishing beyond the gender binary. There are limits to how much and in what ways we can identify ourselves with people who lived hundreds of years ago. The terms we use for desire and who we are aren't the same. The norms and pressures aren't the same. Even so, I find it inspiring to read about ancestors, real and invented.

I love historical romance because it provides so many ancestors for readers to claim, ancestors who can help us look ahead and imagine even more possibilities for living and loving.

A RARE FIND is my first Regency romance. Like many romance writers with novels set during the Regency, I'm creating a version of Georgian England that owes a lot to Jane Austen. Austen was a delightfully keen observer of village life, and of the mores and manners of the middle and upper classes. Elf and Georgie come from that milieu. The Regency was a volatile, transitional period. Slavery in Britain was abolished in 1807, only four years before the Regency officially began, and money continued to flow to those who owned and invested in Caribbean plantations. The Napoleonic Wars raged, bringing unrest at home and loss of life abroad. War was followed by economic depression, harvest failure, the Corn Laws. The population in newly industrial cities boomed. Elf and Georgie don't play a part in any epoch-defining events, but larger historical forces and social expectations nonetheless shape their daily lives in the small (invented) village of Twynham.

Georgie and their friends, Anne, Rosalie, and Phipps, are all queer, although they couldn't have called themselves *queer* in this way in 1818. Elf finds out, happily, that she is too. All sorts of people were happily committing all sorts of consensual sexual acts in the nineteenth century, but it wasn't something you could talk about in public. The Buggery Act of 1533 made sex between men punishable by death. Despite this looming threat, molly houses proliferated in Georgian London, providing men who desired men with venues for trysts and parties. Lesbian relationships were not illegal, perhaps because lawmakers didn't imagine sex between women was possible (or else didn't want to let the cat out of the bag). The concept of "romantic friendship" emerged in the eighteenth century, describing the intense emotional bonds some women shared. This concept created an allowance for female intimacy by framing it as fundamentally chaste.

Georgie and Anne both mention the Ladies of Llangollen, the era's most famous pair of romantic friends. Born into wealthy families, Eleanor Butler and Sarah Ponsonby refused to marry men and left Ireland to live together in a picturesque cottage in Wales with a series of dogs named Sappho. There they received visits from fascinated guests, including William Wordsworth and the Duke of Wellington. The Ladies both exemplified and challenged the concept of romantic friendship with their domestic bliss, to which some visitors and journalists imputed a sexual component. Anne is particularly eager to claim the Ladies as lesbians, quoting rapturously (and anachronistically) from Wordsworth's 1824 sonnet. She's always on the lookout for women like her, and for unconventional relationship models. During the Regency, women were expected to marry, and marriage was often the only acceptable and materially viable option. Women did, however, by choice or circumstance, remain unmarried, and some of them found alternate living arrangements that suited them much better.

Rigid rules governed women's attire and limited their opportunities for employment. Georgie wears fashionable gowns but also likes to look the dashing gentleman. This is part of why they're drawn to the theater. The theater in England has long provided a space of gender play, with men taking women's roles in all-male companies during the Renaissance, and women performing in breeches roles from the seventeenth century on. Writer and actress Charlotte Charke published an autobiography in 1775, *A Narrative of the Life of Mrs. Charlotte Charke*. Charke wore breeches on the stage, and from time to time dressed *en cavalier* in everyday life. She worked in various male trades as Charles Brown and spent years cohabitating with a woman, the two calling themselves "Mr. and Mrs. Brown." Charlotte Charke provides a well-known precedent for dressing in ways that challenge norms, one Georgie could have accessed through her autobiography.

Aspects of Georgie's character are based loosely on Anne Lister (1791-1840), someone they *wouldn't* have read about. Anne Lister became a lesbian icon in the 1980s after historians decoded her sexually explicit diaries. Finally, firsthand proof that participants in romantic friendships were sometimes *more* than friends! Lister visited the Ladies of Llangollen in 1822, wore masculine clothing, and proved herself shrewd and business-minded as she ran her family's estate. The symbolic communion she took at York's Holy Trinity Church with longtime partner Ann Walker in 1834 has been memorialized as the first recorded lesbian marriage in Britain. Anne Lister is now even more firmly entrenched in popular culture thanks to the BBC-HBO series *Gentleman Jack*.

Georgie uses they/them pronouns among close friends. This wasn't a practice during the Regency, but it's not impossible that a friend group would have hit upon the usage. I wanted to show how a discussion of pronouns might have come about in the past to underscore the importance of respecting people's pronouns today. The English language doesn't have a gender-neutral third-person singular pronoun, which has led to grammarians and writers trying out *they*, *it*, and the generic *he* across the centuries. Invented pronouns have also been in the running, including e/es/em (1841), ve/vis/vim (1864), ita (1877), and thon (1884). Grammar books from the eighteenth century through the twentieth went with "he" for indefinite subjects, e.g., "The student forgot *his* books on the school bus." The women's suffrage movement challenged the inherent sexism of this choice, as did several waves of subsequent feminism. Today, the singular *they* is recognized as correct usage by such grammatical gatekeepers as the APA, MLA, and OED. All this is to say, conversations about gender-neutral third-person singular pronouns have been unfolding, in politically charged ways, for a very long time. These conversations didn't focus on the needs of trans and nonbinary people until the 1970s, when some began to use ze, hir, e, ve, and other new and old creations. Feminist philosopher Amia Srinivasan beautifully summarizes this history and the political implications of pronoun usage in her *London Review of Books* response to Dennis Baron's book, *What's Your Pronoun?: Beyond He and She.*

The Albion Society of Antiquaries is my invention, but it bears a resemblance to the Society of Antiquaries of London, founded in 1707. I recommend *Antiquaries: The Discovery of the Past in Eighteenth-Century Britain* by Rosemary Sweet for anyone interested in learning more about these wealthy and eccentric devotees of antiquity. Victorian archaeologist Sir Thomas Bateman uncovered numerous Anglo-Saxon graves in the Peak District and was known as the Barrow Knight. His papers informed my research. Elf's grandfather borrows certain characteristics from William Stukeley, an early Fellow of the Society of

Antiquaries of London. Stukeley did important fieldwork at Stonehenge, but his later fixation on druid practices and beliefs—along with his adoption of the druid pseudonym Chynodax—undermined his credibility with his peers and future, more professionalized, historians and archaeologists. British antiquarianism and archaeology have themselves a complicated history. These fields contributed to the formation of enduring ideas about England's origin and national identity, and their development was bound up with colonialism, racism, and cultural looting. *A Rare Find* attempts to dramatize a few of the different points of view and priorities espoused by antiquaries at the time. With Georgie's help, Elf comes to think more critically and creatively about how knowledge is made, what stories get told, and why.

For people in the Anglo-Saxon kingdoms, the Viking age began with the raid on the monastery at Lindisfarne in 793, and ended in 1066 with the death of King Harald at the Battle of Stamford Bridge. *The Anglo-Saxon Chronicle* records the movements of the "Mycel hæþen here," the Great Heathen Army, through the kingdoms, but archaeological evidence has remained elusive and debates about the size of the army continue. Only two winter camps have been discovered in England to this day, one at Repton in the 1970s and one at Torksey in 2013. Making such a discovery in 1818, and becoming a female Fellow of an antiquarian society, puts Elf way ahead of her time.

Women weren't admitted as members to the Society of Antiquaries of London (or the Royal Society, or many other learned societies) until the twentieth century. Women were, however, making contributions to antiquarian studies long before this. For example, Elizabeth Elstob published the first Old English grammar book in modern English (rather than Latin) in 1715. Intellectually and materially supported by her brother in her scholarly pursuits, Elstob was burdened with debts upon his death, put aside her scholarship, and died a governess. She was an advocate for women's education, and her work bridges the divide between antiquarian and early feminist writing. Women also participated in archaeological fieldwork, despite resistance to their involvement in dirty physical labor. For example, songwriter and song collector Alicia Ann, Lady John Scott directed nineteenth-century excavations on her own estate. Elf is ahead of her time, but she is inspired by her grandmother's precedent, which had its corollaries in real life.

A RARE FIND

JOANNA LOWELL

READERS GUIDE

QUESTIONS FOR DISCUSSION

1. As childhood neighbors, Elf and Georgie think they know a lot about each other's motivations and the meanings behind their actions. What experiences lead them to rethink what they thought they knew? Have you ever been very wrong in your assumptions about who someone else really is?

2. Elf is deeply focused on, even obsessed with, archaeological pursuits, and rarely leaves her family's crumbling property. Georgie lights up every room but can't stay in any room for too long. Why do these opposites attract? What does each one have to offer the other?

3. Elf's inadvertent discovery in the pergola leads her to new territories of sexual possibility. What unexpected discoveries have you made that opened new possibilities for you, sexual or otherwise?

4. What kind of buried treasure would you be most excited to find?

5. Georgie, Phipps, Anne, Rosalie, and multiple other characters have powerful reasons for wishing to live outside of heterosexual marriage, and they find various solutions to the pressures of their time. What other possibilities might have been available to them,

beyond the arrangements discussed in the book? What relationships have you seen in today's world that are more complicated than they appear at first? Which have you seen work particularly well, and why?

6. Elf idolizes her father, and her greatest passion is to work with him. How does she come to see him differently, and how does this change her relationship to her work?

7. How do Elf and her father remember his parents differently? Are there members of your family who look very different depending on who is telling the story?

8. Why does Elf see something different in her grandmother's writing than her father does? How might her experiences in the world as a young woman enable her to see different things in archaeological digs and writings than the men of the Albion Society?

9. Archaeology requires a special way of seeing, to notice the traces of a wolf pit in a field or a barrow on a moor. What have you learned in your life that has given you special ways of seeing?

10. Agnes may finally be able to realize her dream of going to London and having a Season. What do you think she will find when she gets there? What successes and challenges might she have?

11. Georgie thinks they are a city mouse but comes to realize that they may be a country mouse after all. What aspects of city life do you miss when you are in the country, and vice versa?

12. Do you think any of the nuns at the abbey fell in love with each other?

13. Georgie says there are "two kinds of fashionable," one "everyone agrees on" and one "everyone disagrees on." Which do you prefer, and what are your favorite things to wear to demonstrate this preference? If you could try the other style for a day, or perhaps for a London Season, what would you wear?

14. Do you have a favorite riddle?

15. Why was Elf's birthday present to Georgie so risky for her? What is the most romantic place you have ever kissed?

16. Which would be worse: being buried in a cave under a mudslide or spending the same amount of time listening to a sixteen-year-old play and sing their own romantic songs on the lute?

ACKNOWLEDGMENTS

I needed extra time and extra care to finish this book. Thanks to my agent, Tara Gelsomino, who should go down in history as the absolute best person to have in your corner. Thanks to my editor, Kate Seaver, who gave me the insights I needed to reconceptualize Elf's character and journey, and begin again. Thanks to Amanda Maurer, who also edited *A Rare Find* and offered pitch-perfect feedback. Thanks to my team at Berkley for all you do on behalf of my books, and for the encouragement and know-how. Thanks to the Berkletes, and to Elizabeth Everett for feminist malarkey, and friendship, and for reminding me why I love this big, beautiful genre, and historical romance in particular.

Thanks to Wake Forest University for funding my research trip to England, and to my colleagues and students for so many inspiring conversations. Special thanks to Amy Clark, who introduced me to perambulatory boundary clauses and medieval riddles and gave me a sense of the historical context I needed to develop my plot.

Georgie reads a riddle by Symphosius transcribed in English in Elf's grandmother's notes. That translation is actually by Craig Williamson, and you can find it in *A Feast of Creatures: Anglo-Saxon Riddle-Songs*.

While this book was germinating, I watched *The Dig*, a lovely movie about the mid-twentieth-century excavation of Sutton Hoo. I realized after I drafted *A Rare Find* that Elf echoes a character from *The Dig*, Basil Brown, who says, "From the first human handprint on a cave wall, we're part of something continuous." I left Elf's phrasing as is, but she and I owe it to Basil Brown, or rather to Moira Buffini, the screenwriter, and John Preston, whose novel Buffini adapted for the screen.

Elf's line about becoming a hum comes from the title of a book by one of my favorite poets, Eric Baus: *How I Became a Hum*.

Thanks to Mir Yarfitz for deep collaboration, brainstorming, feedback on multiple drafts, huge helpings of historical knowledge, and the discussion questions.

Thanks to my first reader, Sarah Evenson, for offering suggestions and thinking with me about queer identities past, present, and future. I am in awe of your insight and imagination.

Thanks to Jessica Richard for reading the manuscript as both a romance lover and an eighteenth-century British fiction specialist. All mistakes are my own, but there are fewer of them than there would have been without your generosity and expertise.

Thanks to Renee Gladman for stretching my ideas about romance and narration. And thanks for writing *My Lesbian Novel*, which changed my brain.

Thanks to Joanna and John for taking me to the Peak District and especially for the magical stay at Rocking Stone Cottage in Birchover, my new favorite place on Earth. *The Princess Bride* was filmed right behind the cottage! We beheld the very spot where Buttercup fell in love with Westley. And met the descendants of Fezzik's white horses. We wandered the moors and saw the druidic sites that would have inspired generations of Marsdens, and certainly inspired me. A peak experience in every way. Thanks as well to Rachael, our host, for the flowers and brownies and local lore.

I wouldn't have survived this year without my friends and family, particularly my cousins and my aunt Rhetta. My endless beyond-words gratitude for all of you. Thanks to Radhika for the plotting (the book kind and other kinds) and witchery. Thanks to each of you, Caren and Julia, for the narrative support and well-timed walks. Thanks to Brian Conn for Brian Conning. Thanks to Dona and Brad for creating a circle of protection in the gate. Thanks to the girl gang. Thanks to my grief guides, Rian, Jen, Jason, Joanna, Jayne, and Miriam. And fellow travelers, Corinne, Art, Kathy, Kate, Chelsea, Cristina, and Nico. Thanks to Chemlawn, Stiv, Ian, Hana, and the Admiral, for being who you are and being there. Thanks to Sarah and Frankie for bringing the joy. Thanks, Mama, for keeping on. Thanks to my little brother, Jesse, for holding this all with me. Thanks to my sister, Anna, for sharing those summer days. Mir, my dad was right about so many things, and he was definitely right about you.

Joanna Lowell lives among the fig trees in North Carolina, where she teaches in the English department at Wake Forest University. When she's not writing historical romance, she writes collections and novels as Joanna Ruocco. Those books include *Dan*, *Another Governess / The Least Blacksmith*, *The Week*, and *Field Glass*, coauthored with Joanna Howard.

Ready to find
your next great read?

Let us help.

Visit prh.com/nextread

Penguin
Random
House